ACROSS AND DOWN

THROUGH THE BOOK OF MORMON

"... and they had waxed strong in the knowledge of the truth; for they were men of a sound understanding and they had searched the scriptures diligently, that they might know the word of God."

Alma 17:2

BY SUSAN B. NIELSEN

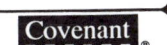

ACKNOWLEDGMENTS

Across and Down Through The Book of Mormon is not only *for families*, but it is *by a family*. I am very grateful for the patience, support, and diligent help of my family, immediate and extended. This book may never have come to pass without their encouragement to see it through and their dedication during its numerous revisions.

At times it seemed that graph paper and a pencil might have been easier; but by stretching and learning, the puzzles in this book were successfully computerized. Many thanks to my husband, Brett, and to Warren Bingham and Dave Packham for their technical support. Also to Centron Software Technologies for their great program, *Puzzle Power*.

Puzzles in this book may be copied for use in the classroom or within individual families only. Copying for any other use is prohibited.

Cover illustration by Val Chadwick Bagley

Published by Covenant Communications, Inc.
American Fork, Utah

Copyright © 1999 by Susan B. Nielsen
All rights reserved

Printed in Canada
First Printing: January 1999

06 05 04 03   10 9 8 7 6 5 4 3

ISBN 1-57734-444-8

CONTENTS

SECTION ONE:	Crossword Puzzles	1
SECTION TWO:	Scripture Falls (for Seminary Scripture Mastery)	106
SECTION THREE:	Word Search - Clueless - Cryptograms	137
SECTION FOUR:	Solutions	193

LEVEL OF DIFFICULTY

Crossword Puzzles	Moderate
Scripture Falls	Moderate
Word Search	Moderately easy
Clueless	Moderate
Cryptograms	Moderately difficult

Week:	Puzzles Related To:	Are Found on These Pages:
1	1 Nephi 1-4	2, 108, 138
2	1 Nephi 5-10	4, 139
3	1 Nephi 11-14	6, 140
4	1 Nephi 15-18	8, 141
5	1 Nephi 19-22	10, 109, 142
6	2 Nephi 1-5	12, 110, 111, 143
7	2 Nephi 6-9	14, 112, 144
8	2 Nephi 10-16	16, 145
9	2 Nephi 17-25	18, 146
10	2 Nephi 26-28	20, 113, 148
11	2 Nephi 29 - Jacob 1	22, 115, 116, 149
12	Jacob 2-7	24, 118, 150
13	Enos - Words of Mormon	26, 151
14	Mosiah 1-3	28, 119, 120, 152
15	Mosiah 4-6	30, 121, 153
16	Mosiah 7-9	32, 154
17	Mosiah 10-14	34, 155
18	Mosiah 15-18	36, 156
19	Mosiah 19-22	38, 157
20	Mosiah 23-26	40, 158
21	Mosiah 27-29	42, 159
22	Alma 1-4	44, 160
23	Alma 5-8	46, 161
24	Alma 9-12	48, 162
25	Alma 13-16	50, 163
26	Alma 17-19	52, 164
27	Alma 20-24	54, 165
28	Alma 25-29	56, 166
29	Alma 30-32	58, 122, 167
30	Alma 33-36	60, 123, 168
31	Alma 37-40	62, 125, 126, 169
32	Alma 41-44	64, 127, 170
33	Alma 45-48	66, 171
34	Alma 49-52	68, 172
35	Alma 53-57	70, 173
36	Alma 58-63	72, 174
37	Helaman 1-4	74, 175
38	Helaman 5-7	76, 128, 176
39	Helaman 8-12	78, 177
40	Helaman 13-16	80, 178
41	3 Nephi 1-5	82, 179
42	3 Nephi 6-10	84, 180
43	3 Nephi 11-12	86, 129, 181
44	3 Nephi 13-16	88, 182
45	3 Nephi 17-20	90, 183
46	3 Nephi 21-28	92, 130, 184
47	3 Nephi 29-Mormon 3	94, 185
48	Mormon 4-9	96, 186
49	Ether 1-8	98, 187
50	Ether 9-15	100, 131, 132, 189
51	Moroni 1-7	102, 133, 135, 191
52	Moroni 8-10	104, 136, 192

SECTION ONE

CROSSWORD PUZZLES

To produce this book, The Book of Mormon was broken down into fifty-two scripture readings (of approximately ten pages each) with corresponding puzzles for each reading so that The Book of Mormon can be studied in one year's time. * Some of the clues/verses are easy enough for young children to answer and some are challenging enough for seminary students and adults. The puzzles can be done with The Book of Mormon open or, for more of a challenge, closed.

To receive the full benefit of this book, read the complete clue no matter where the missing word is in the sentence. In place of the missing word, there is a graphic: ❖ .

The clues used in the crossword puzzles are direct quotes from The Book of Mormon. Some verses are lengthy, which necessitated dividing them into two clues. In this case, the end of the first half of the clue/verse states in which clue the balance of the verse is found. If a word in a verse of scripture is the same as a word found somewhere else in the puzzle, then the number of that clue/word may be shown in brackets, i.e. [12A] for 12 Across or [3D] for 3 Down.

To produce a crossword puzzle, the words are scrambled to fit in with each other; for this reason, the clues are not in the order they are found in the scriptures. In the back of the book, in section four, the solutions to the puzzles are found, along with the clues in actual sequential order and the reference from which they were taken. So clues may be read in actual order, if preferred.

*NOTE: Each of the fifty-two scripture readings will have at least two puzzles that can be used. For example, for the first reading, 1 Nephi 1-4, there is a crossword puzzle (pp. 2-3), a scripture falls (p. 108), and a word search (p. 138).

ONE
1 Nephi 1–4

Across

4 "Now ❖ was the name of the servant; and he promised that he would go down into the wilderness unto our father."

5 "And [the twelve others] came down and went forth upon the face of the earth; and the first came and stood before my father, and gave unto him a ❖ , and bade him that he should read."

9 "For behold, Laban hath the record of the [14A] and also a ❖ of my forefathers, and they are engraven upon plates of brass."

10 A scriptural word for "you".

12 "And it came to pass that as [Lehi] read, he was filled with the ❖ of the Lord."

13 "And I know that the record which I make is ❖ ; and I make it with mine own hand; and I make it according to my knowledge."

14 "Yea, I make a record in the language of my father, which consists of the learning of the ❖ and language of the Egyptians."

15 "I, Nephi, having been born of goodly ❖ , therefore I was taught somewhat in all the learning of my father..." (continued in 8D)

16 "And inasmuch as ye shall keep my commandments, ye shall ❖ , and shall be led to a land of promise; yea, even a land which I have prepared for you; yea, a land which is choice above all other lands."

19 "And it came to pass that he saw One descending out of the midst of heaven, and he beheld that his ❖ was above that of the sun at noon–day."

20 "Yea, and many things did my father read concerning Jerusalem—that it should be destroyed, and the inhabitants thereof; many should ❖ by the sword, and many should be carried away captive into Babylon."

22 "Let us go up again unto Jerusalem, and let us be faithful in keeping the commandments of the Lord; for behold he is ❖ than all the earth, then why not ❖ than Laban and his fifty, yea, or even than his tens of thousands?"

23 "It is better that one man should perish than that a ❖ should dwindle and perish in unbelief."

24 "And it came to pass that the Lord commanded my father, even in a dream, that he should take his ❖ and depart into the wilderness."

26 "And when the Jews heard these things they were angry with [Lehi]; yea, even as with the prophets of old, whom they had cast out, and stoned, and slain; and they also sought his ❖, that they might take it away."

27 (continued from 10D) "...for I know that the ❖ giveth no commandments unto the children of men, save he shall prepare a way for them that they may accomplish the thing which he commandeth them."

28 "And after this manner was the language of my father in the praising of his God; for his soul did rejoice, and his whole ❖ was filled, because of the things which he had seen, yea, which the Lord had shown unto him."

Down

1 "Blessed art thou, Nephi, because of thy ❖ , for thou hast sought me diligently, with lowliness of heart."

2 "Wherefore it came to pass that my father, Lehi, as he went forth ❖ unto the Lord, yea, even with all his heart, in behalf of his people."

3 "And it came to pass as he prayed unto the Lord, there came a ❖ of fire and dwelt upon a rock before him; and he saw and heard much; and because of the things which he saw and heard he did quake and tremble exceedingly."

6 "And it came to pass that [Lehi] was ❖ unto the word of the Lord, wherefore he did as the Lord commanded him."

7 "And I spake unto Sam, making known unto him the things which the Lord had manifested unto me by his Holy Spirit. And it came to pass that he ❖ in my words."

8 (continued from 15A) "...and having seen many afflictions in the course of my days, nevertheless, having been highly favored of the Lord in all my days; yea, having had a great knowledge of the ❖ and the mysteries of God, therefore I make a record of my proceedings in my days."

10 "And it came to pass that I, Nephi, said unto my father: I will go and do the ❖ which the Lord hath commanded..." (continued in 27A)

11 "Wherefore, the Lord hath commanded me that thou and thy brothers should go unto the house of Laban, and seek the ❖, and bring them down hither into the wilderness."

15 "...after the Lord had shown so many marvelous things unto my father, Lehi, yea, concerning the destruction of Jerusalem, behold he went forth among the people, and began to ❖ ..."

17 (continued from 18D) "...and he thought he saw God sitting upon his ❖ , surrounded with numberless concourses of angels in the attitude of singing and praising their God."

18 "And being thus overcome with the Spirit, he was carried away in a ❖ , even that he saw the heavens open..." (continued in 17D)

21 "As the Lord liveth, and as we live, we will not go down unto our ❖ in the wilderness until we have accomplished the thing which the Lord hath commanded us."

25 Nephi said: "And I was ❖ by the Spirit, not knowing beforehand the things which I should do."

3

TWO
1 Nephi 5–10

Across

3 "And it came to pass that when I, Nephi, had spoken these words unto my brethren, they were ❖ with me."

7 "And it came to pass that I did go forth and partake of the fruit thereof; and I beheld that it was most ❖ , above all that I ever before tasted."

10 "And it came to pass that I saw a man, and he was dressed in a white ❖ ; and he came and stood before me."

12 "And after they had tasted of the fruit they were ❖ , because of those that were scoffing at them; and they fell away into forbidden paths and were lost."

14 "And he beheld that [the plates of brass] did contain the five books of ❖ , which gave an account of the creation of the world, and also of Adam and Eve, who were our first parents..."

18 "And it came to pass that I did frankly forgive them all that they had done, and I did ❖ them that they would pray unto the Lord their God for forgiveness."

19 "Yea, and how is it that ye have forgotten that the Lord is able to do all things according to his ❖ , for the children of men, if it so be that they exercise faith in him? Wherefore, let us be faithful to him."

21 "...and they did press forward through the mist of darkness, ❖ to the rod of [28D], even until they did come forth and partake of the fruit of the tree."

25 "And it came to pass that I beheld a ❖ , whose fruit was desirable to make one happy."

26 "Yea, and I beheld that the fruit thereof was ❖ , to exceed all the ❖ ness that I had ever seen."

29 "And after the house of Israel should be scattered they should be ❖ together again..."

31 "And it came to pass that they were ❖ , because of their wickedness, insomuch that they did bow down before me, and did plead with me that I would forgive them of the thing that they had done against me."

32 "That these plates of brass should go forth unto all ❖ , kindreds, tongues, and people who were of his seed."

Down

1 "For the fulness of mine intent is that I may persuade men to come unto the God of Abraham...and be ❖ ."

2 "...Lehi, also found upon the plates of brass a genealogy of his fathers; wherefore he knew that he was a descendant of ❖ ; yea, even that ❖ who was the son of Jacob, who was sold into Egypt..."

4 "...I beheld a ❖ of water; and it ran along, and it was near the tree of which I was partaking the fruit."

5 "And it came to pass after I had prayed unto the Lord I beheld a large and spacious ❖ ."

6 They "...did plead with my brethren, insomuch that they did soften their hearts; and they did cease striving to take away my ❖ ."

8 (continued from 15D) "...wherefore, I began to be desirous that my ❖ should partake of it also; for I knew that it was desirable above all other fruit."

9 "And after they had slain the Messiah, who should come, and after he had been slain he should ❖ from the dead, and should make himself manifest, by the Holy Ghost, unto the Gentiles."

11 "...the house of Israel...should be compared like unto an olive—tree, whose branches should be ❖ off and should be scattered upon all the face of the earth."

13 "But it came to pass that I prayed unto the Lord, saying: O Lord, according to my faith which is in thee, wilt thou deliver me from the hands of my brethren; yea, even give me ❖ that I may burst these bands with which I am bound."

15 "And as I partook of the fruit thereof it filled my ❖ with exceedingly great joy..." (continued in 8D)

16 "...the Lord did ❖ the heart of [22D], and also his household insomuch that they took their journey with us down into the wilderness to the tent of our father."

17 Lehi's "...sons should take daughters to wife, that they might ❖ up seed unto the Lord in the land of promise."

20 "And it came to pass that there arose a mist of ❖ ; yea, even an exceedingly great mist of ❖ , insomuch that they who had commenced in the path did lose their way, that they wandered off and were lost."

22 "And it came to pass that the Lord commanded him that I, Nephi, and my brethren, should again return unto the land of Jerusalem, and bring down ❖ and his family into the wilderness."

23 "And he spake also concerning a prophet who should come before the Messiah, to ❖ the way of the Lord—"

24 "And I also beheld a strait and ❖ path, which came along by the rod of [28D], even to the tree by which I stood..."

27 "Wherefore, he said that these plates of brass should never ❖ ; neither should they be dimmed any more by time."

28 "And I beheld a rod of ❖, and it extended along the bank of the river, and led to the tree by which I stood."

30 "Yea, even ❖ hundred years from the time that my father left Jerusalem, a prophet would the Lord God raise up among the Jews—even a Messiah, or, in other words, a Savior of the world."

5

THREE
1 Nephi 11–14

Across

1 "...I beheld that the rod of iron, which my father had seen, was the ❖ of God, which led to the fountain of living waters, or to the tree of life; which waters are a representation of the love of God; and I also beheld that the tree of life was a representation of the love of God."

4 "The book that thou beholdest is a ❖ of the Jews, which contains the covenants of the Lord, which he hath made unto the house of Israel..."

7 "And I also beheld ❖ others following him."

8 "And the mists of darkness are the temptations of the ❖, which blindeth the eyes, and hardeneth the hearts of the children of men, and leadeth them away into broad roads, that they perish and are lost."

10 "...I beheld this great and ❖ church; and I saw the devil that he was the founder of it."

12 "...I beheld the wrath of God, that it was upon the seed of my brethren; and they were ❖ before the Gentiles and were smitten."

13 "And also for the ❖ of the world do they destroy the saints of God, and bring them down into captivity."

15 "...I beheld multitudes gathered together to battle, one against the other; and I beheld ❖, and rumors of ❖ ..."

16 "For it came to pass after I had desired to know the things that my father had seen, and believing that the Lord was able to make them known unto me, as I sat pondering in mine heart I was caught away in the Spirit of the Lord, yea, into an exceedingly high ❖ ..."

18 "...after they had dwindled in unbelief they became a dark, and loathsome, and a filthy ❖, full of idleness and all manner of abominations."

22 "These last records, which thou has seen among the Gentiles, shall establish the ❖ of the first, which are of the [7A] apostles of the Lamb, and shall make known the plain and [14D] things which have been taken away from them; and shall make known to all kindreds, tongues, and people, that the Lamb of God is the son of the Eternal Father, and the Savior of the world..."

24 "...because of the pride of my seed, and the ❖ of the devil, I beheld that the seed of my brethren did overpower the people of my seed."

28 "And I also saw and bear record that the Holy Ghost fell upon twelve others; and they were ❖ of God, and chosen."

29 "...I will be merciful unto the Gentiles in that day, insomuch that I will bring ❖ unto them, in mine own power, much of my gospel, which shall be plain and precious, saith the Lamb."

30 "...I beheld other ❖, which came forth by the power of the Lamb, from the Gentiles unto them..."

Down

1 "Behold the fountain of filthy ❖ which thy father saw; yea, even the river of which he spake; and the depths thereof are the depths of hell."

2 "For the time cometh, saith the Lamb of God, that I will work a ❖ and a marvelous work among the children of men; a work which shall be everlasting, either on the one hand or on the other—either to the convincing of them unto peace and life eternal, or unto the deliverance of them to the hardness of their hearts and the blindness of their minds unto their being brought down into captivity..."

3 "Behold the gold, and the silver, and the silks, and the scarlets...are the ❖ of this great and [10A] church."

5 "And the Lamb of God went forth and was baptized of him; and after he was baptized, I beheld the heavens open, and the Holy Ghost come down out of heaven and abide upon him in the form of a ❖."

6 "Thus shall be the destruction of all nations, kindreds, tongues, and people, that shall fight against the twelve ❖ of the Lamb."

8 Another word for "seed".

9 "And the time cometh that he shall manifest himself unto all nations, both unto the Jews and also unto the Gentiles...and the ❖ shall be first, and the first shall be ❖ ."

11 "And I beheld the city of ❖ ; and in the city of ❖ I beheld a virgin, and she was exceedingly fair and white."

14 "...they have taken away from the gospel of the Lamb many parts which are plain and most ❖ ; and also many covenants of the Lord have they taken away."

17 "...I beheld the Spirit of God, that it wrought upon other Gentiles; and they went forth out of ❖ , upon the many waters."

19 "And I beheld that he went forth ministering unto the people, in ❖ and great glory; and the multitudes were gathered together to hear him; and I beheld that they cast him out from among them."

20 "And it came to pass that I looked and beheld many ❖ ; and they divided the Gentiles from the seed of my brethren."

21 (continued from 27D) "...and if they endure unto the end they shall be lifted up at the last day, and shall be saved in the everlasting ❖ of the Lamb; and whoso shall publish peace, yea, tidings of great joy, how beautiful upon the upon the mountains shall they be."

23 "And they were ❖ by the power of the Lamb of God; and the devils and the unclean spirits were cast out."

25 "And [❖] shall also write concerning the end of the world."

26 "...and after thy seed shall be destroyed, and dwindle in unbelief, and also the seed of thy brethren, behold, these things shall be ❖ up, to come forth unto the Gentiles, by the gift and power of the Lamb."

27 "And blessed are they who shall seek to bring forth my ❖ at that day, for they shall have the gift and the power of the Holy Ghost..." (continued in 21D)

FOUR
1 Nephi 15–18

Across

5 "And now, my father had begat two sons in the wilderness; the elder was called ❖ and the younger Joseph."

6 "Ye are swift to do iniquity but slow to ❖ the Lord your God."

8 "In the name of the Almighty God, I command you that ye touch me not, for I am filled with the ❖ of God, even unto the consuming of my flesh; and whoso shall lay his hands upon me shall wither even as a dried reed; and he shall be as naught before the ❖ of God, for God shall smite him."

9 "And when my brethren saw that I was about to build a ❖, they began to murmur against me, saying: Our brother is a fool, for he thinketh that he can build a ship..."

11 "...I, ❖, said unto them that they should murmur no more against their father; neither should they withhold their labor from me, for God had commanded me that I should build a ship."

12 "...they began to dance, and to sing, and to speak with much ❖, yea, even that they did forget by what power they had been brought thither; yea, they were lifted up unto exceeding ❖."

14 "And I said unto them that the water which my father saw was ❖ ; and so much was his mind swallowed up in other things that he beheld not the ❖ of the water."

16 "...as my father arose in the morning, and went forth to the tent door, to his great astonishment he beheld upon the ground a round ❖ of curious workmanship; and it was of fine brass."

17 "...I ❖ unto the Lord; and after I had ❖ the winds did cease, and the storm did cease, and there was a great calm."

20 "...I said unto them that I knew that I had spoken hard things against the wicked, according to the truth; and the righteous have I justified, and testified that they should be lifted up at the last day; wherefore, the ❖ taketh the truth to be hard, for it cutteth them to the very center."

22 "...after I had finished the [9A], according to the word of the Lord, my brethren beheld that it was good, and that the workmanship thereof was exceedingly fine; wherefore, they did ❖ themselves again before the Lord."

25 "Wherefore, the wicked are rejected from the righteous, and also from that tree of life, whose fruit is most precious and most desirable above all other fruits; yea, and it is the greatest of all the ❖ of God."

26 "For he truly spake many great things unto them, which were ❖ to be understood, save a man should inquire of the Lord; and they being hard in their hearts, therefore they did not look unto the Lord as they ought."

27 "Yea, do ye suppose that they would have been led out of bondage, if the Lord had not commanded ❖ that he should lead them out of bondage?"

Down

1 "And if it so be that the children of men keep the commandments of God he doth nourish them, and strengthen them, and provide means whereby they can ❖ the thing which he has commanded them..."

2 "...I, Nephi, was exceedingly sorrowful because of the ❖ of their hearts..."

3 "Wherefore, I, Nephi, did exhort them to give heed unto the ❖ of the Lord; yea, I did exhort them with all the energies of my soul, and with all the faculty which I possessed, that they would give heed to the ❖ of God and remember to keep his commandments always in all things."

4 "...whoso would ❖ unto the word of God, and would hold fast unto it, they would never perish; neither could the temptations and the fiery darts of the adversary overpower them unto blindness, to lead them away to destruction."

7 "...when they saw that they were about to be swallowed up in the depths of the sea they ❖ of the thing which they had done, insomuch that they loosed me."

10 "What meaneth the tree which he saw? And I said unto them: It was a representation of the tree of ❖ ."

8

13 "...and if they be filthy it must needs be that they cannot dwell in the ❖ of God; if so, the kingdom of God must be filthy also."

15 "And thus we see that by ❖ means the Lord can bring about great things."

17 "And after we had been driven back upon the waters...my brethren began to see that the judgments of God were upon them, and that they must ❖ save that they should repent of their iniquities..."

18 "Nevertheless, I did look unto God, and I did praise him all day long; and I did not ❖ against the Lord because of mine afflictions."

19 "And it came to pass that we did find upon the land of promise ...that there were ❖ in the forests of every kind..."

21 "And I said unto them: If God had commanded me to do all ❖ I could do them."

22 "...worship the Lord thy God, and ❖ thy father and thy mother, that thy days may be long in the land which the Lord thy God shall give thee."

23 "...as I, Nephi, went forth to slay food, behold, I did break my ❖ , which was made of fine steel; and after I did break my ❖, behold, my brethren were angry with me because of the loss of my ❖, for we did obtain no food."

24 "And it came to pass that we did begin to ❖ the earth, and we began to plant seeds; yea, we did put all our seeds into the earth, which we had brought from the land of Jerusalem."

9

FIVE
1 Nephi 19–22

Across

5 "For the time soon cometh that the fulness of the ❖ of God shall be poured out upon all the children of men; for he will not suffer that the wicked shall destroy the righteous."

7 "Wherefore, the righteous need not ❖ ; for thus saith the prophet, they shall be saved, even if it so be as by fire."

9 "For the time speedily shall come that all churches which are built up to get ❖ , and all those who are built up to get power over the flesh...are they who need to fear, and tremble, and quake..."

10 "And the God of our fathers...yieldeth himself...as a man, into the hands of wicked men, to be ❖ up...and to be crucified..."

11 (continued from 3D) "...and there shall be one fold and one ❖ ; and he shall feed his sheep, and in him they shall find pasture."

14 "...I, Nephi, did teach my brethren these things...which were engraven upon the plates of ❖, that they might know concerning the doings of the Lord in other lands, among people of old."

15 "Wherefore, if ye shall be obedient to the commandments, and endure to the end, ye shall be saved at the ❖ day."

16 "...yea, in fine, all those who belong to the ❖ of the devil are they who need fear, and tremble, and quake; they are those who must be brought low in the dust; they are those who must be consumed as stubble; and this is according to the words of the prophet."

17 "Behold they were manifest unto the prophet by the voice of the ❖ ; for by the ❖ are all things made known unto the prophets..."

19 "Nevertheless, when that day cometh...that they no more turn aside their hearts against the Holy One of Israel, then will he remember the covenants which he made to their ❖ ."

24 "...and those [churches] who are built up to become ❖ in the eyes of the world...are they who need fear, and tremble, and quake..."

25 (continued from 26A) "...and they shall be brought out of obscurity and out of darkness; and they shall know that the Lord is their ❖ and their Redeemer, the Mighty One of Israel."

26 "Wherefore, he will bring them again out of captivity, and they shall be gathered together to the lands of their ❖ ..." (continued in 25A)

27 "But, behold, all nations, kindreds, tongues, and people shall dwell safely in the Holy One of Israel if it so be that they will ❖ ."

28 "And as for those who are at Jerusalem, saith the prophet, they shall be scourged by all people, because they crucify the God of Israel, and turn their hearts aside, rejecting signs and ❖ , and the power and glory of the God of Israel."

29 "...the time cometh speedily that Satan shall have no more power over the hearts of the children of men; for the day soon cometh that all the proud and they who do wickedly shall be as ❖ ; and the cometh that they must be burned."

Down

1 "Wherefore, the things of which I have ❖ are things pertaining to things both temporal and spiritual..."

2 "A ❖ shall the Lord your God raise up unto you, like unto me; him shall ye hear in all things whatsoever he shall say unto you."

3 "And he gathereth his children from the four quarters of the earth; and he numbereth his ❖ , and they know him..." (continued in 11A)

4 "And notwithstanding he hath done all this, and greater also, there is no ❖ , saith the Lord, unto the wicked."

5 "...and those who seek the lusts of the flesh and the things of the ❖, and to do all manner of iniquity...are they who need fear, and tremble, and quake..."

6 "Wherefore, I, Nephi, did make a record upon the other ❖ , which gives an account, or which gives a greater account of the wars and contentions and destructions of my people."

8 "And because they turn their ❖ aside, saith the prophet, and have despised the Holy One of Israel, they shall wander in the flesh, and perish, and become a hiss and a by–word, and be hated among all nations."

12 "And because of the ❖ of his [11A] people, Satan has no power; wherefore, he cannot be loosed for the space of many years; for he hath no power over the hearts of the people, for they dwell in righteousness, and the Holy One of Israel reigneth."

13 "And the blood of that great and abominable church...shall turn upon their own heads; for they shall ❖ among themselves..."

18 "And behold he ❖ , according to the words of the angel, in six hundred years from the time my father left Jerusalem."

20 "Yea, then will he remember the isles of the sea; yea, and all the people who are of the house of Israel, will I gather in...from the ❖ quarters of the earth."

21 "...I did read unto them that which was written by the prophet ❖ ; for I did liken all scriptures unto us, that it might be for our profit and learning."

22 "And it came to pass that the Lord commanded me, wherefore I did make plates of ❖ that I might engraven upon them the record of my people."

23 "For the things which some men esteem to be of great worth, both to the body and soul, others set at naught and ❖ under their feet."

11

SIX
2 Nephi 1–5

Across

4 "And we did observe to keep the judgments, and the statutes, and the commandments of the Lord in all things, according to the law of ❖."

5 "Yea, my God will give me, if I ask not amiss; therefore I will lift up my ❖ unto thee; yea, I will cry unto thee, my God, the rock of my righteousness."

7 "Nevertheless, Jacob, my firstborn in the wilderness, thou knowest the greatness of God; and he shall consecrate thine afflictions for thy ❖."

9 "Behold, my soul delighteth in the things of the Lord; and my heart ❖ continually upon the things which I have seen and heard."

12 "Wherefore, the Lord God gave unto man that he should ❖ for himself."

13 "Awake, my sons; put on the ❖ of righteousness. Shake off the chains with which ye are bound, and come forth out of obscurity, and arise from the dust."

14 "...when the time cometh that they shall dwindle in ❖, after they have received so great blessings from the hand of the Lord...having power given them to do all things by faith...if the day come that they will reject the Holy One of Israel...the judgments of him that is just shall rest upon them."

15 "A ❖ shall the Lord my God raise up, who shall be a choice ❖ unto the fruit of my loins."

17 "Inasmuch as they will not ❖ unto thy words they shall be cut off from the presence of the Lord."

18 "But behold, my sons and my daughters, I cannot go down to my grave save I should leave a blessing upon you; for behold, I know that if ye are brought up in the way ye should go ye will not ❖ from it."

22 "For it must needs be, that there is an ❖ in all things."

23 "...arise from the dust, my sons, and be men, and be determined in one mind and in one ❖, united in all things, that ye may not come down into captivity..."

24 "Wherefore, men are free according to the flesh; and all things are given them which are expedient unto man. And they are free to choose [3D] and ❖ life, through the great Mediator of all men, or to choose captivity and death, according to the captivity and power of the devil; for he seeketh that all men might be miserable like unto himself."

26 "And I, Nephi, did build a ❖; and I did construct it after the manner of the ❖ of Solomon..."

27 "And now, my sons, I speak unto you these things for your profit and learning; for there is a God, and he hath created all ❖, both the heavens and the earth, and all ❖ that in them are, both ❖ to [12A] and ❖ to be [12A] upon."

Down

1 "Yea, he will bring other nations unto them, and he will give unto them power, and he will take away from them the lands of their possessions, and he will cause them to be scattered and ❖."

2 "Adam fell that men might be; and men are, that they might have ❖."

3 "And if it so be that they shall serve him according to the commandments which he hath given, it shall be a land of ❖ unto them; wherefore, they shall never be brought down into captivity; if so, it shall be because of iniquity; for if iniquity shall abound cursed shall be the land for their sakes, but unto the righteous it shall be blessed forever."

4 "If not so...righteousness could not be brought to pass, neither wickedness, neither holiness nor ❖, neither good nor bad."

6 "But, said he, notwithstanding our afflictions, we have obtained a land of promise, a land which is ❖ above all other lands; a land which the Lord God hath covenanted with me should be a land for the inheritance of my seed."

8 "O Lord, I have trusted in ❖, and I will trust in ❖ forever."

10 "And it came to pass that we lived after the manner of ❖ ."

11 "And because that they are [19D] from the fall they have become ❖ forever, knowing good from evil; to [12A] for themselves and not to be [12A] upon, save it be by the punishment of the law at the great and last day, according to the commandments which God hath given."

15 "For my soul delighteth in the ❖ , and my heart pondereth them, and writeth them for the learning and the profit of my children."

16 "Inasmuch as ye shall keep my commandments ye shall ❖ in the land; but inasmuch as ye will not keep my commandments ye shall be cut off from my presence."

19 "And the Messiah cometh in the fulness of time, that he may ❖ the children of men from the fall."

20 "Wherefore, man could not [12A] for himself save it should be that he was ❖ by the one or the other."

21 "Wherefore, redemption cometh in and through the Holy Messiah; for he is full of grace and ❖ ."

23 "And it came to pass that I, Nephi, did cause my people to be industrious, and to labor with their ❖ ."

25 "Wherefore, I, Lehi, prophesy according to the workings of the Spirit which is in me, that there shall none come into this ❖ save they shall be brought by the hand of the Lord."

13

SEVEN
2 Nephi 6–9

Across

3 "And blessed are the Gentiles ...if it so be that they shall repent and fight not against ❖, and do not unite themselves to that great and abominable church, they shall be saved..."

5 "For the atonement satisfieth the demands of his ❖ upon all those who have not the law given to them..."

8 "Wherefore, do not spend money for that which is of no ❖, nor your labor for that which cannot satisfy."

10 "And whoso knocketh, to him will he open; and the wise, and the learned, and they that are rich, who are ❖ up because of their learning, and their wisdom, and their riches—yea, they are they whom he despiseth; and save they shall cast these things away, and consider themselves fools before God, and come down in the depths of humility, he will not open unto them."

11 "Behold, who art thou, that thou shouldst be afraid of ❖ ...and forgettest the Lord thy maker..."

13 "But, behold, the righteous, the ❖ of the Holy One of [18A], they who have believed in the Holy One of [18A], they who have endured the crosses of the world, and despised the shame of it, they shall inherit the kingdom of God..." (continued in 27D)

15 "Behold, the way for man is narrow, but it lieth in a straight course before him, and the ❖ of the gate is the Holy One of [18A]; and he employeth no servant there; and there is none other way save it be by the gate..."

16 "But wo unto him that has the ❖ given, yea, that has all the commandments of God, like unto us, and that transgresseth them, and that wasteth the days of his probation, for awful is his state!"

17 (continued from 15D) "...and the ❖ shall have a perfect knowledge of their enjoyment, and their righteousness, being clothed with purity, yea, even with the robe of righteousness."

18 "...the Lord God, the Holy One of ❖, should manifest himself unto them in the flesh...they should scourge him and crucify him..."

21 "But wo unto the rich, who are rich as to the things of the world. For because they are rich they despise the poor, and they persecute the meek, and their hearts are upon their ❖; wherefore, their ❖ is their god. And behold, their ❖ shall perish with them also."

24 "The Lord God hath given me the tongue of the ❖, that I should know how to speak a word in season unto thee, O house of [18A]."

26 "Wherefore, it must needs be an infinite ❖—save it should be an infinite ❖ this corruption could not put on incorruption."

28 "For the Lord God will ❖ me, therefore shall I not be confounded. Therefore have I set my face like a flint, and I know that I shall not be ashamed."

29 "...and the bodies and the spirits of men will be ❖ one to the other; and it is by the power of the resurrection of the Holy One of [18A]."

30 "O how great the holiness of our God! For he knoweth all things, and there is not anything save he ❖ it."

Down

1 "And, in fine, wo unto all those who die in their ❖ ..."

2 "Remember, to be carnally–minded is death, and to be spiritually–minded is ❖ eternal."

4 "And because of the way of deliverance of our God, the Holy One of [18A], this death...which is the temporal, shall deliver up its dead; which death is the ❖ ."

6 "But to be learned is good if they hearken unto the ❖ of God."

7 "Behold, I will lift up mine hand to the Gentiles, and set up my ❖ to the people; and they shall bring thy sons in their arms, and thy daughters shall be carried upon their shoulders."

8 "O that cunning plan of the evil one! O the vainness, and the frailties, and the foolishness of men! When they are learned they think they are ❖, and they hearken not unto the counsel of God, for they set it aside, supposing they know of themselves, wherefore, their wisdom is foolishness and it profiteth them not. And they shall perish."

9 "And he commandeth all men that they must ❖, and be baptized in his name, having perfect faith in the Holy One of [18A], or they cannot be saved in the kingdom of God."

12 "Wherefore, they that fight against Zion and the covenant people of the Lord shall lick up the dust of their feet; and the people of the Lord shall not be ❖."

14 "...the Lord will be ❖ unto them, that when they shall come to the knowledge of their Redeemer, they shall be gathered together again to the lands of their inheritance."

15 "Wherefore, we shall have a perfect ❖ of all our guilt, and our uncleanness, and our nakedness..." (continued in 17A)

19 "...that ❖ cometh when they shall believe in him; and none will he destroy that believe in him."

20 "...when all men shall have passed from this first death unto life, insomuch as they have become immortal...then must they be ❖ according to the holy judgment of God."

22 "Behold, my beloved brethren, remember the words of your God; ❖ unto him continually by day, and give thanks unto his holy name by night. Let your hearts rejoice."

23 "Come, my brethren, every one that thirsteth, come ye to the ❖ ..."

25 "...they who are righteous shall be righteous ❖, and they who are filthy shall be filthy ❖ ..."

27 "...they shall inherit the kingdom of God, which was prepared for them from the foundation of the world, and their ❖ shall be full forever."

15

EIGHT
2 Nephi 10–16

Across

2 "Wherefore, by the words of three, God hath said, I will establish my ❖."

5 "And it came to pass in the last days, when the mountain of the Lord's ❖ shall be established in the top of the mountains, and shall be exalted above the hills, and all nations shall flow unto it."

8 "Come ye, and let us go up to the mountain of the Lord...and he will teach us of his ways, and we will walk in his ❖ ; for out of Zion shall go forth the law, and the word of the Lord from Jerusalem."

10 "Wherefore, my beloved brethren, reconcile yourselves to the ❖ of God, and not to the ❖ of the devil and the flesh; and remember, after ye are reconciled unto God, that it is only in and through the grace of God that ye are saved."

11 "And he that fighteth against ❖ shall perish, saith God."

12 "The Lord standeth up to ❖ , and standeth to judge the people."

13 "And it shall come to pass that the lofty looks of man shall be ❖ , and the haughtiness of men shall be bowed down, and the Lord alone shall be exalted in that day."

15 "Wherefore, because of their iniquities, destructions, famines, pestilences, and bloodshed shall come upon them; and they who shall not be destroyed shall be ❖ among all nations."

19 "Wo unto them that call ❖ good, and good ❖ , that put darkness for light, and light for darkness, that put bitter for sweet, and sweet for bitter!"

20 "Behold, my ❖ delighteth in proving unto my people the truth of the coming of Christ; for, for this end hath the law of Moses been given; and all things which have been given of God from the beginning of the world, unto man, are the typifying of him."

22 "Because the [17D] of Zion are ❖, and walk with stretched-forth necks and wanton eyes, walking and mincing as they go, and making a tinkling with their feet—"

23 "And he will lift up an ❖ to the nations from far, and will hiss unto them from the end of the earth; and behold, they shall come with speed swiftly; none shall be weary nor stumble among them."

24 "Wo unto them that rise up early in the morning, that they may follow strong ❖ , that continue until night, and wine inflame them!"

26 "For if there be no Christ there be no God; and if there be no God we are not, for there could have been no ❖ ."

27 "Wo unto the wise in their own ❖ and prudent in their own sight!"

28 "And he laid [the live coal] upon my mouth, and said: Lo, this has touched thy lips; and thine iniquity is taken away, and thy ❖ purged."

29 "...for they who are not for me are ❖ me, saith our God."

Down

1 "Therefore, cheer up your hearts, and remember that ye are ❖ to act for yourselves—to choose the way of everlasting death or the way of eternal life."

3 "But there is a God, and he is Christ, and he ❖ in the fulness of his own time."

4 "When the day cometh that they shall ❖ in me, that I am Christ, then have I covenanted with their fathers that they shall be restored in the flesh, upon the earth, unto the lands of their inheritance."

6 "...and they shall beat their ❖ into plow-shares, and their spears into pruning-hooks—nation shall not lift up ❖ against nation, neither shall they learn war any more."

7 "And this land shall be a land of ❖ unto the Gentiles, and there shall be no [25D] upon the land, who shall raise up unto the Gentiles."

8 "And [the Lord] said: Go and tell this ❖ —Hear ye indeed, but they understood not; and see ye indeed, but they perceived not."

9 Isaiah: "Also I heard the voice of the Lord, saying: Whom shall I ❖ , and who will go for us? Then I

16

said: Here am I; ❖ me."

14 "Then said I: Wo is unto me! for I am undone; because I am a man of ❖ lips; and I dwell in the midst of a people of ❖ lips; for mine eyes have seen the King, the Lord of Hosts."

16 "...it must needs be expedient that Christ...should come among the Jews, among those who are the more wicked part of the world; and they shall ❖ him..."

17 "And it shall come to pass, they that are left in Zion and remain in Jerusalem shall be called holy, every one that is written among the living in Jerusalem— When the Lord shall have washed away the filth of the ❖ of Zion, and shall have purged the blood of Jerusalem from the midst thereof by the spirit of judgment and by the spirit of burning."

18 "And I will fortify this land against all other ❖ ."

21 "But because of priestcrafts and iniquities, they at Jerusalem will stiffen their ❖ against him, that he be crucified."

25 "For he that raiseth up a ❖ against me shall perish, for I, the Lord, the ❖ of heaven, will be their ❖ , and I will be a light unto them forever, that hear my words."

17

NINE
2 Nephi 17–25

Across

3 "And when they shall say unto you: ❖ unto them that have familiar spirits, and unto wizards that peep and mutter—should not a people ❖ unto their God for the living to hear from the dead?"

4 "For the stars of heaven and the constellations thereof shall not give their ❖ ; the sun shall be darkened in his going forth, and the moon shall not cause her ❖ to shine."

6 "And it shall come to pass in that day that the Lord shall set his hand again the ❖ time to recover the remnant of his people which shall be left..."

9 "And now behold, I say unto you that the right way is to believe in Christ, and deny him not; and Christ is the Holy One of Israel; wherefore ye must bow down before him, and ❖ him with all your might, mind, and strength, and your whole soul; and if ye do this ye shall in nowise be cast out."

10 "For according to the words of the prophets, the Messiah cometh in ❖ hundred years from the time that my father left Jerusalem; and according to the words of the prophets, and also the word of the angel of God, his name shall be Jesus Christ, the Son of God."

13 "...my soul delighteth in plainness unto my people, that they may ❖ ."

15 "And we talk of ❖ , we rejoice in ❖ , we preach of ❖ , we prophesy of ❖ ..." (continued in 16D)

19 "They shall not hurt nor destroy in all my holy mountain, for the ❖ shall be full of the knowledge of the Lord, as the waters cover the sea."

21 "Behold, God is my salvation; I will trust, and not be afraid; for the Lord JEHOVAH is my ❖ and my song; he also has become my salvation."

22 "Therefore, the Lord himself shall give you a sign—Behold, a virgin shall conceive, and shall bear a son, and shall call his name ❖ ."

24 "And there shall come forth a rod out of the stem of ❖ , and a branch shall grow out of his roots."

25 "And after they have been scattered, and the Lord God hath scourged them by other nations for the space of many generations, yea, even down from generation to generation until they shall be persuaded to believe in Christ, the Son of God, and the ❖ , which is infinite for all mankind..."

26 "...these things are true, and as the Lord God liveth, there is none other name given under heaven save it be this Jesus Christ, of which I have spoken, whereby man can be ❖ ."

Down

1 "For unto us a child is born, unto us a son is given; and the government shall be upon his shoulder; and his name shall be called, Wonderful, Counselor, The Mighty God, The Everlasting Father, The Prince of ❖ ."

2 "The wolf also shall dwell with the lamb, and the leopard shall lie down with the kid, and the calf and the young lion and fatling together; and a little ❖ shall lead them."

5 "And I will punish the world for evil, and the wicked for their iniquity; I will cause the arrogancy of the ❖ to cease, and will lay down the haughtiness of the terrible."

6 "Wherefore , hearken, O my people, which are of the house of Israel, and give ear unto my words; for because the words of Isaiah are not plain unto you, nevertheless they are plain unto all those that are filled with the ❖ of prophecy."

7 "...wo unto them that fight against God and the people of his ❖ ."

8 "And he shall be for a sanctuary; but for a ❖ of stumbling, and for a rock of offense to both the houses of Israel, for a gin and a snare to the inhabitants of Jerusalem."

11 "And the Lord will set his hand again the second time to restore his people from their lost and

18

fallen state. Wherefore, he will proceed to do a marvelous work and a ❖ among the children of men."

12 "How art thou ❖ from heaven, O Lucifer, son of the morning!"

14 "And it shall come to pass in that day that the Lord shall give thee ❖ , from thy sorrow, and from thy fear, and from the hard bondage wherein thou wast made to serve."

16 (continued from 15A) "...and we write according to our prophecies, that our children may know to what source they may look for a ❖ of their sins."

17 "Wherefore, the Jews shall be ❖ among all nations; yea, and also Babylon shall be destroyed; wherefore, the Jews shall be ❖ by other nations."

18 "To the law and to the ❖ ; and if they speak not according to this word, it is because there is no light in them."

20 "For we labor diligently to write, to persuade our ❖ , and also our brethren, to believe in Christ, and to be reconciled to God..." (continued in 23D)

23 (continued from 20D) "...for we know that it is by grace that we are saved, after ❖ we can do."

19

TEN
2 Nephi 26–28

Across

2 "And the Gentiles are lifted up in the pride of their eyes, and have stumbled, because of the greatness of their stumbling block, that they have built up many churches; nevertheless, they put down the ❖ and miracles of God, and preach up unto themselves their own wisdom and their own learning, that they may get gain and grind upon the face of the poor."

4 "And they shall contend one with another; and their priests shall contend one with another, and they shall teach with their learning, and ❖ the Holy Ghost, which giveth utterance."

7 "...priestcrafts are that men ❖ and set themselves up for a a light unto the world, that they may get gain and praise of the world; but they seek not the welfare of Zion."

8 "And there are many ❖ built up which cause envyings, and strifes, and malice."

12 "...the book shall be hid from the eyes of the world, that the eyes of none shall behold it save it be that ❖ witnesses shall behold it, by the power of God, besides him to whom the book shall be delivered; and they shall testify to the truth of the book and the things therein."

13 "For behold, my beloved brethren, I say unto you that the Lord God worketh not in ❖ ."

14 "Wherefore, all those who are ❖ , and that do wickedly, the day that cometh shall burn them up, saith the Lord of Hosts, for they shall be as stubble."

15 "And the day cometh that the words of the book which were ❖ shall be read upon the house tops; and they shall be read by the power of Christ; and all things shall be revealed unto the children of men which ever have been among the children of men, and which ever will be even unto the end of the earth."

17 "...the words of the righteous shall be written, and the prayers of the ❖ shall be heard, and all those who have dwindled in unbelief shall not be forgotten."

18 "Forasmuch as this people draw near unto me with their mouth, and with their lips do honor me, but have removed their ❖ far from me, and their fear towards me is taught by the precepts of men—"

21 "And there shall also be many which shall say: Eat, drink, and be merry; nevertheless, fear God—he will justify in committing a little ❖ ..." (continued in 22D)

23 "He doeth not anything save it be for the ❖ of the world; for he loveth the world, even that he layeth down his own life that he may draw all men unto him."

25 "I will give unto the children of men ❖ upon ❖ , precept upon precept, here a little and there a little..." (continued in 26A)

26 (continued from 25A)"...and blessed are those who hearken unto my precepts, and lend an ear unto my counsel, for they shall learn ❖ ; for unto him that receiveth I will give more; and from them that shall say, We have enough, from them shall be taken away even that which they have."

27 "Yea, and there shall be many which shall teach after this manner, false and ❖ and foolish doctrines, and shall be puffed up in their hearts, and shall seek deep to hide their counsels from the Lord; and their works shall be in the dark."

29 "Yea, and there shall be many which shall say: Eat, drink, and be merry, for tomorrow we ❖ ; and it shall be well with us."

30 "But the laborer in Zion shall labor for Zion; for if they labor for ❖ they shall perish."

Down

1 "Therefore, I will proceed to do a marvelous work among this people, yea, a marvelous work and a wonder, for the wisdom of their wise and learned shall ❖ , and the understanding of their prudent shall be hid."

3 "Wo be unto him that shall say: We have ❖ the word of God, and we need no more of the word of God, for we have enough!"

5 "But behold, the righteous that hearken unto the words of the ❖ , and destroy them not, but look forward unto Christ with stead-

20

fastness for the signs which are given, not withstanding all persecution—behold, they are they which shall not perish."

6 "And wo unto them that seek deep to hide their ❖ from the Lord!"

9 "And behold the book shall be sealed; and in the book shall be a ❖ from God, from the beginning of the world to the ending thereof."

10 "And it shall come to pass that the Lord God shall bring forth unto you the ❖ of a book, and they shall be the ❖ of them which have slumbered."

11 "Yea, wo be unto him that hearkeneth unto the ❖ of men, and denieth the power of God, and the gift of the Holy Ghost!"

16 "And after Christ shall have risen from the dead he shall show himself unto you, my children, and my beloved brethren; and the words which he shall speak unto you shall be the ❖ which ye shall do."

19 "Therefore, wo be unto him that is at ❖ in Zion!"

20 "For the Spirit of the Lord will not always ❖ with man."

22 (continued from 21A) "...yea, lie a little, take the advantage of one because of his words, dig a pit for thy neighbor; there is no harm in this; and do all these things, for tomorrow we die; and if it so be that we are ❖ , God will beat us with a few stripes, and at last we shall be saved in the kingdom of God."

23 "They shall write the things which shall be done among them, and they shall be written and sealed up in a ❖ , and those who have dwindled in unbelief shall not have them, for they seek to destroy the things of God."

24 "...and I [God] work not among the children of men save it be according to their ❖ ."

25 "The Lord God hath given a commandment that all men should have charity, which charity is ❖ And except they should have charity they were nothing."

28 "Hath he commanded any that they should not partake of his salvation? Behold I say unto you, Nay; but he hath given it free for all men; and he hath commanded his people that they should persuade all ❖ to repentance."

21

ELEVEN
2 Nephi 29 – Jacob 1

Across

2 "And I heard a voice from the Father, saying: Yea, the words of my Beloved are true and faithful. He that endureth to the end, the same shall be ❖ ."

3 "...as many of the Gentiles as will repent are the ❖ people of the Lord; and as many of the Jews as will not repent shall be cast off; for the Lord covenanteth with none save it be with them that repent and believe in his Son..."

4 "Wherefore, if ye shall press forward, feasting upon the word of Christ, and endure to the end...Ye shall have ❖ life."

6 "...this is the way; and there is none other way nor name given under ❖ whereby man can be saved in the kingdom of God."

8 "Wherefore, because that ye have a Bible ye need not suppose that it contains all my ❖ ; neither need ye suppose that I have not caused more to be written."

10 "...the Lord God shall commence his work among all nations, kindreds, tongues, and people, to bring about the ❖ of his people upon the earth."

11 "...and many generations shall not pass away among [the Lamanites], save they shall be a ❖ and a delightsome people."

12 "...when a man speaketh by the power of the Holy Ghost the power of the Holy Ghost carrieth it unto the ❖ of the children of men."

13 "... ❖ upon the words of Christ; for behold, the words of Christ will tell you all things what ye should do."

14 "And now, if the Lamb of God, he being holy, should have need to be ❖ by water, to fulfil all righteousness, O then, how much more need have we, being unholy, to be ❖, yea, even by water!"

15 "And he gave me, Jacob, a commandment that I should write upon these [small] plates a few of the things which I considered to be most ❖ ..."

19 " ❖ speak by the power of the Holy Ghost; wherefore, they speak the words of Christ."

22 (continued from 21D) "...ye must not perform any thing unto the Lord save in the first place ye shall pray unto the Father in the name of Christ, that he will consecrate thy performance unto thee, that thy performance may be for the ❖ of thy soul."

23 "For if ye would hearken unto the Spirit which teacheth a man to ❖ ye would know that ye must ❖ ..." (continued in 7D)

24 "...the Jews...as many as shall ❖ in Christ shall also become a delightsome people."

25 "And again, it showeth unto the children of men the straitness of the path, and the narrowness of the ❖ , by which they should enter, he having set the example before them."

Down

1 "And because my words shall hiss forth—many of the Gentiles shall say: A ❖! A ❖ ! We have got a ❖ , and there cannot be anymore ❖ ."

2 "Wherefore, ye must press forward with a ❖ in Christ, having a perfect brightness of hope, and a love of God and of all men."

4 "...if ye will ❖ in by the way, and receive the Holy Ghost, it will show unto you all things what ye should do."

5 "And we did ❖ our office unto the Lord, taking upon us the responsibility, answering the sins of the people upon our own heads if we did not teach them the word of God with all diligence; wherefore, by laboring with our might their blood might not come upon our garments; otherwise their blood would come upon our garments, and we would not be found spotless at the last day."

6 "...the people of Nephi...began to grow ❖ in their hearts, and indulge themselves somewhat in wicked practices..."

7 (continued from 23A) "...for the ❖ spirit teacheth not a man to pray, but teacheth him that he must not pray."

22

8 "...for out of the books which shall be written I will judge the world, every man according to their ❖ , according to that which is written."

9 "And the words which I have written in weakness will be made ❖ unto them; for it persuadeth them to do good..."

15 "Yea, and they also began to search much gold and silver, and began to be lifted up somewhat in ❖ ."

16 "...I know by this that unless a man shall endure to the end, in following the ❖ of the Son of the living God, he cannot be saved."

17 "After ye have repented...and witnessed unto the Father that ye are willing to keep my commandments, by the baptism of water , and have received the baptism of fire and of the Holy Ghost, and can speak with a new tongue, yea, even with the tongue of angels, and after this should deny me, it would have been better for you that ye had not ❖ me."

18 "Follow thou me. Wherefore, my beloved brethren, can we follow Jesus save we shall be ❖ to keep the commandments of the Father?"

20 "And if there were preaching which was ❖ , or revelation which was great, or prophesying, that I should engraven the heads of them upon these plates..."

21 "But behold, I say unto you that ye must pray always, and not ❖ ..." (continued in 22A)

TWELVE
Jacob 2–7

Across

4 "I knew that it was a ❖ spot of ground; wherefore...I have nourished it this long time, and thou beholdest that it hath brought forth much fruit."

5 "But before ye ❖ for riches, ❖ ye for the kingdom of God."

9 "...into the nethermost parts of the [10A]...they beheld that the fruit of the natural branches had become ❖ also..."

10 "Come, let us go to the nethermost part of the ❖ , and behold if the natural branches of the tree have not brought forth much fruit also, that I may lay up of the fruit thereof against the season, unto mine own self."

12 "...the master of the vineyard... said: I will ❖ it, and dig about it, and nourish it, that perhaps it may shoot forth young and tender branches, and it perish not."

15 "Wherefore, brethren, seek not to counsel the ❖ , but to take counsel from his hand."

16 "...we will pluck off those main ❖ which are beginning to wither away, and we will cast them into the fire that they may be burned."

19 "And how blessed are they who have ❖ diligently in his [10A]..."

21 "And after ye have obtained a ❖ in Christ ye shall obtain riches, if ye seek them..." (continued in 23D)

25 "...I fear lest I have committed the unpardonable sin, for I have ❖ unto God; for I denied the Christ, and said that I believed the scriptures; and they truly testify of him."

26 "For I, the Lord God, delight in the chastity of ❖ ."

27 "...the tree in the which the [29A] olive branches had been [2D]; ...had sprung forth and begun to bear ❖ ."

29 "Take thou the branches of the ❖ olive–tree, and [2D] them in, in the stead thereof..."

30 "And [Sherem] preached many things which were ❖ unto the people; and this he did that he might overthrow the doctrine of Christ."

Down

1 "O all ye that are ❖ in heart, lift up your heads and receive the pleasing word of God, and feast upon his love; for ye may, if your minds are firm, forever."

2 "...I will take away many of these young and tender branches, and I will ❖ them whithersoever I will..."

3 "...I will liken thee, O house of ❖ , like unto a tame olive–tree, which a man took and nourished in his vineyard; and it grew, and waxed old, and began to decay."

6 "Look unto God with firmness of mind, and pray unto him with exceeding ❖, and he will console you in your afflictions, and he will console you in your afflictions, and he will plead your cause, and send down justice upon those who seek your destruction."

7 "Wherefore, go to, and call servants, that we may labor diligently with our might in the vineyard, that we may ❖ the way, that I may bring forth again the natural [27A], which natural [27A] is good and the most precious above all other [27A]."

8 "And when the time cometh that evil fruit shall again come into my [10A], then will I cause the good and the bad to be gathered; and the good will I ❖ unto myself, and the bad will I cast away into its own place."

11 "For behold, ye yourselves know that he counseleth in wisdom, and in justice, and in great ❖ , over all his works."

13 "But behold, this time [the old tree] hath brought forth much [27A], and there is ❖ of it which is good... notwithstanding all our labor..."

14 "...and because some of you have obtained more abundantly than that of your brethren ye are lifted up in the ❖ of your hearts, and wear stiff necks and high heads because of the costliness of your apparel, and persecute your brethren because ye suppose that ye are better than they."

17 "Think of your brethren like unto yourselves, and be familiar with all and free with your ❖ , that they may be rich like unto you."

18 "Behold, [the Lamanite] husbands love their wives, and their wives love their husbands, and their husbands and their wives love their ❖ ..."

20 "...I know that the roots are good...and because of their much ❖ they have hitherto brought forth, from the wild branches, good [27A]."

22 "And there began to be the natural fruit again in the [10A]; and the natural branches began to ❖ and thrive exceedingly..."

23 (continued from 21A) "...and ye will seek them for the intent to do ❖ —to clothe the naked, and to feed the hungry, and to liberate the captive, and administer relief to the sick and the afflicted."

24 "And he had hope to shake me from the faith, notwithstanding the many revelations and the many things which I had seen concerning these things; for I truly had seen ❖ , and they had ministered unto me."

28 "Wherefore, let us take of the branches of these which I have planted in the nethermost parts of my vineyard, and let us [2D] them into the ❖ from whence they came..."

25

THIRTEEN
Enos – Words of Mormon

Across

2 "And as many as are not stiffnecked and have faith, have communion with the Holy ❖, which maketh manifest unto the children of man, according to their faith."

6 "And my soul hungered; and I kneeled down before my ❖, and I cried unto him in mighty prayer and supplication for mine own soul; and all the day long did I cry unto him; yea, and when the night came I did still raise my voice high that it reached the heavens."

7 "Wherefore, the prophets, and the priests, and the teachers, did ❖ diligently, exhorting with all long–suffering the people to diligence; teaching the law of Moses, and the intent for which it was given; persuading them to look forward unto the Messiah, and believe in him to come as though he already was."

10 (continued from 20A) "...for there is nothing which is good save it comes from the Lord: and that which is ❖ cometh from the devil."

12 "And they departed out of the land into the wilderness, as many as would hearken unto the ❖ of the Lord; and they were led by many preachings and prophesyings."

14 "Whatsoever thing ye shall ❖ in faith, believing that ye shall receive in the name of Christ, ye shall receive it."

17 (continued from 9D) "...and there were many holy men in the land, and they did speak the word of God with power and with ❖ ; and they did use much sharpness because of the stiffneckedness of the people—"

19 "And now, I do not know all things; but the Lord knoweth all things which are to come; wherefore, he worketh in me to do according to his ❖ ."

20 (continued from 16D) "...exhorting all men to... believe in...the gift of speaking with ❖ , and in the gift of interpreting languages, and in all things which are good..." (continued in 10A)

21 "And I know that they will be ❖ ; for there are great things written upon them, out of which my people and their brethren shall be judged at the great and last day, according to the word of God which is written."

22 "Now, it came to pass that when I had heard these words I began to ❖ a desire for the welfare of my brethren, the Nephites; wherefore, I did pour out my whole soul unto God for them."

24 "And it came to pass that I [Mosiah] began to be old; and, having no seed, and knowing king ❖ to be a just man before the Lord, wherefore, I shall deliver up these plates unto him..." (continued in 16D)

27 "Enos, thy sins are ❖ thee, and thou shalt be blessed."

28 "And it came to pass that by so doing they kept them from being destroyed upon the face of the land; for they did prick their hearts with the ❖ , continually stirring them up unto repentance."

29 "Behold, it came to pass that I, Enos, knowing my father that he was a just man—for he taught me in his ❖ , and also in the nurture and admonition of the Lord—and blessed be the name of my God for it—"

Down

1 "And he said unto me: Because of thy faith in Christ, whom thou hast never before heard nor seen. And many years pass away before he shall manifest himself in the flesh; wherefore, go to, thy faith hath made thee ❖ ."

3 "Wherefore, with the help of these, king [24A], by laboring with all the might of his body and the faculty of his whole soul, and also the ❖ , did once more establish peace in the land."

4 "Wherefore, I chose these things, to finish my record upon them, which remainder of my record I shall take from the plates of [25D]; and I cannot ❖ the hundredth part of the things of my people."

5 "...I would that ye should come unto Christ, who is the Holy One of Israel, and partake of his salvation, and the ❖ of his redemption."

8 (continued from 25D) "...which contained this small account of the prophets, from ❖ down to the reign of this king [24A], and also many of the words of [25D]."

9 "For behold, king [24A] was a ❖ man, and he did reign over his people in righteousness..." (continued in 17A)

11 "...and [King [24A]] did fight with the strength of his own arm, with the sword of ❖ . And in the strength of the Lord they did contend against their enemies..."

13 "But behold, I shall take these plates, which contain these prophesyings and revelations, and put them with the remainder of my record, for they are ❖ unto me; and I know they will be ❖ unto my brethren."

15 "And after there had been ❖ prophets, and ❖ preachers and teachers among the people, and all these having been punished according to their crimes..."

16 (continued from 24A) "...exhorting all men to come unto God, the Holy One of Israel, and believe in prophesying, and in revelations, and in the ❖ of angels..." (continued in 20A)

18 "...in the days of Mosiah, there was a large ❖ brought unto him with engravings on it; and he did interpret the engravings by the gift and power of God."

23 "Inasmuch as ye will keep my commandments ye shall prosper in the ❖ ."

25 "...after I [Mormon] had made an abridgment from the plates of ❖ , down to the reign of this king [24A], of whom Amaleki spake, I searched among the records which had been delivered into my hands, and I found these plates..." (continued in 8D)

26 "Yea, come unto him, and offer your whole ❖ as an offering unto him, and continue in fasting and praying, and endure to the end; and as the Lord liveth ye will be saved."

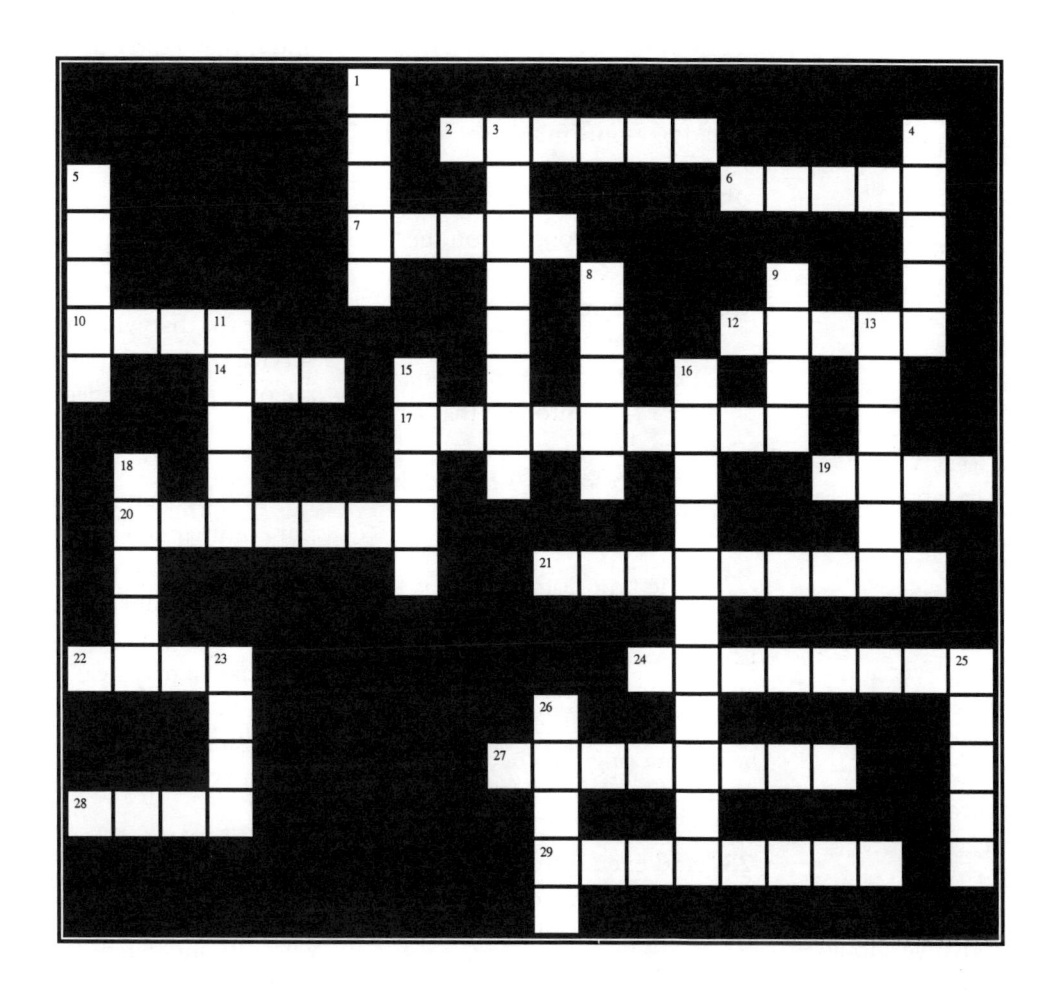

27

FOURTEEN
Mosiah 1–3

Across

3 "I say unto you, my sons, were it not for these things, which have been kept and preserved by the hand of God, that we might ❖ and understand of his mysteries, and have his commandments always before our eyes, that even our fathers would have dwindled in unbelief..."

5 "And if they be evil they are consigned to an awful view of their own ❖ and abominations, which doth cause them to shrink from the presence of the Lord into a state of misery and endless torment, from whence they can no more return..."

8 "For behold, and also his blood ❖ for the sins of those who have fallen by the transgression of Adam, who have died not knowing the will of God concerning them, or who have ignorantly sinned."

10 "Behold, ye have called me your ❖ ; and if I, whom ye call your ❖ , do labor to serve you, then ought not ye to labor to serve one another?"

12 "For the ❖ man is an enemy to God, and has been from the fall of Adam, and will be, forever and ever, unless he yields to the enticings of the Holy Spirit, and putteth off the ❖ man and becometh a saint through the atonement of Christ the Lord..." (continued in 24D)

14 "...and I would that ye should keep the commandments of God, that ye may prosper in the land according to the ❖ which the Lord made unto our fathers."

17 "And the things which I shall tell you are made known unto me by an ❖ from God."

18 "...and he never doth vary from that which he hath said; therefore, if ye do keep his commandments he doth ❖ you and prosper you."

19 "And lo, he shall suffer temptations, and ❖ of body, hunger, thirst, and fatigue, even more than man can suffer, except it be unto death..." (continued in 13D)

22 "...I say, if ye should serve him with all your whole souls yet ye would be unprofitable ❖ ."

25 "And moreover, I would desire that ye should consider on the blessed and ❖ state of those that keep the commandments of God."

26 "Behold, I say unto you that because I said unto you that I had spent my days in your service, I do not desire to ❖ , for I have only been in the service of God."

27 "...the time cometh, and is not far distant, that with power, the Lord ❖ who reigneth, who was, and is from all eternity to all eternity, shall come down from heaven among the children of men..." (continued in 21D)

28 "And even I, myself, have labored with mine own hands that I might ❖ you, and that ye should not be laden with taxes..."

Down

1 "And now, my sons, I would that ye should remember to ❖ them diligently, that ye may profit thereby..." (continued in 14A)

2 (continued from 15D) "...and even after all this they shall consider him a man, and say that he hath a devil, and shall scourge him, and shall ❖ him."

4 "And he shall cast out devils, or the evil spirits which ❖ in the hearts of the children of men."

6 "For behold, they are blessed in all things, both ❖ and spiritual; and if they hold out faithful to the end they are received into heaven, that thereby they may dwell with God in a state of never ending happiness."

7 "And behold, I tell you these things that ye may learn ❖ ; that ye may learn that when ye are in the service of your fellow beings ye are only in the service of your God."

9 King Benjamin: "...for I have not commanded you to come up hither to ❖ with the words which I shall speak, but that you should hearken unto me, and open your ears that ye may hear, and your hearts that ye may understand, and your minds that the mysteries of God may be unfolded to your view."

11 "O, all ye old men, and also ye young men, and you little children who can understand my words, for I have spoken ❖ unto you that ye

might understand, I pray that ye should awake to a remembrance of the awful situation of those that have fallen into transgression."

13 (continued from 19A) "...blood cometh from every pore, so great shall be his ❖ for the wickedness and the abominations of his people."

15 "And lo, he cometh unto his own, that ❖ might come unto the children of men even through faith on his name..." (continued in 2D)

16 "And [King Benjamin] caused that [his sons] should be taught in all the ❖ of his fathers, that thereby they might become men of understanding..."

19 "And the Lord God hath sent his holy ❖ among all the children of men, to declare these things to every kindred, nation, and tongue, that thereby whosoever should believe that Christ should come, the same might receive remission of their sins, and rejoice with exceedingly great joy, even as though he had already come among them."

20 "And he shall be called Jesus Christ, the Son of God, the Father of heaven and earth, the ❖ of all things from the beginning; and his mother shall be called Mary."

21 (continued from 27A) "...and [he] shall dwell in a tabernacle of ❖ , and shall go forth amongst men, working mighty miracles, such as healing the sick, raising the dead, causing the lame to walk, the blind to receive their sight, and the deaf to hear, and curing all manner of diseases."

23 "And moreover, I say unto you, that the time shall come when the knowledge of a ❖ shall spread throughout every nation, kindred, tongue, and people."

24 (continued from 12A) "...and becometh as a child, submissive, meek, humble, patient, full of ❖ , willing to submit to all things which the Lord seeth fit to inflict upon him, even as a child doeth submit to his father."

29

FIFTEEN
Mosiah 4–6

Across

3 (continued from 2D) "...and ye will not suffer that the beggar putteth up his petition to you in vain, and turn him out to ❖."

8 (continued from 27A) "...neither will ye suffer that they transgress the ❖ of God, and fight and quarrel one with another, and serve the devil, who is the master of sin or who is the evil spirit which hath been spoken of by our fathers, he being an enemy to all righteousness."

10 (continued from 7D) "...and ask in sincerity of ❖ that he would forgive you..." (continued in 20A)

11 "And see that all these things are done in wisdom and ❖ ; for it is not requisite that a man should run faster than he has strength."

12 "For how knoweth a man the master whom he has not ❖ , and who is a stranger unto him, and is far from the thoughts and intents of his heart?"

14 " And it came to pass that king ❖ did walk in the ways of the Lord, and did observe his judgments and his statutes, and did keep his commandments in all things whatsoever he commanded him."

15 "And now, because of the [25A] which ye have made ye shall be called the children of Christ, his sons, and his daughters; for behold, this day he hath spiritually ❖ you..." (continued in 23D)

19 "...the Spirit of the Lord came upon them, and they were filled with joy, having received a ❖ of their sins, and having peace of conscience, because of the exceeding faith which they had in Jesus Christ who should come..."

20 (continued from 10A) "...and now, if you believe all these things ❖ that ye do them."

22 "Believe in God; believe that he is, and that he ❖ all things, both in heaven and in earth..." (continued in 24A)

24 (continued from 22A) "...believe that he has all ❖ , and all power, both in heaven and in earth; believe that man doth not comprehendeth all the things which the Lord can comprehend."

25 "And we are willing to enter into a ❖ with our God to do his will, and to be obedient to his commandments in all things that he shall command us..."

26 "But ye will ❖ them to walk in the ways of truth and soberness; ye will teach them to love one another, and to serve one another."

27 "And ye will not suffer your children that they go ❖ , or naked..." (continued in 8A)

28 "For behold, are we not all ❖ ? Do we not all depend upon the same Being, even God, for all the substance which we have, for both food and raiment, and for gold, and for silver, and for all the riches which we have of every kind?"

Down

1 "Perhaps thou shalt say: The man has brought upon himself his ❖ ; therefore I will stay my hand, and will not give unto him of my food, nor impart unto him of my substance that he may not suffer, for his punishments are just—"

2 (continued from 16D) "...you will administer of your substance unto him that standeth in ❖ ..." (continued in 3A)

3 "And again, I say unto the ❖ , ...I would that ye say in your hearts that: I give not because I have not, but if I had I would give."

4 "Therefore, I would that ye should be steadfast and immovable, always abounding in good works, that Christ, the Lord God Omnipotent, may ❖ you his, that you may be brought to heaven, that ye may have everlasting salvation and eternal life, through the wisdom, and power, and justice, and mercy of him who created all things, in heaven and in earth, who is God above all."

5 "And again, it is expedient that he should be ❖ , that thereby he might win the prize; therefore, all things must be done in order."

6 "O have mercy, and apply the ❖ blood of Christ that we may receive forgiveness of our sins, and our hearts may be purified; for we believe in Jesus Christ..."

7 "And again, believe that ye must repent of your sins and ❖ them, and humble yourselves before God..." (continued in 10A)

9 "And it came to pass that there was not one ❖ , except it were little children, but who had entered into the [25A] and had taken upon them the name of Christ."

13 "...humble yourselves even in the depths of humility, calling on the name of the Lord ❖ , and standing steadfastly in the faith of that which is to come..."

15 "And king [14A] did cause his people that they should till the earth. And he also, himself, did till the earth, that thereby he might not become ❖ to his people..."

16 "And also, ye yourselves will ❖ those that stand in need of your ❖ ..."

17 "And ye will not have a mind to ❖ one another, but to live peaceably, and to render to every man according to that which is his due."

18 "...if you do not watch yourselves, and your thoughts, and your words, and your ❖ , and observe the commandments of God, and continue in faith of what ye have heard concerning the coming of our Lord, even unto the end of your lives, ye must perish."

21 "Yea, we believe all the words which thou hast spoken unto us; and also, we know of their surety and truth, because of the Spirit of the Lord Omnipotent, which has wrought a ❖ change in us, or in our hearts, that we have no more disposition to do evil, but to do good continually."

23 (continued from 15A) "...for ye say that your hearts are changed through ❖ on his name; therefore, ye are born of him and have become his sons and his daughters."

31

SIXTEEN
Mosiah 7-9

Across

1 "For behold, the Lord hath said: I will not succor my people in the day of their [23A]; but I will hedge up their ways that they ❖ not; and their doings shall be as a stumbling block before them."

5 "But a [19A] can know of things which are past, and also of things which are to come, and by them shall all things be ❖ ..." (continued in 6A)

6 (continued from 5A) "...or, rather, shall secret things be made manifest, and hidden things shall come to ❖ , and things which are not known shall be made known by them, and also things shall be made known by them which otherwise could not be known."

7 "And again, he saith: If my people shall sow filthiness they shall reap the chaff thereof in the whirlwind; and the effect thereof is ❖ ."

9 "And Ammon took three of his brethren, and their names were Amaleki, ❖ , and Hem, and they went down into the land of Nephi."

10 "Now, as soon as Ammon had read the record, the king inquired of him to know if he could interpret languages, and Ammon told him that he could ❖ ."

13 "And we began to till the ground, yea, even with all manner of seeds, with seeds of corn, and of ❖ , and of barley, and with neas, and with sheum, and with seeds of all manner of fruits; and we did begin to multiply and prosper in the land."

14 "And God did hear our ❖ and did answer our prayers; and we did go forth in his might..."

17 "And because [a prophet] said unto them that Christ was the God, the Father of all things, and said that he should take upon him the ❖ of man, and it should be the ❖ after which man was created in the beginning...they did put him to death; and many more things did they do which brought down the wrath of God upon them."

18 "Yea, in the strength of the Lord did we go forth to battle against the Lamanites; for I and my people did cry mightily to the Lord that he would ❖ us out of the hands of our enemies, for we were awakened to a remembrance of the deliverance of our fathers."

19 "And the king said that a ❖ is greater than a prophet."

20 "And it came to pass that on the morrow they started to go up, having with them one Ammon, he being a ❖ and mighty man, and a descendant of Zarahemla; and he was also their leader."

22 "Thus God has provided a means that man, through ❖ , might work mighty miracles; therefore he becometh a great benefit to his fellow beings."

23 "For if this people had not fallen into ❖ the Lord would not have suffered that this great evil should come upon them."

Down

2 "And it came to pass that he caused that the ❖ which contained the record of his people...should be brought before Ammon, that he might read them."

3 King Limhi: "Now, I know of a surety that my brethren who were in the land of ❖ are yet alive. And now, I will rejoice; and on the morrow I will cause that my people shall rejoice also."

4 "And yet, I being over–zealous to inherit the land of our fathers, collected as many as were desirous to go up to possess the land, and started again on our journey into the [13D] to go up to the land; but we were smitten with famine and sore afflictions; for we were slow to ❖ the Lord our God."

8 "And the things are called ❖ , and no man can look in them except he be commanded, lest he should look for that he ought not and he should perish."

11 "And Ammon said that a [19A] is a ❖ and a prophet also; and a gift which is greater can no man have, except he should possess the power of God, which no man can; yet a man may have great power given him from God."

12 "But if ye will turn to the Lord with full purpose of heart, and put your trust in him, and serve him with all ❖ of mind, if ye do this, he will, according to his own will

32

and pleasure, deliver you out of bondage."

13 "And now, they knew not the course they should travel in the ❖ to go up to the land of Lehi–Nephi; therefore they wandered many days in the ❖ , even forty days did they wander."

15 "And it came to pass that king Mosiah granted that ❖ of their strong men might go up to the land of Lehi–Nephi, to inquire concerning their brethren."

16 "Therefore, lift up your heads, and rejoice, and put your trust in God, in that God who was the God of Abraham, and Isaac, and ❖ ; and also, that God who brought the children of Israel out of the land of Egypt, and caused that they should walk through the Red Sea on dry ground, and fed them with manna that they might not perish in the [13D]; and many more things did he do for them."

21 "And behold, the king of the people who are in the land of Zarahemla is the man that is commanded to do these things, and who has this high ❖ from God."

33

SEVENTEEN
Mosiah 10–14

Across

3 "He was oppressed, and he was afflicted, yet he opened not his mouth; he is brought as a ❖ to the slaughter, and as a sheep before her shearers is dumb so he opened not his mouth."

7 "Thou shalt not ❖ thy neighbor's house, thou shalt not ❖ thy neighbor's wife, nor his man–servant, nor his maid–servant, not his ox, nor his ass, nor anything that is thy neighbor's."

8 "❖ thy father and thy mother, that thy days may be long upon the land which the Lord thy God giveth thee."

9 "And I did cause that the women should ❖ , and toil, and work, and work all manner of fine linen, yea, and cloth of every kind, that we might clothe our nakedness; and thus we did prosper in the land—thus we did have continual peace in the land for the space of twenty and two years."

12 Abinadi: "I say unto you, wo be unto you for perverting the ways of the Lord! For if ye understand these things ye have not taught them; therefore, ye have ❖ the ways of the Lord."

14 "Thou shalt not bear ❖ witness against thy neighbor."

17 "And I did cause that the men should till the ground, and ❖ all manner of grain and all manner of fruit of every kind."

18 "He is despised and rejected of men; a man of ❖ , and acquainted with grief; and we hid as it were our faces from him; he was despised, and we esteemed him not."

19 "Thou shalt not ❖ ."

20 "All we, like sheep, have gone ❖ ; we have turned every one to his own way; and the Lord hath laid on him the iniquities of us all."

21 "For behold, [King Noah] did not keep the commandments of God, but he did walk after the ❖ of his own heart."

22 "Thou shalt not ❖ adultery."

24 "And it came to pass that [King Noah] placed his heart upon his ❖ , and he spent his time in riotous living with his wives and his concubines; and so did also his priests spend their time with harlots."

Down

1 "Thou shalt not take the name of the Lord thy God in ❖ ; for the Lord will not hold him guiltless that taketh his name in ❖ ."

2 "And it came to pass that we did go up in the strength of the Lord to ❖ ."

4 "Surely he has ❖ our griefs, and carried our sorrows; yet we did esteem him stricken, smitten of God, and afflicted."

5 Abinadi: "Ye have not applied your hearts to understanding; therefore, ye have not been ❖ ."

6 "Now it came to pass after Abinadi had spoken these words that the people of king Noah durst not lay their hands on him, for the Spirit of the Lord was upon him; and his face ❖ with exceeding luster, even as Moses' did while in the mount of Sinai, while speaking with the Lord."

10 "And now, ye remember that I said unto you: Thou shalt not make unto thee any graven ❖ , or any likeness of things which are in heaven above, or which are in the earth beneath, or which are in the water under the earth."

11 "But he was wounded for our ❖ , he was bruised for our iniquities; the chastisement of our peace was upon him; and with his stripes we are healed."

13 "For he shall grow up before him as a tender ❖ , and as a root out of dry ground; he hath no form nor comeliness; and when we shall see him there is no beauty that we should desire him."

15 "Thou shalt not ❖ ."

16 "Remember the sabbath day, to keep it ❖ . Six days shalt thou labor, and do all thy work."

23 "But the seventh day, the sabbath of the Lord thy God, thou shalt not do any ❖ , thou, nor thy son, nor thy daughter, thy

34

man–servant, nor thy maid–servant, nor thy cattle, nor thy stranger that is within thy gates; for in six days the Lord made heaven and earth, and the sea, and all that in them is; wherefore the Lord blessed the sabbath day, and hallowed it."

EIGHTEEN
Mosiah 15–18

Across

1 Baptism: "...a witness before [God] that ye have entered into a covenant with him, that ye will serve him and keep his commandments, that he may ❖ out his Spirit more abundantly upon you."

2 He "...suffereth temptation, and yieldeth not to the temptation, but suffereth himself to be ❖ , and scourged, and cast out, and disowned by his people."

5 "And after Alma had said these words, both Alma and Helam were buried in the ❖ ; and they arose and came forth out of the ❖ rejoicing, being filled with the Spirit."

6 "The ❖ , because he was conceived by the power of God; and the Son, because of the flesh; thus becoming the ❖ and Son—"

10 "Yea, and are willing to ❖ with those that ❖ ; yea, and comfort those that stand in need of comfort..." (continued in 20D)

11 (continued from 20D) "...that ye may be ❖ of God, and be numbered with those of the first resurrection, that ye may have eternal life—"

12 "...there should be no contention one with another, but that they should look forward with one eye, having one faith and one ❖ ..." (continued in 28D)

14 "And after all this, after working many mighty miracles among the children of men, he shall be led, yea, even as ❖ said, as a sheep before the shearer is dumb, so he opened not his mouth."

17 "And he also commanded them that the priests whom he had ordained should ❖ with their own hands for their support."

18 "Alma...repented of his sins and iniquities, and went about ❖ among the people, and began to teach the words of Abinadi—"

20 "...and they did walk uprightly before God, imparting to one another both temporally and spiritually according to their needs and their ❖ ."

21 "...whosoever has heard the words of the prophets...[and] hearkened unto their words, and believed that the Lord would redeem his people and have looked forward to that day for a remission of their sins, I say unto you, that these are his ❖ , or they are the heirs of the kingdom."

22 "And it came to pass that he said unto them: Behold, here are the waters of [2D] (for thus were they called) and now, as ye are desirous to come into the fold of God, and to be called his people, and are willing to bear one another's ❖ , that they may be light..."

25 "And he did teach them, and did preach unto them repentance, and ❖ , and faith on the Lord."

29 "...O Lord, pour out thy Spirit upon thy ❖ , that he may do this work with holiness of heart."

30 "And these are those who have part in the [16D] resurrection; and these are they that have died before Christ came, in their ignorance, not having ❖ declared unto them."

31 Abinadi "...having been put to death because he would not deny the commandments of God, having ❖ the truth of his words by his death."

Down

2 "And it came to pass that as many as did believe him did go forth to a place which was called ❖ ..."

3 "And now I say unto you that the time shall come that the [30A] of the Lord shall be declared to every nation, kindred, tongue, and ❖ ."

4 "And they were called the church of God, or the church of ❖ , from this time forward."

7 "He is the light and the ❖ of the world; yea, a light that is endless, that can never be darkened; yea, and also a life which is endless, that there can be no more death."

8 "Having ascended into heaven, having the bowels of mercy; being filled with compassion towards the children of men; standing betwixt them and justice; having broken the bands of death, taken upon himself their iniquity and their transgressions, having redeemed, and satisfied the demands of ❖."

9 "And because he dwelleth in ❖ he shall be called the Son of God, and having subjected the ❖ to the will of the Father, being the Father and the Son—"

13 "And he commanded [the priests] that they should teach nothing save it were the things which he had taught, and which had been spoken by the mouth of the holy ❖."

15 "But remember that he that persists in his own ❖ nature, and goes on in the ways of sin and rebellion against God, remaineth in his fallen state and the devil hath all power over him."

16 "And now, the resurrection of all the prophets, and all those that have believed in their words, or all those that have kept the commandments of God, shall come forth in the ❖ resurrection..."

19 (continued from 26D) "...if he have more ❖ he should [26D] more ❖ ; and of him that had but little, but little should be required; and to him that had not should be given."

20 (continued from 10A) "...and to stand as ❖ of God at all times and in all things, and in all places that ye may be in, even until death..." (continued in 11A)

23 Alma "...began to ❖ with the king that he would not be angry with Abinadi, but suffer that he might depart in peace."

24 "And thus God breaketh the bands of ❖ , having gained the victory over ❖ ; giving the Son power to make intercession for the children of men—"

26 "And again Alma commanded that the people of the church should ❖ of their substance, every one according to that which he had..." (continued in 19D)

27 "Yea, even so he shall be led, crucified, and slain, the flesh becoming subject even unto death, the ❖ of the Son being swallowed up in the ❖ of the Father."

28 (continued from 12A) "...having their hearts ❖ together in unity and in love one towards another."

37

NINETEEN
Mosiah 19–22

Across

1 "Therefore the Lamanites did spare their lives, and took them captives and carried them back to the land of ❖ ..."

6 "And they did humble themselves even in the depths of humility; and they did ❖ mightily to God; yea, even all the day long did they ❖ unto their God that he would deliver them out of their afflictions."

7 "And they did humble themselves even to the dust, subjecting themselves to the ❖ of bondage, submitting themselves to be smitten and to be driven to and fro, and burdened, according to the desires of their enemies."

8 "And the king commanded the people that they should ❖ before the Lamanites, and he himself did go before them, and they did ❖ into the wilderness, with their women and their children."

11 "But they fought for their lives, and for their wives, and for their children; therefore they exerted themselves and like ❖ did they fight."

12 "Now they durst not slay them, because of the oath which their king had made unto Limhi; but they would smite them on their cheeks, and exercise authority over them; and began to put heavy ❖ upon their backs..."

15 "And now Limhi told the king all the things concerning his ❖ , and the priests that had fled into the wilderness, and attributed the carrying away of their daughters to them."

16 "Yea, all this was done that the word of the Lord might be ❖ ."

18 Gideon: "And I will go according to thy command and pay the last tribute of wine to the Lamanites, and they will be ❖ ; and we will pass through the secret pass on the left of their camp when they are ❖ and asleep."

19 "They were desirous to be baptized as a witness and a ❖ that they were willing to serve God with all their hearts..."

22 "And it came to pass that they began to prosper by degrees in the land, and began to raise grain more ❖ , and flocks, and herds, that they did not suffer with hunger."

25 "...twenty and four of the ❖ of the Lamanites [were] carried into the wilderness [by the priests of King Noah]."

26 "And after being many days in the wilderness they arrived in the land of [27A], and joined Mosiah's people, and became his ❖ ."

27 "But when he found that they were not [the priests of King Noah], but that they were his brethren, and had come from the land of ❖ , he was filled with exceeding great joy."

28 "And it came to pass that Mosiah received them with joy; and he also received their records, and also the records which had been ❖ by the people of Limhi."

Down

2 "And it came to pass that Limhi began to establish the kingdom and to establish ❖ among his people."

3 "And it came to pass that the people began to ❖ with the king because of their afflictions; and they began to be desirous to go against them to battle."

4 "Now there was a great number of women, more than there was of men; therefore king Limhi commanded that every man should impart to the support of the ❖ and their children, that they might not perish with hunger..."

5 "And now the Lord was slow to hear their cry because of their iniquities; nevertheless the Lord did hear their cries, and began to ❖ the hearts of the Lamanites that they began to ease their burdens; yet the Lord did not see fit to deliver them out of bondage."

9 "Nevertheless they did find a land which had been peopled; yea, a land which was covered with dry ❖ ..."

10 "...the Lamanites had granted unto them that they might possess the land by paying a ❖ to

38

the Lamanites of one half of all they possessed."

13 "And the people told the men of ❖ that they had slain the king and his priests had fled from them farther into the wilderness."

14 "And the king having been without the gates of the city with his guard, discovered ❖ and his brethren; and supposing them to be the priests of Noah therefore he caused that they should be taken, and bound, and cast into prison."

17 "For are not the words of Abinadi fulfilled, which he prophesied against us—and all this because we would not hearken unto the words of the Lord, and turn from our ❖ ."

20 "Now there were many that would not leave [their wives and their children], but had rather stay and ❖ with them. And the rest left their wives and their children and fled."

21 "And [King Limhi] caused that his people should watch the land round about, that by some means they might take those priests that ❖ into the wilderness, who had stolen the daughters of the Lamanites..."

23 "Now king Limhi had sent, previous to the coming of [14D], a small number of men to search for the land of [27A]; but they could not find it, and they were ❖ in the wilderness."

24 "And they brought a ❖ with them, even a ❖ of the people whose [9D] they had found..."

39

TWENTY
Mosiah 23–26

Across

2 "Nevertheless, if it were possible that ye could always have ❖ men to be your kings it would be well for you to have a king."

3 "And Alma and his people did not raise their voices to the Lord their God, but did ❖ out their hearts to him; and he did know the thoughts of their hearts."

4 "For behold, this is my church; whosoever is [26A] shall be [26A] unto repentance. And whomsoever ye receive shall believe in my name; and him will I freely ❖ ."

6 "Nevertheless—whosoever putteth his trust in him the same shall be ❖ up at the last day."

7 "And now the spirit of Alma was again troubled; and he went and inquired of the Lord what he should do concerning this matter, for he feared that he should do wrong in the ❖ of God."

9 "Ye shall not esteem one flesh ❖ another, or one man shall not think himself ❖ another; therefore I say unto you it is not expedient that ye should have a king."

10 "And now because of their unbelief [many of the rising generation] could not understand the word of God; and their hearts were ❖ ."

12 "...and [Amulon] put guards over them to watch them, that whosoever should be found ❖ upon God should be put to death."

13 "Thus did Alma teach his people, that every man should ❖ his neighbor as himself, that there should be no contention among them."

14 "And Amulon and his brethren did join the Lamanites, and they were traveling in the wilderness in search of the land of Nephi when they discovered the land of ❖ , which was possessed by Alma and his brethren."

16 "And they were called the people of God. And the Lord did pour out his Spirit upon them, and they were ❖ , and prospered in the land."

18 "And also trust no one to be your ❖ nor your minister, except he be a man of God, walking in his ways and keeping his commandments."

21 "And it came to pass that the voice of the Lord came to them in their afflictions, saying: Lift up your heads and be of good comfort, for I know of the ❖ which ye have made unto me; and I will ❖ with my people and deliver them out of bondage."

22 "But Alma went forth and stood among them, and exhorted them that they should not be frightened, but that they should remember the Lord their God and he would ❖ them."

23 "And it came to pass that so great were their afflictions that they began to cry ❖ to God."

24 "...the Lord did strengthen them that they could bear up their burdens with ease, and they did submit ❖ and with patience to all the will of the Lord."

25 "And those that would not ❖ their sins and repent of their iniquity, the same were not numbered among the people of the church, and their names were blotted out."

26 "...after Alma had taught the people many things...king Limhi ...and all his people were desirous that they might be ❖ also."

27 "...stand fast in this ❖ wherewith ye have been made free, and that ye trust no man to be a king over you."

Down

1 "Now Alma, having been warned of the ❖ that the armies of king Noah would come upon them, and having made it known to his people, therefore they gathered together their flocks, and took their grain, and departed into the wilderness..."

2 "And they do not repent of their iniquities; therefore we have brought them before thee, that thou mayest ❖ them according to their crimes."

3 "Nevertheless the Lord seeth fit to chasten his people; yea, he

trieth their ❖ and their faith."

5 "And I will also ❖ the burdens which are put upon your shoulders, that even you cannot feel them upon your backs, even while you are in bondage; and this will I do that ye may stand as witnesses for me hereafter, and that ye may know of a surety that I, the Lord God, do visit my people in their afflictions."

8 "Yea, in the valley of Alma they poured out their ❖ to God because he had been merciful unto them, and eased their burdens, and had delivered them out of bondage; for they were in bondage, and none could deliver them except it were the Lord their God."

11 "And thus, not withstanding there being many churches they were all one church, yea, even the church of God; for there was nothing ❖ in all the churches except it were repentance and faith in God."

15 "And now the name of the king of the Lamanites was ❖ ..."

17 "And they pitched their tents, and began to till the ground, and began to build buildings; yea, they were industrious, and did ❖ exceedingly."

19 "Nevertheless, after much tribulation, the Lord did hear my cries, and did answer my prayers, and has made me an ❖ in his hands in bringing so many of you to a knowledge of his truth."

20 "And thus the Lamanites began to increase in ❖ , and began to trade one with another and wax great, and began to be a cunning and a wise people, as to the wisdom of the world..."

TWENTY–ONE
Mosiah 27–29

Across

1 "For, said he, I have repented of my sins, and have been redeemed of the Lord; behold I am born of the ❖."

2 "And the Lord did visit them and ❖ them, and they became a large and wealthy people."

3 "And even I myself have labored with all the power and faculties which I have possessed, to teach you the commandments of God, and to establish ❖ throughout the land..."

7 [21D] "...zealously striving to repair all of the injuries which they had done to the church, confessing all their sins, and publishing all things which they had seen, and explaining the prophecies and the ❖ to all those who desired to hear them."

10 "And they rehearsed unto his father all that had happened unto them; and his father rejoiced, for he knew that it was the ❖ of God."

13 "And he was a man of many words, and did speak much ❖ to the people; therefore he led many of the people to do after the manner of his iniquities."

14 (continued from 15A) "...yea, born of God, changed from their ❖ and fallen state, to a state of righteousness, being redeemed of God, becoming his sons and daughters..."

15 "...Marvel not that all mankind, yea, men and women, all nations, kindreds, tongues and people, must be ❖ again..." (continued in 14A)

16 "...Alma, ❖ and stand forth, for why persecutest thou the church of God?"

18 "And whosoever has these [12D] is called a ❖, after the manner of old times."

20 "And thus they were instruments in the hands of God in bringing many to the ❖ of the truth, yea, to the ❖ of their Redeemer."

24 "...as they were going about rebelling against God, behold, the ❖ of the Lord appeared unto them; and he descended as it were in a cloud; and he spake as it were with a voice of thunder, which caused the earth to shake upon which they stood..."

25 "Therefore he took the records which were engraven on the plates of ❖, and also the plates of Nephi, and all the things which he had kept and preserved according to the commandments of God..."

26 "Now it is not common that the ❖ of the people desireth anything contrary to that which is right; but it is common for the lesser part of the people to desire that which is not right..."

Down

1 "Now the ❖ of Mosiah were numbered among the unbelievers; and also one of the ❖ of Alma..."

2 "For the Lord hath said: This is my church, and I will establish it; and nothing shall overthrow it, save it is the transgression of my ❖."

4 "Yea, and all their priests and teachers should labor with their own hands for their support, in all cases save it were in ❖, or in much want; and doing these things, they did abound in the grace of God."

5 "Now it is better that a man should be judged of God than of man, for the ❖ of God are always just, but the ❖ of man are not always just."

6 "Behold, the Lord hath heard the prayers of his people, and also the prayers of his servant, Alma, who is thy father; for he has prayed with much faith concerning thee that thou mightest be brought to the knowledge of the ❖; therefore, for this purpose have I come to convince thee of the power and authority of God, that the prayers of his servants might be answered according to their faith."

8 "And thus they become new ❖; and unless they do this, they can in nowise inherit the kingdom of God."

9 "Now they were desirous that ❖ should be declared to every creature, for they could not bear that any human soul should perish; yea, even the very thoughts that any soul should endure endless torment did cause them to quake and tremble."

11 "...and thus an unrighteous king doth pervert the ❖ of all righteousness."

12 "And now he translated them by the means of those two ❖ which were fastened into the two rims of a bow."

15 "And were it not for the interposition of their all–wise Creator, and this because of their sincere repentance, they must unavoidably remain in ❖ until now."

17 "And now I say unto thee, Alma, go thy way, and seek to ❖ the church no more, that their prayers may be answered..."

19 "Therefore they relinquished their desire for a king, and became exceedingly anxious that every man should have an ❖ chance throughout all the land; yea, and every man expressed a willingness to answer for his own sins."

21 "And four of them were the sons of Mosiah; and their names were Ammon, and Aaron, and ❖ , and Himni..."

22 "That they should let no ❖ nor haughtiness disturb their peace; that every man should esteem his neighbor as himself, laboring with their own hands for their support."

23 "And now it came to pass that Alma did ❖ in the ways of the Lord, and he did keep his commandments, and he did judge righteous judgments; and there was continual peace through the land."

43

TWENTY-TWO
Alma 1–4

Across

1 "...and were ❖ to be enforced among this people it would prove their entire destruction."

5 "...they did not send away any who were naked, or that were hungry, or that were ❖, or that were sick, or that had not been nourished; and they did not set their hearts upon riches; therefore they were liberal to all, both old and young, both bond and free, both male and female, whether out of the [20A] or in the [20A], having no respect to persons as to those who stood in need."

7 "And the Amlicites were distinguished from the Nephites, for they had marked themselves with ❖ in their foreheads after the manner of the Lamanites..."

8 "...a certain man, being called ❖, he being a very cunning man, yea, a wise man as to the wisdom of the world..."

9 "...and the priest, not esteeming himself above his hearers, for the preacher was no ❖ than the hearer, neither was the teacher any ❖ than the learner; and thus they were all equal..." (continued in 12D)

10 "And they began to establish the [20A] more fully; yea, and many were ❖ in the waters of Sidon and were joined to the [20A] of God; yea, they were ❖ by the hand of Alma..."

13 "Looking forward to that day, thus retaining a remission of their sins; being filled with great joy because of the resurrection of the ❖, according to the will and power and deliverance of Jesus Christ from the bands of death."

14 "For they saw and beheld with great sorrow that the people of the church began to be ❖ up in the pride of their eyes, and to set their hearts upon riches and upon the vain things of the world..."

15 "And when the priests left their labor to impart the ❖ of God unto the people, the people also left their labors to hear the ❖ of God."

16 "And they did impart of their ❖, every man according to that which he had, to the poor, and the needy, and the sick, and the afflicted..." (continued in 21D)

18 "...and that [Alma] might pull down, by the word of God, all the pride and craftiness and all the contentions which were among his people, seeing no way that he might reclaim them save it were in bearing down in ❖ testimony against them."

19 "...❖...did acknowledge, between the heavens and the earths, that what he had taught to the people was contrary to the word of God..."

20 "And now, because of the steadiness of the ❖ they began to be exceedingly rich, having abundance of all things whatsoever they stood in need..."

22 "Yea, they did persecute them, and afflict them with all manner of words, and this because of their ❖; because they were not proud in their own eyes, and because they did impart the word of God, one with another, without money and without price."

26 "Nevertheless, the Nephites being strengthened by the hand of the Lord, having prayed mightily to him that he would ❖ them out of the hands of their enemies, therefore the Lord did hear their cries, and did strengthen them..."

27 "And [11D] also testified unto the people that ❖ mankind should be saved at the last day, and that they need not fear nor tremble, but that they might lift up their heads and rejoice; for the Lord had created ❖ men, and had also redeemed ❖ men; and, in the end, ❖ men should have eternal life."

28 "And in one year were thousands and tens of thousands of souls sent to the eternal world, that they might reap their rewards according to their ❖, whether they were good or whether they were bad, to reap eternal happiness or eternal misery, according to the spirit which they listed to obey..."

Down

1 "But it came to pass that whosoever did not belong to the church of God began to ❖ those that did belong to the church of God, and had taken upon them the name of Christ."

2 "And this was done that their

44

seed might be distinguished from the seed of their brethren, that thereby the Lord God might preserve his people, that they might not mix and believe in incorrect ❖ which would prove their destruction."

3 "And he began to be lifted up in the pride of his heart, and to wear very costly ❖ , yea, and even began to establish a church after the manner of his preaching."

4 "Now this was a great trial to those that did stand fast in the ❖ ; nevertheless, they were steadfast and immovable in keeping the commandments of God, and they bore with patience the persecution which was heaped upon them."

6 "And so great were their afflictions that every soul had cause to mourn; and they believed that it was the judgments of God sent upon them because of their ❖ and their abominations; therefore they were awakened to a remembrance of their duty."

11 "...and it was [❖] who was an instrument in the hands of God in delivering the people of Limhi out of bondage."

12 (continued from 9A) "...and thus they were all equal, and they did all labor, every man according to his ❖ ."

16 "...there was a man...declaring unto the people that every priest and teacher ought to become popular; and they ought not to labor with their hands, but that they ought to be ❖ by the people."

17 "...[King Mosiah] had established laws, and they were acknowledged by the people; therefore they were obliged to ❖ by the laws which he had made."

21 (continued from 16A) "...and they did not wear costly apparel, yet they were neat and ❖ ."

23 "And the ❖ of the Lamanites were dark, according to the mark which was set upon their fathers, which was a curse upon them because of their transgression and their rebellion against their brethren..."

24 "And it came to pass that Alma, being a man of God, being exercised with much faith, cried, saying: O Lord, have ❖ and spare my life, that I may be an instrument in thy hands to save and preserve this people."

25 "...for there were many who loved the ❖ things of the world, and they went forth preaching false doctrines; and this they did for the sake of riches and honor."

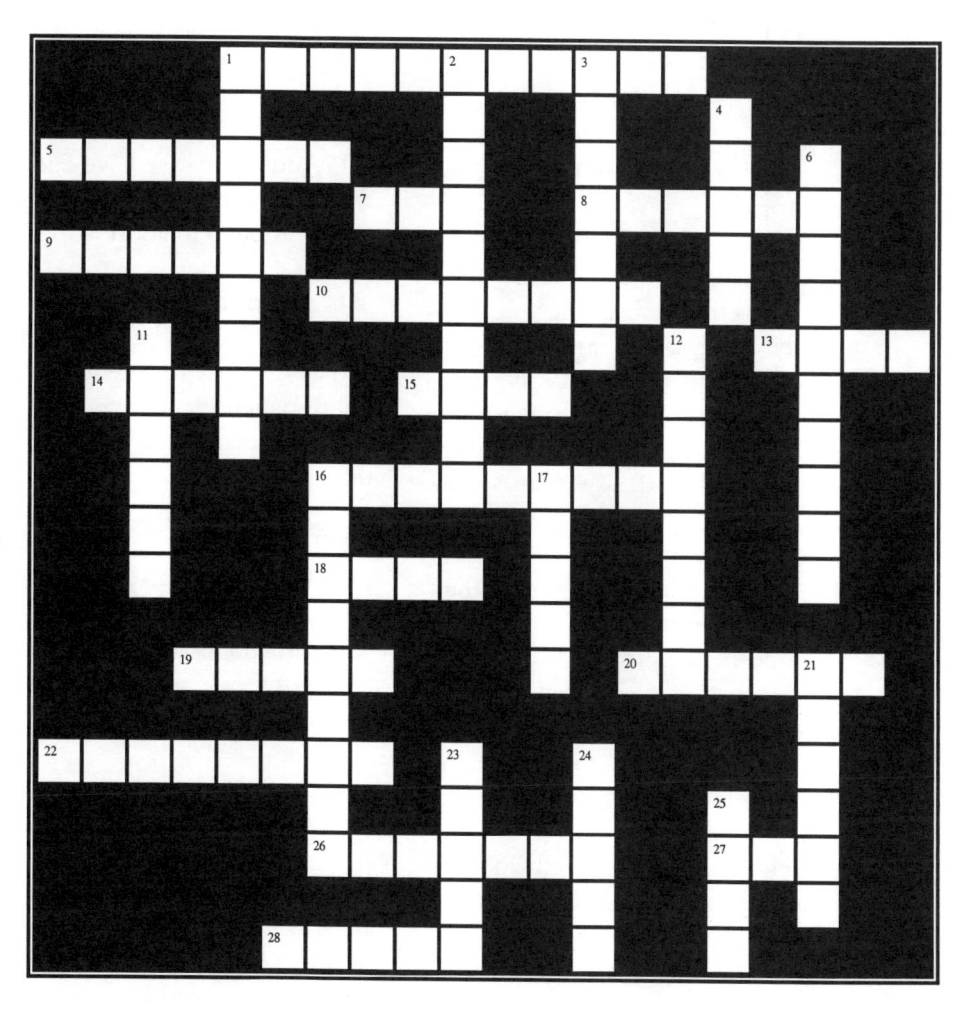

45

TWENTY-THREE
Alma 5–8

Across

6 "Or do ye imagine to yourselves that ye can ❖ unto the Lord in that day, and say—Lord, our works have been righteous works upon the face of the earth—and that he will save you?"

7 "And [Alma] began to teach the people in the land of ❖ according to the holy order of God, by which he had been called..."

8 "...is there one among you that doth make a ❖ of his brother, or that heapeth upon him persecutions?"

10 "...can you imagine to yourselves that ye hear the voice of the Lord, saying unto you, in that day: Come unto me ye ❖ , for behold, your works have been the works of righteousness upon the face of the earth?"

12 (continued from 20A) "...being diligent in keeping the commandments of God at all times; asking for whatsoever things ye stand in need, both spiritual and temporal; always returning ❖ unto God for whatsoever things ye do receive."

14 "Behold, he sendeth an invitation unto all men, for the arms of mercy are extended towards them, and he saith: ❖ , and I will receive you."

15 "And now, may the ❖ of God rest upon you, and upon your houses and lands, and upon your flocks and herds, and all that you possess, your women and your children, according to your faith and good works, from this time forth and forever."

16 "Or otherwise, can ye imagine yourselves brought before the tribunal of God with your souls filled with ❖ and remorse, having a remembrance of all your ❖ , yea, a perfect remembrance of all your wickedness, yea, a remembrance that ye have set at defiance the commandments of God?"

19 "And see that ye have faith, ❖ , and charity, and then ye will always abound in good works."

20 "And now I would that ye should be ❖ , and be submissive and gentle; easy to be entreated; full of patience and long–suffering; being temperate in all things..." (continued in 12A)

21 "I say unto you, can ye look up to God at that day with a ❖ heart and clean hands? I say unto you, can you look up, having the [24D] of God engraven upon your countenances?"

22 "Do ye exercise faith in the ❖ of him who created you?"

26 "...thou art the man whom an angel said in a vision: Thou shalt receive. Therefore, go with me into my house and I will impart unto thee of my ❖ ; and I know that thou wilt be a blessing unto me and my house."

27 "Behold the ❖ of the King of all the earth; and also the King of heaven shall very soon shine forth among all the children of men."

28 "Behold, I say, is there one among you who is not stripped of ❖ ? I say unto you that such an one is not prepared; and I would that he should prepare quickly, for the hour is close at hand, and he knoweth not when the time shall come; for such an one is not found guiltless."

29 "I trust that ye are not lifted up in the pride of your hearts; yea, I trust that ye have not set your hearts upon riches and the vain things of the world; yea, I trust that you do not worship idols, but that ye do worship the true and the ❖ God..."

Down

1 "Behold, I have fasted and prayed many days that I might know these things of myself. And now I do know of myself that they are ❖ ; for the Lord God hath made them manifest unto me by his Holy Spirit; and this is the spirit of revelation which is in me."

2 "And behold, he shall be born of Mary, at Jerusalem which is the land of our forefathers, she being a virgin, a precious and chosen ❖ , who shall be overshadowed and conceive by the power of the Holy Ghost, and bring forth a son, yea, even the Son of God."

3 "Nevertheless the children of God were commanded that they should gather themselves together oft, and join in fasting and mighty prayer in behalf of the ❖ of the souls of those who knew not God."

4 "Do you look forward with an eye of faith, and view this mortal body raised in immortality, and this corruption raised in incorruption, to stand before God to be judged according to the ❖ which have been done in the mortal body?"

5 "For I say unto you that whatsoever is ❖ cometh from God, and whatsoever is evil cometh from the devil."

9 "Repent ye, and prepare the way of the Lord, and walk in his paths, which are ❖ ; for behold, the kingdom of heaven is at hand, and the Son of God cometh upon the face of the earth."

10 "And now behold, I ask of you, my brethren of the church, have ye spiritually been ❖ of God?"

11 "...all you that are desirous to follow the voice of the good ❖ , come ye out from the wicked, and be ye separate, and touch not their unclean things..."

13 "Yea, will ye persist in supposing that ye are ❖ one than another; yea, will ye persist in the persecution of your brethren, who humble themselves and do walk after the holy order of God, wherewith they have been brought into this church, having been sanctified by the Holy Spirit, and they do bring forth works which are meet for repentance—"

17 "And now behold, I say unto you, my brethren, if ye have experienced a change of heart, and if ye have felt to sing the song of ❖ love, I would ask, can ye feel so now?"

18 "Have ye experienced this mighty ❖ in your hearts?"

23 "...can ye lay aside these things, and trample the Holy One under your feet; yea, can ye be ❖ up in the pride of your hearts; yea, will ye still persist in wearing costly apparel and setting your hearts upon the vain things of the world, upon your riches?"

24 "Have ye received his ❖ in your countenances?"

25 "Behold, are ye stripped of ❖ ? I say unto you, if ye are not ye are not prepared to meet God."

47

TWENTY–FOUR
Alma 9–12

Across

4 "Therefore, prepare ye the way of the Lord, for the time is at hand that all men shall reap a reward of their ❖ , according to that which they have been..." (continued in 22A)

6 "Repent ye, repent, for the kingdom of ❖ is at hand."

7 (continued from 17D) "...and he that will not harden his heart, to him is given the ❖ portion of the word, until it is given unto him to know the mysteries of God until he know them in full."

12 "And behold, I am also a man of no small reputation among all those who know me; yea, and behold, I have many kindreds and ❖ , and I have also acquired much riches by the hand of my industry."

15 "...he would rather suffer that the Lamanites might destroy all his people who are called the people of ❖ , if it were possible that they could fall into sins and transgressions, after having had so much light and so much knowledge given unto them of the Lord their God."

16 "Now these are the words which Amulek preached unto the people who were in the land of ❖ ..."

19 "It is given unto many to know the ❖ of God; nevertheless they are laid under a strict command that they shall not impart only according to the portion of his word which he doth grant unto the children of men, according to the heed and diligence which they give unto him."

22 (continued from 4A) "—if [they] have been righteous they shall reap the salvation of their souls, according to the power and ❖ of Jesus Christ..." (continued in 14D)

23 "...he hath said that no unclean thing can ❖ the kingdom of heaven; therefore, how can ye be saved, except ye ❖ the kingdom of heaven? Therefore, ye cannot be saved in your sins."

24 "...then cometh a death, even a second death, which is a ❖ death; then is a time that whosoever dieth in his sins, as to a temporal death, shall also die a ❖ death; yea, he shall die as to things pertaining unto righteousness."

25 "And not many days hence the Son of God shall come in his glory; and his glory shall be the glory of the Only Begotten of the Father, full of grace, ❖ , and truth, full of patience, mercy, and long–suffering, quick to hear the cries of his people and to answer their prayers."

26 "O ye wicked and perverse generation, why hath Satan got such great hold upon your hearts? Why will ye yield yourselves unto him that he may have power over you, to blind your eyes, that ye will not ❖ the words which are spoken, according to their truth?"

Down

1 King Mosiah said "...that if the time should come that the ❖ of this people should chose iniquity, that is, if the time should come that this people should fall into transgression, they would be ripe for destruction."

2 "The spirit and the body shall be ❖ again in its perfect form; both limb and joint shall be restored to its proper frame, even as we are at this time; and we shall be brought to stand before God, knowing even as we know now, and have a bright recollection of all our guilt."

3 (continued from 9D) "...the foundation of the destruction of this people is beginning to be laid by the unrighteousness of your lawyers and your ❖ ."

5 "And at some period of time they [the Lamanites] will be brought to believe in his word, and to know of the incorrectness of the traditions of their fathers; and many of them will be ❖ , for the Lord will be merciful unto all who call on his name."

6 "Nevertheless, I did ❖ my heart, for I was called many times and I would not hear..."

8 "And he shall come into the world to ❖ his people; and he shall take upon him the transgressions of those who will believe on his name; and these are they that shall have eternal life, and salvation cometh to none else."

9 (continued from 2D) "...and we shall be brought to stand before God, knowing even as we know now, and have a ❖ recollection of all our guilt."

10 "Therefore the wicked remain as though there had been no redemption made, except it be the loosing of the bands of ❖ ; for behold, the day cometh that all shall rise from the dead and stand before God, and be judged according to their works."

11 "Now the object of these lawyers was to get gain; and they got gain according to their ❖ ."

13 "For our words will ❖ us, yea, all our works will ❖ us; we shall not be found spotless; and our thoughts will also ❖ us; and in this awful state we shall not dare look up to our God; and we would fain be glad if we could command the rocks and the mountains to fall upon us to hide us from his presence."

14 (continued from 22A) "...and if [they] have been evil they shall reap the damnation of their souls, according to the power and ❖ of the devil."

17 "And therefore, he that will harden his heart, the same receiveth the ❖ portion of the word..." (continued in 7A)

18 "...nevertheless there was a space granted unto man in which he might ❖ ; therefore this life became a probationary state; a time to prepare to meet God; a time to prepare for that endless state which has been spoken of by us, which is after the resurrection of the dead."

20 "And behold, he cometh to redeem those who will be ❖ unto repentance, through faith on his name."

21 "Now, there is a death which is called a ❖ death; and the death of Christ shall loose the bands of this ❖ death, that all shall be raised from this ❖ death."

49

TWENTY-FIVE
Alma 13–16

Across

2 "And there was no inequality among them; the Lord did pour out his Spirit on all the face of the land to ❖ the minds of the children of men, or to ❖ their hearts to receive the word which should be taught among them at the time of his coming—"

4 "And then Alma cried unto the Lord, saying: O Lord our God, have ❖ on this man, and heal him according to his faith which is in Christ."

6 "And many of the people did inquire concerning the place where the Son of God should come; and they were taught that he would appear unto them after his ❖ ; and this people did hear with great joy and gladness."

8 "But Melchizedek having exercised mighty faith, and received the ❖ of the high priesthood according to the holy order of God, did preach repentance unto his people."

9 "And Alma and Amulek went forth preaching ❖ to the people in their temples, and in their sanctuaries, and also in their synagogues, which were built after the manner of the Jews."

10 "Now they, after being sanctified by the Holy Ghost, having their garments made white, being pure and ❖ before God, could not look upon sin save it were with abhorrence..."

13 "...Amulek having forsaken all his gold, and silver, and his precious things...for the word of God, he being ❖ by those who were once his friends and also by his father and his kindred..."

14 "...they were ordained—being called and prepared from the ❖ of the world according to the foreknowledge of God, on account of their exceeding faith and good works; in the first place being left to choose good or evil; therefore they having chosen good, and exercising exceedingly great faith, are called with a holy calling, yea, with that holy calling which was prepared with, and according to, a preparatory redemption for such."

15 (continued from 19D) "And he doth suffer...that the people may do this thing unto them, according to the hardness of their hearts, that the ❖ which he shall exercise upon them in his wrath may be just; and the blood of the innocent shall stand as a witness against them, yea, and cry mightily against them at the last day."

19 "And this great sin, and his many other sins, did harrow up his mind until it did become exceedingly sore, having no deliverance; therefore he began to be ❖ with a burning heat."

21 "And as many as would hear their words, unto them they did impart the word of God, without any ❖ of persons, continually."

22 "...and the people of Ammonihah were destroyed; yea, every living soul of the Ammonihahites was destroyed, and also their great ❖ , which they said God could not destroy, because of its greatness."

23 "...seeing that the people were checked as to the pride of their hearts, and began to ❖ themselves before God, and began to assemble themselves together at their sanctuaries to worship God before the altar, watching and praying continually, that they might be delivered from Satan, and from death, and from destruction—"

24 "And it came to pass that [❖] began to cry unto the people, saying: Behold, I am guilty, and these men are spotless before God."

Down

1 "...and I would that ye should remember that the Lord God ordained ❖ , after his holy order, which was after the order of his Son, to teach these things unto the people."

3 "...I wish from the inmost part of my heart, yea, with great anxiety even unto pain, that ye would hearken unto my words, and cast off your sins, and not ❖ the day of your repentance..."

5 "And the chief judge...said unto them: If ye have the power of God ❖ yourselves from these bands, and then we will believe that the Lord will destroy this people according to your words."

7 "...having faith on the Lord; having a hope that ye shall receive

50

eternal life; having the ❖ of God always in your hearts, that ye may be lifted up at the last day and enter into his rest."

11 "But that ye would humble yourselves before the Lord, and call on his holy name, and watch and ❖ continually, that ye may not be tempted above that which ye can bear, and thus be led by the Holy Spirit, becoming humble, meek, submissive, patient, full of love and all long–suffering..."

12 "And it was this same Melchizedek to whom Abraham paid ❖ ; yea, even our father Abraham paid ❖ of one–tenth part of all he possessed."

14 "How long shall we suffer these great afflictions, O Lord? O Lord, give us strength according to our ❖ which is in Christ, even unto deliverance."

16 "That they might not be hardened against the word, that they might not be unbelieving, and go on to destruction, but that they might receive the word with joy, and as a branch be ❖ into the true vine, that they might enter into the rest of the Lord their God."

17 "And when Amulek saw the pains of the women and children who were consuming in the fire, he also was pained; and he said unto Alma: How can we witness this awful scene? Therefore let us stretch forth our hands, and ❖ the power of God which is in us, and save them from the flames."

18 "And many such things, yea, all manner of such things did they say unto them; and thus they did ❖ them for many days."

19 "But Alma said unto him: The ❖ constraineth me that I must not stretch forth mine hand; for behold the Lord receiveth them up unto himself, in glory..." (continued in 15A)

20 "...the church had been established throughout all the land—having got the victory over the ❖ , and the word of God being preached in its purity in all the land, and the Lord pouring out his blessing upon the people..."

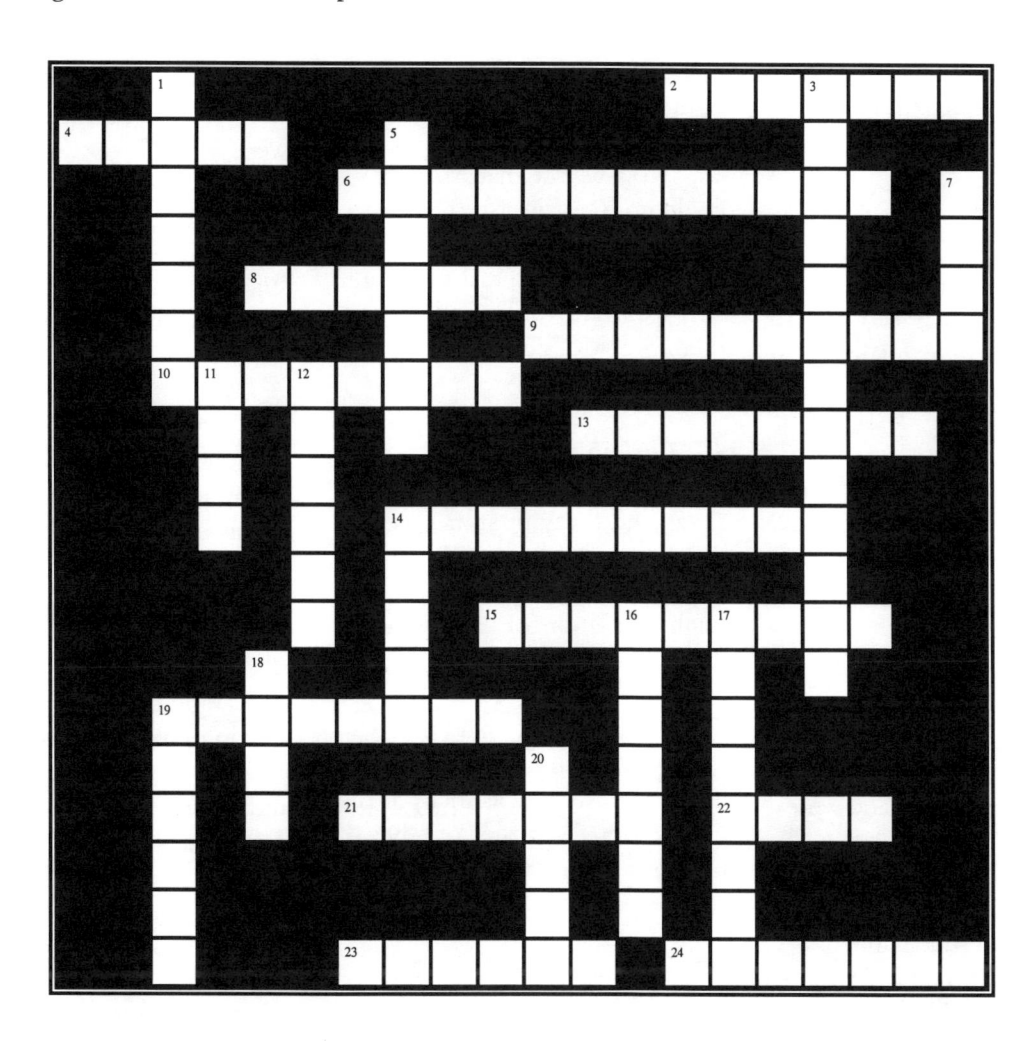

51

TWENTY-SIX
Alma 17–19

Across

1 "...he knew that king Lamoni was under the power of God; he knew that the dark ❖ of unbelief was being cast away from his mind, and the light which did light up his mind, which was the light of the glory of God..." (continued in 21D)

3 "And it came to pass that when Ammon arose he also administered unto them...and they did all declare unto the people the self–same thing—that their hearts had been ❖ ; that they had no more desire to do evil."

6 "And it came to pass that the Lord did visit them with his Spirit, and said unto them: Be ❖ . And they were ❖ ."

11 "...and [they] took their swords, and their ❖ , and their bows, and their arrows, and their slings; and this they did that they might provide food for themselves while in the wilderness."

15 "And a portion of that Spirit ❖ in me, which giveth me knowledge, and also power according to my faith and desires which are in God."

16 "...and [God] looketh down upon all the children of men; and he knows all the thoughts and ❖ of the heart; for by his hand were they all created from the beginning."

17 "...they fasted much and prayed much that the Lord would grant unto them a ❖ of his Spirit to go with them, and abide with them, that they might be an instrument in the hands of God to bring, if it were possible, their brethren...to the knowledge of the truth..."

19 "...yet ye shall be patient in long–suffering and ❖ , that ye may show forth good examples unto them in me, and I will make an instrument of thee in my hands unto the salvation of many souls."

20 "And behold, many did declare unto the people that they had seen ❖ and had conversed with them; and thus they had told them things of God, and of his righteousness."

25 "Now we see that Ammon could not be slain, for the Lord had said unto Mosiah, his father: I will spare him, and it shall be unto him according to thy faith—therefore, Mosiah ❖ him unto the Lord."

27 The Lamanites' "...hearts were set upon riches, or upon gold and silver, and precious stones; yet they sought to obtain these things by murdering and ❖ , that they might not labor for them with their own hands."

28 "And it came to pass that there were many that did believe in their words; and as many as did believe were baptized; and they became a ❖ people, and they did establish a church among them."

29 "...and we see that his ❖ is extended to all people who will repent and believe on his name."

Down

2 "...Alma did rejoice exceedingly to see his brethren [the sons of Mosiah]; and what added more to his joy, they were still his brethren in the ❖ ..." (continued in 25D)

4 The queen "...arose and stood upon her feet, and cried with a loud voice, saying: O blessed Jesus, who has saved me from an ❖ hell! O blessed God, have mercy on this people!"

5 King Lamoni: "Yea, I will believe all thy words. And thus he was caught with ❖ ."

7 "And now, when he had said this, he fell unto the earth, as if he were ❖ ."

8 "Now Ammon being wise, yet harmless, he said unto Lamoni: Wilt thou hearken unto my words, if I tell thee by what ❖ I do these things?"

9 King Lamoni: "Surely there has not been any servant among all my servants that has been so ❖ as this man; for even he doth remember all my commandments to execute them."

10 "Now Ammon...fell upon his knees, and began to pour out his soul in prayer and ❖ to God for what he had done for his brethren; and he was also overpowered with joy..."

12 "But this is not all; they had given themselves to much prayer, and fasting; therefore they had the spirit of ❖ , and the spirit of

52

revelation, and when they taught, they taught with power and authority of God."

13 "Now Ammon...did ❖ unto them, and he departed from them, after having blessed them according to their several stations, having imparted the word of God unto them..."

14 King Lamoni said: "Surely, this is more than a man. Behold, is not this the Great ❖ who doth send such great punishments upon this people, because of their murders?"

18 "...for, said [Ammon], I will show forth my power unto these my fellow–servants, or the power which is in me, in restoring these flocks unto the king, that I may ❖ the hearts of these my fellow servants, that I may lead them to believe in my words."

21 (continued from 1A) "...which was a marvelous light of his goodness—yea, this light had infused such joy into his soul, the cloud of ❖ having been dispelled, and that the light of everlasting life was lit up in his soul, yea, he knew that this had overcome his natural frame, and he was carried away in God—"

22 "And Ammon said unto [the queen]: Blessed art thou because of thy exceeding faith; I say unto thee, woman, there has not been such great faith among all the people of the ❖ ."

23 King Lamoni arose and said: "Blessed be the name of God, and blessed art thou. For as sure as thou livest, behold, I have seen my ❖ ..."

24 "And [King Lamoni] began to cry unto the Lord, saying: O Lord, have ❖ ; according to thy abundant ❖ which thou hast had upon the people of Nephi, have upon me, and my people."

25 (continued from 2D) "...yea, and they had waxed strong in the knowledge of the ❖ ; for they were men of a sound understanding and they had searched the scriptures diligently, that they might know the word of God."

26 "Whether he be the Great [14D] or a man, we know not; but this much we do know, that he cannot be slain by the enemies of the king; neither can they scatter the king's ❖ when he is with us, because of his expertness and great strength..."

53

TWENTY-SEVEN
Alma 20–24

Across

2 "For the king was greatly astonished at the words which he had ❖ , and also at the words which had been ❖ by his son Lamoni, therefore he was desirous to learn them."

3 "And he did exhort them daily, with all diligence; and they gave heed unto his word, and they were ❖ for keeping the commandments of God."

4 "...the Lord began to bless them, insomuch that they brought many to the knowledge of the ❖ ; yea, they did convince many of their sins, and of the traditions of their fathers, which were not correct."

5 "What shall I do that I may have this eternal ❖ of which thou hast spoken?"

9 "...as the Lord liveth, as many of the Lamanites as believed in their preaching, and were converted unto the Lord, ❖ did fall away."

13 "And thus we see that, when these Lamanites were brought to believe and to know the truth, they were ❖ , and would suffer even unto death rather than commit sin; and thus we see that they buried their weapons of peace, or they buried the weapons of war, for peace."

14 "Now Aaron began to open the scriptures unto them concerning the coming of Christ, and also concerning the resurrection of the dead, and that there could be no redemption for ❖ save it were through the death and sufferings of Christ, and the atonement of his blood."

16 The father of Lamoni to Aaron: "Yea, I believe that the Great Spirit ❖ all things, and I desire that ye should tell me concerning all these things, and I will believe thy words."

18 "Behold, said he, I will give up all that I ❖ , yea, I will forsake my kingdom, that I may receive this great joy."

22 (continued from 28D) "...and that he breaketh the bands of death, that the ❖ shall have no victory, and that the sting of death should be swallowed up in the hopes of glory..."

23 "And Ammon said unto him: No one hath told me, save it be God; and he said unto me—Go and deliver thy brethren, for they are in ❖ in the land of Middoni."

27 "Now there was not one soul among all the people who had been converted unto the Lord that would take up ❖ against their brethren; nay, they would not even make any preparations for war...."

29 "If thou desirest this thing, if thou wilt bow down before God, yea, if thou wilt repent of all thy sins, and will bow down before God, and call on his name in faith, believing that ye shall ❖ , then shalt thou ❖ the hope which thou desirest."

30 "And it came to pass that they called their names ❖ ; and they were called by this name and were no more called Lamanites."

Down

1 "And behold, I thank my great God that he has given us a portion of His Spirit to ❖ our hearts, that we have opened a correspondence with these brethren, the Nephites."

6 "...after a people have been once enlightened by the Spirit of God, and have had great knowledge of things pertaining to righteousness, and then have ❖ away into sin and transgression, they become more hardened and thus their state becomes worse than though they had never known these things."

7 "Yea, what shall I do that I may be born of God, having this wicked spirit ❖ out of my breast, and receive his Spirit, that I may be filled with joy, that I may not be cast off at the last day?"

8 "For they became a righteous people; they did lay down the ❖ of their rebellion, that they did not fight against God any more, neither against any of their brethren."

10 "...and if thou art God, wilt thou make thyself known unto me, and I will give away all my sins to know thee, and that I may be ❖ from the dead, and be saved at the last day."

11 "And Aaron did expound unto him the scriptures from the creation of ❖ , laying the fall of man before him, and their carnal state and also the plan of redemption, which was prepared from the foundation of the world, through Christ, for all whosoever would believe on his name."

12 "But Ammon stood forth and said unto [King Lamoni's father]: Behold, thou shalt not slay thy son; nevertheless it were better that he should fall than thee, for behold, he has repented of his sins; but if thou shouldst fall at this time, in thine ❖ , thy soul could not be saved."

15 "And they began to be a very ❖ people; yea, and they were friendly with the Nephites..."

17 "And thousands were brought to the knowledge of the Lord, yea, thousands were brought to believe in the ❖ of the Nephites; and they were taught the records and prophecies which were handed down even to the present time."

19 "And when Ammon did meet [his brethren] he was exceedingly ❖ ... And they had also suffered hunger, thirst, and all kinds of afflictions; nevertheless they were patient in all their sufferings."

20 "And the king stood forth, and began to ❖ unto them. And he did ❖ unto them, insomuch that his whole household were converted unto the Lord."

21 "And now it came to pass that the king and those who were ❖ were desirous that they might have a name, that thereby they might be distinguished from their brethren..."

24 "And he also declared unto them that they might have the ❖ of worshiping the Lord their God according their desires, in whatsoever place they were in..."

25 "I thank my God, my beloved people, that our great God has in goodness sent these our brethren, the Nephites, unto us to ❖ unto us, and to convince us of the traditions of our wicked fathers."

26 "...for perhaps, if we should stain our swords again they can no more be washed ❖ through the blood of the Son of our great God, which shall be shed for the atonement of our sins."

28 "And since man had fallen he could not ❖ anything of himself; but the sufferings and death of Christ atone for their sins, through faith and repentance..." (continued in 22A)

55

TWENTY–EIGHT
Alma 25–29

Across

2 "But Ammon said unto him: I do not boast in my own ❖, nor in my own wisdom; but behold, my joy is full, yea, my heart is brim with joy, and I will rejoice in my God."

6 "For behold, the Lord doth grant unto all nations, of their own nation and ❖, to teach his word, yea, in wisdom, all that he seeth fit that they should have; therefore we see that the Lord doth counsel in wisdom, according to that which is just and true."

7 "...and my joy is carried away, even unto boasting in my God; for he has all power, all ❖, and all understanding; he comprehendeth all things, and he is a merciful Being, even unto salvation, to those who will repent and believe on his name."

11 "Now when our hearts were ❖, and we were about to turn back, behold, the Lord comforted us, and said: Go amongst thy brethren, the Lamanites, and bear with patience thine afflictions, and I will give unto you success."

13 "Yea, he that repenteth and exerciseth faith, and bringeth forth good works, and prayeth continually without ceasing—unto such it is given to know the ❖ of God..."

19 (continued from 1D) "...and thus we see the great reason of sorrow, and also of rejoicing–sorrow because of death and destruction among men, and joy because of the ❖ of Christ unto life."

20 "...the voice of the people came, saying: Behold, we will give up the land of Jershon...and this land Jershon is the land which we will give unto our brethren for an ❖."

21 "Yea, and I know that good and evil have come before all men; but he that knoweth not good from evil is ❖; but he that knoweth good and evil, to him it is given according to his desires, whether he desireth good or evil, life or death, joy or remorse of conscience."

23 "And we have suffered all manner of afflictions, and all this, that perhaps we might be the means of saving some ❖; and we supposed that our joy would be full if perhaps we could be the means of saving some."

26 "For many of them, after having suffered much loss and so many afflictions, began to be stirred up in ❖ of the words which Aaron and his brethren had preached to them in their land; therefore they began to disbelieve the traditions of their fathers, and to believe in the Lord..."

28 "And among the Lamanites who were slain were almost all the ❖ of Amulon and his brethren, who were the priests of Noah..."

29 "Behold, this is ❖ which none receiveth save it be the truly penitent and humble seeker of happiness."

30 "Now, seeing that I know these things, why should I desire more than to perform the ❖ to which I have been called?"

31 "And [the people of Ammon] were also distinguished for their ❖ towards God, and also towards men; for they were perfectly honest and upright in all things; and they were firm in the faith of Christ, even unto the end."

Down

1 "And thus we see the great call of diligence of men to labor in the ❖ of the Lord..." (continued in 19A)

3 "Yea, I would declare unto every soul, as with the voice of ❖, repentance and the plan of redemption, that they should repent and come unto our God, that there might not be more sorrow upon all the face of the earth."

4 "But notwithstanding the law of Moses, they did look forward to the ❖ of Christ, considering that the law of Moses was a type of his ❖, and believing that they must keep those outward performances until the time that he should be revealed unto them."

5 "Behold, the field was ❖, and blessed are ye, for ye did thrust in the sickle, and did reap with your might, yea, all the day long did ye labor; and behold the number of your sheaves!"

8 "And thus we see how great the inequality of man is because of sin and ❖, and the power of the devil, which comes by the

56

cunning plans which he hath devised to ensnare the hearts of men."

9 "Yea, blessed is the name of my God, who has been mindful of this people, who are a branch of the tree of ❖ , and has been lost from its body in a strange land..."

10 "Yea, I know that I am ❖ ; as to my strength I am weak; therefore I will not boast of myself, but I will boast of my God, for in his strength I can do all things; yea, behold, many mighty miracles we have wrought in this land, for which we will praise his name forever."

12 "But behold, I am a man, and do sin in my ❖ ; for I ought to be content with the things which the Lord hath allotted unto me."

14 The people of Anti–Nephi–Lehi "...did keep the law of Moses; for it was expedient that they should keep the law of Moses as yet, for it was not all ❖ ."

15 "And thus there was a tremendous ❖ ..."

16 "I ought not to harrow up in my desires, the firm decree of a just God, for I know that he granteth unto men according to their desire, whether it be unto death or unto ❖ ..."

17 "Now they did not suppose that ❖ came by the law of Moses; but the law of Moses did serve to strengthen their faith in Christ; and thus they did retain a hope through faith, unto eternal ❖ , relying upon the spirit of prophecy, which spake of those things to come."

18 "And this is the blessing which hath been ❖ upon us, that we have been made instruments in the hands of God to bring about this great work."

22 "And it came to pass that as Ammon was going forth into the land, that he and his brethren met Alma, over in the place of which has been spoken; and behold, this was a joyful ❖ ."

24 "And now surely this was a sorrowful day; yea, a time of solemnity, and a time of much fasting and ❖ ."

25 "...and they never did look upon ❖ with any degree of terror, for their hope and views of Christ and the resurrection; therefore, ❖ was swallowed up to them by the victory of Christ over it."

27 "O that I were an ❖ , and could have the wish of mine heart, that I might go forth and speak with the trump of God, with a voice to shake the earth, and cry repentance unto every people!"

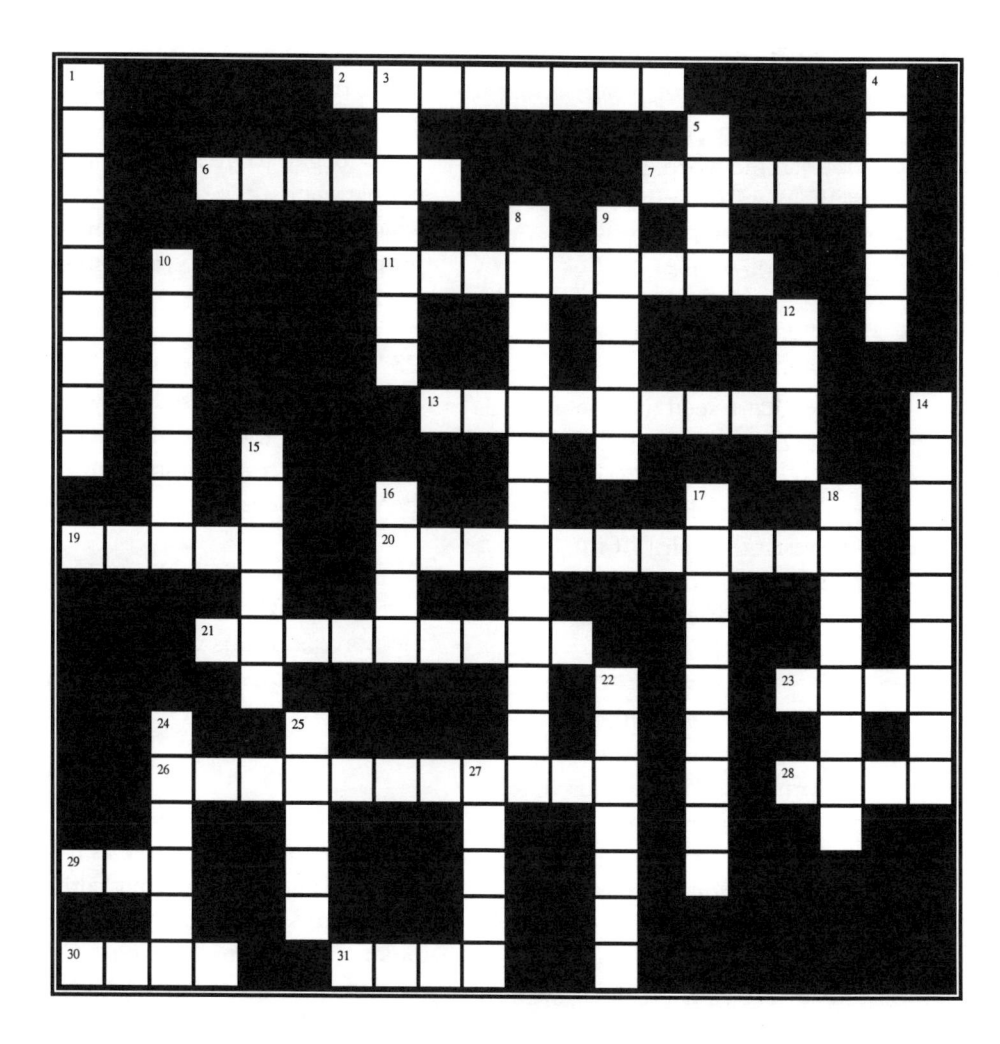

TWENTY-NINE
Alma 30–32

Across

1 "Behold, O Lord, their souls are precious, and many of them are our brethren; therefore, give unto us, O Lord, ❖ and wisdom that we may bring these, our brethren, again unto thee."

8 "And now as I said concerning faith— ❖ is not to have a perfect knowledge of things; therefore if ye have ❖ ye hope for things which are not seen, which are true."

9 "And thus, if ye will not nourish the word, looking forward with an eye of faith to the fruit thereof, ye can never pluck of the fruit of the tree of ❖ ."

10 "Now, we will compare the word unto a seed. Now, if ye give place, that a seed may be planted in your heart, behold, if it be a true seed, or a good seed, if ye do not cast it out by your ❖ , that ye will resist the spirit of the Lord, behold, it will begin to swell within your breasts..." (continued in 10D)

11 "Neither would [the Zoramites] observe the performances of the church, to continue in prayer and supplication to God daily, that they might not enter into ❖ ."

12 "But behold, if ye will awake and arouse your faculties, even to an ❖ upon my words, and exercise a particle of faith, yea, even if ye can no more than desire to believe, let this desire work in you, even until ye believe in a manner that ye can give place for portion of my words."

15 "And now, if we do not receive anything for our labors in the church, what doth it profit us to labor in the church save it were to declare the ❖ , that we may have rejoicings in the joy of our brethren?"

19 "Choose ye this day, whom ye will ❖ ."

20 "...there came a man into the land of Zarahemla, and he was ❖ , for he began to preach unto the people against the prophecies which had been spoken by the prophets, concerning the coming of Christ."

23 "...because ye were ❖ to be humble ye were blessed, do ye not suppose that they are more blessed who truly humble themselves because of the word?"

26 "And thus we see the end of him who perverteth the ways of the Lord; and thus we see that the ❖ will not support his children at the last day, but doth speedily drag them down to hell."

27 "But if ye will nourish the word, yea, nourish the tree as it beginneth to grow, by your faith with great ❖ , and with patience, looking forward to the fruit thereof, it shall take root; and behold it shall be a tree springing up unto everlasting life."

28 "Now if a man desired to serve God, it was his privilege; or rather, if he believed in God it was his privilege to serve him; but if he did not believe in him there was no ❖ to punish him."

29 "And behold, as the tree beginneth to grow, ye will say: Let us nourish it with great care, that it may get ❖ , that it may grow up, and bring forth fruit unto us."

Down

1 "Now behold, would not this increase your faith? I say unto you, Yea; nevertheless it hath not grown up to a ❖ knowledge."

2 "And now, as the preaching of the ❖ had a great tendency to lead the people to do that which was just—yea, it had had more powerful effect upon the minds of the people than the sword, or anything else, which had happened unto them—therefore Alma thought it was expedient that they should try the virtue of the word of God."

3 "...they have cast us out of our synagogues which we have labored abundantly to build with our own hands; and they have cast us out because of our exceeding ❖ ; and we have no place to worship our God; and behold, what shall we do?"

4 "And this [20A], whose name was Korihor...began to preach unto the people that there should be no ❖ ."

5 "...for if a man ❖ a thing he hath no cause to believe, for he ❖ it."

58

6 "But Alma said unto him: Thou hast had signs enough; will ye tempt your God? Will ye say, Show unto me a ❖ , when ye have the testimony of all these thy brethren, and also all the holy prophets? The scriptures are laid before thee, yea, and all things denote there is a God; yea, even the earth, and all things that are upon the face of it, yea, and its motion, yea, and also all the planets which move in their regular form do witness that there is a Supreme Creator."

7 "For [the Zoramites] had a place built up in the center of their synagogue, a place for standing, which was high above the head; and the top thereof would only admit one person." It was called ❖ .

10 (continued from 10A) "...and when you feel these swelling motions, ye will begin to say within yourselves—It must needs be that this is a good seed, or that the word is good, for it beginneth to enlarge my soul; yea, it beginneth to enlighten my ❖, yea, it beginneth to be delicious to me."

13 "This will I give unto thee for a sign, that thou shalt be struck ❖ ..."

14 "Then, my brethren, ye shall reap the ❖ of your faith, and your diligence, and patience, and long–suffering, waiting for the tree to bring forth fruit unto you."

16 "Therefore, blessed are they who ❖ themselves without being [23A] to be ❖ ..."

17 "Behold, O God, they cry unto thee, and yet their hearts are swallowed up in their pride. Behold, O God, they cry unto thee with their mouths, while they are puffed up, even to greatness, with the ❖ things of the world."

18 "...behold, by and by ye shall pluck the fruit thereof, which is most precious, which is sweet above all that is sweet, and which is ❖ above all that is ❖, yea, and pure above all that is pure; and ye shall feast upon this fruit even until ye are filled, that ye hunger not, neither shall ye thirst."

21 "And the Lord provided for [Alma and his brethren] that they should ❖ not, neither should they thirst; yea, and he also gave them strength, that they should suffer no manner of afflictions, save it were swallowed up in the joy of Christ."

22 "And he did rise up in great swelling words before Alma, and did revile against the priests and teachers, accusing them of leading away the people after the ❖ traditions of their fathers, for the sake of glutting on the labors of the people."

23 Korihor told them that "...every man prospered according to his genius, and that every man conquered according to his strength; and whatsoever a man did was no ❖ ."

24 "Yea, and he also saw that their hearts were lifted up unto great boasting, in their ❖ ."

25 Alma to Korihor: "Behold, I know that thou believest, but thou art possessed with a ❖ spirit, and ye have put off the Spirit of God that it may have no place in you; but the devil has power over you..."

59

THIRTY
Alma 33–36

Across

5 Alma: "...I do know that whosoever shall put their trust in God shall be supported in their ❖, and their troubles, and their afflictions, and shall be lifted up at the last day."

8 "Yea, and I also exhort you, my brethren, that ye be watchful unto prayer continually, that ye may not be led away by the temptations of the devil, that he may not ❖ you..."

10 "Cry unto him when ye are in your ❖, yea, over all your flocks."

12 "And then may God grant unto you that your burdens may be ❖, through the joy of his Son."

13 "And now, as I said unto you before, as ye have had so many witnesses, therefore, I beseech of you that ye do not ❖ the day of your repentance until the end; for after this day of life, which is given us to prepare for eternity, behold, if we do not improve our time while in this life, then cometh the night of darkness wherein there can be no labor performed."

15 "Yea, and from that time even until now, I have labored without ceasing, that I might bring souls unto repentance; that I might bring them to ❖ of the exceeding joy of which I did ❖; that they might also be born of God, and be filled with the Holy Ghost."

16 "And now, my brethren, I desire that ye shall plant this ❖ in your hearts, and as it beginneth to swell even so nourish it by your faith."

17 "And thus mercy can satisfy the demands of ❖, and encircles them in the arms of safety, while he that exercises no faith unto repentance is exposed to the whole law of the demands of ❖..."

18 "...if ye turn away the needy, and the naked, and visit not the sick and afflicted, and impart of your substance, if ye have, to those who stand in need—I say unto you, if ye do not any of these things, behold, your prayer is vain, and availeth you nothing, and ye are as ❖ who do deny the faith."

20 "Therefore may God grant unto you, my brethren, that ye may begin to exercise your faith unto ❖, that ye begin to call upon his holy name, that he would have mercy upon you..."

22 "Yea, ❖ yourselves, and continue in prayer unto him."

23 "Yea, cry unto him against the power of your ❖."

25 "Now Alma...seeing that the hearts of the people began to wax hard, and that they began to be offended because of the strictness of the word, his heart was exceedingly ❖."

26 "...the Lord hath said he dwelleth not in unholy ❖, but in the hearts of the righteous doth he dwell..."

27 "Yea, and when you do not cry unto the Lord, let your hearts be ❖, drawn out in prayer unto him continually for your welfare, and also for the welfare of those who are around you."

Down

1 "And behold, this is the whole meaning of the law, every whit pointing to that great and last ❖; and that great and last ❖ will be the Son of God, yea, infinite and eternal."

2 "Yea, methought I saw...God sitting upon his throne, surrounded with numberless concourses of ❖, in the attitude of singing and praising their God; yea, and my soul did long to be there."

3 "That ye contend no more against the Holy Ghost, but that ye receive it, and take upon you the ❖ of Christ..."

4 "But this is not all; ye must pour out your souls in your ❖, and your secret places, and in your wilderness."

6 "Cry unto him over the crops of your fields, that ye may ❖ in them. Cry over the flocks of your fields, that they may increase."

7 "Nay, ye cannot say this; for the same ❖ which doth possess your bodies at the time that ye go out of this life, that same ❖ will have power to possess your body in that eternal world."

9 "Yea, cry unto him against the devil, who is an enemy to all ❖ ."

11 "Yea, thou art ❖ unto thy children when they cry unto thee, to be heard of thee and not of men, and thou wilt hear them."

12 "...inasmuch as ye shall keep the commandments of God ye shall prosper in the ❖ ..."

13 "But that ye have ❖ , and bear with those afflictions, with a firm hope that ye shall one day rest from all your afflictions."

14 "...inasmuch as ye will not keep the commandments of God ye shall be ❖ off from his presence."

19 "Cry unto him in your ❖ , yea, over all your household, both morning, mid–day, and evening."

20 "Ye cannot say, when ye are brought to that awful crisis, that I will repent, that I will ❖ to my God."

21 "...according to the great plan of the ❖ God there must be an atonement made, or else all mankind must unavoidably perish; yea, all are hardened; yea, all are fallen and lost..."

24 "For behold, this life is the time for men to prepare to ❖ God; yea, behold the day of this life is the day for men to perform their labors."

61

THIRTY–ONE
Alma 37–40

Across

2 "O, remember, my son, and learn ❖ in thy youth; yea, learn in thy youth to keep the commandments of God."

4 "Seek not after riches nor the vain things of this world; for behold, you cannot ❖ them with you."

5 "And then...the spirits of the wicked, yea, who are evil...these shall be ❖ out into outer darkness; there shall be weeping, and wailing, and gnashing of teeth, and this because of their own iniquity, being led captive by the will of the devil."

8 "Do not say: O God, I thank thee that we are better than our brethren; but rather say: O Lord, ❖ my unworthiness, and remember my brethren in mercy—yea, acknowledge your unworthiness before God at all times."

9 "...if ye ❖ the Holy Ghost when it once has had place in you, and ye know that ye ❖ it, behold this is a sin which is unpardonable." (continued in 8D)

10 (continued from 24A) "...yea, when thou liest down at night lie down unto the Lord, that he may ❖ over you in your sleep..." (continued in 28A)

11 "...I command you that ye retain all their oaths, and their covenants, and their agreements in their secret abominations; yea, and all their signs and their wonders ye shall keep from this people, that they know them not, lest peradventure they should fall into ❖ also and be destroyed."

12 "Behold, O my son, how great ❖ you brought upon the Zoramites; for when they saw your conduct they would not believe in my words."

17 (continued from 16D) "...yea, let all thy thoughts be directed unto the Lord; yea, let the ❖ of thy heart be placed upon the Lord forever."

18 "The soul shall be restored to the ❖ , and the ❖ to the soul; yea, and every limb and joint shall be restored to its ❖ ; yea, even a hair of the head shall not be lost; but all things shall be restored to their proper and perfect frame."

20 "And the Lord God doth work by means to bring about his great and eternal purposes; and by very small means the Lord doth confound the wise and bringeth about the ❖ of many souls."

23 "...is not a soul at this time as ❖ unto God as a soul will be at the time of his of his coming?"

24 "Counsel with the Lord in all thy doings, and he will direct thee for ❖ ..." (continued in 10A)

25 "...I would that ye should understand that these things are not without a ❖ ; for as our fathers were slothful to give heed to this compass (now these things were temporal) they did not prosper; even so it is with things which are spiritual."

27 "...there is a space between death and the resurrection of the body, and a state of the soul in happiness or in misery until the time which is appointed of God that the ❖ shall come forth, and be reunited, both soul and body, and be brought to stand before God, and be judged according to their works."

28 (continued from 10A) "...and when thou ❖ in the morning let thy heart be full of thanks unto God; and if ye do these things, ye shall be lifted up at the last day."

29 "But behold, ye cannot ❖ your crimes from God; and except ye repent they will stand as a testimony against you at the last day."

Down

1 "Do not pray as the Zoramites do, for ye have seen that they pray to be heard of men, and to be ❖ for their wisdom."

3 "And now remember, my son, that God has entrusted you with these things, which are ❖ , which he has kept ❖ , and also which he will keep and preserve for a wise purpose in him, that he may show forth his power unto future generations."

6 "Teach them to never be weary of good works, but to be meek and lowly in heart; for such shall find ❖ to their souls."

7 "And behold, [the ❖] was

prepared to show unto our fathers the course which they should travel in the wilderness."

8 (continued from 9A) "...yea, and whosoever murdereth against the light and knowledge of God, it is not easy for him to obtain ❖ ..."

13 "See that ye are not lifted up unto pride; yea, see that ye do not ❖ in your own wisdom, nor of your much strength."

14 "For behold, it is as easy to give heed to the word of Christ, which will point to you a ❖ course to eternal bliss, as it was for our fathers to give head to this compass, which would point unto them a ❖ course to the promised land."

15 "And then shall it come to pass, that the spirits of those who are righteous are received into a state of happiness, which is called ❖ , a state of rest, a state of peace, where they shall rest from all their troubles and from all care, and sorrow."

16 "Yea, and cry unto God for all thy support; yea, let all thy ❖ be unto the Lord, and whithersoever thou goest let it be in the Lord..." (continued in 17A)

19 "Use boldness, but not over-bearance; and also see that ye ❖ all your passions, that ye may be filled with love; see that ye refrain from idleness."

21 "...the wicked...are unclean, and no unclean thing can ❖ the kingdom of God; but they are cast out, and consigned to partake of the fruits of their labors or their works, which have been evil; and they drink the dregs of a bitter cup."

22 "...the spirits of all men, as soon as they are departed from this mortal body, yea, the spirits of all men, whether they be good or evil, are taken ❖ to that God who gave them life."

26 "Now ye may suppose that this is foolishness in me; but behold I say unto you, that by small and simple things are great things brought to pass; and small means in many instances doth confound the ❖ ."

63

THIRTY-TWO
Alma 41–44

Across

4 "If he hath repented of his sins, and desired righteousness until the end of his ❖, even so he shall be rewarded unto righteousness."

5 "For that which ye do ❖ out shall return unto you again, and be restored..."

8 "...the meaning of the word ❖ is to bring back again evil for evil, or carnal for carnal, or devilish for devilish—good for that which is good; righteous for that which is righteous; just for that which is just; merciful for that which is merciful."

9 "Therefore, according to justice, the plan of redemption could not be brought about, only on conditions of ❖ of men in this [6D] state, yea, this preparatory state..."(continued in 11D)

13 "I say unto thee, my son, that the plan of restoration is requisite with the ❖ of God; for it is requisite that all things should be restored to their proper order."

15 "But God ceaseth not to be God, and mercy claimeth the penitent, and mercy cometh because of the atonement; and the atonement bringeth to pass the ❖ of the dead; and the ❖ of the dead bringeth back men into the presence of God..." (continued in 1D)

17 "...see that you are merciful unto your brethren; deal ❖, judge righteously, and do good continually; and if ye do all these things then shall ye receive your reward..."

18 "And now the design of the Nephites was to support their lands, and their houses, and their wives, and their children, that they might ❖ them from the hands of their enemies; and also that they might ❖ their rights and their privileges, yea, and also their liberty, that they might worship God according to their desires."

20 "Do not suppose, because it has been spoken concerning restoration, that ye shall be restored from ❖ to happiness."

24 "And now, the plan of mercy could not be brought about except an ❖ should be made; therefore God himself atoneth for the sins of the world...to appease the demands of justice, that God might be a perfect, just God, and a merciful God also."

25 "Now, we see that the man had become as God, knowing good and evil; and lest he should put forth his ❖, and take also of the tree of life, and eat and live forever, the Lord God placed cherubim and the flaming sword, that he should not partake of the fruit—"

26 "Behold, I say unto you, wickedness never was ❖."

Down

1 (continued from 15A) "...and thus [men] are restored into his presence, to be ❖ according to their works, according to the law and justice."

2 "...whosoever will come may come and ❖ of the waters of life freely; and whosoever will not come the same is not compelled to come; but in the last day it shall be restored unto him according to his deeds."

3 "But behold, it was appointed unto man to die—therefore, as they were cut off from the tree of life they should be cut off from the face of the earth—and man became ❖ forever, yea, they became fallen man."

6 "And thus we see, that there was a time granted unto man to repent, yea, a ❖ time, a time to repent and serve God."

7 "Nevertheless, the Nephites were inspired by a better ❖, for they were not fighting for monarchy or power but they were fighting for their homes and their liberties, their wives and their children, and their all, yea, for their rights of worship and their church."

10 "Now, there was a punishment affixed, and a just law given, which brought remorse of ❖ unto man."

11 (continued from 9A) "...for except it were for these conditions, ❖ could not take effect except it should destroy the work of justice."

12 "...the Lord God sent our first ❖ forth from the garden of Eden, to till the ground, from whence they were taken..."

14 "And they were doing that which they felt was the ❖ which they owed to their God; for the Lord had said unto them, and also unto their fathers, that: Inasmuch as ye are not guilty of the first offense, neither the second, ye shall not suffer yourselves to be slain by the hands of your enemies."

16 "...for as he has desired to do evil all the day long even so shall he have his ❖ of evil when the night cometh."

18 "And now, ye see by this that our first parents were cut off both temporally and spiritually from the ❖ of the Lord; and thus we see they became subjects to follow after their own will."

19 "And if their [22D] are ❖ they shall be restored unto them for ❖ ."

21 "Now ye see that this is the true ❖ of God; yea, ye see that God will support, and keep, and preserve us, so long as we are faithful unto him, and unto our ❖ , and our religion; and never will the Lord suffer that we shall be destroyed except we should fall into transgression and deny our ❖ ."

22 "And it is requisite with the [13A] of God that men should be judged according to their ❖ ; and if their ❖ were good in this life, and the desires of their hearts were good, that they should also, at the last day, be restored unto that which is good."

23 "Now, the decrees of God are unalterable; therefore, the way is prepared that whosoever will may ❖ therein and be saved."

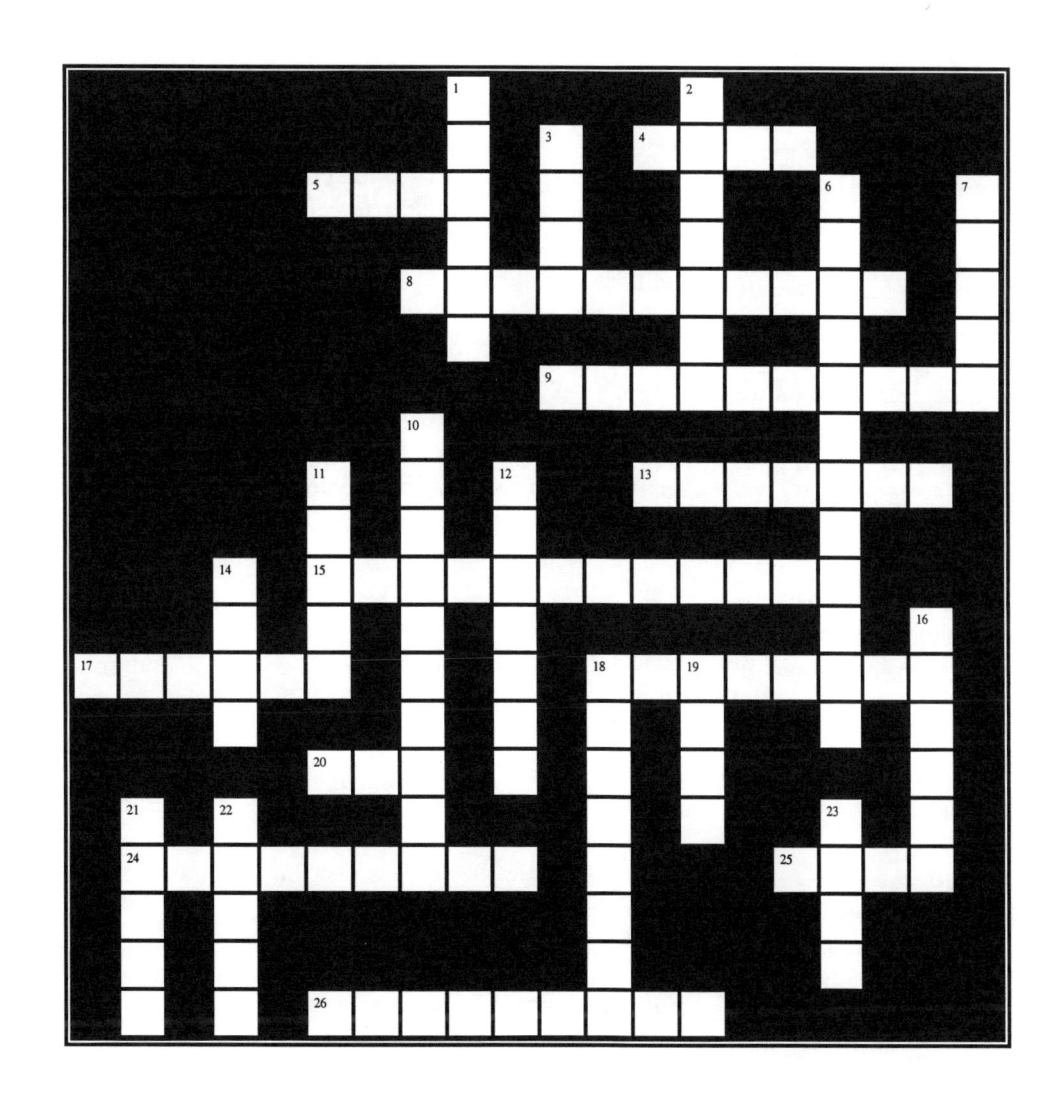

65

THIRTY-THREE
Alma 45–48

Across

2 "And it came to pass also, that he caused the [8A] of liberty to be hoisted upon every tower which was in all the land, which was possessed by the Nephites; and thus Moroni planted the ❖ of liberty among the Nephites."

5 "But they grew proud, being lifted up in their hearts, because of their exceedingly great riches; therefore they grew rich in their own eyes, and would not give heed to their ❖ , to walk uprightly before God."

6 "Therefore [18A] had accomplished his design, for he had hardened the hearts of the Lamanites and blinded their ❖ , and stirred them up to anger..."

8 "And [Moroni] fastened on his headplate, and his breastplate, and his shields, and girded on his armor about his loins; and he took the pole, which had on the end thereof his rent [15D], (and he called it the ❖ of liberty)..." (continued in 15A)

9 Alma: "Behold, I perceive that this very people, the Nephites, according to the spirit of revelation which is in me, in ❖ hundred years from the time that Jesus Christ shall manifest himself unto them, shall dwindle in unbelief."

11 "Now these dissenters, having the same instruction and the same information of the Nephites, yea, having been instructed in the same ❖ of the Lord, nevertheless, it is strange to relate, not long after their dissensions they became more hardened and impenitent..."

14 "Yea, a man whose heart did swell with thanksgiving to his God, for the many privileges and blessings which he ❖ upon his people; a man who did labor exceedingly for the welfare and safety of his people."

15 (continued from 8A) "...and [Moroni] bowed himself to the earth, and he prayed mightily unto God for the blessings of liberty to rest upon his brethren, so long as there should a band of ❖ remain to possess the land—"

16 "Yea, and we also see the great wickedness one very ❖ man can cause to take place among the children of men."

18 "And it came to pass that ❖ sought the favor of the queen, and took her unto him to wife; and thus by his fraud, and by the assistance of his cunning servants, he obtained the kingdom..."

19 "...the Lord had again delivered them out of the hands of their enemies; therefore they gave ❖ unto the Lord their God; yea, and they did fast much and pray much, and they did worship God with exceedingly great joy."

20 "And those who did belong to the church were faithful; yea, all those who were true ❖ in Christ took upon them, gladly, the name of Christ, or [15A] as they were called, because of their belief in Christ who should come."

23 "And there were some who died with fevers, which at some seasons of the year were very frequent in the land—but not so much so with fevers, because of the excellent qualities of the many plants and roots which God had prepared to remove the cause of ❖ ..."

24 "...for the Lord cannot look upon sin with the least degree of ❖ ."

25 (continued from 3D) "...yea, and they were also taught never to give an ❖ , yea, and never to raise the sword except it were against an enemy, except it were to preserve their lives."

27 "Now it came to pass that while [18A] had thus been obtaining power by fraud and deceit, Moroni, on the other hand, had been ❖ the minds of the people to be faithful unto the Lord their God."

Down

1 "Yea, verily, verily I say unto you, if all men had been, and were, and ever would be, like unto Moroni, behold, the very powers of hell would have been shaken forever; yea, the devil would never have ❖ over the hearts of the children of men."

2 "Now, they were ❖ to take up arms against the Lamanites, because they did not delight in the shedding of blood..."

3 "Now the Nephites were taught to ❖ themselves against their enemies, even to the shedding of blood if it were necessary..." (continued in 25A)

4 "...and the people did ❖ themselves because of their words, insomuch that they were highly favored of the Lord, and thus they were free from wars and contentions among themselves..."

7 "In memory of our God, our religion, and ❖ , and our peace, our wives, and our children..."

10 "...and this was not all—they were sorry to be the means of sending so many of their brethren out of this world into an eternal world, ❖ to meet their God."

12 "And Moroni was a strong and a mighty man; he was a man of a perfect understanding; yea, a man that did not ❖ in bloodshed; a man whose soul did joy in the liberty and the freedom of his country..."

13 "Behold, whosoever will maintain this [8A] upon the land, let them come forth in the strength of the Lord, and enter into a ❖ that they will maintain their rights, and their religion, that the Lord God may bless them."

15 "And it came to pass that [Moroni] rent his ❖ ; and he took a piece thereof, and wrote upon it [all of 7D] and he fastened it upon the end of a pole."

17 "And this was their faith, that by so doing God would prosper them in the land...yea, warn them to ❖ , or to prepare for war, according to their danger..."

21 "And it came to pass that there were many who died, firmly believing that their souls were ❖ by the Lord Jesus Christ; thus they went out of the world rejoicing."

22 "Thus we see how quick the children of men do ❖ the Lord their God, yea, how quick to do iniquity, and to be led away by the evil one."

24 "And it came to pass that [❖] was never heard of more; as to his death or burial we know not of."

26 "Yea, and he was a man who was ❖ in the faith of Christ, and he had sworn with an oath to defend his people, his rights, and his country, and his religion, even to the loss of his blood."

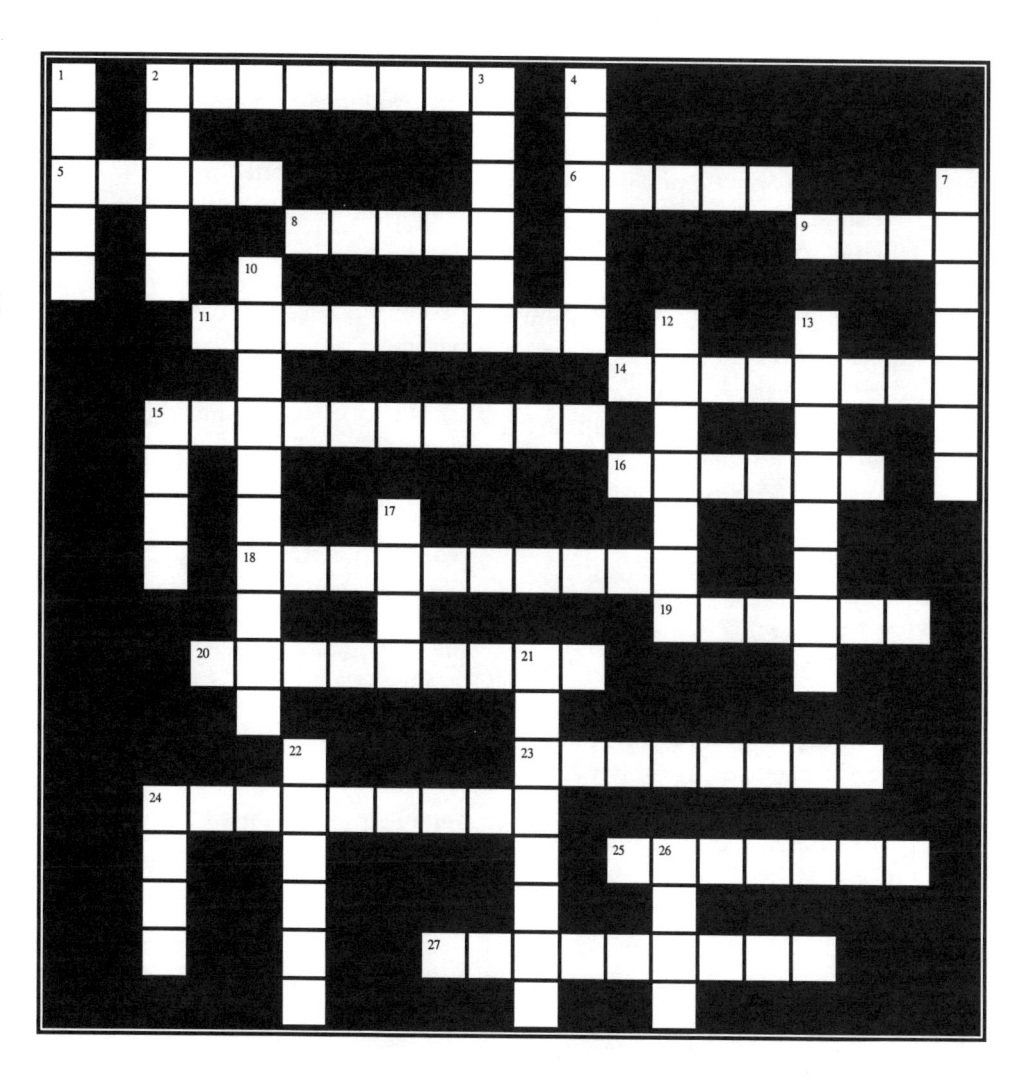

67

THIRTY-FOUR
Alma 49-52

Across

5 "Behold, it came to pass that the son of Nephihah...was appointed chief judge and governor over the people, with an oath and sacred ordinance to judge righteously, and to keep the peace and the ❖ of the people, and to grant unto them their sacred privileges to worship the Lord their God, yea, to support and maintain the cause of God all his days, and to bring the wicked to justice according to their crime."

7 "But behold there never was a ❖ time among the people of Nephi, since the days of Nephi, than in the days of Moroni..."

10 "And those who were faithful in keeping the commandments of the Lord were ❖ at all times, whilst thousands of their wicked brethren have been consigned to bondage, or to perish by the sword, or to dwindle in unbelief, and mingle with the Lamanites."

11 "And we see that these ❖ have been verified to the people of Nephi; for it has been their quarrelings and their contentions, yea, their murderings and their plunderings, their idolatry, their whoredoms, and their abominations, which were among themselves, which brought upon them their wars and their destructions."

13 "Yea, and there was continual peace among them, and exceedingly great ❖ in the church because of their heed and diligence which they gave unto the word of God..."

15 "But remember, inasmuch as they will not keep my commandments they shall be ❖ off from the presence of the Lord."

16 "And it came to pass, that on the other hand, the people of Nephi did thank the Lord their God, because of his ❖ power in delivering them from the hands of their enemies."

18 "And it came to pass that those who were desirous that Pahoran should be dethroned from the judgment–seat were called ❖ ..."

19 "...there were a part of the people who desired that a few particular points of the ❖ should be altered. But behold, Pahoran would not alter nor suffer the ❖ to be altered..."

22 "Thus Moroni, with his armies, which did increase daily because of the assurance of ❖ which his works did bring forth unto them, did seek to cut off the strength and the power of the Lamanites from off the lands of their possessions..."

23 "And Moroni also sent unto [1D], desiring him that he would be faithful in maintaining that quarter of the land, and that he would seek every opportunity to scourge the Lamanites in that quarter, as much as was in his power, that perhaps he might take again by ❖ or some other way those cities which had been taken out of their hands..."

Down

1 "And it came to pass that the army which was sent by Moroni, which was led by a man whose name was ❖ , did meet the people of Morianton..." (continued in 9D)

2 "Now those who were in favor of kings were those of high ❖ , and they sought to be kings; and they were supported by those who sought for power and authority over the people."

3 "Now Moroni seeing [the Lamanites'] confusion, he said unto them: If ye will bring forth your weapons of war and deliver them up, behold we will ❖ shedding your blood."

4 "And it came to pass that in the same year that the people of Nephi had ❖ restored unto them, that Nephihah, the second chief judge, died, having filled the judgment–seat with perfect uprightness before God."

5 "And those who were desirous that Pahoran should remain chief judge over the land took upon them the name of ❖ ..."

6 "But behold, there were many that would not; and those who would not deliver up their ❖ were taken and bound..."

8 "For it was [Moroni's] first care to put an end to such contentions and ❖ among the people; for behold, this had been hitherto a cause of all their destruction."

68

9 (continued from 1D) "...and so stubborn were the people of Morianton, (being inspired by his wickedness and his flattering words) that a battle commenced between them, in the which [1D] did slay Morianton and ❖ his army..."

12 "And it came to pass that this matter of their contention was settled by the ❖ of the people."

14 "And it came to pass that the brother of Amalickiah was appointed king over the people; and his name was ❖ ..."

15 "Blessed art thou and thy ❖ ; and they shall be blessed, inasmuch as they shall keep my commandments they shall prosper in the land."

17 "Yea, [Amalickiah] was exceedingly wroth, and he did curse God, and also Moroni, swearing with an oath that he would drink his blood; and this because Moroni had kept the commandments of God in preparing for the ❖ of his people."

20 "And it came to pass that when the Lamanites had heard these words, their chief captains, all those who were not slain, came forth and threw down their weapons of war at the ❖ of Moroni..."

21 "For behold, the people who possessed the land of Morianton did claim a part of the land of Lehi; therefore there began to be a ❖ contention between them..."

69

THIRTY-FIVE
Alma 53–57

Across

3 "Yea, they were men of truth and soberness, for they had been taught to keep the commandments of God and to ❖ uprightly before him."

4 "Nevertheless, we may console ourselves in this point, that they have died in the ❖ of their country and of their God, yea, and they are happy."

5 "Now they were determined to conquer in this place or die; therefore you may well suppose that this little force which I brought with me, yea, those ❖ of mine, gave them great hopes and much joy."

7 "...and [Lehi] was a man like unto Moroni, and they rejoiced in each other's ❖ ; yea, they were beloved by each other, and also beloved by all the people of Nephi."

9 "And Helaman feared lest by so doing they should lose their ❖ ; therefore all those who had entered into this covenant were compelled to behold their brethren wade through their afflictions, in their dangerous circumstances at this time."

13 "Now they never had ❖ , yet they did not fear death; and they did think more upon the liberty of their fathers than they did upon their lives..." (continued in 8D)

14 "And they were all young men, and they were exceedingly valiant for ❖ , and also for strength and activity; but behold, this was not all—they were men who were true at all times in whatsoever thing they were entrusted."

16 "And they rehearsed unto me the words of their [8D], saying: We do not ❖ our [8D] knew it."

17 "But behold, as they were about to take their weapons of war, they were overpowered by the persuasions of Helaman and his brethren, for they were about to ❖ the [22A] which they had made."

21 "...they had many sons, who had not entered into a covenant that they would not take their weapons of war to defend themselves against their ❖ ..."

22 "...they had taken an ❖ that they never would shed blood more; and according to their ❖ they would have perished...had it not been for the pity and exceeding love which Ammon and his brethren had had for them."

23 "And now when Laman and his men saw that they were all drunken, and were in a deep ❖ , they returned to Moroni and told him all the things that had happened."

25 "Now this was the faith of these of whom I have spoken; they are young, and their minds are ❖ , and they do put their trust in God continually."

26 "And I did join my two [29A] sons, (for they are worthy to be called sons) to the army of Antipus, in which strength Antipus did ❖ exceedingly; for behold, his army had been reduced by the Lamanites..."

28 "And thus because of iniquity amongst themselves [the Nephites], yea, because of dissensions and intrigue among themselves they were placed in the most ❖ circumstances."

29 "Now behold, there were two ❖ of those young men ..."

Down

1 "But behold, to my great joy, there had not one soul of them ❖ to the earth; yea, and they had fought as if with the strength of God; yea, never were men known to have fought with such miraculous strength..."

2 "Now Moroni caused that Laman and a small number of his men should go forth unto the ❖ who were over the Nephites."

6 "...[Moroni] did not delight in murder or bloodshed, but he delighted in the ❖ of his people from destruction; and for this cause he might not bring upon him injustice, he would not fall upon the Lamanites and destroy them in their drunkenness."

7 Helaman's stripling warriors said: "Father, behold our God is with us, and he will not ❖ that we should fall; then let us go forth; we would not slay our brethren if they would let us alone..."

8 (continued from 13A) "...yea, they had been taught by their ❖, that if they did not doubt, God would deliver them."

10 "But behold, the Nephites were not ❖ to remember the Lord their God in this their time of affliction. They could not be taken in their snares..."

11 Concerning "...the people of Ammon, who, in the beginning, were Lamanites; but by Ammon and his ❖ , or rather by the power and word of God, they had been converted unto the Lord..." (continued in 15D)

12 "...I, Helaman...was filled with exceeding joy because of the ❖ of God in preserving us, that we might not all perish; yea, and I trust that the souls of them who have been slain have entered into the rest of their God."

15 (continued from 11D) The people of Ammon "...had been brought down into the land of ❖ , and had ever since been protected by the Nephites."

18 "And this city became an exceeding stronghold ever after; and in this city they did guard the ❖ of the Lamanites; yea, even within a wall which they had caused them to build with their own hands."

19 Moroni: "...I will not ❖ prisoners, save it be on conditions that ye will deliver up a man and his wife and his children, for one prisoner; if this be the case that ye will do it, I will ❖ ."

20 "But it came to pass that when they saw the danger, and the many afflictions and tribulations which the Nephites bore for them, they were moved with compassion and were ❖ to take up arms in the defence of their country."

24 "...after the Lamanites had finished burying their dead and also the dead of the Nephites, they were marched back into the land Bountiful; and Teancum, by the orders of Moroni, caused that they should commence laboring in digging a ❖ round about the land..."

27 "And they entered into a covenant to fight for the liberty of the Nephites, yea, to protect the ❖ unto the laying down of their lives..."

THIRTY-SIX
Alma 58–63

Across

1 "See that ye strengthen Lehi and Teancum in the Lord; tell them to ❖ not, for God will deliver them..."

4 "And the people of Nephi began to prosper again in the land, and began to multiply and to ❖ exceedingly strong again in the land."

6 "Behold, I am Moroni, your chief captain. I seek not for ❖ , but to pull it down."

8 "Now it came to pass that when Lehi and Moroni knew that ❖ was dead they were exceedingly sorrowful..." (continued in 20A)

10 "...the Lord our God did visit us with assurances that he would deliver us; yea, insomuch that he did speak ❖ to our souls, and did grant unto us great faith, and did cause us that we should hope for our deliverance in him."

15 "Therefore we did pour out our souls in ❖ to God, that he would strengthen us and deliver us out of the hands of our enemies..."

18 "And [❖] was a just man, and he did walk uprightly before God; and he did observe to do good continually, to keep the commandments of the Lord his God..."

20 (continued from 8A) "...he had been a man who had fought valiantly for his country, yea, a true ❖ to liberty; and he had suffered very many exceedingly sore afflictions."

25 (continued from 27A) "...they do observe to keep his statutes, and his judgments, and his commandments continually; and their faith is strong in the ❖ concerning that which is to come."

27 "But behold, they have received many ❖ ; nevertheless they stand fast in that liberty wherewith God has made them free; and they are strict to remember the Lord their God from day to day..." (continued in 25A)

29 "But behold, because of the exceedingly great ❖ of the war between the Nephites and the Lamanites many had become hardened..."

30 "And now, my beloved brother, Moroni, may the Lord our God, who has redeemed us and made us ❖ , keep you continually in his presence..."

31 "And there had been murders, and contentions, and dissensions, and all manner of iniquity among the people of Nephi; nevertheless for the righteous' ❖ , yea, because of the prayers of the righteous, they were spared."

Down

1 "...give unto [Lehi and [8A]] power to conduct the war in that part of the land, according to the Spirit of God, which is also the spirit of ❖ which is in them."

2 "And they did pray unto the Lord their God continually, insomuch that the Lord did bless them, according to his ❖ , so that they did wax strong and prosper in the land."

3 "Now we do not know the cause that the government does not ❖ us more strength..."

5 "And those sons of the people of ❖ , of whom I have so highly spoken, are with me in the city of Manti; and the Lord has supported them, yea, and kept them from falling by the sword, insomuch that even one soul has not been slain."

7 "Now I would that ye should remember that God has said that the inward ❖ should be cleansed first, and then shall the outer ❖ be cleansed also."

9 Pahoran: "And now, in your epistle you have censured me, but it mattereth not; I am not ❖ , but do rejoice in the greatness of your heart."

10 "...we did wait in these difficult circumstances for the space of many months, even until we were about to ❖ for the want of food."

11 "...whosoever would not take up arms in the defence of their ❖ , but would fight against it, were put to death."

12 "Or do ye suppose that the Lord will still deliver us, while we sit upon our ❖ and do not make use of the means which the Lord has provided for us?"

13 "I, Pahoran, do not seek for power, save only to retain my judgment–seat that I may ❖ the rights and the liberty of my people."

14 "Therefore, my beloved brother, Moroni, let us resist ❖ , and whatsoever ❖ we cannot resist with our words, yea, such as rebellions and dissensions, let us resist them with our swords, that we may retain our freedom, that we may rejoice in the great privilege of our church, and in the cause of our Redeemer and our God."

16 "Yea, behold I do not fear your power nor your ❖ , but it is my God whom I fear..."

17 "But, behold, it mattereth not—we trust God will deliver us, notwithstanding the ❖ of our armies, yea, and deliver us out of the hands of our enemies."

19 Moroni to Pahoran: "And now, my ❖ brethren—for ye ought to be ❖ ; yea, and ye ought to have stirred yourselves more diligently for the welfare and the freedom of this people..."

21 (continued from 29A) "...and many were softened because of their afflictions, insomuch that they did humble themselves before God, even in the ❖ of humility."

22 "Therefore, Helaman and his brethren went forth, and did declare the word of God with much power unto the convincing of many people of their wickedness, which did cause them to repent of their ❖ and to be baptized unto the Lord their God."

23 "I seek not for ❖ of the world, but for the glory of my God, and the freedom and welfare of my country."

24 "Yea, they did remember how great things the Lord had done for them, that he had delivered them from death, and from ❖ , and from prisons, and from all manner of afflictions, and he had delivered them out of the hands of their enemies."

26 "Or is it that ye have neglected us because ye are in the ❖ of our country and ye are surrounded by security, that ye do not cause food to be sent unto us, and also men to strengthen our armies?"

28 "But notwithstanding their riches, or their strength, or their prosperity, they were not lifted up in the pride of their eyes; neither were they ❖ to remember the Lord their God; but they did humble themselves exceedingly before him."

73

THIRTY-SEVEN
Helaman 1–4

Across

6 "For there was one Gadianton, who was exceedingly expert in many ❖ , and also in his craft, to carry on the secret work of murder and of robbery; therefore he became the leader of the band of Kishkumen."

7 (continued from 19A) "...and smiting their humble brethren upon the cheek, making a ❖ of that which was sacred, denying the spirit of prophecy and of revelation, murdering, plundering, lying, stealing, committing adultery, rising up in great contentions..."

10 "...they sent forth one Kishkumen, even to the judgment seat of [22D], and ❖ [22D] as he sat upon the judgment seat."

14 "...because of the greatness of the destruction of the people who had before inhabited the land it was called ❖ ."

16 "But behold, a hundredth part of the proceedings of this people, yea, the account of the Lamanites and of the Nephites...cannot be contained in this ❖ ."

18 "...there was peace also, save it were the pride which began to enter into the church—not into the church of God, but into the hearts of the people who professed to ❖ to the church of God—"

19 "And it was because of the pride of their hearts, because of their exceeding riches, yea, it was because of their oppression to the ❖ , withholding their food from the hungry, withholding their clothing from the naked..." (continued in 7A)

20 "And when the servant of Helaman had known all the heart of Kishkumen, and how that it was his object to murder, and also that it was the object of all those who belonged to his band to murder, and to rob, and to ❖ power..."

22 "...there was no contention among the people of Nephi save it were a little ❖ which was in the church..."

24 "And there being but little timber upon the face of the land, nevertheless the people who went forth became exceedingly expert in the working of ❖ ; therefore they did build houses of ❖ , in the which they did dwell."

26 "And it came to pass as timber was exceedingly scarce in the land northward, they did send forth much by the way of ❖ ."

27 "...and they did suffer whatsoever ❖ should spring up upon the face of the land that it should grow up, that in time they might have timber to build their houses, yea, their cities, and their temples, and their synagogues, and their sanctuaries, and all manner of their buildings."

28 "And behold, in the end of this book ye shall see that this Gadianton did prove the overthrow, yea, almost the entire ❖ of the people of Nephi."

Down

1 "Nevertheless Helaman did fill the judgment-seat with ❖ and equity; yea, he did observe to keep the statutes, and the judgments, and the commandments of God..." (continued in 23D)

2 "Yea, we see that whosoever will may lay hold upon the word of God, which is ❖ and powerful, which shall divide asunder all the cunning and the snares and the wiles of the devil, and lead the man of Christ in a strait and narrow course across that everlasting gulf of misery which is prepared to engulf the wicked—"

3 "And they saw that they had become weak, like unto their brethren, the Lamanites, and that the Spirit of the Lord did no more preserve them; yea, it had withdrawn from them because the Spirit of the Lord doth not dwell in unholy ❖ —"

4 "And land their souls, yea, their immortal souls, at the right hand of God in the kingdom of heaven, to sit down with Abraham, and ❖ , and with Jacob, and with all our holy fathers, to go no more out."

5 "And so great was the prosperity of the church, and so many the blessings which were poured out upon the people, that even the high priests and the ❖ were themselves astonished beyond measure."

8 "And they were ❖ up in pride, even to the persecution of many of their brethren."

9 "And it came to pass that Moronihah took possession of the city of ❖ again, and caused that the Lamanites who had been taken prisoners should depart out of the land in peace."

11 "And it came to pass that in this same year there was exceedingly great prosperity in the church, insomuch that there were thousands who did ❖ themselves unto the church and were baptized unto repentance."

12 "Nevertheless they did fast and pray oft, and did wax stronger and stronger in their humility, and ❖ and ❖ in the faith of Christ, unto the filling their souls with joy and consolation, yea, even to the purifying and the sanctification of their hearts..." (continued in 13D)

13 (continued from 12D) "...which sanctification cometh because of their ❖ their hearts unto God."

15 "Thus we may see that the Lord is merciful unto all who will, in the ❖ of their hearts, call upon his holy name."

17 "Now this great loss of the Nephites, and the great slaughter which was among them, would not have happened had it not been for their wickedness and their abomination which was among them; yea, and it was among those also who ❖ to belong to the church of God."

18 "And because of this their great wickedness, and their ❖ in their own strength, they were left in their own strength; therefore they did not prosper, but were afflicted and smitten..."

21 "And it came to pass in the forty and sixth [year], yea, there was much contention and many dissensions; in the which there were an exceedingly great many who departed out of the land of [9D], and went forth unto the land northward to ❖ the land."

22 "Nevertheless, it came to pass that ❖ was appointed by the voice of the people to be chief judge and a governor over the people of Nephi."

23 (continued from 1D) "...and [Helaman] did do that which was right in the sight of God continually; and he did walk after the ways of his ❖ , insomuch that he did prosper in the land."

25 "For behold, [22D] had died, and gone the way of all the ❖ ; therefore there began to be a serious contention concerning who should have the judgment-seat among the brethren, who were the sons of Pahoran."

75

THIRTY-EIGHT
Helaman 5–7

Across

1 "And thus we see that the Nephites did begin to ❖ in unbelief, and grow in wickedness and abominations, while the Lamanites began to grow exceedingly in the knowledge of their God; yea, they did begin to keep his statutes and commandments, and to walk in truth and uprightness before him."

3 "Yea, wo shall come unto you because of that ❖ which ye have suffered to enter your hearts, which has lifted you up beyond that which is good because of your exceedingly great riches!"

5 "And when they saw that they were encircled about with a ❖ of fire, and that it burned them not, their hearts did take courage."

7 "And it came to pass that Nephi and Lehi did preach unto the Lamanites with such great power and ❖ , for they had power and ❖ given unto them that they might speak, and they also had what they should speak given unto them—"

9 "For as their laws and their governments were established by the voice of the people, and they who chose evil were more numerous than they who chose good, therefore they were ❖ for destruction, for the laws had become corrupted."

11 "Yea, and this was not all; they were a ❖ people, insomuch that they could not be governed by the law nor justice, save it were to their destruction."

13 "For behold, the Lord had blessed them so long with the ❖ of the world that they had not been stirred up to anger, to wars, nor to bloodshed; therefore they began to set their hearts upon their ❖ ; yea, they began to seek to get gain that they might be lifted up one above another..."

14 "And now, my sons, remember, remember that it is upon the ❖ of our Redeemer, who is Christ, the Son of God, that ye must build your foundation..." (continued in 24A)

15 "...that ye may not do these things that ye may boast, but that ye may do these things to lay up for yourselves a ❖ in heaven, yea, which is eternal and which fadeth not away; yea, that ye may have that precious gift of eternal life..."

16 "You must repent, and cry unto the voice, even until ye shall have ❖ in Christ, who was taught unto you by Alma, and Amulek, and Zeezrom; and when ye shall do this, the cloud of darkness shall be removed from overshadowing you."

17 (continued from 24A) "...because of the [14A] upon which ye are built, which is a sure foundation, a foundation whereon if men build they cannot ❖ ."

18 "And it came to pass when they heard this voice, and beheld that it was not a voice of thunder, neither was it a voice of a great tumultuous noise, but behold, it was a still voice of ❖ mildness, as if it had been a whisper, and it did pierce even to the very soul—"

19 "And behold, there was ❖ in all the land..."

20 "...remember that there is no other way nor means whereby man can be saved, only through the ❖ blood of Jesus Christ, who shall come; yea, remember that he cometh to redeem the world."

22 "...the Lord surely should come to redeem his people, but that he should not come to redeem them in their ❖, but to redeem them from their ❖ ."

24 (continued from 14A) "...that when the devil shall send forth his mighty winds, yea, his shafts in the whirlwind, yea, when all his hail and his mighty ❖ shall beat upon you, it shall have no power over you to drag you down to the gulf of misery and endless woe..." (continued in 17A)

26 "Condemning the righteous because of their righteousness; letting the guilty and the wicked go unpunished because of their ❖ ; and moreover to be held in office at the head of government, to rule and do according to their wills, that they might get gain and glory of the world..."

27 "And after [Nephi and Lehi] had been cast into prison many days without food, behold, [the Lamanites] went forth into the prison to take them that they might ❖ them."

76

Down

2 "And it came to pass that there came a voice as if it were above the cloud of ❖ , saying: Repent ye, repent ye, and seek no more to destroy my servants whom I have sent unto you to declare good tidings."

3 "And thus we see that the Lord began to ❖ out his Spirit upon the Lamanites, because of their easiness and willingness to believe in his words."

4 "Now behold, those secret ❖ and covenants...were put into the heart of Gadianton by that same being who did entice our first parents to partake of the forbidden fruit—"

6 "...there were eight thousand of the Lamanites who were in the land of Zarahemla and round about baptized unto repentance, and were ❖ of the wickedness of the traditions of their fathers."

8 "And he hath power given unto him from the Father to redeem them from their sins because of ❖ ..."

10 "For behold, [the Lamanites] are more righteous than you, for they have not sinned against that great knowledge which ye have received; therefore the Lord will be ❖ unto them; yea, he will lengthen out their days and increase their seed..."

12 "O, how could you have ❖ your God in the very day that he has delivered you?"

15 "And thus [the Gadianton robbers] did obtain the sole management of the government, insomuch that they did ❖ under

their feet and smite and rend and turn their backs upon the poor and the meek, and the humble followers of God."

18 "But behold, it is to get gain, to be ❖ of men, yea, and that ye might get gold and silver."

21 "...and this I have done that when you remember your ❖ ye may remember [our first parents who came out of Jerusalem]; and when you remember them ye may remember their works...that they were good."

23 "And behold, the ❖ Spirit of God did come down from heaven, and did enter into their hearts, and they were filled as if with fire, and they could speak forth marvelous words."

25 "...and they were filled with that ❖ which is unspeakable and full of glory."

THIRTY-NINE
Helaman 8–12

Across

1 "And it came to pass that when Nephi had declared unto them the word, behold, they did still ❖ their hearts and would not hearken unto his words..."

3 "And thus we see that except the Lord doth ❖ his people with many afflictions...they will not remember him."

6 "Blessed art thou, Nephi, for those things which thou hast done; for I have beheld how thou hast with ❖ declared the word, which I have given unto thee, unto this people."

11 "Yea, and we may see at the very time when he doth prosper his people...yea, then is the time that they do harden their hearts, and do ❖ the Lord their God, and do trample under their feet the Holy One—yea, and this because of their ease, and their exceedingly great prosperity."

12 "And thus we can behold how false, and also the unsteadiness of the hearts of the children of men; yea, we can see that the Lord in his great infinite goodness doth bless and prosper those who put their ❖ in him."

13 "Yea, how quick to be lifted up in pride; yea, how quick to ❖, and do all manner of that which is iniquity; and how slow are they to remember the Lord their God, and to give ear unto his counsels, yea, how slow to walk in wisdom's paths!"

18 "Behold, now we will know of a surety whether this man be a prophet and God hath commanded him to ❖ such marvelous things unto us."

20 "And now behold, Moses did not only testify of these things, but also all the holy ❖, from his days even to the days of Abraham."

21 "And thus, if ye shall say unto this temple it shall be rent in ❖, it shall be done."

22 "And thou hast not feared them, and has not sought thine own ❖, but hast sought my will, and to keep my commandments."

24 "And it came to pass that...the Lord did turn away his anger from the people, and caused that ❖ should fall upon the earth, insomuch that it did bring forth her fruit in the season of her fruit."

25 "And now, seeing ye know these things and cannot ❖ them except ye shall lie, therefore in this ye have sinned, for ye have rejected all these things, notwithstanding so many evidences which ye have received..."

26 "And now behold, I command you, that ye shall go and declare unto this people, that thus saith the Lord God, who is the Almighty: Except ye repent ye shall be ❖, even unto destruction."

27 "...we do not believe that he is a prophet; nevertheless, if this thing which he has said concerning the chief judge be true, that he be ❖, then will we believe that the other words which he has spoken are true."

Down

2 "For the earth was smitten that it was ❖, and did not yield forth the grain in the season of grain; and the whole earth was smitten..."

3 "And as many as should look upon that [16D] should live, even so as many as should look upon the Son of God with faith, having a ❖ spirit, might live, even unto that life which is eternal."

4 "And now, because thou hast done this with such [6A], behold, I will bless thee ❖; and I will make thee mighty in word and in deed, in faith and in works; yea, even that all things shall be done unto thee according to thy word, for thou shalt not ask that which is contrary to my will."

5 "O how foolish, and how vain, and how evil, and devilish, and how quick to do ❖, and how slow to do good, are the children of men; yea, how quick to hearken unto the words of the evil one, and to set their hearts upon the vain things of the world!"

7 "...and they did no more seek to destroy Nephi, but they did esteem him as a great prophet, and as a man of God, having great power and ❖ given unto him from God."

8 "...the contentions did ❖,

78

insomuch that there were wars throughout all the land among all the people of Nephi."

9 "...when Nephi saw that the people had repented and did humble themselves in ❖ , he cried again unto the Lord..."

10 "And may God grant, in his great fulness, that men might be brought unto repentance and good ❖ , that they might be restored unto grace for grace, according to their ❖ "

14 "And there were some of the Nephites who believed on the words of Nephi; and there were some also, who believed because of the ❖ of the five, for they had been converted while they were in prison."

15 "But behold, ye have rejected the truth, and rebelled against your holy god; and even at this time, instead of laying up for yourselves ❖ in heaven, where nothing doth corrupt, and where nothing can come which is unclean, ye are heaping up for yourselves wrath against the day of judgment."

16 "Yea, did [Moses] not bear record that the Son of God should come? And as he lifted up the brazen ❖ in the wilderness, even so shall he be lifted up who should come."

17 "And if ye shall say unto this ❖ , Be thou cast down and become smooth, it shall be done."

19 "And those judges were angry with [Nephi] because he spake ❖ unto them concerning their secret works of darkness..."

20 Nephi: "And now behold, if God gave unto [Moses] such ❖, then why should ye dispute among yourselves, and say that he hath given unto me no ❖ whereby I may know concerning the judgments that shall come upon you except ye repent?"

23 "O Lord, do not suffer that this people shall be destroyed by the sword; but O Lord, rather let there be a ❖ in the land, to stir them up in remembrance of the Lord their God, and perhaps they will repent and turn unto thee."

26 "Behold, I give unto you power, that whatsoever ye shall ❖ on earth shall be ❖ in heaven; and whatsoever ye shall loose on earth shall be loosed in heaven; and thus shall ye have power among this people."

FORTY
Helaman 13–16

Across

2 "He hath given unto you that ye might ❖ good from evil, and he hath given unto you that ye might choose life or death..."

6 "Therefore, as many [of the Lamanites] as have come to this, ye know of yourselves are firm and steadfast in the ❖, and in the thing wherewith they have been made free."

8 "...if a prophet come among you and declareth unto you the word of the Lord...ye are angry with him, and cast him out...yea, you will say that he is a ❖ prophet, and that he is a sinner, and of the devil, because he testifieth that your deeds are evil."

10 "...[the Lord] saith...that ye are cursed because of your ❖, and also are your ❖ cursed because ye have set your hearts upon them, and have not hearkened unto the words of him who gave them unto you."

11 "Nevertheless, the people began to harden their hearts, all save it were the most believing part of them, both of the Nephites and also of the Lamanites, and began to depend upon their own ❖ and upon their own wisdom..."

12 "Ye do not remember the Lord your God in the things with which he hath blessed you, but ye do always remember your riches, not to ❖ the Lord your God for them; yea, your hearts are not drawn out unto the Lord..."

17 "And behold this is not all, there shall be many signs and ❖ in heaven."

18 "...for behold, ye are ❖ ; ye are permitted to act for yourselves; for behold, God hath given unto you a knowledge and he hath made you ❖ ."

20 "...they would not suffer that he should enter into the city; therefore he went and got upon the ❖ thereof, and stretched forth his hand and cried with a loud voice, and prophesied unto the people whatsoever things the Lord put into his [7D]."

21 "Yea, behold, this death bringeth to pass the resurrection, and redeemeth all mankind from the first death—that ❖ death; for all mankind, by the fall of Adam being cut off from the presence of the Lord, are considered as dead, both as to things temporal and to things ❖ ."

22 "...saith the Lord of Hosts...that whoso shall ❖ up treasures in the earth shall find them again no more, because of the great curse of the land, save he be a righteous man and shall ❖ it up unto the Lord."

24 "And angels did appear unto men, wise men, and did declare unto them glad ❖ of great joy; thus in this year the scriptures began to be fulfilled."

26 "...in that day that he shall suffer death the sun shall be darkened and refuse to give his light unto you; and also the moon and the stars; and there shall be no light upon the ❖ of this land, even from the time that he shall suffer death, for the space of three days, to the time that he shall rise again from the dead."

27 "And many ❖ shall be opened, and shall yield up many of their dead; and many saints shall appear unto many."

28 "Because of the hardness of the hearts of the people of the Nephites, except they repent I will take away my ❖ from them, and I will withdraw my Spirit from them..."

Down

1 "Behold, I give unto you a ❖ ; for five years more cometh, and behold, then cometh the Son of God to redeem all those who shall believe on his name."

3 (continued from 11D) "...for ye have sought all the days of your lives for that which ye could not ❖ ; and ye have sought for happiness in doing iniquity, which thing is contrary to the nature of that righteousness which is in our great and Eternal Head."

4 "...yea, in the days of their iniquities hath he chastened [the people of Nephi] because he ❖ them."

5 "But behold, if a man shall come among you and shall say: Do this, and there is no iniquity... Walk after the ❖ of your own hearts...and do whatsoever your heart desireth—and if a man shall

80

come among you and say this, ye will receive him, and say that he is a prophet."

6 "And it shall come to pass that ye shall all be amazed, and wonder, insomuch that ye shall ❖ to the earth."

7 "But behold, the voice of the Lord came unto [Samuel], that he should return again, and prophesy unto the people whatsoever things should come into his ❖ ."

9 "And behold, this will I give unto you for a sign at the time of his coming; for behold, there shall be great ❖ in heaven, insomuch that in the night before he cometh there shall be no darkness, insomuch that it shall appear unto man as if it was day."

11 "But behold, your days of probation are past; ye have procrastinated the day of your ❖ until it is everlastingly too late..." (continued in 3D)

13 "And behold, there shall a new ❖ arise, such an one as ye never have beheld; and this also shall be a sign unto you."

14 "And as many as believed on his word went forth and sought for Nephi; and when they had come forth and found him they confessed unto him their sins and denied not, desiring that they might be ❖ unto the Lord."

15 "And this is according to the prophecy, that [the Lamanites] shall again be brought to the true ❖ , which is the ❖ of their Redeemer, and their great and true shepherd, and be numbered among his sheep."

16 "For behold, he surely must die that salvation may come; yea, it behooveth him and becometh expedient that he dieth, to bring to pass the resurrection of the dead, that thereby men may be brought into the ❖ of the Lord."

19 "...four hundred years pass not away save the sword of ❖ falleth upon this people."

23 "But as many as there were who did not believe in the words of Samuel were ❖ with him; and they cast stones at him upon the wall...but the Spirit of the Lord was with him, insomuch that they could not hit him with their stones neither with their arrows."

25 "That it is not reasonable that such a being as a Christ shall come; if so, and he be the Son of God, the Father of heaven and of earth, as it has been spoken, why will he not ❖ himself unto us as well as unto them who shall be at Jerusalem?"

FORTY-ONE
3 Nephi 1-5

Across

2 "...[Lachoneus] did cause that his people should cry unto the Lord for ❖ against the time that the robbers should come down against them."

5 "And their hearts were swollen with joy, unto the gushing out of many ❖ , because of the great goodness of God..."

6 "Behold, I [Mormon] am a disciple of Jesus Christ, the Son of God. I have been called of him to declare his word among his people, that they might have everlasting ❖ ."

8 "And it came to pass that the ❖ which came unto Nephi were fulfilled...for behold, at the going down of the sun there was no darkness; and the people began to be astonished because there was no darkness when the night came."

10 "...even so shall the covenant wherewith he hath covenanted with the house of Jacob be fulfilled in his own due ❖ , unto the restoring all the house of Jacob unto the knowledge of the covenant that he hath covenanted with them."

14 "And insomuch as the children of ❖ have kept [the Savior's] commandments he hath blessed them and prospered them according to his word."

16 "Now it came to pass that there was a day set apart by the unbelievers, that all those who believed in those ❖ should be put to death except the sign should come to pass..."

17 "...Lachoneus, the governor, was a just man, and could not be frightened by the demands and threatenings of a ❖ ..."

18 "And it came to pass that the sun did ❖ in the morning again, according to its proper order; and they knew that it was the day that the Lord should be born..."

20 "...and the people began to forget those signs and ❖ which they had heard, and began to be less and less astonished at a sign or a ❖ from heaven, insomuch that they began to be hard in their hearts, and blind in their minds..."

22 "Lift up your head and be of good ❖ ; for behold, the time is at hand, and on this night shall the sign be given, and on the morrow come I into the world, to show unto the world that I will fulfill all that which I have caused to be spoken by the mouth of my holy prophets."

23 "And thus were the Lamanites afflicted also, and began to decrease as to their faith and righteousness, because of the wickedness of the ❖ generation."

25 "Therefore, all the Lamanites who had become converted unto the Lord did unite with their brethren, the Nephites, and were compelled, for the ❖ of their lives and their women and their children, to take up arms against those Gadianton robbers..." (continued in 11D)

27 "And as surely as the Lord liveth, will he gather in from the four quarters of the earth all the remnant of the ❖ of Jacob, who are scattered abroad upon all the face of the earth."

28 "And it came to pass that they did break forth, all as one, in ❖ , and praising their God for the great thing which he had done for them, in preserving them from falling into the hands of their enemies."

29 "...it was impossible for the robbers to lay siege sufficiently long to have any effect upon the Nephites, because of their much provision which they had laid up in ❖ ..."

Down

1 "And they did rejoice and cry again with one voice, saying: May the God of Abraham, and the God of Isaac, and the God of ❖ , protect this people in righteousness, so long as they shall call on the name of their God for protection."

3 "May the Lord preserve his people in righteousness and in ❖ of heart, that they may cause to be felled to the earth all who shall seek to slay them because of power and secret combinations..."

4 "...and they knew it was because of their repentance and their ❖ that they had been delivered from an everlasting destruction."

7 "And there was also a cause of much sorrow among the Lamanites; for behold, they had many children who did grow up and began to wax strong in years, that they became for themselves, and were led away by some who were Zoramites, by their lyings and their ❖ words, to join those Gadianton robbers."

9 "...and thus did Satan get possession of the hearts of the people again, insomuch that he did blind their eyes and lead them away to believe that the ❖ of Christ was a foolish and a vain thing."

11 (continued from 25A) "...yea, and also to maintain their rights, and the privileges of their ❖ and of their worship, and their freedom and their liberty."

12 "...and they did fear the words which had been spoken by Lachoneus, insomuch that they did repent of all their sins; and they did put up their ❖ unto the Lord their God, that he would deliver them in the time that their enemies should come down against them to battle."

13 "Now it was the custom among all the Nephites to appoint for their chief captains...some one that had the spirit of revelation and also ❖ ; therefore, this Gidgiddoni was a great prophet among them, as also was the chief judge."

15 "I [Mormon] have reason to bless my God and my Savior Jesus Christ, that he brought our ❖ out of the land of Jerusalem...and that he hath given me and my people so much knowledge unto the salvation of our souls."

19 "Therefore they did forsake all their sins, and their abominations, and their whoredoms, and did ❖ God with all diligence day and night."

20 "And their curse was taken from [the Lamanites who had united with the Nephites], and their skin became ❖ like unto the Nephites."

21 "Yea, [Lachoneus] said unto them: As the Lord liveth, except ye ❖ of all your iniquities, and cry unto the Lord, ye will in nowise be delivered out of the hands of those Gadianton robbers."

24 "But behold, they did watch steadfastly for that day and that night and that day which should be as one day as if there were no night, that they might know that their faith had not been ❖ ."

26 "But in this thing they were disappointed, for the Nephites did not ❖ them; but they did ❖ their God and did supplicate him for protection..."

27 "And it came to pass also that a new ❖ did appear, according to the word."

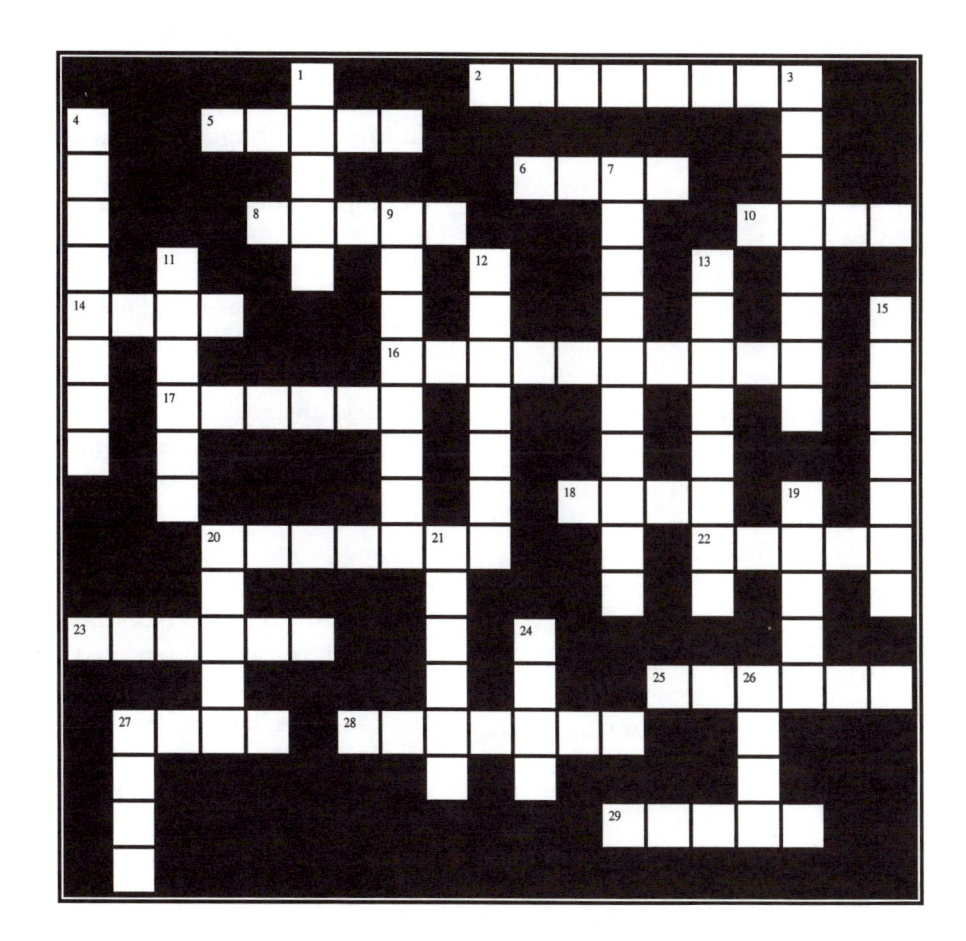

83

FORTY–TWO

3 Nephi 6–10

Across

4 "...I will show unto you that the people of Nephi who were ❖ , and also those who had been called Lamanites, who had been ❖ , did have great favors shown unto them..." (continued in 11A)

5 "Now they did not sin ignorantly, for they knew the will of God concerning them, for it had been taught unto them; therefore they did willfully ❖ against God."

7 "And the people began to look with great earnestness for the sign which had been given by the prophet Samuel, the Lamanite, yea, for the time that there should be ❖ for the space of three days..."

8 "...and some were lifted up unto ❖ and boastings because of their exceedingly great riches, yea, even unto great persecutions..."

10 "...all these great and terrible things were done in about the space of ❖ hours—and then behold, there was darkness upon the face of the land."

11 (continued from 4A) "...and great blessings poured out upon their heads, insomuch that soon after the ascension of Christ into ❖ he did truly manifest himself unto them—"

12 "And thus the face of the whole earth became deformed, because of the tempests, and the thunderings, and the lightnings, and the ❖ of the earth."

13 "...O ye people of the house of ❖ , ye that dwell at Jerusalem, as ye that have fallen; yea, how oft would I have gathered you as a hen gathereth her chickens, and ye would not."

16 Nephi "...began to testify, boldly, repentance and remission of sins through ❖ on the Lord Jesus Christ."

18 "Therefore, whoso repenteth and cometh unto me as a little ❖ , him will I receive, for of such is the kingdom of God."

19 (continued from 2D) "...for the devil laugheth, and his angels rejoice, because of the slain of the fair sons and daughters of my people; and it is because of their ❖ and abominations that they are fallen!"

20 "And many great and notable cities were sunk, and many were ❖ , and many were shaken till the buildings thereof had fallen to the earth, and the inhabitants thereof were slain, and the places were left desolate."

21 "And in another place they were heard to cry and mourn, saying: O that we had repented before this great and terrible day, and had not killed and ❖ the prophets, and cast them out; then would our mothers and our fair daughters, and our children have been spared..."

22 "And the people began to be distinguished by ranks, according to their ❖ and their chances for learning; yea, some were ignorant because of their poverty, and others did receive great learning because of their ❖ ."

25 "I am the light and the life of the world. I am ❖ and Omega, the beginning and the end."

27 "Behold, I am Jesus Christ the Son of God. I ❖ the heavens and the earth, and all things that in them are."

28 "And now, whoso readeth, let him understand; he that hath the scriptures, let him ❖ them, and see and behold if all these deaths and destructions...and all these things are not unto the fulfilling of the prophecies of many of the holy prophets."

29 "And it was the more righteous part of the people who were ❖ , and it was they who received the prophets and stoned them not; and it was they who had not shed the blood of the saints, who were spared—"

Down

1 "And these things which testify of us, are they not written upon the plates of ❖ which our father Lehi brought out of Jerusalem?"

2 "Wo, wo, wo unto this ❖ ; wo unto the inhabitants of the whole earth except they shall repent..." (continued in 19A)

3 "...how oft will I gather you as a hen gathereth her chickens under her wings, if ye will repent and return unto me with ❖ purpose of heart."

6 "...all such as should come unto

84

them should be ❖ with water, and this as a witness and a testimony before God, and unto the people, that they had repented and received a remission of their sins."

9 "Now the cause of this iniquity of the people was this—Satan had great ❖ , unto the stirring up of the people to do all manner of iniquity, and to the puffing them up with pride, tempting them to seek for ❖ , and authority, and riches, and the vain things of the world."

11 "And ye shall offer for a sacrifice unto me a broken ❖ and a contrite spirit. And whoso cometh unto me with a broken ❖ and a contrite spirit, him will I baptize with fire and with the Holy Ghost..."

14 "I came unto my own, and my own received me not. And the ❖ concerning my coming are fulfilled."

15 Concerning the great destruction: "...that their wickedness and abominations might be hid from before my face, that the ❖ of the prophets and the saints whom I sent among them might not cry unto me from the ground against them."

16 "I was with the ❖ from the beginning. I am in the ❖ , and the ❖ in me; and in me hath the ❖ glorified his name."

17 "Some were lifted up in pride, and others were exceedingly ❖ ; some did return railing for railing, while others would receive railing and persecution and all manner of afflictions, and would not turn and revile again, but were ❖ and penitent before God."

23 "O all ye that are spared because ye were more righteous than they, will ye not now return unto me, and repent of your sins, and be converted, that I may ❖ you?"

24 "And as many as have received me, to them have I given to become the ❖ of God; and even so will I to as many as shall believe on my name, for behold, by me redemption cometh, and in me is the law of Moses fulfilled."

26 "Behold, for such I have laid down my ❖ , and have taken it up again; therefore repent, and come unto me ye ends of the earth, and be saved."

85

FORTY-THREE
3 Nephi 11–12

Across

2 "...whoso repenteth of his sins through your words, and desireth to be baptized in my ❖ , on this wise shall ye baptize them— Behold, ye shall go down and stand in the water, and in my ❖ shall ye baptize them."

4 "...and this they did do, going forth one by one until they had all gone forth, and did see with their eyes and did feel with their hands, and did know of a surety and did bear ❖ , that it was he, of whom it was written by the prophets, that should come."

5 "And whosoever shall compel thee to go a mile, go with him ❖ ."

9 "And again, blessed are all they that ❖ , for they shall be comforted."

10 "And blessed are the ❖ , for they shall inherit the earth."

11 "...I give unto you to be the ❖ of the earth; but if the ❖ shall lose its savor wherewith shall the earth be ❖ ? The ❖ shall be thenceforth good for nothing, but to be cast out and to be trodden under foot of men."

12 "And blessed are all the pure in ❖ , for they shall see God."

16 "...I give unto you to be the light of this people. A city that is set on a ❖ cannot be hid."

17 "Behold, I am Jesus Christ, whom the ❖ testified shall come into the world."

19 (continued from 31A) "...and notwithstanding it being a [31A] voice it did pierce them that did hear to the center, insomuch that there was no part of their frame that it did not cause to quake; yea, it did pierce them to the very ❖ , and did cause their hearts to burn."

21 "Therefore let your light so shine before this people, that they may see your ❖ works and glorify your Father who is in heaven."

22 "And the Lord said unto [Nephi]: I give unto you power that ye shall ❖ this people when I am again ascended into heaven."

23 "Verily, verily, I say unto you, that this is my doctrine, and whoso buildeth upon this buildeth upon my ❖ , and the gates of hell shall not prevail against them."

26 "For verily, verily I say unto you, he that hath the spirit of ❖ is not of me, but is of the devil, who is the father of ❖ , and he stirreth up the hearts of men to contend with anger, one with another."

29 "...thou shalt not kill, and whosoever shall kill shall be in ❖ of the judgment of God; But I say unto you, that whosoever is angry with his brother shall be in ❖ of his judgment."

31 "...for they understood not the voice which they heard; and it was not a harsh voice, neither was it a loud voice; nevertheless, and notwithstanding it being a ❖ voice it did pierce them that did hear to the center..." (continued in 19A)

32 "And again I say unto you, ye must repent, and be baptized in my name, and become as a little child, or ye can in nowise ❖ the kingdom the God."

33 "Yea, blessed are the ❖ in spirit who come unto me, for theirs is the kingdom of heaven."

Down

1 "But I say unto you, that ye shall not resist evil, but whosoever shall smite thee on thy right cheek, ❖ to him the other also..."

2 "Old things are done away, and all things have become ❖ ."

3 "Therefore I would that ye should be ❖ even as I, or your Father who is in heaven is ❖ ."

6 "Behold, it is written by them of old time, that thou shalt not commit ❖ ; But I say unto you, that whosoever looketh on a woman, to lust after her, hath committed ❖ already in his heart."

7 "And it came to pass, as they understood they cast their eyes up again towards heaven; and behold, they saw a Man descending out of heaven; and he was clothed in a ❖ robe; and he came down and stood in the midst of them..."

8 "Behold, do men light a ❖ and put it under a bushel? Nay, but on a ❖ stick, and it giveth light to all that are in the house..."

86

13 "And now behold, these are the words which ye shall say, calling them by name, saying: Having ❖ given me of Jesus Christ, I baptize you in the name of the Father, and of the Son, and of the Holy Ghost. Amen. And then shall ye immerse them in the water, and come forth again out of the water."

14 "And blessed are all the peacemakers, for they shall be called the ❖ of God."

15 "And behold, the third time they did understand the voice which they heard; and it said unto them: Behold my Beloved Son, in whom I am well pleased, in whom I have ❖ my name—hear ye him."

18 "And behold, I am the light and the life of the world; and I have drunk out of that bitter ❖ which the Father hath given me, and have glorified the Father in taking upon me the sins of the world…"

20 "And blessed are the ❖ , for they shall obtain mercy."

22 "Therefore, if ye shall come unto me, or shall desire to come unto me, and rememberest that thy ❖ hath aught against thee —Go thy way unto thy ❖ , and first be reconciled to thy ❖ , and then come unto me with full purpose of heart, and I will receive you."

24 "But behold I say unto you, love your ❖ , bless them that curse you, do good to them that hate you, and pray for them who despitefully use you and persecute you…"

25 "And blessed are all they who do hunger and ❖ after righteousness, for they shall be filled with the Holy Ghost."

27 "Give to him that asketh thee, and from him that would ❖ of thee turn thou not away."

28 "But verily, verily, I say unto you, ❖ not at all; neither by heaven, for it is God's throne; Nor by the earth, for it is his footstool…"

30 "And thus will the Father bear record of me, and the Holy Ghost will bear record unto him of the Father and me; for the Father, and I, and the Holy Ghost are ❖ ."

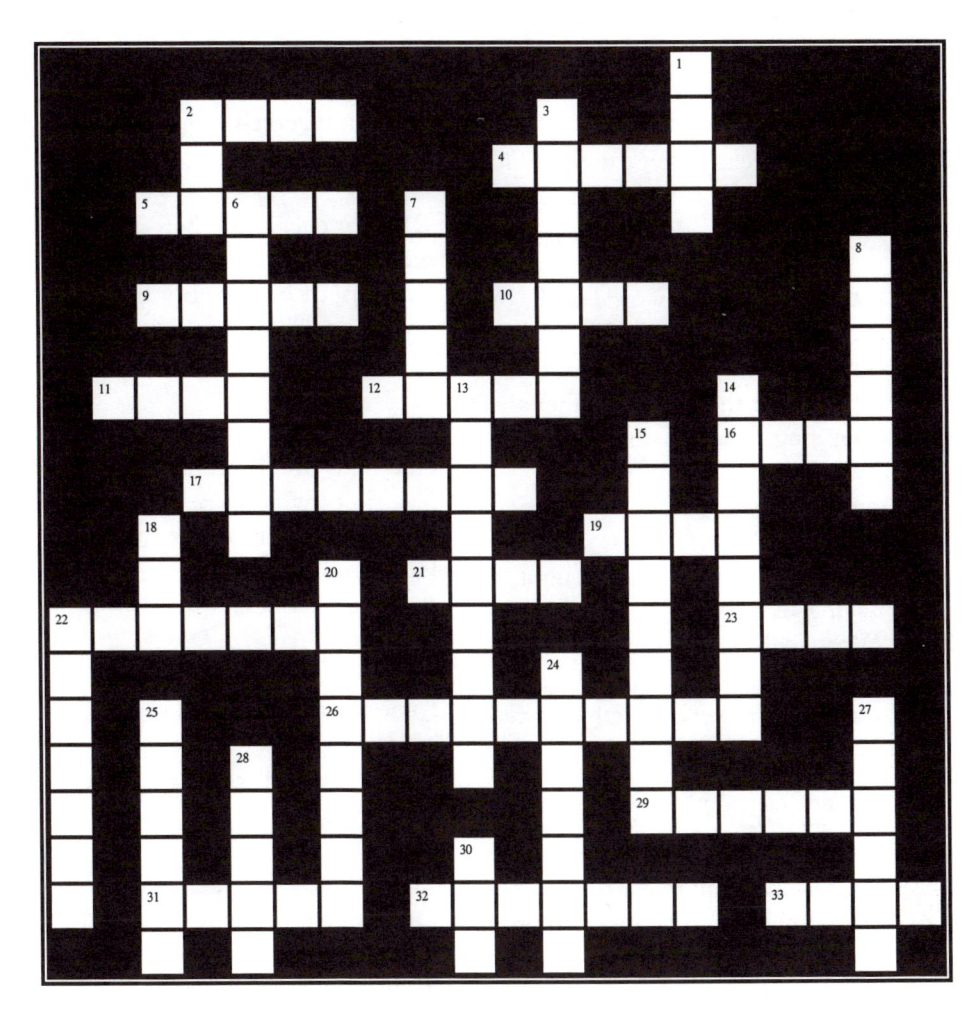

87

FORTY–FOUR
3 Nephi 13–16

Across

1 "Behold, I am the law, and the ❖. Look unto me, and endure to the end, and ye shall live; for unto him that endureth to the end will I give eternal life."

3 (continued from 14A) "And lead us not into temptation, but deliver us from ❖. For thine is the kingdom, and the power, and the glory, forever. Amen."

6 "But seek ye first the ❖ of God and his righteousness, and all these things shall be added unto you."

8 "And then the words of the prophet ❖ shall be fulfilled, which say: Thy watchmen shall lift up the voice; with the voice together shall they sing, for they shall see eye to eye when the Lord shall bring again Zion."

10 "Therefore take no thought, saying, What shall we eat? or, What shall we ❖? or, Wherewithal shall we be clothed? For your heavenly Father knoweth that ye have need of all these things."

12 "...At that day when the Gentiles shall sin against my gospel, and shall reject the ❖ of my gospel, and shall be lifted up in the pride of their hearts above all nations...behold, saith the Father, I will bring the ❖ of my gospel from among them."

14 "After this manner therefore pray ye: Our Father who art in heaven, hallowed be thy name. Thy will be done on earth as it is in heaven. And ❖ us our debts, as we ❖ our debtors." (continued in 3A)

15 " And then will I remember my ❖ which I have made unto my people, O house of Israel, and I will bring my gospel unto them."

18 "No man can serve two ❖ ; for either he will hate the one and love the other, or else he will hold to the one and despise the other. Ye cannot serve God and Mammon."

21 "Not every one that saith unto me, Lord, Lord, shall ❖ into the kingdom of heaven; but he that doeth the will of my Father who is in heaven."

23 "But thou, when thou prayest, enter into thy ❖ , and when thou hast shut thy door, pray to thy Father who is in secret; and thy Father, who seeth in secret, shall reward thee openly."

24 "Beware of ❖ prophets, who come to you in sheep's clothing, but inwardly they are ravening wolves. Ye shall know them by their fruits."

26 "...Verily, verily, I say unto you, Judge not, that ye be not ❖. For with what judgment ye judge, ye shall be ❖ ; and with what measure ye mete, it shall be measured to you again."

27 "That other sheep I have which are not of this ❖ ; them also I must bring, and they shall hear my voice; and there shall be one ❖ , and one shepherd."

Down

2 "Be not ye therefore like unto them, for your Father knoweth what ❖ ye have need of before ye ask him."

3 "Behold, I am he that gave the law, and I am he who covenanted with my people Israel; therefore, the law in me is fulfilled, for I have come to fulfil the law; therefore it hath an ❖."

4 "But thou, when thou fastest, anoint thy ❖ , and wash thy face; That thou appear not unto men to fast, but unto thy Father, who is in secret; and thy Father, who seeth in secret, shall reward thee openly."

5 "But when ye pray, use not ❖ repetitions, as the heathen, for they think that they shall be heard for their much speaking."

7 "And verily, verily, I say unto you that I have other sheep, which are not of this land, neither of the land of Jerusalem, neither in any parts of that land round about whither I have been to ❖ ."

9 "Therefore, whoso heareth these sayings of mine and doeth them, I will liken him unto a wise man, who built his ❖ upon a rock—And the rain descended, and the floods came, and the winds blew, and beat upon that ❖ ; and it fell not, for it was founded upon a rock."

11 "Ask, and it shall be given unto you; seek, and ye shall find; ❖ , and it shall be opened unto you."

88

13 "Behold, because of their belief in me, saith the Father, and because of the unbelief of you, O house of Israel, in the ❖ day shall the truth come unto the Gentiles, that the fulness of these things shall be made known unto them."

15 "But lay up for yourselves treasures in heaven, where neither moth nor rust doth ❖ , and where thieves do not break through nor steal. For where your treasure is, there will your heart be also."

16 "And why beholdest thou the ❖ that is in thy brother's eye, but considerest not the beam that is in thine own eye?"

17 "For, if ye forgive ❖ their trespasses your heavenly Father will also forgive you; But if ye forgive not ❖ their trespasses neither will your Father forgive your trespasses."

19 "But when thou doest ❖ let not thy left hand know what thy right hand doeth; That thine ❖ may be in secret; and thy Father who seeth in secret, himself shall reward thee openly."

20 "Give not that which is holy unto the dogs, neither cast ye your pearls before ❖ , lest they trample them under their feet, and turn again and rend you."

22 "If ye then, being evil, know how to give ❖ gifts unto your children, how much more shall your Father who is in heaven give ❖ things to them that ask him?"

24 "And every one that heareth these sayings of mine and doeth them not shall be likened unto a foolish man, who built his house upon the sand—And the rain descended, and the floods came, and the winds blew, and beat upon that house; and it fell, and great was the ❖ of it."

25 "Therefore, all things whatsoever ye would that men should do to you, do ye even so to them, for this is the ❖ and the prophets."

89

FORTY-FIVE
3 Nephi 17-20

Across

2 "But now I go unto the Father, and also to show myself unto the ❖ tribes of Israel, for they are not ❖ unto the Father, for he knoweth whither he hath taken them."

6 "And it came to pass that he commanded that their ❖ children should be brought."

7 "...and [Jesus] said: Father, I thank thee that thou hast given the Holy Ghost unto these whom I have ❖ ; and it is because of their belief in me that I have ❖ them out of the world. Father, I pray thee that thou wilt give the Holy Ghost unto all them that shall believe in their words."

8 "And I give unto you a commandment that ye shall do these things. And if ye shall always do these things blessed are ye, for ye are built upon my ❖ ."

9 "And whatsoever ye shall ask the Father in my name, which is ❖ , believing that ye shall receive, behold it shall be given unto you."

12 "...Behold there shall one be ❖ among you, and to him will I give power that he shall break bread and bless it and give it unto the people of my church, unto all those who shall believe and be baptized in my name."

14 "Behold, verily, verily, I say unto you, ye must ❖ and pray always lest ye enter into temptation; for Satan desireth to have you, that he may sift you as wheat."

17 "...ye shall not suffer any one knowingly to partake of my flesh and blood unworthily, when ye shall ❖ it; For whoso eateth and drinketh my flesh and blood unworthily eateth and drinketh damnation to his soul..."

18 "And it came to pass when they were all baptized and had come up out of the water, the Holy Ghost did fall upon them, and they were filled with the Holy Ghost and with ❖ ."

19 "And as they looked to behold they cast their eyes towards heaven, and they saw the heavens open, and they saw ❖ descending out of heaven as it were in the midst of fire; and they came down and encircled those little ones about, and they were encircled about with fire; and the ❖ did minister unto them."

22 "Pray in your families unto the Father, always in my name, that your wives and your children may be ❖ ."

24 "...ye shall not cast him out of your synagogues, or your places of ❖ , for unto such shall ye continue to minister; for ye know not but what they will return and repent, and come unto me with full purpose of heart, and I shall heal them; and ye shall be the means of bringing salvation unto them."

27 "And when he had said these words, he himself also ❖ upon the earth; and behold he prayed unto the Father, and the things which he prayed cannot be written, and the multitude did bear record who heard him."

28 "And now Father, I pray unto thee for them, and also for all those who shall believe on their words, that they may believe in me, that I may be in them as thou, Father, art in me, that we may be ❖ ."

29 "And behold, ye shall ❖ together oft; and ye shall not forbid any man from coming unto you when ye shall ❖ together, but suffer them that they may come unto you and forbid them not; But ye shall pray for them..."

30 "...neither can the hearts of men conceive so great and marvelous things as we both saw and heard Jesus speak; and no one can conceive of the joy which filled our ❖ at the time we heard him pray for us unto the Father."

Down

1 "Have ye any that are ❖ among you?...Bring them hither and I will heal them, for I have compassion upon you; my bowels are filled with mercy."

3 "And [the Gentiles] shall be a ❖ unto the people of this land. Nevertheless, when they shall have received the fulness of my gospel, then if they shall harden their hearts against me I will return their iniquities upon their own heads..."

4 "Behold I am the ❖ ; I have set an example for you."

90

5 "And tongue cannot speak the words which he prayed, neither can be written by man the words which he prayed. And the multitude did hear and do bear ❖ ; and their hearts were open and they did understand in their hearts the words which he prayed."

10 "How beautiful upon the mountains are the feet of him that bringeth good ❖ unto them, that publisheth peace; that bringeth good ❖ unto them of good, that publisheth salvation; that saith unto Zion: Thy God reigneth!"

11 "And I will remember the covenant which I have made with my people; and I have covenanted with them that I would ❖ them together in mine own due time, that I would give unto them again the land of their fathers for their inheritance, which is the land of Jerusalem, which is the promised land unto them forever..."

13 "And this shall ye do in remembrance of my body, which I have shown unto you. And it shall be a testimony unto the Father that ye do always ❖ me. And if ye do always ❖ me ye shall have my Spirit to be with you."

15 "For I perceive that ye desire that I should show unto you what I have done unto your brethren at Jerusalem, for I see that your ❖ is sufficient that I should heal you."

16 "And it shall come to pass that the time cometh, when the fulness of my gospel shall be preached unto them; And they shall believe in me, that I am Jesus Christ, the Son of God, and shall ❖ unto the Father in my name."

20 "And behold, ye are the children of the prophets; and ye are of the house of Israel; and ye are of the covenant which the Father made with your fathers, saying unto Abraham: And in thy ❖ shall all the kindreds of the earth be blessed."

21 "And behold, this people will I establish in this land, unto the fulfilling of the covenant which I made with your father Jacob; and it shall be a ❖ Jerusalem."

23 "And when he had said these words, he ❖ , and the multitude bare record of it, and he took their little children, one by one, and blessed them, and prayed unto the Father for them."

24 "...Jesus said unto them: Blessed are ye for this thing which ye have done, for this is fulfilling my commandments, and this doth ❖ unto the Father that ye are willing to do that which I have commanded you."

25 "...Jesus blessed them as they did pray unto him; and his countenance did smile upon them, and the light of his countenance did ❖ upon them, and behold they were as white as the countenance and also the garments of Jesus..."

26 "Therefore, go ye unto your homes, and ❖ upon the things which I have said, and ask of the Father, in my name, that ye may understand, and prepare your minds for the morrow, and I come unto you again."

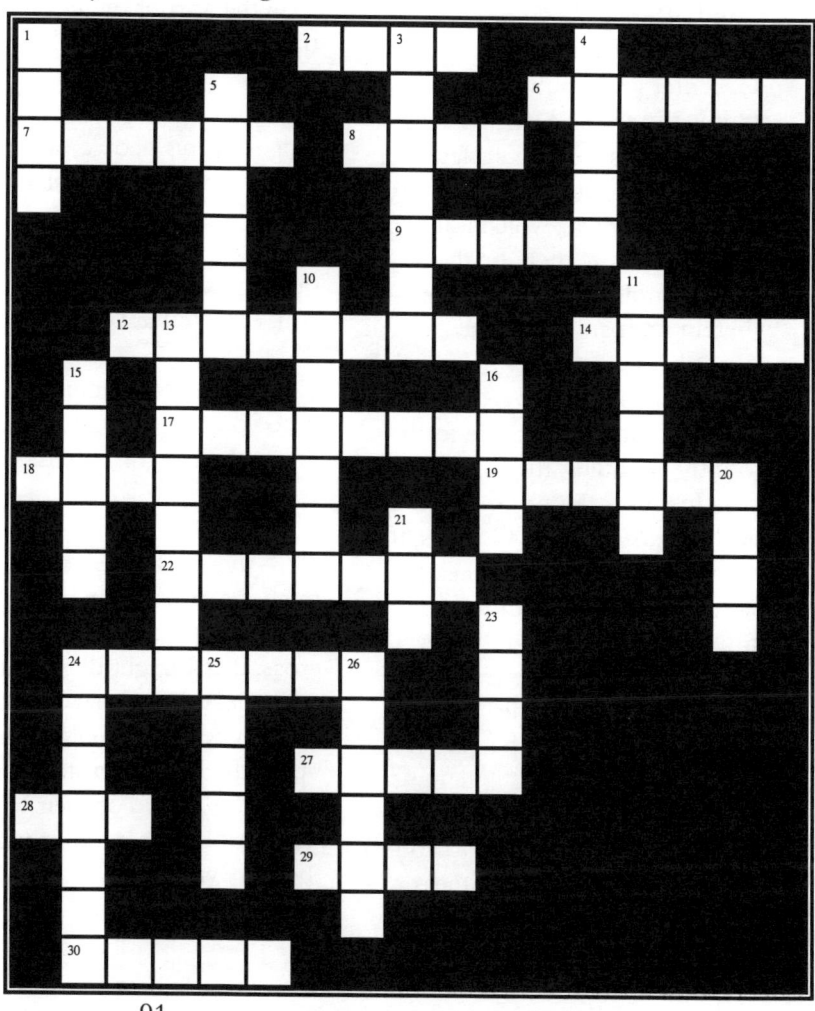

91

FORTY–SIX
3 Nephi 21–28

Across

7 "Bring ye all the [10A] into the storehouse, that there may be meat in my house; and prove me now herewith, saith the Lord of Hosts, if I will not ❖ you the windows of heaven, and pour you out a blessing that there shall not be room enough to receive it."

8 "And how be it my church save it be called in my name? For if a church be called in ❖' name then it be ❖' church; or if it be called in the name of a man then it be the church of a man..."

10 "Will a man rob God? Yet ye have robbed me. But ye say: Wherein have we robbed thee? In ❖ and offerings."

13 "Enter ye in at the strait ❖ ; for strait is the ❖ , and narrow is the way that leads to life, and few there be that find it; but wide is the gate, and broad the way which leads to death, and many there be that travel therein, until the night cometh, wherein no man can work."

18 "For thus it behooveth the Father that it should come forth from the Gentiles, that he may show forth his ❖ unto the Gentiles, for this cause that the Gentiles, if they will not harden their hearts, that they may repent and come unto me and be baptized in my name and know of the true points of my doctrine, that they may be numbered among my people, O house of Israel..."

20 "And I will come near to you to ❖ ; and I will be a swift witness against the sorcerers, and against the adulterers, and against false swearers, and against those that oppress the hireling in his wages, the widow and the fatherless, and that turn aside the stranger, and fear not me..."

23 [❖ of the twelve disciples]: "We desire that after we have lived unto the age of man, that our ministry, wherein thou hast called us, may have an end, that we may speedily come unto thee in thy kingdom."

24 "And when they shall have received this, which is expedient that they should have first, to try their ❖ , and if it shall so be that they shall believe these things then shall the greater things be made manifest unto them."

25 "And know ye that ye shall be judges of this people, according to the judgment which I shall give unto you, which shall be just. Therefore, what manner of ❖ ought ye to be? Verily I say unto you, even as I am."

26 "Yea, a commandment I give unto you that ye ❖ these things diligently; for great are the words of Isaiah."

27 "And my Father sent me that I might be ❖ up upon the cross; and after that I had been ❖ up upon the cross, that I might draw all men unto me, that as I have been ❖ up by men even so should men be ❖ up by the Father, to stand before me, to be judged of their works, whether they be good or whether they be evil—"

28 "And even unto the great and last day, when all people, and all kindreds, and all nations and tongues shall ❖ before God, to be judged of their works, whether they be good or whether they be evil "

Down

1 "If they be ❖ , to the resurrection of everlasting life; and if they be evil, to the resurrection of damnation; being on a parallel, the one on the one hand and the other on the other hand, according to the mercy, and the justice, and the holiness which is in Christ, who was before the world began."

2 "For behold, out of the ❖ which have been written, and which shall be written, shall this people be judged, for by them shall their works be known unto men."

3 "And whoso taketh upon him my ❖ , and endureth to the end, the same shall be saved at the last day."

4 "And they taught, and did minister one to another; and they had all things common among them, every man dealing ❖ , one with another."

5 "And all thy children shall be taught of the Lord; and ❖ shall be the peace of thy children."

6 "And no unclean thing can enter into his kingdom; therefore nothing entereth into his ❖ save it be those who have washed their garments in my blood, because of their faith, and the repentance of all their sins, and their faithfulness unto the end."

9 "And when these things come to pass that thy seed shall begin to know these things—it shall be a ❖ unto them, that they may know that the work of the Father hath already commenced unto the fulfilling of the covenant which he hath made unto the people who are of the house of Israel."

11 [To ❖ of the twelve disciples]: "Therefore, more blessed are ye, for ye shall never taste of death; but ye shall live to behold all the doings of the Father unto the children of men, even until all things shall be fulfilled according to the will of the Father, when I shall come in my glory with the powers of heaven."

12 "But who may abide the day of his coming, and who shall stand when he appeareth? For he is like a refiner's fire, and like fuller's ❖ ."

14 "Behold, I will send you ❖ the prophet before the coming of the great and dreadful day of the Lord; And he shall turn the heart of the fathers to the children, and the heart of the children to their fathers, lest I come and smite the earth with a curse."

15 "But if they will repent and hearken unto my words, and ❖ not their hearts, I will establish my church among them..."

16 "...he did teach and minister unto the children of the multitude of whom hath been spoken, and he did loose their tongues, and they did speak unto their ❖ great and marvelous things, even greater than he had revealed unto the people..."

17 "What have we spoken against thee? Ye have said: It is vain to serve God, and what doth it ❖ that we have kept his ordinances and that we have walked mournfully before the Lord of Hosts? And now we call the proud happy; yea, they that work wickedness are set up; yea, they that tempt God are even delivered."

19 "For behold, the day cometh that shall burn as an ❖ ; and all the proud, yea, and all that do wickedly, shall be stubble; and the day that cometh shall burn them up, saith the Lord of Hosts, that it shall leave them neither root nor branch."

21 "Thus said the Father unto ❖ —Behold, I will send my messenger, and he shall prepare the way before me, and the Lord whom ye seek shall suddenly come to his temple, even the messenger of the covenant, whom ye delight in..."

22 "For it is ❖ in the Father that they should be established in this land, and be set up as a free people by the power of the Father, that these things might come forth from them unto a remnant of your seed, that the covenant of the Father may be fulfilled which he hath covenanted with his people, O house of Israel..."

26 "And whosoever will hearken unto my words and repenteth and is baptized, the same shall be ❖ . Search the prophets, for many there be that testify of these things."

FORTY-SEVEN
3 Nephi 29 – Mormon 3

Across

1 "...there began to be among them those who were lifted up in pride, such as the wearing of costly apparel, and all manner of fine pearls, and of the fine things of the ❖ ."

5 "And there were no envyings, nor strifes, nor tumults, nor whoredoms, nor lyings, nor murders, nor any manner of lasciviousness; and surely there could not be a happier people among all the people who had been created by the ❖ of God."

7 (continued from 28A) "...and your envyings, and your strifes, and from all your wickedness and abominations, and come unto me, and be baptized in my name, that ye may receive a remission of your sins, and be ❖ with the Holy Ghost, that ye may be numbered with my people who are of the house of Israel."

9 "And now, because of this great thing which my people, the Nephites, had done, they began to ❖ in their own strength, and began to swear before the heavens that they would avenge themselves of the blood of their brethren..."

10 "...nevertheless the strength of the Lord was not with us; yea, we were left to ourselves, that the Spirit of the Lord did not abide in us; therefore we had become ❖ like unto our brethren."

11 "And it came to pass that my sorrow did return unto me again, and I saw that the day of ❖ was passed with them, both temporally and spiritually; for I saw thousands of them hewn down in open rebellion against their God..."

13 "And it came to pass that the Lord did say unto [Mormon]: Cry unto this people—repent ye, and come unto me, and be ye baptized, and build up again my church, and ye shall be ❖ ."

14 "And again, there was another church which denied the Christ; and they did persecute the ❖ church of Christ, because of their humility and their belief in Christ; and they did despise them because of the many miracles which were wrought among them."

15 "...and all manner of ❖ did they work among the children of men; and in nothing did they work ❖ save it were in the name of Jesus."

17 "Yea, wo unto him that shall deny the revelations of the Lord, and that shall say the Lord no longer worketh by revelation, or by prophecy, or by gifts, or by tongues, or by ❖ , or by the power of the Holy Ghost!"

19 "...when the Lord shall see fit, in his wisdom, that these sayings shall come unto the ❖ according to his word, then ye may know that the covenant which the Father hath made with the children of Israel, concerning their restoration to the lands of their inheritance, is already beginning to be fulfilled."

20 "And it came to pass that when I, Mormon, saw their lamentation and their mourning and their ❖ before the Lord, my heart did begin to rejoice within me, knowing the mercies and the long–suffering of the Lord, therefore supposing that he would be merciful unto them..."

21 "And I did ❖ unto this people, but it was in vain; and they did not realize that it was the Lord that had spared them, and granted unto them a chance for repentance."

23 "But wickedness did prevail upon the face of the whole land, insomuch that the Lord did take away his beloved disciples, and the work of miracles and of healing did cease because of the ❖ of the people."

25 "Yea, and wo unto him that shall say at that day, to get gain, that there can be no miracle wrought by Jesus Christ; for he that doeth this shall become like unto the son of ❖ , for whom there was no mercy, according to the word of Christ!"

26 "And they did not walk any more after the performances and ordinances of the law of ❖ ; but they did walk after the commandments which they had received from their Lord and their God, continuing in fasting and prayer, and in meeting together oft both to pray and to hear the word of the Lord."

28 "Turn, all ye Gentiles, from your wicked ways; and repent of your evil doings, of your ❖ and deceivings, and of your whoredoms, and of your secret abominations, and your idolatries, and of your murders, and your

94

priestcrafts..." (continued in 7A)

Down

2 "...and [I, Mormon] had loved them, according to the ❖ of God which was in me, with all my heart; and my soul had been poured out in prayer unto my God all the day long for them; nevertheless, it was without faith, because of the hardness of their hearts."

3 "Wo unto him that spurneth at the doings of the Lord; yea, wo unto him that shall ❖ the Christ and his works!"

4 "And they had all things common among them; therefore there were not rich and poor, bond and free, but they were all made free, and partakers of the heavenly ❖ ."

5 "And also the people who were called the people of Nephi began to be proud in their ❖ , because of their exceeding riches, and become vain like unto their brethren, the Lamanites."

6 "Nevertheless, the people did ❖ their hearts, for they were led by many priests and false prophets to build up many churches, and to do all manner of iniquity. And they did smite upon the people of Jesus; but the people of Jesus did not smite again."

8 "And it came to pass that there was no contention in the land, because of the love of God which did ❖ in the hearts of the people."

12 "Vengeance is mine, and I will repay; and because this people repented not after I had delivered them, behold, they shall be ❖ off from the face of the earth."

13 "And these Gadianton robbers, who were among the Lamanites, did infest the land, insomuch that the inhabitants thereof began to hide up their treasures in the earth; and they became ❖ , because the Lord had cursed the land, that they could not hold them, nor retain them again."

16 "...in the thirty and sixth year, the people were all ❖ unto the Lord, upon all the face of the land, both Nephites and Lamanites, and there were no contentions and disputations among them, and every man did deal justly one with another."

18 "Yea, behold, I write unto all the ends of the earth; yea, unto you, twelve tribes of Israel, who shall be judged according to your ❖ by the twelve whom Jesus chose to be his disciples in the land of Jerusalem."

22 "And I write also unto the ❖ of this people, who shall also be judged by the twelve whom Jesus chose in this land; and they shall be judged by the other twelve whom Jesus chose in the land of Jerusalem."

24 "And they did not come unto Jesus with broken hearts and contrite ❖ , but they did curse God, and wish to die."

27 "But behold this my joy was vain, for their sorrowing was not unto repentance, because of the goodness of God; but it was rather the sorrowing of the damned, because the Lord would not always suffer them to take happiness in ❖ ."

FORTY–EIGHT
Mormon 4–9

Across

2 "Yea, it shall come in a day when there shall be [12A] built up that shall say: Come unto me, and for your ❖ you shall be forgiven of your sins."

5 "Behold I say unto you, he that denieth these things knoweth not the ❖ of Christ; yea, he has not read the scriptures; if so, he does not understand them."

6 "And ye will also know that ye are a remnant of the seed of ❖ ; therefore ye are numbered among the people of the first covenant..." (continued in 26A)

7 (continued from 17A) "...therefore I made this record out of the ❖ of Nephi, and hid up in the hill [17A] all the records which had been entrusted to me by the hand of the Lord, save it were these few ❖ which I gave unto my son [2D]."

8 "Be wise in the days of your probation; strip yourselves of all uncleanness; ask not, that ye may consume it on your lusts, but ask with a firmness unshaken, that ye will yield to no temptation, but that ye will serve the true and ❖ God."

9 "Behold, I say unto you that whoso believeth in Christ, doubting nothing, whatsoever he shall ask the Father in the name of Christ it shall be granted him; and this promise is unto all, even unto the ends of the ❖ ."

10 "For behold, ye do love money, and your substance, and your fine ❖ , and the adorning of your churches, more than ye love the poor and the needy, the sick and the afflicted."

12 "Yea, it shall come in a day when the power of God shall be denied, and ❖ become defiled and be lifted up in the pride of their hearts; yea, even in a day when leaders of ❖ and teachers shall rise in the pride of their hearts, even to the envying of them who belong to their ❖ ."

16 "...he that is found guiltless before him at the judgment day hath it given unto him to dwell in the presence of God in his ❖ , to sing ceaseless praises with the choirs above, unto the Father, and unto the Son, and unto the Holy Ghost, which are one God, in a state of happiness which hath no end."

17 "And it came to pass that when we had gathered in all our people in one to the land of ❖ , behold I, Mormon, began to be old; and knowing it to be the last struggle of my people, and having been commanded of the Lord that I should not suffer the records which had been handed down by our fathers, which were sacred, to fall into the hands of the Lamanites..." (continued in 7A)

20 "See that ye are not baptized unworthily; see that ye partake not of the sacrament of Christ unworthily; but see that ye do all things in worthiness, and do it in the name of Jesus Christ, the Son of the living God; and if ye do this, and ❖ to the end, ye will in nowise be cast out."

22 "O ye fair ones, how could ye have departed from the ways of the Lord! O ye fair ones, how could ye have rejected that Jesus, who stood with open ❖ to receive you!"

23 "But behold, I was without ❖ , for I knew the judgments of the Lord which should come upon them; for they repented not of their iniquities, but did struggle for their lives without calling upon that Being who created them."

25 "But, behold, the judgments of God will overtake the ❖ ; and it is by the ❖ that the ❖ are punished; for it is the ❖ that stir up the hearts of the children of men unto bloodshed."

26 (continued from 6A) "...if it so be that ye believe in Christ, and are baptized, first with ❖ , then with fire and with the Holy Ghost, following the example of our Savior, according to that which he hath commanded us, it shall be well with you in the day of judgment. Amen."

27 "Do ye suppose that ye could be happy to dwell with that holy Being, when your ❖ are racked with a consciousness of guilt that ye have ever abused his laws?"

Down

1 "Behold, I ❖ unto you as if ye were present, and yet ye are not. But behold, Jesus Christ hath shown you unto me, and I know your doing."

2 "And my father also was killed

96

by them, and I [✤] even remain alone to write the sad tale of the destruction of my people."

3 "And I know that ye do walk in the ✤ of your hearts; and there are none save a few only who do not lift themselves up in the ✤ of their hearts, unto the wearing of very fine apparel, unto envying, and strifes, and malice, and persecutions, and all manner of iniquities..."

4 "They were once a delightsome ✤, and they had Christ for their shepherd; yea, they were led even by God the Father."

5 "For he truly saith that no one shall have them to get ✤ ; but the record thereof is of great worth; and whoso shall bring it to light, him will the Lord bless."

8 "...for this people shall be scattered, and shall become a dark, a filthy, and a ✤ people...and this because of their unbelief and idolatry."

11 "Why do ye adorn yourselves with that which hath no life, and yet suffer the hungry, and the ✤ , and the naked, and the sick and the afflicted to pass by you, and notice them not?"

13 "For behold, the same that judgeth rashly shall be judged rashly again; for according to his works shall his wages be; therefore, he that smiteth shall be ✤ again, of the Lord."

14 "And whoso receiveth this ✤, and shall not condemn it because of the imperfections which are in it, the same shall know of greater things than these."

15 "Why are ye ashamed to take upon you the name of Christ? Why do ye not think that greater is the value of an endless happiness than that misery which never dies—because of the ✤ of the world?"

18 "And now behold, I, Mormon, do not desire to ✤ up the souls of men in casting before them such an awful scene of blood and carnage as was laid before mine eyes; but I, knowing that these things must surely be made known, and that all things which are hid must be revealed upon the house-tops—"

19 "Know ye that ye must come to the knowledge of your fathers, and repent of all your sins and iniquities, and believe in Jesus Christ, that he is the Son of God, and that he was slain by the Jews, and by the power of the Father he hath risen again, whereby he hath gained the victory over the grave; and also in him is the sting of ✤ swallowed up."

21 " ✤ not, but be believing, and begin as in times of old, and come unto the Lord with all your heart, and work out your own salvation with fear and trembling before him."

24 "And behold, they shall go unto the unbelieving of the ✤ ; and for this intent shall they go—that they may be persuaded that Jesus is the Christ, the Son of the living God; that the Father may bring about, through his most Beloved, his great and eternal purpose, in restoring the ✤ , or all the house of Israel, to the land of their inheritance..."

97

FORTY-NINE

Ether 1–8

Across

3 "And they were taught to ❖ humbly before the Lord; and they were also taught from on high."

4 "And I take mine account from the twenty and ❖ plates which were found by the people of Limhi, which is called the Book of Ether."

6 "Go to and gather together thy flocks, both male and female, of every kind; and also of the ❖ of the earth of every kind; and thy families..."

11 "And unto ❖ shall they be shown by the power of God; wherefore they shall know of a surety that these things are true."

12 "Wherefore, I, Moroni, am commanded to write these things that evil may be done away, and that the time may come that Satan may have no ❖ upon the hearts of the children of men, but that they may be persuaded to do good continually, that they may come unto the fountain of all righteousness and be saved."

13 "And behold, these two ❖ will I give unto thee, and ye shall seal them up also with the things which ye shall write."

15 "And the ❖ was taken from off the eyes of the brother of Jared, and he saw the finger of the Lord; and it was as the finger of a man, like unto flesh and blood..."

16 "...whoso should possess this land of promise, from that time henceforth and forever, should serve him, the true and only God, or they should be ❖ off when the fulness of his wrath should come upon them."

18 "And the Lord said unto him: Because of thy ❖ thou hast seen that I shall take upon me flesh and blood; and never has man come before me with such exceeding ❖ as thou hast; for were it not so ye could not have seen my finger."

23 "And there will I meet thee, and I will go before thee into a land which is ❖ above all the lands of the earth."

24 "And because of the knowledge of this man he could not be kept from beholding within the veil; and he saw the finger of Jesus, which, when he saw, he fell with fear; for he ❖ that it was the finger of the Lord; and he had faith no longer, for he ❖ , nothing doubting."

25 "For because of my Spirit he shall know that these things are true; for it persuadeth men to do ❖ ."

27 "And in that day that they shall exercise faith in me, saith the Lord, even as the brother of Jared did, that they may become sanctified in me, then will I manifest unto them the things which the brother of Jared saw, even to the unfolding unto them all my ❖ ..."

28 (continued from 2D) "...yea, when ye shall call upon the Father in my name, with a broken heart and a contrite spirit, then shall ye know that the Father hath remembered the covenant which he made unto your ❖ , O house of Israel."

Down

1 "Which Jared came forth with his brother and their families, with some others and their families, from the great ❖ , at the time the Lord confounded the language of the people..."

2 "Behold, when ye shall rend that veil of unbelief which doth cause you to remain in your awful state of wickedness, and hardness of heart, and blindness of ❖ , then shall the great and marvelous things which have been hid up from the foundation of the world from you..." (continued in 28A)

5 "And they were kept up by the power of the devil to administer these ❖ unto the people, to keep them in darkness, to help such as sought power to gain power..."

6 "Behold, this is a choice land, and whatsoever nation shall possess it shall be free from bondage, and from captivity, and from all other nations under heaven, if they will but ❖ the God of the land, who is Jesus Christ..."

7 "Wherefore, the Lord commandeth you, when ye shall see these things come among you that ye shall awake to a sense of your ❖ situation, because of this secret combination which shall be among you..."

98

8 "...the brother of Jared did sing praises unto the Lord, and he did thank and ❖ the Lord all the day long; and when the night came, they did not cease to ❖ the Lord."

9 "Yea, even all men were created in the beginning after mine own ❖ ."

10 "Therefore what will ye that I should prepare for you that ye may have ❖ when ye are swallowed up in the depths of the sea?"

14 "And there shall be none greater than the ❖ which I will raise up unto me of thy seed, upon all the face of the earth."

17 "And also in the reign of Shule there came ❖ among the people, who were sent from the Lord, prophesying that the wickedness and idolatry of the people was bringing a curse upon the land, and they should be destroyed if they did not repent."

19 "Now behold, O Lord, and do not be angry with thy servant because of his ❖ before thee; for we know that thou art holy and dwellest in the heavens, and that we are unworthy before thee; because of the fall our natures have become evil continually..."

20 "And they did also carry with them ❖ , which, by interpretation, is a honey bee..."

21 "And it came to pass that they formed a ❖ combination, even as they of old; which combination is most abominable and wicked above all, in the sight of God..."

22 "For it cometh to pass that whoso buildeth [this secret combination] up seeketh to overthrow the ❖ of all lands, nations, and countries; and it bringeth to pass the destruction of all people, for it is built up by the devil, who is the father of all lies..."

26 "...there was no water that could hurt them, their vessels being tight like unto a ❖ , and also they were tight like unto the ark of Noah; therefore when they were encompassed about by many waters they did cry unto the Lord, and he did bring them forth again upon the top of the waters."

99

FIFTY
Ether 9–15

Across

3 "And there came forth poisonous ❖ also upon the face of the land, and did poison many people."

5 "And after [❖] had anointed Coriantum to reign in his stead he lived four years, and he saw peace in the land; yea, and he even saw the Son of Righteousness, and did rejoice and glory in his day and he died in peace."

7 "For if there be no faith among the children of ❖ God can do no miracle among them; wherefore, he showed not himself until after their faith."

8 "Behold, I will show unto the Gentiles their weakness, and I will show unto them that faith, hope and ❖ bringeth unto me—the fountain of all righteousness."

10 "...Fools ❖ , but they shall mourn; and my grace is sufficient for the meek, for they shall take no advantage of your weakness; And if men come unto me I will show unto them their weakness."

11 "...Riplakish did not do that which was right in the sight of the Lord, for he did have many wives and concubines, and did lay that upon men's shoulders which was grievous to be borne; yea, he did tax them with heavy taxes; and with the taxes he did ❖ many spacious buildings."

13 "❖ began to repent of the evil which he had done; he began to remember the words which had been spoken by the mouth of all the prophets..."

15 "Now when the people saw that they must ❖ they began to repent of their iniquities and cry unto the Lord."

16 "Wherefore, whoso believeth in God might with surety hope for a better world, yea, even a place at the right hand of God, which hope cometh of faith, maketh an ❖ to the souls of men, which would make them sure and steadfast, always abounding in good works, being led to glorify God."

18 "And [Ether] went forth, and beheld that the words of the Lord had all been fulfilled; and he finished his record; (and the hundredth part I have not written) and he hid them in a manner that the people of ❖ did find them."

19 "For it was by faith that Christ ❖ himself unto our fathers, after he had risen from the dead; and he ❖ not himself unto them until after they had faith in him..."

21 "And it came to pass that there began to be a great ❖ upon the land, and the inhabitants began to be destroyed exceedingly fast because of the ❖..."

23 "And the people began to repent of their iniquity; and inasmuch as they did the Lord did have ❖ on them."

25 "And they were exceedingly industrious, and they did buy and ❖ and traffic one with another, that they might get gain."

26 "And it came to pass that Lib also did that which was good in the ❖ of the Lord."

27 "And that a ❖ Jerusalem should be built up upon this land, unto the remnant of the seed of Joseph, for which things there has been a type."

Down

1 "Whether the Lord will that I be translated, or that I suffer the will of the Lord in the flesh, it mattereth not, if it so be that I am saved in the kingdom of God. ❖ ."

2 "And thus we see that the Lord did visit them in the fulness of his wrath, and their wickedness and abominations had prepared a way for their everlasting ❖ ."

4 "And now there began to be a great curse upon all the land because of the iniquity of the people, in which, if a man should lay his tool or his ❖ upon his shelf, or upon the place whither he would keep it, behold, upon the morrow, he could not find it..."

6 "And as he dwelt in the cavity of a ❖ he made the remainder of this record..."

9 "But behold, the Spirit of the Lord had ceased striving with them, and Satan had full ❖ over the hearts of the people; for they were given up unto the hardness of their hearts, and the blindness of their minds that they might be destroyed..."

12 "And now, I, Moroni, would speak somewhat concerning these things; I would show unto the world that faith is things which are hoped for and not seen; wherefore, dispute not because ye see not, for ye receive no witness until after the ❖ of your faith."

13 "And thus the Lord did pour out his blessings upon this land, which was ❖ above all other lands; and he commanded that whoso should possess the land should possess it unto the Lord, or they should be destroyed when they were ripened in iniquity..."

14 "And it came to pass that when they had humbled themselves sufficiently before the Lord he did send ❖ upon the face of the earth; and the people began to revive again..."

17 "And there came prophets in the land again, crying repentance unto them—that they must prepare the way of the Lord or there should come a ❖ upon the face of the land..."

19 "...and [Ether] began to prophesy unto the people, for he could not be restrained because of the ❖ of the Lord which was in him."

20 "I give unto men weakness that they may be humble; and my ❖ is sufficient for all men that humble themselves before me; for if they humble themselves before me, and have faith in me, then will I make weak things become strong unto them."

22 "And it came to pass that the army of [13A] did pitch their tents by the ❖ Ramah; and it was the same ❖ where my father Mormon did hide up the records unto the Lord, which were sacred."

24 "And there came also in the days of Com many prophets, and prophesied of the destruction of that great people except they should repent, and ❖ unto the Lord, and forsake their murders and wickedness."

25 "And it came to pass that Ether did prophesy great and marvelous things unto the people, which they did not believe, because they ❖ them not."

101

FIFTY-ONE
Moroni 1–7

Across

1 "...it is by faith that miracles are wrought; and it is by faith that angels appear and minister unto men; wherefore, if these things have ceased wo be unto the children of men, for it is because of unbelief, and all is ❖ ."

3 "For I remember the word of God which saith by their works ye shall know them; for if their works be ❖ , then they are ❖ also."

7 "Wherefore, my beloved brethren, if ye have not charity, ye are nothing, for charity never ❖ ."

9 "For behold, the Spirit of Christ is given to every man, that he may know good from evil; wherefore, I show unto you the way to judge; for every thing which inviteth to do good, and to persuade to believe in Christ, is sent forth by the power and gift of Christ; wherefore ye may know with a ❖ knowledge it is of God."

11 "In the name of Jesus Christ I ❖ you to be a priest, (or, if he be a teacher) I ❖ you to be a teacher, to preach repentance and remission of sins through Jesus Christ, by the endurance of faith on his name to the end. Amen."

12 "For behold, God hath said a man being evil cannot do that which is good; for if he offereth a gift, or prayeth unto God, except he shall do it with real ❖ it profiteth him nothing."

13 "...because of their hatred they put to death every Nephite that will not ❖ the Christ. And I, Moroni, will not ❖ the Christ..."

15 "And now, my brethren, seeing that ye know the ❖ by which ye may judge, which ❖ is the ❖ of Christ, see that ye do not judge wrongfully; for with that same judgment which ye judge ye shall also be judged."

19 "And after they had been received unto baptism, and were wrought upon and cleansed by the power of the Holy Ghost, they were numbered among the people of the church of Christ; and their names were taken, that they might be remembered and ❖ by the good word of God, to keep them in the right way, to keep them continually watchful unto prayer, relying alone upon the merits of Christ, who was the author and the finisher of their faith."

20 "And the church did meet together oft, to fast and to pray, and to speak one with another concerning the welfare of their ❖ ."

22 "Wherefore, my beloved brethren, have miracles ceased because Christ hath ascended into heaven, and hath sat down on the right ❖ of God, to claim of the Father his rights of mercy which he hath upon the children of men?"

23 "...pray unto the Father with all the energy of heart, that ye may be ❖ with this love, which he hath bestowed upon all who are true followers of his Son, Jesus Christ..."

24 "But charity is the ❖ love of Christ, and it endureth forever; and whoso is found possessed of it at the last day, it shall be well with him."

26 "For behold, [the angels] are subject unto him, to minister according to the word of his command, showing themselves unto them of strong faith and a ❖ mind in every form of godliness."

Down

2 "O God, the Eternal Father, we ask thee in the ❖ of thy Son, Jesus Christ, to bless and sanctify this bread to the souls of all those who partake of it; that they may eat in remembrance of the body of thy Son, and witness unto thee, O God, the Eternal Father, that they are willing to take upon them the ❖ of thy Son, and always remember him, and keep his commandments which he hath given them, that they may always have his Spirit to be with them. Amen."

3 "For behold, if a man being evil giveth a ❖ , he doeth it grudgingly; wherefore it is counted unto him the same as if he had retained the ❖ ; wherefore he is counted evil before God."

4 "Behold I say unto you that ye shall have ❖ through the atonement of Christ and the power of his resurrection, to be raised unto life eternal, and this because of your faith in him according to the promise."

5 "And Christ hath said: If ye will have faith in ❖ ye shall have power to do whatsoever thing is expedient in ❖."

6 "Wherefore, I beseech of you, brethren, that ye should search diligently in the light of Christ that ye may know good from evil; and if ye will lay hold upon every good thing, and condemn it not, ye certainly will be a ❖ of Christ."

7 "But as oft as they repented and sought forgiveness, with real intent, they were ❖ ."

8 "Ye shall call on the Father in my name, in mighty ❖ ; and after ye have done this ye shall have power that to him upon whom ye shall lay your hands, ye shall give the Holy Ghost; and in my name shall ye give it..."

10 "Neither did they receive any unto baptism save they came forth with a broken heart and a ❖ spirit, and witnessed unto the church that they truly repented of all their sins."

14 "But whatsoever thing persuadeth men to do ❖ , and believe not in Christ, and deny him, and serve not God, then ye may know with a perfect knowledge it is of the devil; for after this manner doth the devil work, for he persuadeth no man to do good, no, not one; neither do his angels; neither do they who subject themselves unto him."

16 "O God, the Eternal Father, we ask thee, in the name of thy Son, Jesus Christ, to bless and sanctify this wine to the souls of all those who drink of it, that they may do it in remembrance of the ❖ of thy Son, which was shed for them; that they may witness unto thee, O God, the Eternal Father, that they do always remember him, that they may have his Spirit to be with them. Amen."

17 "Wherefore, by the ministering of ❖ , and by every word which proceeded forth out of the mouth of God, men began to exercise faith in Christ; and thus by faith, they did lay hold upon every good thing..."

18 "And charity suffereth long, and is kind, and envieth not, and is not ❖ up, seeketh not her own, is not easily provoked, thinketh no evil, and rejoiceth not in iniquity but rejoiceth in the truth, beareth all things, believeth all things, hopeth all things, endureth all things."

21 "And none were received unto baptism save they took upon them the name of Christ, having a determination to ❖ him to the end."

22 "And likewise also is it counted evil unto a man, if he shall pray and not with real intent of ❖ ; yea, and it profiteth him nothing, for God receiveth none such."

23 "Behold, elders, priests, and teachers were baptized; and they were not baptized save they brought forth ❖ meet that they were worthy of it."

24 "...for as the power of the Holy Ghost led them whether to ❖ , or to exhort, or to pray, or to supplicate, or to sing, even so it was done."

25 "Wherefore, I would speak unto you that are of the church, that are the peaceable followers of Christ, and that have obtained a sufficient hope by which ye can enter into the ❖ of the Lord..."

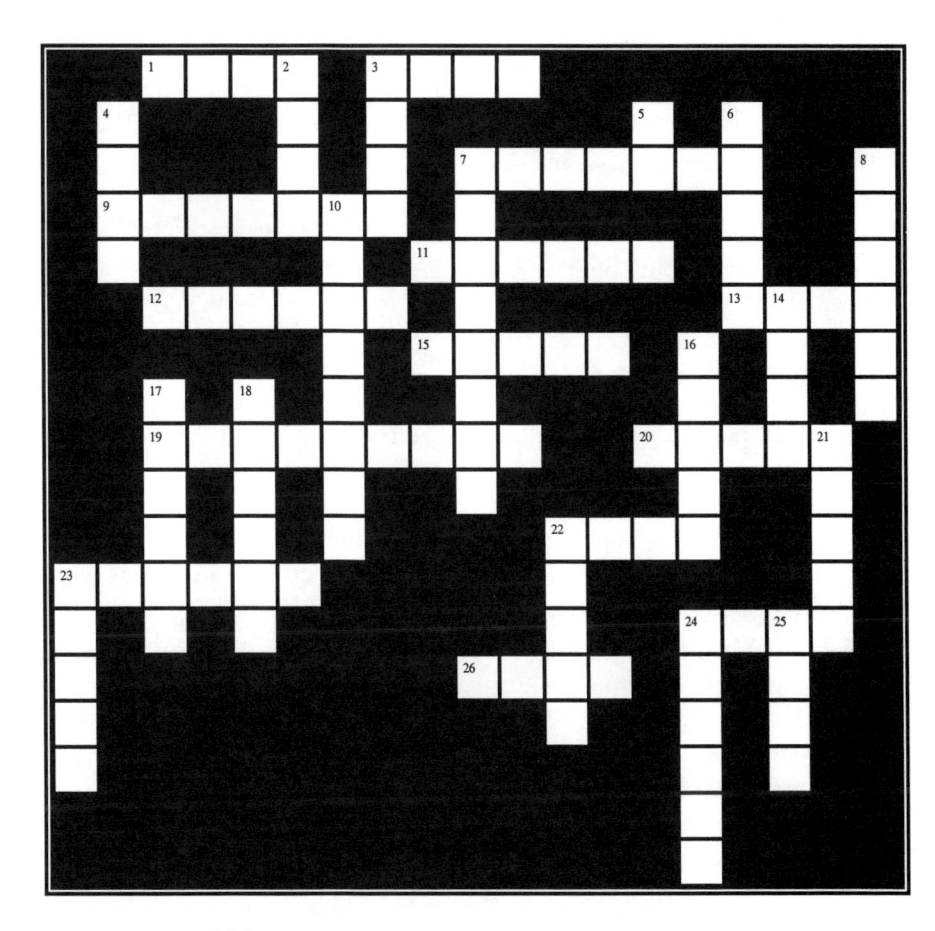

103

FIFTY-TWO
Moroni 8–10

Across

2 "For the power of redemption cometh on all them that have no ❖ ; wherefore, he that is not condemned, or he that is under no condemnation, cannot repent; and unto such baptism availeth nothing—"

3 "And the remission of sins bringeth meekness, and lowliness of heart; and because of meekness and lowliness of heart cometh the visitation of the Holy Ghost, which Comforter filleth with hope and perfect love, which love endureth by diligence unto prayer, until the end shall come, when all the ❖ shall dwell with God."

5 "Wherefore, there must be ❖ ; and if there must be ❖ there must also be hope; and if there must be hope there must also be charity."

10 "And now, my beloved son, notwithstanding their hardness, let us ❖ diligently; for if we should cease to ❖ , we should be brought under condemnation..."

12 "And now behold, my son, I fear lest the Lamanites shall destroy this people; for they do not repent, and Satan stirreth them up continually to ❖ one with another."

13 "...to one is given by the Spirit of God, that he may teach the word of wisdom; And to another, that he may teach the word of knowledge...and to another, exceedingly great faith; and to another, the gifts of healing...to another, that he may work mighty miracles...to another, that he may prophesy concerning all things...to another, the beholding of angels and ministering spirits...to another, all kinds of ❖ ...to another, the interpretation of languages and of divers kinds of ❖ ."

16 "And he that saith that little children need baptism denieth the mercies of Christ, and setteth at naught the ❖ of him and the power of his redemption."

17 "And again I would exhort you that ye would come unto Christ, and lay hold upon every good gift, and touch not the evil gift, nor the ❖ thing."

18 "And I am filled with ❖ , which is everlasting love; wherefore, all children are alike unto me; wherefore, I love little children with a perfect love; and they are all alike and partakers of salvation."

19 "I soon go to rest in the paradise of God, until my spirit and body shall again ❖ , and I am brought forth triumphant through the air, to meet you before the pleasing bar of the great Jehovah, the Eternal Judge of both quick and dead. Amen."

20 "...this thing shall ye teach—repentance and ❖ unto those who are accountable and capable of committing sin; yea, teach parents that they must repent and be baptized, and humble themselves as their little children, and they shall all be saved with their little children."

25 "Behold, I would exhort you that when ye shall read these things, if it be ❖ in God that ye should read them, that ye would remember how merciful the Lord hath been unto the children of men..."

27 "And when ye shall receive these things, I would exhort you that ye would ask God, the Eternal Father, in the name of Christ, if these things are not ❖ ; and if ye shall ask with a sincere heart, with real intent, having faith in Christ, he will manifest the truth of it unto you, by the power of the Holy Ghost."

28 "I am mindful of you always in my prayers, continually praying unto God the Father in the name of his Holy Child, Jesus, that he, through his infinite goodness and ❖ , will keep you through the endurance of faith on his name to the end."

29 "For so exceedingly do they anger that it seemeth me that they have no fear of ❖; and they have lost their love, one towards another..."

Down

1 "...I fear not what man can do; for perfect love casteth out all ❖ ."

2 "My son, be faithful in Christ; and may not the things which I have written grieve thee, to weigh thee down unto death; but may Christ ❖ thee up..."

4 "But behold, I fear lest the ❖ hath ceased striving with them..."

6 "For behold that all little children are ❖ in Christ, and also all they that are without the law."

7 "And may the grace of God the Father, whose ❖ is high in the heavens, and our Lord Jesus Christ, who sitteth on the right hand of his power, until all things shall become subject unto him, be, and abide with you forever. Amen!"

8 "And there are different ways that these gifts are administered; but it is the same God who worketh all in all; and they are given by the manifestations of the Spirit of God unto men, to ❖ them."

9 "And except ye have charity ye can in nowise be ❖ in the kingdom of God; neither can ye be ❖ in the kingdom of God if ye have not faith; neither can ye if ye have no hope."

11 "Behold, I came into the world not to call the righteous but ❖ners to repentance; the whole need no physician, but they that are sick; wherefore, little children are whole, for they are not capable of committing ❖..."

14 "And again, if ye by the grace of God are perfect in Christ, and deny not his power, then are ye ❖ in Christ by the grace of God, through the shedding of the blood of Christ, which is in the covenant of the Father unto the remission of your sins, that ye become holy, without spot."

15 "For awful is the wickedness to suppose that God saveth one child because of baptism, and the other must ❖ because he hath no baptism."

21 "Behold, the ❖ of this nation, or the people of the Nephites, hath proven their destruction except they should repent."

22 "And by the ❖ of the Holy Ghost ye may know the truth of all things."

23 "...that which was most ❖ and precious above all things, which is chastity and virtue—"

24 "And the ❖ fruits of repentance is baptism; and baptism cometh by faith unto the fulfilling the commandments; and the fulfilling the commandments bringeth remission of sins..."

26 "...and if ye shall deny yourselves of all ungodliness, and love God with all your might, ❖ and strength, then is his grace sufficient for you, that by his grace ye may be perfect in Christ..."

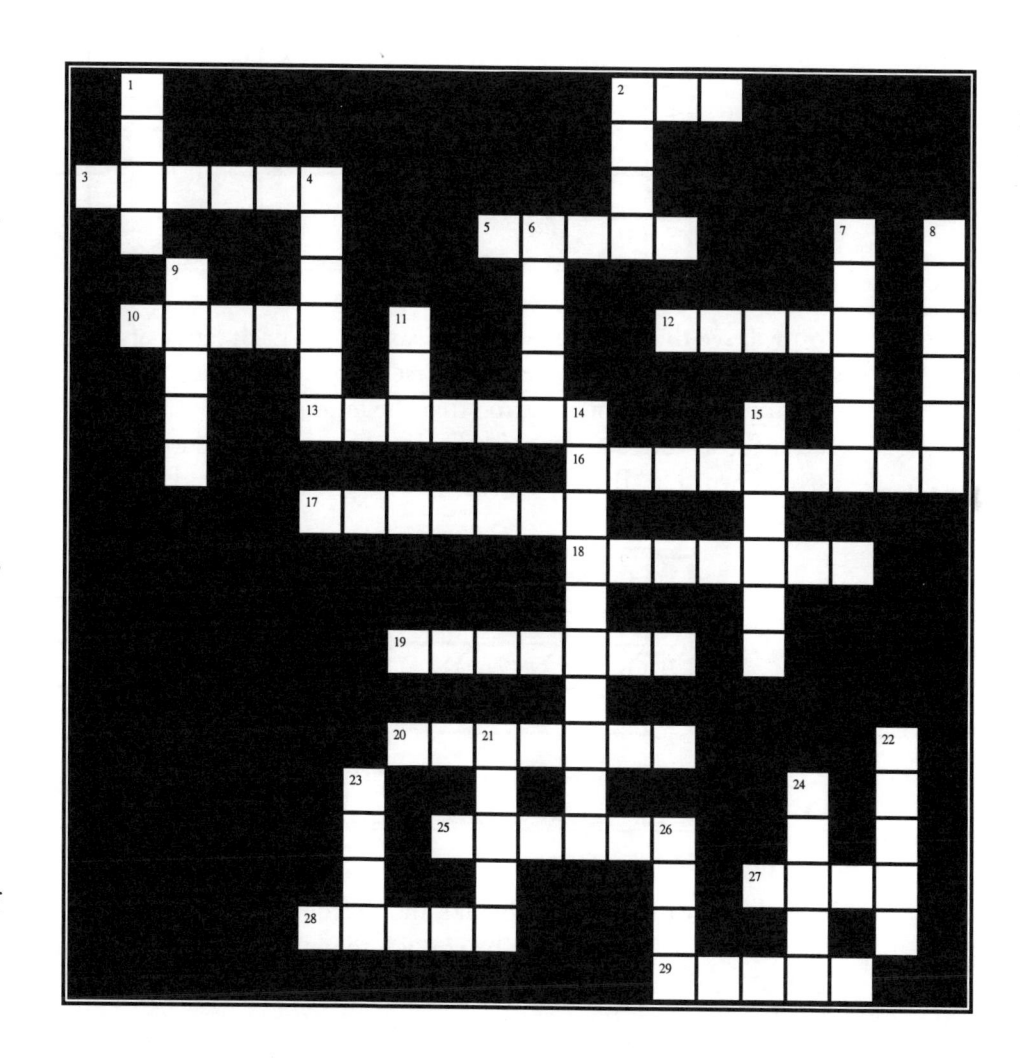

SECTION TWO

SCRIPTURE FALLS

"Scripture Falls" are a type of puzzle where the letters in the scripture are scrambled and arranged in columns across the top half of the puzzle. There are no punctuation marks, and some words are "wrapped" around to the next line. Some scriptures are longer, so appear in two or three sections. The actual scripture references are listed in the solution section at the back of the book.

To solve the puzzle, drag the letters straight down to their proper position, creating the (horizontal) words of the scripture. For example, to begin, look at the first empty row of squares.

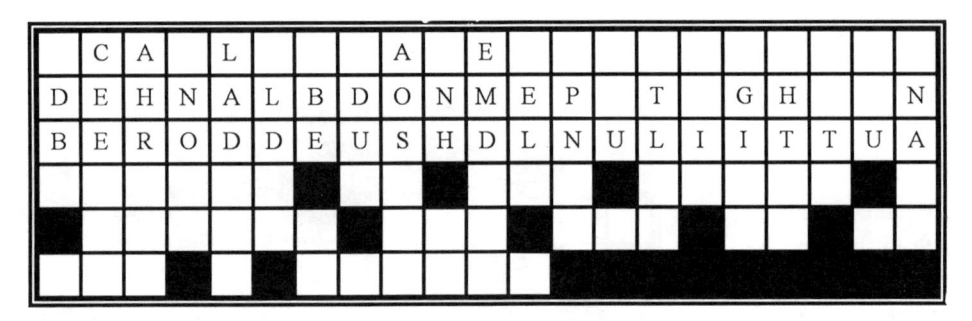

	C	A		L			A		E									
D	E	H	N	A	L	B	D	O	N	M	E	P		T		G	H	N
B	E	R	O	D	D	E	U	S	H	D	L	N	U	L	I	I	T	T	U	A

You will see that the first word has six letters. Each letter of the first word is among the letters in the squares immediately above those first six blank squares. Look over the letters to create a possible beginning word, remembering that the letters must be brought straight down into the blanks. Can you make a word starting with D? If not, can you make a word starting with B? Yes! The only possible word is "Behold." Write in those six letters and cross out the ones you have used from above.

	C	A		~~L~~			A		E									
D	E	~~H~~	N	A	L	B	~~D~~	O	N	M	E	P		T		G	H	N
~~B~~	~~E~~	R	~~O~~	D	~~D~~	E	U	S	H	D	L	N	U	L	I	I	T	T	U	A
B	E	H	O	L	D		D	O										

Now, look at the next two blanks and decide what letters should "fall" down into the blanks to make the next word. That should be enough to get you started. And once you get started, you'll enjoy them so much you may never want to stop!

* This section contains the 25 scriptures chosen by the Church Education System for seminary students to learn and memorize. For that reason, there isn't a scripture falls for every reading.

SCRIPTURE FALLS

Scripture Falls: Found in: Accompanies Crossword:

1......................1 Nephi 1–4..........................Puzzle ONE
2......................1 Nephi 19–22......................Puzzle FIVE
3......................2 Nephi 1–5..........................Puzzle SIX
4......................2 Nephi 1–5..........................Puzzle SIX
5......................2 Nephi 6–9..........................Puzzle SEVEN
6......................2 Nephi 26–28......................Puzzle TEN
7......................2 Nephi 29–Jacob 1..............Puzzle ELEVEN
8......................2 Nephi 29–Jacob 1..............Puzzle ELEVEN
9......................Jacob 2–7.............................Puzzle TWELVE
#10....................Mosiah 1–3...........................Puzzle FOURTEEN
#11....................Mosiah 1–3...........................Puzzle FOURTEEN
#12....................Mosiah 4–6...........................Puzzle FIFTEEN
#13....................Alma 30–32..........................Puzzle TWENTY–NINE
#14....................Alma 33–36..........................Puzzle THIRTY
#15....................Alma 37–40..........................Puzzle THIRTY–ONE
#16....................Alma 37–40..........................Puzzle THIRTY–ONE
#17....................Alma 41–44..........................Puzzle THIRTY–TWO
#18....................Helaman 5–7........................Puzzle THIRTY–EIGHT
#19....................3 Nephi 11–12......................Puzzle FORTY–THREE
#20....................3 Nephi 21–28......................Puzzle FORTY–SIX
#21....................Ether 9–15............................Puzzle FIFTY
#22....................Ether 9–15............................Puzzle FIFTY
#23....................Moroni 1–7...........................Puzzle FIFTY–ONE
#24....................Moroni 1–7...........................Puzzle FIFTY–ONE
#25....................Moroni 10:4–5......................Puzzle FIFTY–TWO

SCRIPTURE FALLS #1

1 Nephi 1–4

SCRIPTURE FALLS #2

1 Nephi 19–22

SCRIPTURE FALLS #3

2 Nephi 1–5

	T		E			E	N	L		M		A			M				M	
A	D	A	B	Y		A	I	D		T	H	H	T	V	E	E	N	O	H	I	T
H	T	H	M	E	F	M	L	G	H	T	E	N	A	A	R	E	J	T	Y	A	G

* This section of scripture study includes two Scripture Falls (#3 and #4)

SCRIPTURE FALLS #4

2 Nephi 1–5

SCRIPTURE FALLS #5

2 Nephi 6–9

SCRIPTURE FALLS #6

2 Nephi 26–28

Scripture Falls #6 (continued)

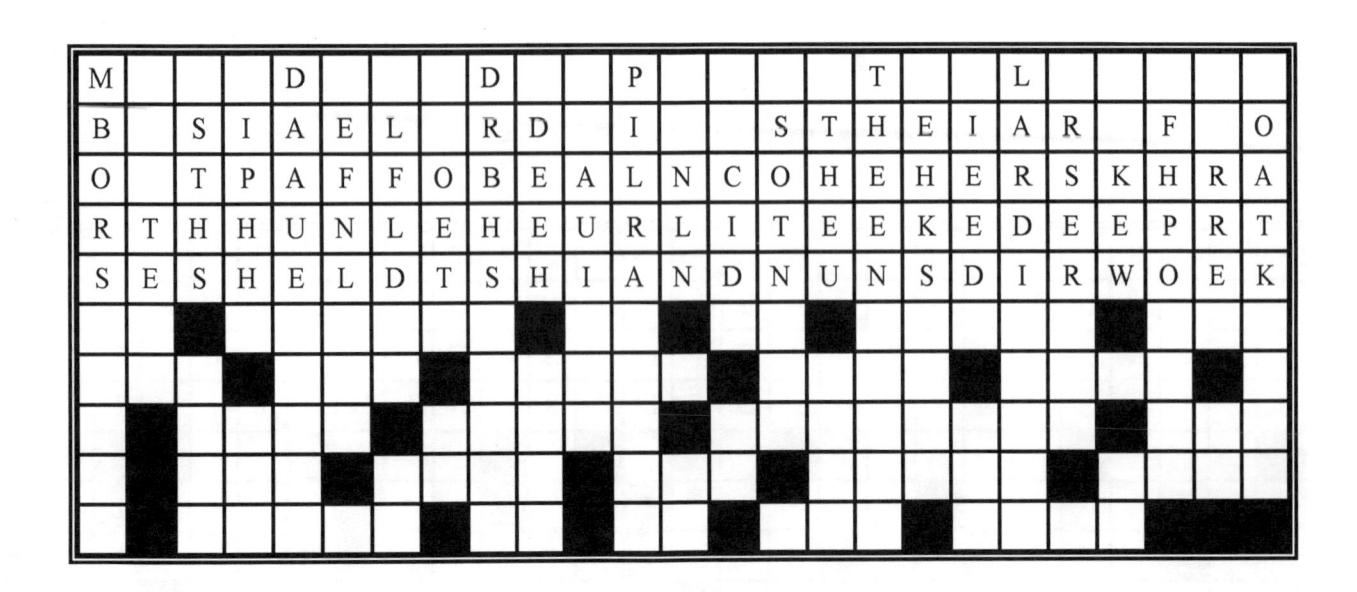

SCRIPTURE FALLS #7

2 Nephi 29–Jacob 1

SCRIPTURE FALLS #8

2 Nephi 29–Jacob 1

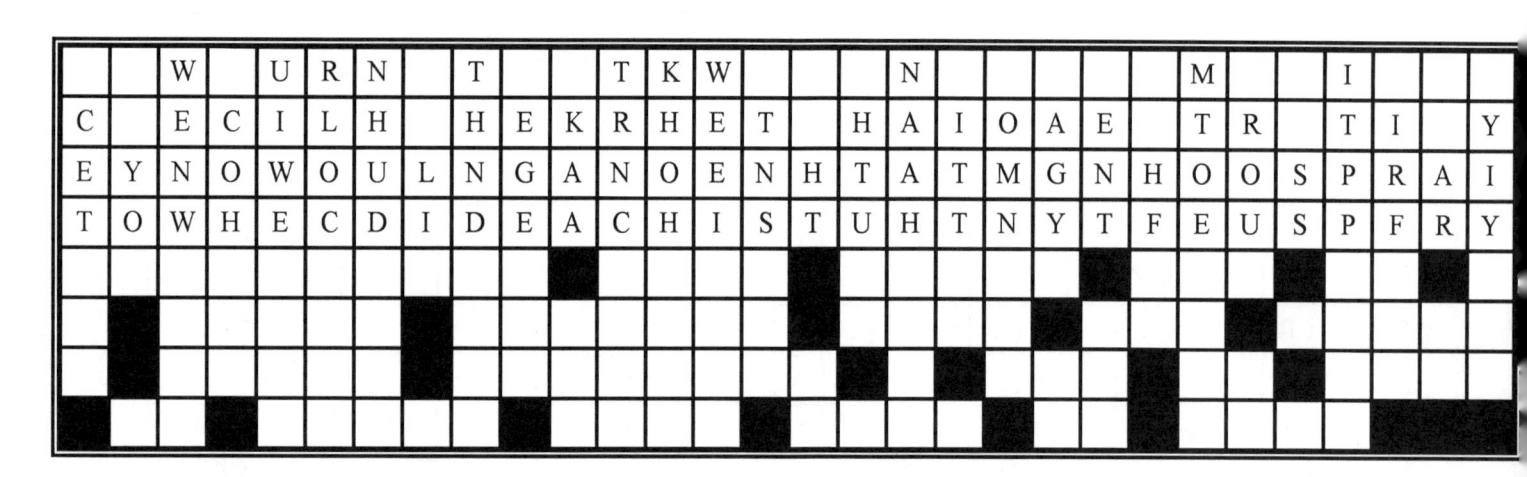

Scripture Falls #8 (continued)

O	R			T			I	A		Y				T	T		O		N		L
T	H	I	A	Y	N	M	H	H	N	R	R	N	Y	O	A	L	W	N	E	A	D	A	S	A
V	E	A	T	N	I	Y	T	T	T	F	I	T	S	T	A	T	M	U	C	H	E	Y	S	O	S	H	E	R	F
O	T	M	F	A	N	E	H	E	U	S	T	G	P	U	E	P	L	A	S	E	A	Y	L	T	R	P	D	L	N

	C	O						F	A			E			H		T		C	
P	F	A	U	N	T	O	Y	E	T	E	A	F	E	T	O	A	R	C	I	M	O	E	B	E
E	E	O	R	F	T	C	E	R	H	Y	P	E	T	H	O	O	H	M	A	C	E	Y	N	H	O	N	A
E	E	A	T	H	A	H	H	H	I	S	H	P	E	R	A	T	R	H	N	T	W	E	U	S	A	U	L	N	S
M	R	R	Y	T	E	T	T	T	W	T	L	F	R	R	F	R	M	F	E	N	I	N	L	L	T	Y	O	T	H

117

SCRIPTURE FALLS #9

Jacob 2–7

SCRIPTURE FALLS #10

Mosiah 1–3

SCRIPTURE FALLS #11

Mosiah 1–3

SCRIPTURE FALLS #12

Mosiah 4–6

SCRIPTURE FALLS #13

Alma 30–32

SCRIPTURE FALLS #14

Alma 33–36

Scripture Falls #14 (continued)

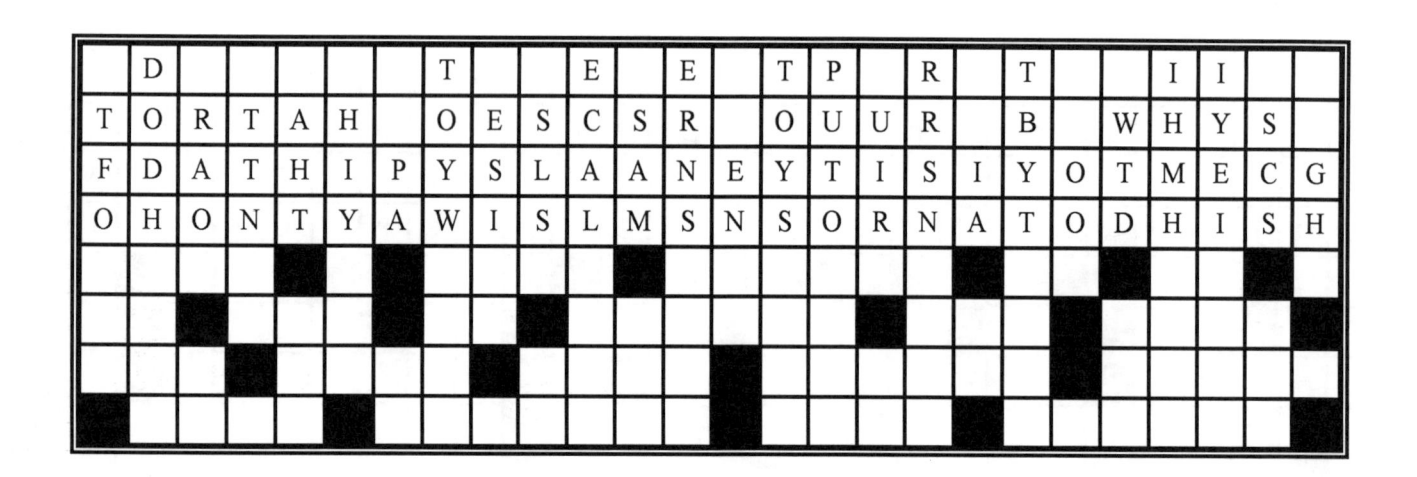

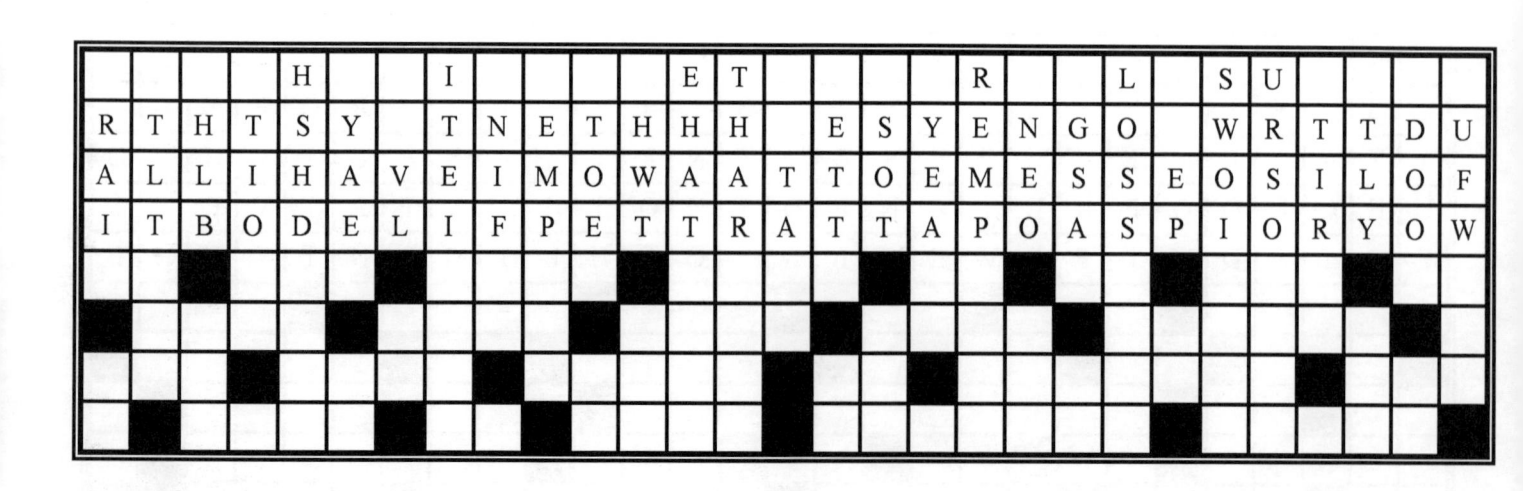

SCRIPTURE FALLS #15

Alma 37–40

SCRIPTURE FALLS #16

Alma 37–40

	W	R		M	B	A				N		N			T		O	E	
N		A	E	N	C	O	N		T	H	M	M	E	Y	T	T		O	N	O		L	E	E
O	E	H	I	M	E	I	M	M	R	N	Y	Y	H	S	O	Y	H	A	F	D		Y	E	A	P
L	T	R	E	S	D	O	M	E	I	N	D	T	Y	O	U	S	O	U	T	H	G	K	D	A	R

SCRIPTURE FALLS #17

Alma 41–44

SCRIPTURE FALLS #18

Helaman 5–7

SCRIPTURE FALLS #19

3 Nephi 11–12

SCRIPTURE FALLS #20

3 Nephi 21–28

SCRIPTURE FALLS #21

Ether 9–15

SCRIPTURE FALLS #22

Ether 9–15

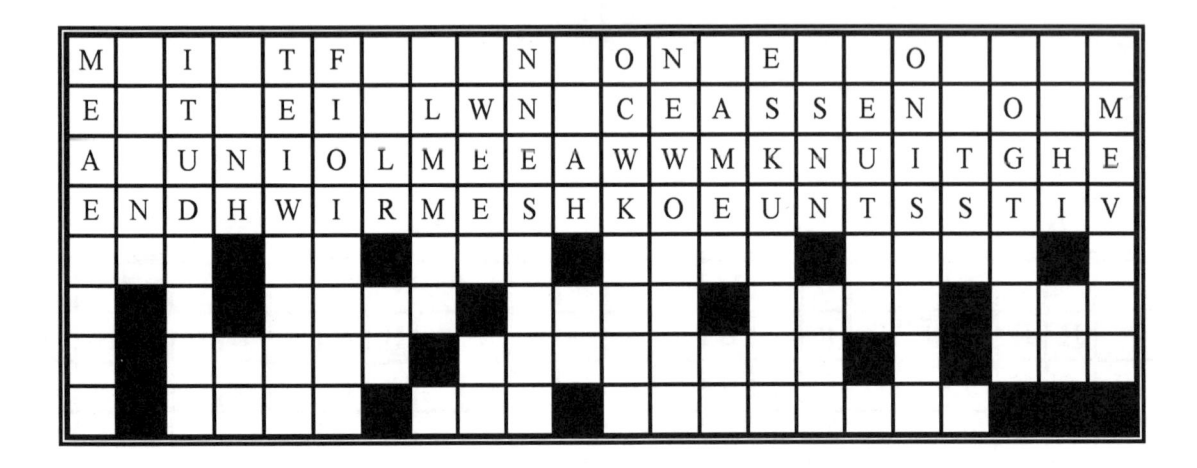

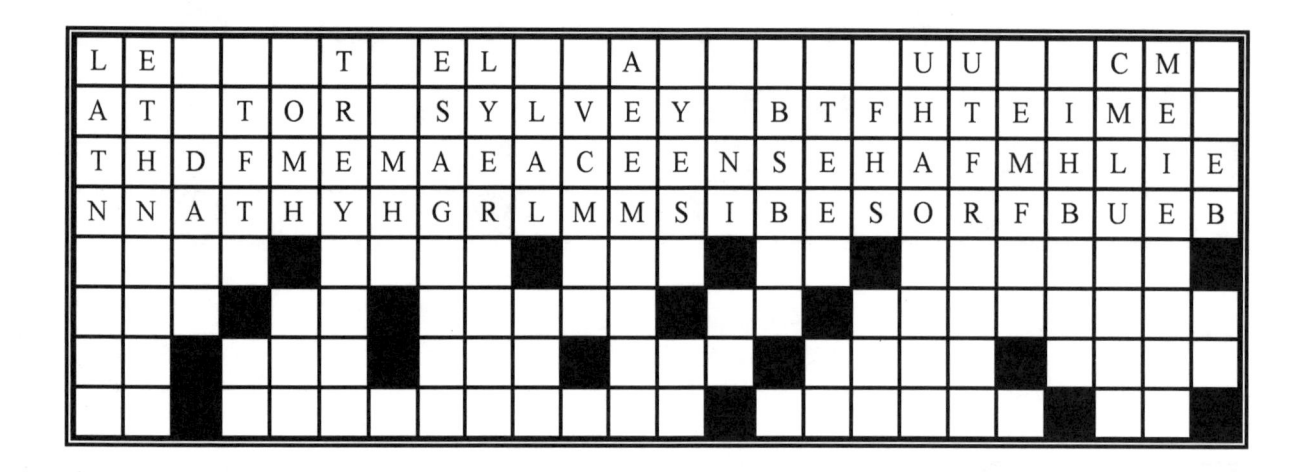

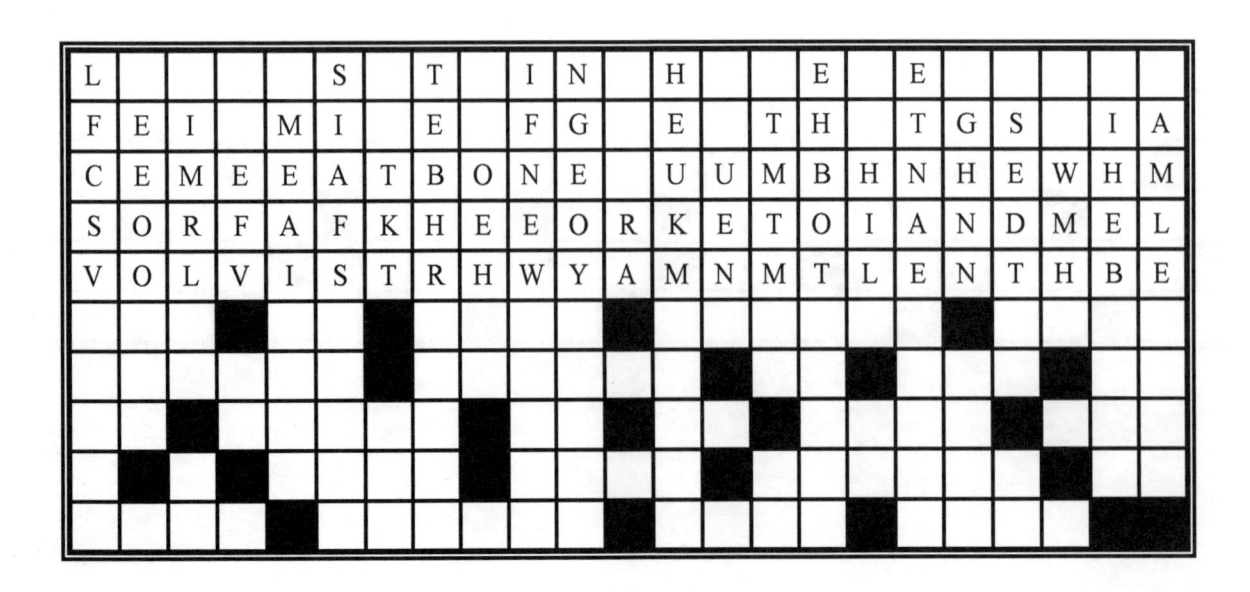

SCRIPTURE FALLS #23

Moroni 1–7

Scripture Falls #23 (continued)

K		F	H	R		D		E				N						O		E				E	
H		A	O	E		D	E	T	O	R		A	O	S	S		F	A	N		E	R		P	V	I
L	U	T	D	E	E		A	F	N	E	I	T	W	H	R	K	O	F	O	R	H	G	E	O	D	E	R
S	N	O	W	L	T	H	G	V	I	L	M	T	I	I	T	O	M	D	T	N	H	O	D	D	O	T

N	G		E	S			E	I	T		E	E		V	E			N	T			H	O		
N	B	J	L	O	T		T	N	E	M	S	R	I	T	H	S	T	H	E	O		W	I	I		A
U	O	E	N	C	T	N	O	H	E	H	N	E	L	D	O	E	R	U	D	Y	O	H	H	S	M	S

SCRIPTURE FALLS #24

Moroni 1–7

SCRIPTURE FALLS #25

Moroni 8–10

SECTION THREE

WORD SEARCH, CLUELESS & CRYPTOGRAMS

In this section there are fifty-two Clueless and Word Search puzzles, one for each section of scripture study. These are fairly easy and suitable for all ages. Several sections also include a Cryptogram. Since these are quite challenging, these are for older children, teens, and adults.

Word Search and Clueless puzzles are made up of the proper names and places found in each particular reading. There is one to correspond with each crossword puzzle. Some reading assignments, like 1 Nephi 11-14, have a Cryptogram in addition to the Word Search or Clueless puzzle.

Each Word Search has a list of words The words are found in the puzzle forwards, backwards, vertically, horizontally, and diagonally. The words are always in a straight line and no letters are skipped over. Circle the words in the puzzle as they are found. Not all the letters in the puzzle will be used, and some will be used more than once.

Clueless (also known as "Kriss-Kross") puzzles consist of a list of words and a blank puzzle structure. The puzzle is solved by placing all of the words in the puzzle where they fit.

A Cryptogram is an encoded puzzle in which a verse of scripture is written using a simple letter substitution code. A clue is given to get started, and one letter is already decoded. With that letter in place, you may be able to guess at the words that use that letter, then see if that letter will help you decipher other words in the puzzle. Place the decoded letters directly above the coded sentence to form words until you've filled in all the blank squares correctly.

In the simplified example below, the letter "A" is the code letter for "O". So, wherever the letter "A" is found in the cryptogram, write "O" directly above it on the line, then try to figure out the rest of the letters.

Clue: "A man would get nearer to God..." **Prophet Joseph Smith**

Cryptogram: ___ OO O O O
              V C R   M A A Y   A Z   D A S D A P

Key:

O																									
A	B	C	D	E	F	G	H	I	J	K	L	M	N	O	P	Q	R	S	T	U	V	W	X	Y	Z

137

ONE

1 Nephi 1–4

B	J	P	H	A	R	A	O	H	U	A	L
A	X	U	H	H	Q	G	L	G	W	J	E
L	B	A	R	D	A	G	W	Y	U	E	Y
Y	G	N	G	A	I	I	P	R	C	B	U
L	J	K	T	Q	H	K	U	D	R	J	E
O	H	V	M	S	N	S	E	E	G	J	L
N	A	M	H	N	A	E	N	D	R	N	N
T	I	A	Q	L	N	S	P	A	E	M	U
V	R	S	E	A	E	O	A	H	M	Z	B
X	A	M	B	S	H	B	X	U	I	A	A
H	S	A	O	L	E	H	I	K	I	V	L
T	L	M	T	U	A	X	M	A	R	O	Z

BABYLON LEHI   SAM
JERUSALEM LEMUEL   SARIAH
JUDAH   MOSES   ZEDEKIAH
LABAN   NEPHI   ZORAM
LAMAN   PHARAOH

138

TWO

1 Nephi 5–10

```
J J E L M A H A R B A J I O
E V O G V I H P E N U S B S
R H A R Y E V E C D R O A V
E A A R D P S B A A U R S L
M I D U A A T H E N I V J E
I K A K X B N L T A R O I A
A E M M Q L A I H N O D H M
H D D Y A H F H L J A U E H
G E C M P U I I T E A B L S
B Z A E L S Y R S E U C A I
A N S J A J M A S E B M O L
D O I A Z O R A M S H E B
J O C B A B Y L O N D O T L
J E R U S A L E M I G D M K
```

ABRAHAM	ISRAEL	LEHI
ADAM	JACOB	LEMUEL
BABYLON	JEREMIAH	MOSES
BETHABARA	JERUSALEM	NEPHI
BOUNTIFUL	JORDAN	PHARAOH
EGYPT	JOSEPH	SAM
EVE	JUDAH	SARIAH
ISAAC	LABAN	ZEDEKIAH
ISHMAEL	LAMAN	ZORAM

THREE

1 Nephi 11–14

ISRAEL   JOHN   NEPHI
JERUSALEM   NAZARETH   ZION
JEW

Clue: The tree of life in Nephi's vision…

"___, __ __ ___ ____ __ ___, _____ _____ _____ _____ __
"SAI, PF PU FTA KCNA CQ LCJ, DTPMT UTAJJAFT PFUAKQ IGOCIJ PR
___ _____ __ ___ _____ __ ___; _____, __ __ ___
FTA TAIOFU CQ FTA MTPKJOAR CQ WAR; DTAOAQCOA, PF PU FTA
____ _____ ____ ___ _____."
WCUF JAUPOIGKA IGCNA IKK FTPRLU."

| | | | | | L | | | | | | | | M | | | |
|A|B|C|D|E|F|G|H|I|J|K|L|M|N|O|P|Q|R|S|T|U|V|W|X|Y|Z|

FOUR

1 Nephi 15–18

```
A I I A S I T R T P Y G E J J
Z B R S M O S E S A M Q O A I
J J R R R X X I H E L R L S L
Y A N A E A C U V D D U A A A
R C E A H A E W I A F I G R M
F O P E R A N L N I A P T K A
N B H P X I M T T H C E M N
R A I B N E W N U J M S Q A W
E Y V Y W L U I H M O R R R L
Z M N F E O S K H O X S T O O
A J J U B H Q Y A G A V E Z R
H H M K M N T F X Q F R S P V
S E Z A Y V E M O H A N A L H
L R E I S A A C A T H N Z H P
I L J E R U S A L E M Y N F P
```

ABRAHAM   ISRAEL   LEMUEL
BOUNTIFUL   JACOB   MOSES
EGYPT   JERUSALEM   NAHOM
IRREANTUM   JORDAN   NEPHI
ISAAC   JOSEPH   PHARAOH
ISAIAH   LAMAN   SHAZER
ISHMAEL   LEHI   ZORAM

141

FIVE

1 Nephi 19–22

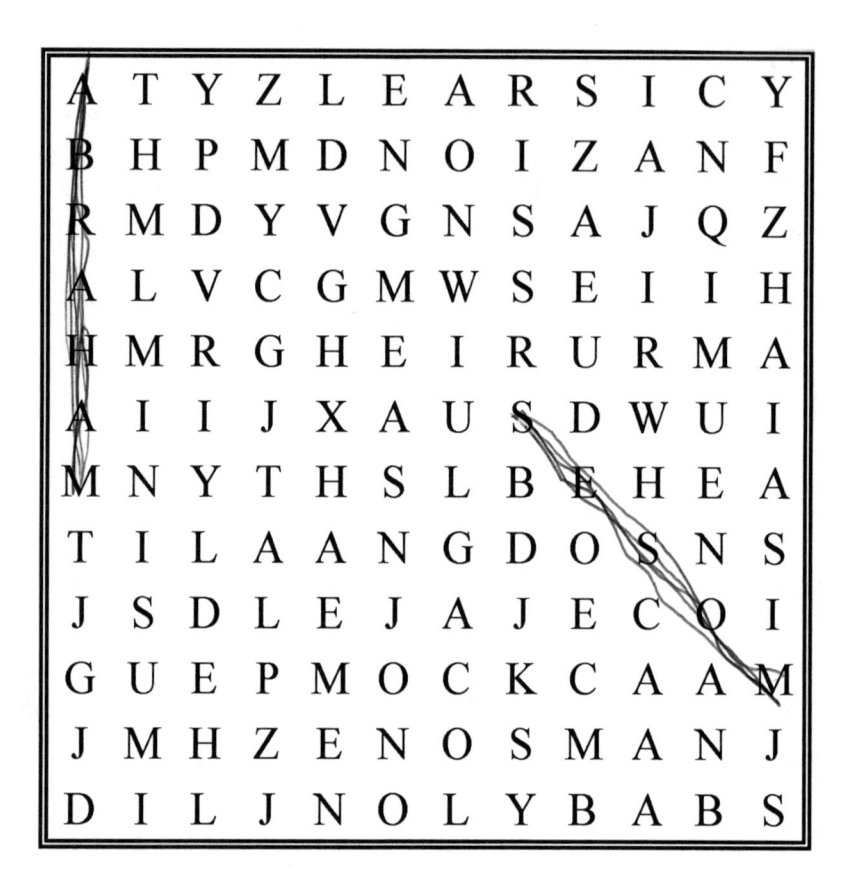

A	T	Y	Z	L	E	A	R	S	I	C	Y
B	H	P	M	D	N	O	I	Z	A	N	F
R	M	D	Y	V	G	N	S	A	J	Q	Z
A	L	V	C	G	M	W	S	E	I	I	H
H	M	R	G	H	E	I	R	U	R	M	A
A	I	I	J	X	A	U	S	D	W	U	I
M	N	Y	T	H	S	L	B	E	H	E	A
T	I	L	A	A	N	G	D	O	S	N	S
J	S	D	L	E	J	A	J	E	C	O	I
G	U	E	P	M	O	C	K	C	A	A	M
J	M	H	Z	E	N	O	S	M	A	N	J
D	I	L	J	N	O	L	Y	B	A	B	S

ABRAHAM   ISAIAH   MOSES
BABYLON   ISRAEL   NEPHI
CHALDEANS   JACOB   NEUM
EGYPT   JERUSALEM   SINIM
ISAAC   JUDAH   ZENOS

SIX

2 Nephi 1–5

```
J O S E P H Z D I D I L
L H D Y I H P E N S A J
C A S P K M A S E B A J
E S M J U B P S A C E L
Z G J A W X O N O R A E
O L Y U N M B B U E D M
R F E P D K S S L V A U
A Z N A T A A Y V E M E
M S M I M L H Y S H L L
K E S P E H T J O R B Z
B O J M Y S S D G I U Q
L E H I Q B M I P C C W
```

ADAM
EGYPT
EVE
ISHMAEL
JACOB
JERUSALEM
JOSEPH
JUDAH
LABAN
LAMAN
LEHI
LEMUEL
MOSES
NEPHI
SAM
ZORAM

SEVEN

2 Nephi 6–9

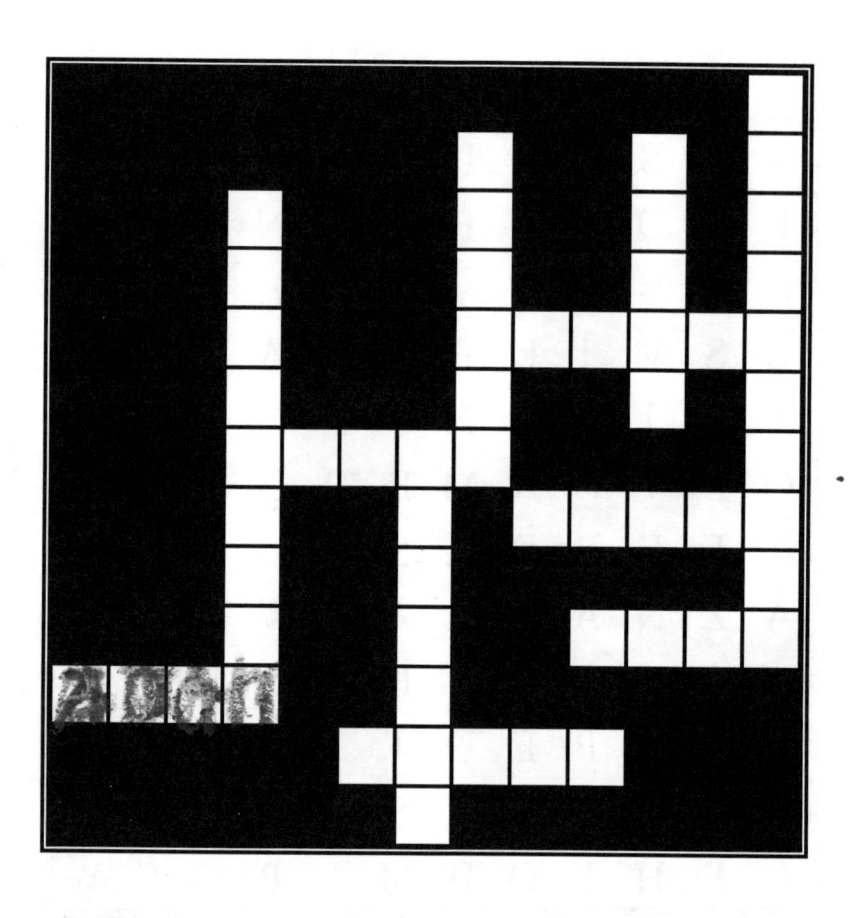

ABRAHAM   ISRAEL   RAHAB
ADAM   JACOB   SARAH
DESOLATION   JERUSALEM   ZION
ISAIAH   NEPHI

EIGHT

2 Nephi 10–16

```
N I H E L N B U J I N W H C M M
E U Y N A O Z O S O N S H E E O
U F V B C Z S A N O I A L K C S
M C A A I E I A L H L A H K H E
G L J A P A B Y S D S F N S Z S
M C H H H E B R E U N U O O B A
S I N Z L A A A R K X F I N A D
A V H O B T N E B L Z H Z E H A
R Q S P I S J E V E F C A Z A M
A Z B Y A T A I P W L T A D R Y
H O N R E R A B S N L E P A U E
A M N P P I E L R H A E U Y S J
C A H Z W E J S O A M H A M G I
Y A O J M I N I S S H A S R E E
H W M A S I H P E N E A E A S L
Z M A R O Z N A M A L D M L B I
```

ABRAHAM	ISRAEL	NEPHI
ADAM	JACOB	NEUM
AMOZ	JERUSALEM	RAHAB
BABYLON	JEW	SAM
BASHAN	JOSEPH	SARAH
CHALDEANS	JUDAH	SERAPHIM
DESOLATION	LABAN	SINIM
EGYPT	LAMAN	TARSHISH
EPHAH	LEBANON	UZZIAH
EVE	LEHI	ZENOS
ISAAC	LEMUEL	ZION
ISAIAH	MOSES	ZORAM
ISHMAEL		

145

NINE

2 Nephi 17–25

```
M A L E M N L M A H A Z I K J H C G G E B A
C U V I A E I Q I M G T C E F A I T Y Z T M
O Y B I B A A N A W B W R F R B O D P U L O
F E D A R S A N I N Z U B C E N R H A Y M D
G I N H S P A M A E S U H A U J M A T P G E
M O P Y H S M I C A H E H L H I O I N A R E
N E R T S A T H L S M J U O G A S S G I I A
T I A E N P A E A I R B E A H A M R E R H A
A L H U Y R M J S X E E Q H F H L A A P O S
I V E G I H R H X Z R K M B O S A L T E H N
Z L E A O A A P P A F T S A V V O O I H L A
I G H N E N A I M A B A O M L N A R L M V W
O D L H A I J A H N L F P X H I O H H I Z E
N A S D R H T U U C O E J T H S A L K T H J
C D R A A H V W D R E I S H H A A H Y A A S
R O M I A H Y L M A L R T T T A N M J B N P
J A A M A H A B C O H V E A I O R E H P A K
S S M I E I M Z O M A S B B L N H R M C W B
I O Z S S S Y R I A B Y E O E O A T O D I W
N Z S H P E K A H B E R O D C J S K A M A M
U E U R I A H V D I H P E N E A F E L N O M
J M O S E S R E Z I N S A U L M J R D I A G
```

146

AHAZ	IMMANUEL	MOSES
AIATH	ISAIAH	NAPHTALI
AMMON	ISRAEL	NEPHI
AMOZ	JACOB	OREB
ANATHOTH	JEBERECHIAH	PALESTINA
ARPAD	JEHOVAH	PATHROS
ASSYRIA	JERUSALEM	PEKAH
BABYLON	JESSE	RAMATH
CALNO	JEW	REMALIAH
CARCHEMISH	JORDAN	REZIN
DESOLATION	JOSEPH	SAMARIA
EDOM	JUDAH	SAUL
EGYPT	LAISH	SHEARJASHUB
EGYPTIAN	LEBANON	SHILOAH
ELAM	MADMENAH	SHINAR
EPHRAIM	MANASSEH	SYRIA
GALLIM	MEDES	URIAH
GEBA	MICHMASH	UZZIAH
GEBIM	MIDIAN	ZEBULUN
GIBEAH	MIGRON	ZECHARIAH
GOMORRAH	MOAB	ZION
HAMATH		

TEN

2 Nephi 26–28

ABRAHAM   JACOB   NEPHI
ISRAEL   LEBANON   ZION

Clue: In the last days

"...MSHQ XVGXOV ALPJ CVPL WCMG DV JHMS MSVHL DGWMS, PCA

JHMS MSVHL OHXQ AG SGCGL DV, FWM SPIV LVDGIV A MSVHL

SVPLMQ RPL RLGD DV..."

D																									
A	B	C	D	E	F	G	H	I	J	K	L	M	N	O	P	Q	R	S	T	U	V	W	X	Y	Z

148

ELEVEN

2 Nephi 29 – Jacob 1

~~ABRAHAM~~   ~~JERUSALEM~~   ~~LABAN~~
~~ISRAEL~~   ~~JEW~~   ~~LEHI~~
~~JACOB~~   ~~JOSEPH~~   ~~NEPHI~~

- -

Clue: "...thus saith the Father"

"_____, _____
"SWIGIUFGI, TI QKLC XGILL UFGSHGA SECW H

_____, _____
LCIHAUHLCDILL ED BWGELC, WHMEDZ H XIGUIBC

_____, _____
NGEZWCDILL FU WFXI, HDA H VFMI FU ZFA HDA FU HVV

____..._____, _____
QID...UIHLCEDZ KXFD CWI SFGA FU BWGELC, HDA IDAKGI CF

_____..."
CWI IDA..."

																							P		
A	B	C	D	E	F	G	H	I	J	K	L	M	N	O	P	Q	R	S	T	U	V	W	X	Y	Z

TWELVE

Jacob 2–7

M	L	C	C	O	M	Q	F	P	B	V	M	B	A	E
S	J	Q	G	A	O	E	T	B	K	F	N	F	Y	Y
X	M	P	R	I	A	F	L	P	X	M	O	Z	R	G
P	K	W	N	K	S	S	E	A	A	J	Q	H	Q	P
X	H	J	P	I	O	H	I	H	S	Y	W	U	D	W
N	R	P	M	U	Y	L	A	V	J	U	Z	O	Z	Q
T	I	N	H	L	M	R	J	S	W	O	R	Z	S	S
R	P	W	Z	F	B	Y	H	U	Z	U	S	E	H	Q
S	S	E	C	A	L	E	E	N	D	O	B	E	J	D
O	O	T	D	E	R	S	G	K	Z	K	R	A	P	D
N	N	B	A	E	I	X	E	M	V	H	G	Z	D	H
E	E	R	M	O	O	T	E	I	G	O	I	H	E	L
Z	S	M	P	E	Z	W	D	R	I	I	H	P	E	N
I	Q	T	B	A	P	J	P	S	T	S	E	S	O	M
F	U	C	I	P	B	F	L	U	H	B	O	C	A	J

ABRAHAM   JACOB   MOSES
ENOS   JERUSALEM   NEPHI
ISAAC   JOSEPH   SHEREM
ISRAEL   LEHI   ZENOS

THIRTEEN

Enos – Words of Mormon

```
M N A B I N A D O M A N N
A O A N E P H I M J O O S
A C R B O M N I E R M E Z
L H C A A E J R A R S E E
M E I O J L U M O O Y H D
E M G C R S A M M T I A E
H I I T A I A L E R H I K
A S Q L J I A M E T E S I
R H E U B J N N A A L O A
A M D O J Z S O T L R M H
Z A C L S O N E R U E S F
H A N O L Y B A B O M K I
J T N I M A J N E B M R I
```

ABINADOM	ISRAEL	MORONI
AMALEKI	JACOB	MOSES
AMARON	JAROM	MOSIAH
BABYLON	JERUSALEM	NEPHI
BENJAMIN	JUDAH	OMNI
CHEMISH	LABAN	ZARAHEMLA
CORIANTUMR	LEHI	ZEDEKIAH
ENOS	MORMON	

151

FOURTEEN

Mosiah 1–3

M	M	O	S	I	A	H	G	Y	N	M
C	M	O	I	S	V	W	F	H	A	C	F
J	A	J	S	O	P	G	R	B	Z	I	T
M	R	U	E	E	S	M	A	A	A	K	T
U	Y	M	T	R	S	L	R	L	E	L	Y
R	B	H	R	B	U	A	Q	Z	Q	U	N
O	L	K	Q	I	H	S	A	Y	U	M	A
L	R	S	H	E	M	R	A	D	N	B	M
E	S	P	M	K	V	F	P	L	A	T	A
H	E	L	J	F	T	N	M	K	E	M	L
N	A	L	E	H	I	E	D	W	M	M	E
B	E	N	J	A	M	I	N	N	K	P	H

ADAM   JERUSALEM   MOSES
BENJAMIN   LABAN   MOSIAH
HELAMAN   LEHI   NEPHI
HELORUM   MARY   ZARAHEMLA

152

FIFTEEN

Mosiah 4–6

ADAM   JERUSALEM   MOSIAH
BENJAMIN   LEHI

Clue: King Benjamin's advice to parents

"_____

"MPX OC FRNN XCGBJ XJCQ XY FGND RE XJC FGOW YK XHPXJ

_____; _____

GEZ WYMCHECWW; OC FRNN XCGBJ XJCQ XY NYLC YEC

_____, _____."

GEYXJCH, GEZ XY WCHLC YEC GEYXJCH."

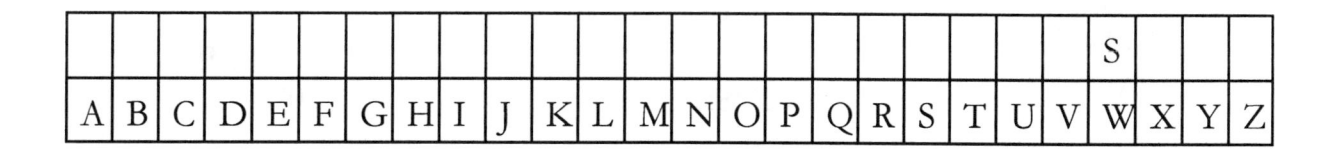

A	B	C	D	E	F	G	H	I	J	K	L	M	N	O	P	Q	R	S	T	U	V	W	X	Y	Z
																		S							

SIXTEEN

Mosiah 7–9

```
T N E A S E O J X M L N A A S
F P N I R W F I E E O M Q M F
Y O Y P D R E L A M E L H A Z
B T D G H C A R M L X P Z L N
O K E D E S S A E O Z P Z E A
J Z P A U I M H E Z H C M K V
P W Y R L O Z D L D B M U I M
I F E N L M O E U A X E E F A
H J D I J C E V N M M H H Z H
P R H A O G I H H I C A S Y A
E S C Y K V J Q A A F A N D R
N O N O A H J K T R I F A U B
B L E H I Y N A T W A S R S A
I L G D C E I H M I L Z O B I
B E N J A M I N S P E V U M Q
```

ABRAHAM
AMALEKI
AMMON
BENJAMIN
EGYPT
HELEM

ISRAEL
JACOB
JERUSALEM
LAMAN
LEHI
LIMHI
MOSIAH

NEAS
NEPHI
NOAH
SHEUM
SHILOM
ZARAHEMLA
ZENIFF

154

SEVENTEEN

Mosiah 10 – 14

```
I H N S H I L O M C O I V H I
S N J E D V V V Y L E A R S I
A F A N P Z I O N D F M X T R
I Y C M O H U I V L P S A Q I
A M E Y A L I E F R G L B A E
H B Z F E L M T Z X Q Q N G I
D I J Y R Q M E I P V I Y D C
H Y S M E E Q E H I S P A Y O
E G Z G V N K Z L S T N D Z P
Z H F I L Y L R U A I H V F S
X A F W V G P G S B S L A L R
V I I F G G E E A D G U U O J
A S N F I I S Z P T S P R R N
U O E I I O N U E V F L Y E X
O M Z Z M F P O U G T S Q J J
```

ABINADI
EGYPT
ISAIAH
ISRAEL
JERUSALEM
LAMAN
MOSES
MOSIAH
NEPHI
NOAH
SHEMLON
SHILOM
SINAI
ZENIFF
ZIFF
ZION

EIGHTEEN

Mosiah 15 – 18

```
I M G D L M H A I S O M
K S O N E P H I L G C H
T J A S H M I Z S V L H
N V E I E J G O S R E N
O E E R A S G O A L P O
X H H I U H D Z A A S A
N R I F X S Z M B Q S H
O G J L U I A I A Q E K
M A U T R I N L H F B G
R M I E I A A P E U R H
O L G R D C E S C M D R
M A X I Z I O N C D S L
```

ABINADI   JERUSALEM   NEPHI
ALMA   MORMON   NOAH
HELAM   MOSES   ZION
ISAIAH   MOSIAH

NINETEEN

Mosiah 19 – 22

```
T M S A M P X D A M L A
T O H I M I W Q B K Y I
P S I C H M D Z A L O Z
J I L X C P O A M I A G
M A O R L K E N N R S L
X H M U R Q W N A I Z G
N V C H C Z J H L T B G
O N G A D Z E I F J L A
E L E O K M M A G P N F
D A B N L H W J B W B I
I R M A I U F F S U Y K
G R S I M N O L M E H S
```

ABINADI   LIMHI   SHEMLON
ALMA   MOSIAH   SHILOM
AMMON   NEPHI   ZARAHEMLA
GIDEON   NOAH

TWENTY

Mosiah 23 – 26

```
A A N V M O X M N O L U M A
B E B O M O S I A H U O J A
R L Z I A K E T F F I N E Z
A A M A N H I S A A C I Z T
H L O T R A J A C O B V B O
A S R S H A D P I H P E N A
M F M M E L H I S A C E L B
L N O Q L A Z E I L T M E M
A O N M A M U M M R A N F U
S L V O M A O K M L J X M L
E M N L E N Y J K A A E S E
S E O I V U W Q M M U I I K
O H T H Q Z T I E X P H Y Z
M S V S O D N L I M H I R H
```

ABINADI	JACOB	NEPHI
ABRAHAM	LAMAN	NOAH
ALMA	LIMHI	SHEMLON
AMULON	MORMON	SHILOM
BENJAMIN	MOSES	ZARAHEMLA
HELAM	MOSIAH	ZENIFF
ISAAC	MULEK	

TWENTY–ONE

Mosiah 27 – 29

```
U N M L E H I M L J T Z N
F I O E J H F P Q B A O L
S Z N M L F J X C R R I A
R D B M M A Q B A A M V L
I W S X I A S H A H K P M
B Y D E Z H E U I R D C A
R R R Q S M H H R M I H J
E M R L L E A X A E Z U T
N A O A L Y Z N K I J Z U
M D E A D X L K M Y S R P
O A M C E L P H A O N O Y
N E P H I I H O N M J Y M
B E N J A M I N N G A X D
```

AARON	HELAM	MOSIAH
ADAM	HIMNI	NEPHI
ALMA	JERUSALEM	NOAH
AMMON	LEHI	OMNER
BENJAMIN	LIMHI	ZARAHEMLA

TWENTY–TWO

Alma 1–4

```
M A N T I U V D M Y A H A N Z
U M I G R O H E N M P M L E A
Z E R A M L I E N E N S I P R
L D A M L A N O S I H I M H A
J G G Z B A R O H E S D H I H
G E I I M O J U R M A O I H E
H N R A D R C M X I M N B A M
S J L U E E O A R E Y Z L H L
Z B A H S U O L J E I Y E Z A
B U M V N A I N E H P S P T O
F I Y T T N L C D M A L Q I Q
L T S I X T I E I G U I X P L
N E P H I C A P M L C E S V V
I G Y Y Q N O N I M M S L O M
S G I W L E A M H S I A Z E M
```

ALMA	JERUSALEM	MOSIAH
AMLICI	JOSEPH	NEHOR
AMNIHU	LAMAN	NEPHI
AMNOR	LEMUEL	NEPHIHAH
GIDEON	LIMHER	SAM
HERMOUNTS	LIMHI	SIDON
ISHMAEL	MANTI	ZARAHEMLA
JACOB	MINON	ZERAM

TWENTY–THREE

Alma 5 – 8

```
D G F B A L M E H A R A Z N W
I N N Q Y I D A N I B A E O G
J I V Z H R N O D I S H Y I W
X K H O L N S Z P J O M D A Q
A E P G O L K P R N E V B J
H M P L E X G J L O O O J R M
N A U N E N Q P R N M M B A U
O W H L O M S A V E V R E H H
A D U I E M A U L W K Z T A A
H O Y Y N K R A U C V Y I M H
L V S W J O S O C X K R H E I
C K E A I U M V M A B A P H H
J U C C R P C M W B A M E Z P
A O B E A O P Z A I E S N Q E
B Z J E G A D W A M L A I P N
```

AARON	ISAAC	NEPHI
ABINADI	JACOB	NEPHIHAH
ABRAHAM	JERUSALEM	NEPHITE
ALMA	MARY	NOAH
AMMONIHAH	MELEK	SIDON
AMULEK	MORMON	ZARAHEMLA
GIDEON	NEHOR	

TWENTY–FOUR

Alma 9 – 12

```
S E N I N E L E H I L Q Y M J U
A M N O R N O A H K I E O O H U
M M R I U D M O R Z E S S R K I
H O S E N U M W U R I E K M S M
A A R S H U M G I A P E U H A M
T N N Z B L U H H H L L M N I H
A J T O E W U S Q U B A A B A H
V M E I D E B X M I E S U M A M
A R I R O D Z A H L S R M A O X
H N S N U N I S B E E O O L H V
R A T H A S A G H H N G N M H K
L U N I I D A H C I D K T A I T
W I X M O B I L H L V M I R H P
K J J V I N L A E L Z O B L P Y
W Q J D N L H O M M V J B O E G
E I N S M A D A N C C Y R S N E
```

ADAM
ALMA
AMINADI
AMMONIHAH
AMNOR
AMULEK
ANTION
ANTIONAH
CHERUBIM
EGYPT

EZROM
GIDDONAH
ISHMAEL
JERUSALEM
JOSEPH
LEHI
LIMNAH
MANASSEH
MOSIAH

NEPHI
NOAH
ONTI
SENINE
SENUM
SHIBLON
SHIBLUM
SHUM
ZEEZROM

162

TWENTY-FIVE

Alma 13 – 16

```
A A F I V Q M O D I S M M M
N M A L M A C P R E E O N K
Q E U K F W H B H L R O Z O
R S P L W O R Z C Z E K O M
C A N H E Y S H E D L X R H
Y L I O I K I E I D D P A A
W Y B V I Z Z G P L U O M H
N A N K E T M V W R C H R I
O H E D M N A A E Z Y A N N
D A E E E K S L H I L O P O
I K L H Z M F H O A T N V M
S A O X C G P K H S R N L M
S R B X K H I H E L E B A A
K U A L M E H A R A Z D A M
```

ABRAHAM
AHA
ALMA
AMMONIHAH
AMULEK
DESOLATION
GIDEON

LEHI
MANTI
MELCHIZEDEK
NEHOR
NEPHI
NOAH

SALEM
SIDOM
SIDON
ZARAHEMLA
ZEEZROM
ZORAM

163

TWENTY–SIX

Alma 17 – 19

```
G L L A M A N H M L J V C E
R I E A R U I A M L A A T M
A M D M C B K Z W E L I O N
B A E E U V C X T M H S F E
B D Y L O E T R E P I T H P
A A T U A N L H E A Q H U H
N M C P A S A N H R E H A I
A X K E R R U I A K C M I S
H V T W A I M R S B V M H
A S R Z N N Y N E H I N E S
W W J O O M S T X J M S L U
D J M M Z R Z Y R B L A H A
V A M K K A G S U B E S E L
L A I Z D M I M I T N A M L
```

ABISH
ADAM
ALMA
AMMON
GIDEON
ISHMAEL
JERUSALEM
LAMAN
LAMONI
LEHI
LEMUEL
MANTI
MOSIAH
NEPHI
NEPHITE
RABBANAH
SEBUS
ZARAHEMLA

164

TWENTY–SEVEN

Alma 20 – 24

```
A T B Z M E L A S U R E J A K M
H D J A L M E H A R A Z M A O L
E J N O N M O I T N A M M R E K
D T H I M N I T U N O O M M Z E
M E I N E H O R S N L O U N T L
S I S K S I D O N I N E O I E A
M L D O E U C E H P L L H A M E
N I N D L L D S Z B U P M U L A
M O N O O A A Z M M E H L P A M
B U N O L N T M A N S O K I M L
N L L A M M I I A I N R E H A A
I R L O I A E Y O I N J P P N M
T E E D K D L H T N H O P E O A
N N H P Q I I E S V F C R N O L
A M I R I V S M A D A M C A R E
M O K M T L U F I T N U O B A H
```

AARON
ADAM
ALMA
AMALEKITE
AMMON
AMULON
AMULONITES
ANTIOMNO
BOUNTIFUL
DESOLATION
HELAM

HIMNI
ISHMAEL
JERUSALEM
LAMAN
LAMONI
LEHI
LEMUEL
MANTI
MIDDONI
MIDIAN

MORMON
MULOKI
NEHOR
NEPHI
NEPHITE
OMNER
SHEMLON
SHILOM
SIDON
ZARAHEMLA

165

TWENTY–EIGHT

Alma 25– 29

```
A L M A J Z M P A V A B Z A
C R U M C O H M L B O J J S
T F K B S A M E I U N K E A
A Z C E C O A N N E P A Y
H Z S A N R A T O O P L L M
F A A P S D I J B A H E M E
Z S H I I F V B N H I A E L
I K P I U A H D O Y F M H A
I G U L N N A I I D Q H A S
H O Q C N O O R M B B S R U
L E H I A D M L O N O I A R
J P R E N M O M U N I C Z E
J E R S H O N D A M I D A J
A B R A H A M I E V A Z Z J
```

AARON
ABINADI
ABRAHAM
ALMA
AMMON
AMMONIHAH
AMULON
BOUNTIFUL
HIMNI
ISAAC
ISHMAEL
ISRAEL
JACOB
JERSHON
JERUSALEM
LEHI
MOSES
NEPHI
NOAH
OMNER
ZARAHEMLA

TWENTY-NINE

Alma 30 – 32

```
Z N Q S H A N O D D I G A N N
S N O M O S E S V B T M O A A
H E Z E V N O M M A U T M M A
I O N A D M C I E L N A Z E A
M M A I G I U P E A L I O L Q
N N S Z N R G K I E P A R E M
I E L H C E A R H T I O A K U
S R E P X O O M N C I Z M Y N
B O N Y N C R N E O S I T V O
C S U I A O A F O U H B B L I
R B D A H I X H Z L M S P S T
T A R I S H A M L A B P R X N
H O R N E P H I I B Z I T E A
N O Z E E Z R O M O K X H O J
K E E K A L M E H A R A Z S M
```

AARON	HELAMAN	ONIDAH
ALMA	HIMNI	RAMEUMPTOM
AMMON	JERSHON	SENINE
AMULEK	KORIHOR	SHIBLON
ANTIONUM	MELEK	ZARAHEMLA
CORIANTON	MOSES	ZEEZROM
GIDDONAH	NEPHI	ZORAM
GIDEON	OMNER	

THIRTY

Alma 33 - 36

```
H J M A U T K P O I H P E N
E E M E M A Z E N O S E Q L
L R E W L M L P V K Z J R E
A S C B P E O M R C E L R H
M H F I E B K N E R S P G I
A O F A V K T H U H M J H Y
N N H C E Q T S B I A M X G
E Y S E F I A M T J S R Q K
W R E T Z L A P A Q N A A E
A A S F E H Y C P O S U A Z
T G O M A G O Y O Z N X A C
O J M R E B V N Q S A M L A
I G B M O S I A H P G V S S
Y A W F X V N T K E L U M A
```

ABRAHAM
ALMA
AMMON
AMULEK
EGYPT
HELAMAN
ISAAC
JACOB
JERSHON
JERUSALEM
LEHI
MELEK
MOSES
MOSIAH
NEPHI
ZARAHEMLA
ZENOS

THIRTY-ONE

Alma 37 - 40

```
M S K F M A D A I U L
S S D R J N U H N E S
V L H F I N P A B Y I
Z C E C K E M A C S R
A N M T N A S T A B O
N O O E L I T H B F N
O L I E L N E H P A X
H B H L T E O Q Z M G
A I I H J N Z M I L L
I H W O I M Z A M A Q
L S F G U E X A G A K
```

ADAM   HELAMAN   NEPHI
ALMA   ISABEL   SHIBLON
AMMON   LIAHONA   SIRON
GAZELEM

169

THIRTY-TWO

Alma 41 - 44

```
C R M M N E Q L B I H P E N
I H D O A S Q I Z I H E L H
S J E K R N S K R P D A A N
H E T R H O T Y Q P O L A A
M R S I U A N I P S P M Y L
A S K D T B N I H I A A T M
E H I X L V I M R L N Z Q A
L O W M V D T M E T N M Y O
O N T H O W R L I H V L U T
C V M A R I E O J A A J T X
H A A O R M N J E Z M R O B
T Z D N U U K I S K V M E E
B O A E M K I P O B E V O Z
D T L S I D O N D M C O H N
```

ADAM   JERSHON   NEPHI
ALMA   LAMAN   NOAH
AMMON   LEHI   RIPLAH
ANTIONUM   LEMUEL   SIDON
CHERUBIM   MANTI   ZERAHEMNAH
ISHMAEL   MORONI

THIRTY-THREE

Alma 45 - 48

```
A M O S E S J R C H R S L H
X M E Y A M T N A M A J G E
X L M I X J T D O P D A G L
H B A O R U I R I E S C Z A
C A Q K N N O T S R Z O J M
Q U I I O N N O H Q A B A A
I J K K I A L Z S O I W L N
X T H B C A M V R M H G M D
A M C E T I J O S I P B E H
M T J I X N L O S P E G H I
L H O L H C X A S I N K A B
A N Z W A T Y Z M E A V R L
M E L E K U S G S A P H A Z
L E H O N T I G V G C H Z K
```

ALMA   JACOB   MOSES
AMALICKIAH   JOSEPH   MOSIAH
AMMON   LEHONTI   NEPHI
ANTIPAS   MELEK   ONIDAH
DESOLATION   MORONI   ZARAHEMLA
HELAMAN

171

THIRTY-FOUR

Alma 49 - 52

```
H Z A M O R I A N T O N F B I N
T E O M R K V G I H P E N N O A
C E L R A K F R I H E L O R N M
G H A A L C N W R T R O O M M
T A S N M M I E S Q O M M A U O
H L I G C A I C N M M M N L L N
L M D I X U N T K A A O P M E I
U E O D G M M S E I I U M A K H
F H N L Z M H K H T A D O C M A
I A U A C I E A A N X H O F U H
T R T I B T H L T T A N A F B A
N A M L I I O A T Y B R O D Q U
U Z O H H S N R I U E O O R I Z
O N P P E N O A H Y V G C H A J
B E E D F X F N R E N M O A A A
N N J O Y N O T N A I R O C J P
```

AARON
ALMA
AMALICKIAH
AMMON
AMMONIHAH
AMMORON
BOUNTIFUL
CORIANTON
DESOLATION
GID
HELAMAN
JACOB
LEHI
MORIANTON
MORONI
MULEK
NEPHI
NEPHIHAH
NEPHITE
NOAH
OMNER
PAHORAN
SHIBLON
SIDON
TEANCUM
ZARAHEMLA
ZORAMITE

172

THIRTY-FIVE

Alma 53 - 57

```
B Z E M O R I A N T O N U U A T
O Y S T M U L E K B N G M M E A
U M H U I A L M A J D L M A M G
N E O A P H X U P C L O N M A G
T M S R R I P T K G N C O M J G
I V I Z Z A T E C O U R A Y N E
F H D L L E P N N M O L Y M R T
U A O F W W E I A N I G K W M I
L H N M W H L Z T C I Z U W A N
B I A Y J A C N K N J N G F R A
U H B X M U A I F V A U O D O M
V P C A M M A N V R P I D R Z A
I E N E A H G I D Y T G T E O L
H N N L Q U I X I H P E N N A M
E I E Z A R A H E M L A G W A S
L H W V W S M E L A S U R E J M
```

ALMA
AMALICKIAH
AMMON
AMMORON
ANTIPARAH
ANTIPUS
BOUNTIFUL
CUMENI
GID

HELAMAN
JERUSALEM
JUDEA
LAMAN
LAMANITE
LEHI
MANTI
MORIANTON
MORONI

MULEK
NEPHI
NEPHIHAH
NEPHITE
SIDON
TEANCUM
ZARAHEMLA
ZEEZROM
ZORAM

THIRTY-SIX

Alma 58 - 63

```
N M N D M O R O N I H A H I H
B O O O E G K I H E L A H A K
O X E R M S T V P Z M E G M Y
U A A D O M O T O A X O G A N
N L L N I N A L L I T X I N O
T M M A U G I I A H O M D T T
I E A Q E X C H N T K G A I N
F H Q D P K E T P O I O O Z A
U A G X I L N R E A R O Z V I
L R K A A O E P J A H O N B R
U A H M L N A Q C I N O M I O
X Z A B M C W K I U B C R M M
M N I O H X J I H P E N U A A
C H E U N E P H I H A H Q M N
S T S C O R I A N T O N L H M
```

ALMA
AMALICKIAH
AMMON
AMMORON
BOUNTIFUL
CORIANTON
DESOLATION
GID

GIDEON
HAGOTH
HELAMAN
LEHI
MANTI
MORIANTON
MORONI
MORONIHAH

NEPHI
NEPHIHAH
PACHUS
PAHORAN
SHIBLON
TEANCUM
TEOMNER
ZARAHEMLA

THIRTY–SEVEN

Helaman 1 – 4

```
G M V H M B A M M O N S D H Z
A K O I E A O I S A A C K P E
D I K S H L H U A L M A T D F
I S Q L I C A A N L E H I N U
A H W A N A N M R T R N U C R
N K H L E G H A A B I X P M B
T U A M P Y S I A N A F U L W
O M H E H J A X M P I T U N H
N E I H I B V C N N N A E L T
P N N A P H L A E A M P N Z O
V P O R J Z R M I M H A L Q L
S R R A Q O U R O I Z A H Q A
D Z O Z H C O R T O A R D L B
S D M A A C O E Q C Z U Q O U
V G P P V N L P L B O C A J T
```

ABRAHAM	HELAMAN	NEPHI
ALMA	ISAAC	NEPHITE
AMMON	JACOB	PAANCHI
AMMORON	KISHKUMEN	PACUMENI
BOUNTIFUL	LEHI	PAHORAN
CORIANTUMR	MORONIHAH	TUBALOTH
GADIANTON	MOSIAH	ZARAHEMLA

THIRTY–EIGHT

Helaman 5 – 7

```
I Z E D E K I A H M L H S B G
N H G I D T I N U E E L A H A
A E M C J Z I L B L T D W I D
L S P I Z O E A A A A C A Y I
M X P H L K M M M N B A L P A
A K B A I O A M I K Y I M M N
L J W O R N O M R P Q N E E T
R G P Z U N A A X K L P H L O
A D E X I N C N M N D A A A N
X E V H A D T E E U Z H R S E
Z K A M Q O B I Z P L I A U Y
X H M G H B H L F O H E Z R L
U O N W D I H E L U R I K E P
N B E N J A M I N V L A T J E
K I S H K U M E N S V E M E L
```

ABEL
ALMA
AMINADAB
AMMON
AMMONIHAH
AMULEK
BENJAMIN
BOUNTIFUL

CAIN
CEZORAM
GADIANTON
GID
HELAMAN
JERUSALEM
KISHKUMEN
LEHI

LIMHI
MULEK
NEPHI
NEPHITE
ZARAHEMLA
ZEDEKIAH
ZEEZROM

176

THIRTY–NINE

Helaman 8 – 12

```
G S S E A N T U M T E K S
L L E O F M L O H Z G P E
J B B S S W W V I X L N E
M J R G O N T A J T X A Z
A Q U G A M S E J T J M O
H I V M G D R N C X C A R
A H P W M U I I E Y C L A
R E A U S K N A S P E E M
B L L A R O P Y N A H H D
A E L U I H Z E D T I I K
K E H F D S O N E Z O A J
M Z E D E K I A H M H N H
J E R E M I A H L R E L H
```

ABRAHAM	JEREMIAH	NEPHI
EZIAS	JERUSALEM	SEANTUM
GADIANTON	LEHI	SEEZORAM
HELAMAN	MOSES	ZEDEKIAH
ISAIAH	MULEK	ZENOS

FORTY

Helaman 13 - 16

```
G I D E O N Z Q V V M S H
B Q P M Q C U I J O X A E
E M O G B E A E S P F M L
I B F D B N R E U X P U A
C J O Q E U S L T I V E M
N G E N S S I M Z Y W L A
K O T A S N O K M K P Q N
O F L O A L D L I V J T O
D E N Z R C J W A H F Z R
M E X Z T P B W Z T P S B
Z F E C L F M A D A I E J
U A C E T I N A M A L O N
U V J A L M E H A R A Z N
```

ADAM   JERUSALEM   SAMUEL
DESOLATION   LAMANITE   ZARAHEMLA
GIDEON   MOSES   ZENOS
HELAMAN   NEPHI

FORTY-ONE

3 Nephi 1 - 5

```
N G L S E T I N A M A L N M D
G A I E E D Z H M E H E O E H
Q D M D U S R B H I P S S P G
S M A A G M O J B H I O E L A
L E L M L I A M I A L S R E D
U L M P N E D S H A O P N H I
F A A E M C H D T J E C S I A
I S A K D J B I O J L O Y F N
T U C Q A G O M T N A N L Z T
N R P F H N A X Y N I C U X O
U E V A I H M B H M O W O S N
O J D S A Q E J N P T M V B Y
B U A R Z E D E K I A H R Y M
J A B W I H N A I D D I G O Y
C A Z E M N A R I H A H G L M
```

ABRAHAM
ALMA
BOUNTIFUL
DESOLATION
GADIANTON
GIDDIANHI
GIDGIDDONI
HELAMAN
HEM

ISAAC
JACOB
JERUSALEM
JOSEPH
JUDAH
LACHONEUS
LAMANITE
LEHI

MORMON
MOSES
MOSIAH
NEPHI
SAMUEL
ZARAHEMLA
ZEDEKIAH
ZEMNARIHAH

FORTY-TWO

3 Nephi 6 - 10

```
V Z H G W R X Z G N E P H I U S
N E J P I D J S A I D T H D A G
T N A Y E L J E U R M J M T E H
S O C P L S G A R E A G K H G H
E S O S E Y O A C U N H I Y L S
S Q B Q H Z T J L O S O E M X O
O E V N I I W X M G B A H M N J
M L I A G P N O I H N U L C L O
H E X M Q J R D A E G E G E A A
A U I A R O G N M A T I M A M L
H M W L N I M U D I S O I B T V
I A C I D O K I N R R Y U R H H
N S H D I H A A A O X A E F L U
O A O D S N M E N O M E G A K S
H N A I D A L I Z R O M U C O M
I G K I L X O F W V J A H P L A
```

ALPHA
GAD
GADIANDI
GADIOMNAH
GIDGIDDONI
GILGAL
GIMGIMNO
ISRAEL
JACOB
JACOBUGATH

JERUSALEM
JOSEPH
JOSH
KISHKUMEN
LACHONEUS
LAMAN
LAMANITE
LEHI
MOCUM

MORONI
MORONIHAH
MOSES
NEPHI
OMEGA
ONIHAH
SAMUEL
ZARAHEMLA
ZENOS

180

FORTY-THREE

3 Nephi 11–12

NEPHI   SENINE
ISRAEL   BOUNTIFUL

Clue: "And behold, the third time they did understand the voice which they heard; and it said unto them:

"_____, _____
"MXOJBG DI MXBJWXG QJP, NP KOJD N UD KXBB
_____, _____--_____
SBXUQXG, NP KOJD N OUWX CBJLNENXG DI PUDX-OXUL
_____."
IX OND."

					Y																				
A	B	C	D	E	F	G	H	I	J	K	L	M	N	O	P	Q	R	S	T	U	V	W	X	Y	Z

181

FORTY–FOUR

3 Nephi 13–16

ISAIAH JOSEPH NEPHI
ISRAEL MOSES   ZION
JERUSALEM

Clue: Seek...

"AYB RGGU SG XPWRB BNG UPVZJIQ IX ZIJ NPR WPZNBGIYRVGRR, HVJ HEE BNGRG BNPVZR RNHEE AG HJJGJ YVBI SIY."

A	B	C	D	E	F	G	H	I	J	K	L	M	N	O	P	Q	R	S	T	U	V	W	X	Y	Z
										K															

182

FORTY–FIVE

3 Nephi 17– 20

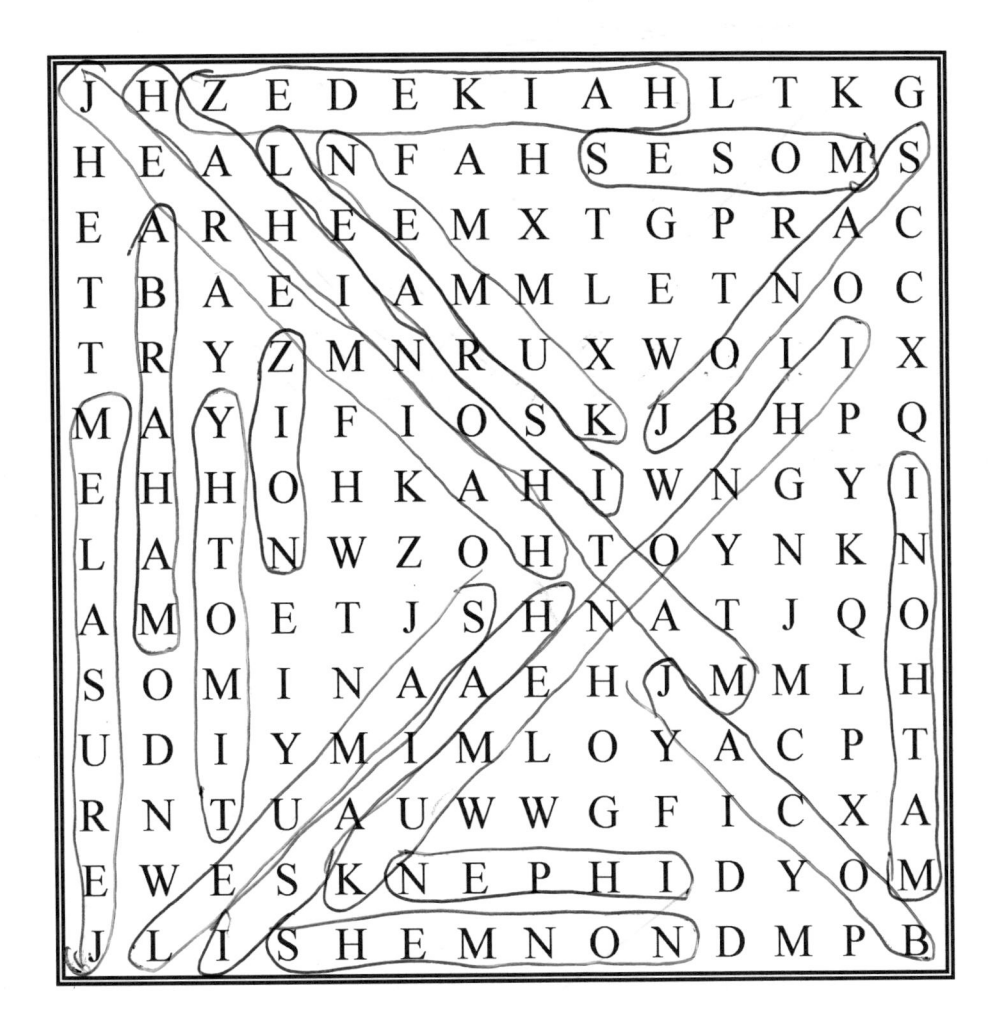

```
J H Z E D E K I A H L T K G
H E A L N F A H S E S O M S
E A R H E E M X T G P R A C
T B A E I A M M L E T N O C
T R Y Z M N R U X W O I I X
M A Y I F I O S K J B H P Q
E H H O H K A H I W N G Y I
L A T N W Z O H T O Y N K N
A M O E T J S H N A T J Q O
S O M I N A A E H J M M L H
U D I Y M I M L O Y A C P T
R N T U A U W W G F I C X A
E W E S K N E P H I D Y O M
J L I S H E M N O N D M P B
```

ABRAHAM   JONAS   NEPHI
ISAIAH   KUMEN   SAMUEL
ISRAEL   KUMENONHI   SHEMNON
JACOB   MATHONI   TIMOTHY
JEREMIAH   MATHONIHAH   ZEDEKIAH
JERUSALEM   MOSES   ZION

183

FORTY-SIX

3 Nephi 21–28

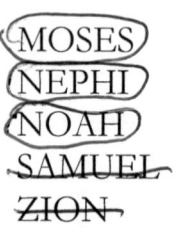

```
H J A C O B Z N P A Z C R I
J A J N O A H U M E O E S L
U J J E S K W M G Z W A E M
D O M I R L M G K L I U Z O
A H U B L U B S A A M P I S
H N Q C X E S M H A Y N O E
J Q A M W X A A S Z L O N S
N R Z C D N M I L T W N J Z
L O Q K I A H M S E T I Q R
Q P I T L O L N O R M I O N
D E E A R U T B Z R A L G X
Q A C E Z L Q W T M M E E I
U H B O J J C I V E L O L B
I N E P H I P O O Q C C N X
```

ELIJAH   JOHN   MOSES
HOREB   JUDAH   NEPHI
ISAIAH   LAMANITE 2 NOAH
ISRAEL   LEVI   SAMUEL
JACOB   MALACHI   ZION
JERUSALEM MORMON

184

FORTY-SEVEN

3 Nephi 29 - Mormon 3

J	Z	L	G	S	M	O	S	E	S	T	I	C	B	Q
E	A	A	N	D	A	A	G	B	W	N	O	D	I	S
R	R	M	L	O	E	M	N	S	H	I	M	N	X	A
U	A	A	A	E	R	S	U	T	M	Q	H	Z	A	A
S	H	N	L	U	A	A	O	E	U	Y	S	R	H	M
A	E	I	J	S	H	R	M	L	L	M	O	C	A	O
L	M	T	U	H	X	S	S	M	A	N	K	G	A	S
E	L	E	E	E	G	A	O	I	A	T	A	F	O	U
M	A	Q	I	M	L	M	E	J	I	D	I	J	J	J
S	D	S	H	C	Q	P	M	D	I	A	A	O	E	Y
N	N	U	P	H	A	O	A	A	L	S	G	J	N	B
T	P	P	E	G	R	N	N	O	H	J	P	M	R	O
G	O	H	N	M	I	T	G	O	L	D	M	D	W	C
C	Q	O	O	B	O	N	N	F	B	S	H	U	S	A
R	U	N	A	N	A	A	D	A	M	R	Q	I	K	J

AARON
ABINADI
ADAM
AMMARON
AMOS
ANGOLA
ANTUM
DESOLATION

GADIANTON
ISRAEL
JACOB
JASHON
JERUSALEM
JOSHUA
LAMANITE
MORMON

MOSES
NEPHI
SAMUEL
SHEM
SHIM
SIDON
ZARAHEMLA

185

FORTY–EIGHT

Mormon 4–9

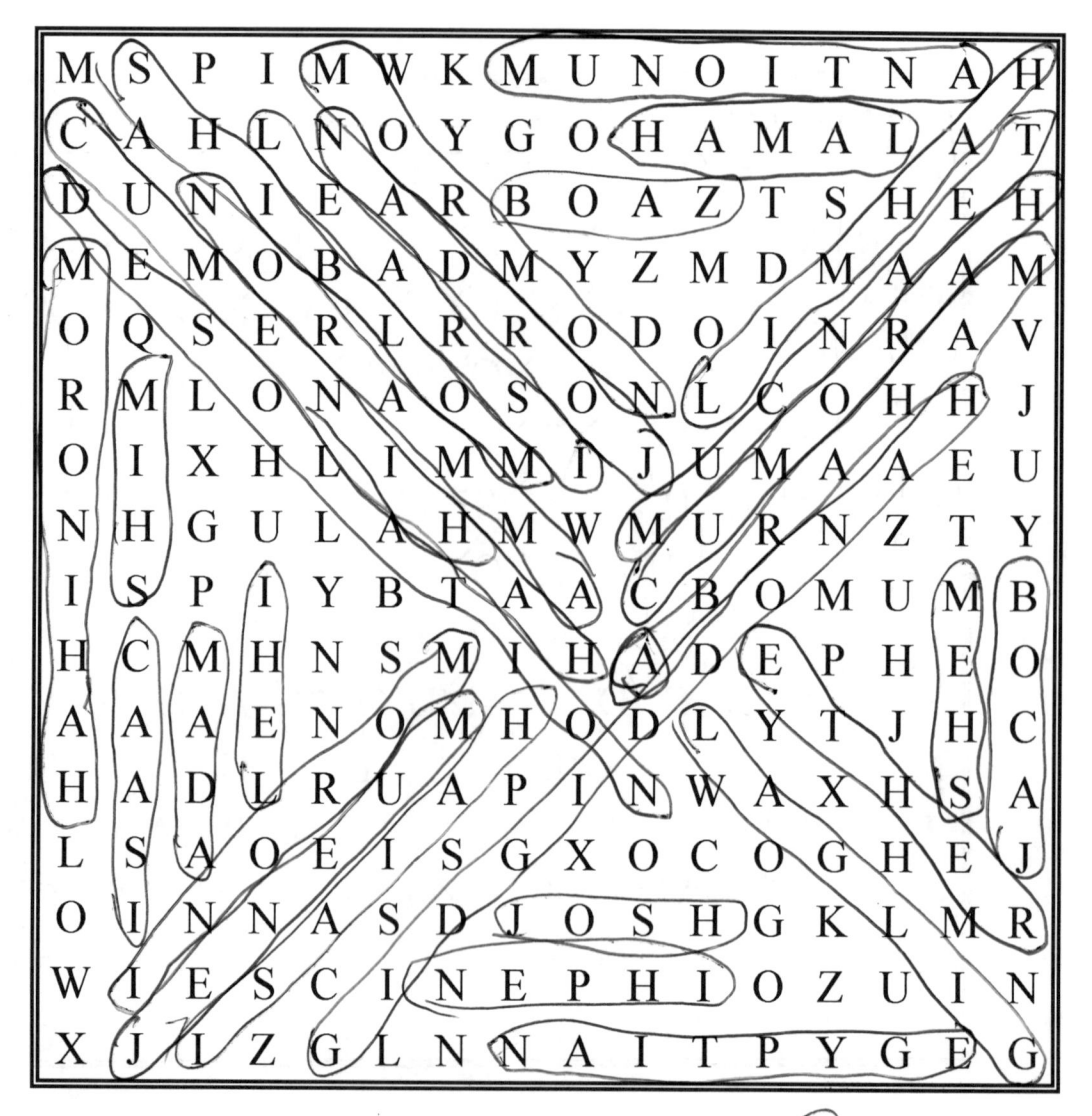

```
M S P I M W K M U N O I T N A H
C A H L N O Y G O H A M A L A T
D U N I E A R B O A Z T S H E H
M E M O B A D M Y Z M D M A A M
O Q S E R L R R O D O I N R A V
R M L O N A O S O N L C O H H J
O I X H L I M M I J U M A A E U
N H G U L A H M W M U R N Z T Y
I S P I Y B T A A C B O M U M B
H C M H N S M I H A D E P H E O
A A A E N O M H O D L Y T J H C
H A D L R U A P I N W A X H S A
L S A O E I S G X O C O G H E J
O I N N A S D J O S H G K L M R
W I E S C I N E P H I O Z U I N
X J I Z G L N N A I T P Y G E G
```

ABRAHAM   GIDGIDDONAH   LEHI
ADAM   GILGAL   LIMHAH
AMMARON   ISAAC   MORMON
ANTIONUM   ISAIAH   MORONI
BOAZ   ISRAEL   MORONIHAH
CUMENIHAH   JACOB   NEPHI
CUMORAH   JENEUM   SHEM
DESOLATION   JORDAN   SHIBLOM
EGYPTIAN   JOSH   SHIM
ETHER   LAMAH   TEANCUM

186

FORTY-NINE

Ether 1 - 8

```
K I M N A G N A A N Y S R M A J H B I L
U K I A I O T H O T R E B A O M A A Q Z
H A R L L E E T R M M M W F K R E C H O
C O G B R A N O U U O I O E M I O H O A
N A I E R A T T C M U S S R D E S C T M
H H S T I N N N R V C Z R O O L H J E
S E H R A A A R Y G O O V I A N R E O A
D O O I I I O Y V H B H V M H E I M H G
M M R R R N L Z O A N M S R I P L F I S
C O O O M H V R E I M O U I O A E H Y N
C C M I A H E T N P C N I T K H R N S Y
F G K I A S H B N E M N I T N A I H E T
E I S H R E K I B I P E O G A A L R P Z
U O I O R S H E Z N K H D U A L I P O E
M R M A D U V X H T E S I H L D O R I C
O B D E H R G J U N O I Z E N I D S O R
D A R A O A Q S H R I V E L L O H A E C
M A H H G J O H N E C O M Z W U R M H D
J A E A N O A H E M Y U H T E H H O I J
M N P K I S H E N O T J V R E M E S M L
```

(Word list on next page)

AARON	ETHER	MORON
ADAM	GILGAH	MORONI
AHAH	HEARTHOM	MOSIAH
AKISH	HETH	NEHOR
AMNIGADDAH	ISRAEL	NEPHI
CAIN	JACOM	NIMROD
COHOR	JARED	NOAH
COM	JOHN	OMER
CORIANTOR	KIB	ORIHAH
CORIANTUM	KIM	PAGAG
CORIANTUMR	KIMNOR	RIPLAKISH
CORIHOR	KISH	SETH
COROM	LEVI	SHELEM
DESERET	LIB	SHEZ
DESOLATION	LIMHI	SHIBLON
EMER	MAHAH	SHULE
EPHRAIM	MORIANCUMER	ZENEPHI
ESROM	MORIANTON	ZION
ETHEM		

FIFTY

Ether 9–15

```
H C G I M A H A H H T E H N M A C R M B
C E O I N O L E H I S F O O B O M U A A
Z O A R L O L C O M E R R R R U C L M A
E A M R I G R B Y R A M A I T N M G T L
R I M N T H A O A A O H A N A E I P N M
I K H N O H O L M N A N A I H D Y M N A
N I S P I R O R R M T I L A J G L B R S
T S H J E G L M M U R P R C E A O I E E
X H I K K N A O M O I A A A O E R L M T
Z Q Z Q H N R D C R Z J J K M R T E O H
E F A S I I I C D C J H O S I M O H D Z
H T O M A S K W H A O E S S D S O M E B
S G R N R D G E A J H R R I E E H N F M
A A T A A K S S Z A M M I U K P R W J Z
H O E E E H I K Q O T S O A S A H A Q E
N L L L R R I S H H H N L N A L R H L
F I U O O E H E T U L K A O B T L P X S
G M N H H M S A R K I M H M R I O E I E
A R O T I X G R L E V I T V A O H R M R
F C E L Y O E M E R R M I H S R M S U Q
```

(Word list on next page)

189

AARON	EMER	MORON
ABLOM	ETHEM	MORONI
ABRAHAM	ETHER	MOSES
AGOSH	GILEAD	NEPHI
AHAH	GILGAL	NIMRAH
AKISH	HEARTHOM	OGATH
ALMA	HESHLON	OMER
AMGID	HETH	RAMAH
AMMON	ISRAEL	RIPLAKISH
AMNIGADDAH	JARED	RIPLIANCUM
AMULEK	JERUSALEM	SETH
COHOR	JOSEPH	SHARED
COM	KIM	SHEZ
COMNOR	KISH	SHIBLOM
CORIANTOR	LEHI	SHIM
CORIANTUM	LEVI	SHIZ
CORIANTUMR	LIB	SHURR
CORIHOR	LIMHI	ZARAHEMLA
COROM	MORIANTON	ZERIN
EGYPT	MORMON	

FIFTY-ONE

Moroni 1–7

JARED   MORONI
MORMON   NEPHITE

Clue: "...charity never faileth"

"_____,
"XDM GSLUPMA PN MSB EDUB JQZB QK GSUPNM, LOT PM
_____;_____
BOTDUBMS KQUBZBU; LOT HSQNQ PN KQDOT EQNNBNNBT QK
_____,_____."
PM LM MSB JLNM TLA, PM NSLJJ XB HBJJ HPMS SPF."

Hard

FIFTY-TWO

Moroni 8 - 10

AARON ISRAEL MORIANTUM
ADAM JEHOVAH MORMON
AMORON JERUSALEM MORONI
ARCHEANTUS LURAM SHERRIZAH
EMRON

SECTION FOUR

SEQUENTIAL ORDER OF CLUES

15A - 1:1	24A - 2:2
8D - 1:1	6D - 2:3
14A - 1:2	7D - 2:17
13A - 1:3	1D - 2:19
2D - 1:5	16A - 2:20
3D - 1:6	9A - 3:3
18D - 1:8	11D - 3:4
17D - 1:8	10D - 3:7
19A - 1:9	27A - 3:7
5A - 1:11	21D - 3:15
12A - 1:12	22A - 4:1
20A - 1:13	25D - 4:6
28A - 1:15	23A - 4:13
15D - 1:18	4A - 4:35
26A - 1:20	

SOLUTIONS

1

Crossword solution 1 contains the words: PILLAR, ZORAM, FAITH, BOOK, PRAYED, TRUE, THEE, GENEALOGY, GOD, SPIRIT, PARENTS, JEWS, PROSPER, LUSTER, PERISH, VISION, MIGHTIER, NATION, FAMILY, LIFE, LORD, HEART.

2

14A - 5:11	25A - 8:10
2D - 5:14	7A - 8:11
32A - 5:18	26A - 8:11
27D - 5:19	15D - 8:12
1D - 6:4	8D - 8:12
17D - 7:1	4D - 8:13
22D - 7:2	28D - 8:19
16D - 7:5	24D - 8:20
19A - 7:12	20D - 8:23
3A - 7:16	21A - 8:24
13D - 7:17	12A - 8:28
6D - 1:19	30D - 10:4
31A - 7:20	23D - 10:7
18A - 7:21	9D - 10:11
10A - 8:5	11D - 10:12
5D - 8:9	29A - 10:14

Crossword solution 2 contains: SAVED, ANGRY, JOSS, FIELD, SWEET, FAMILIES, ROBE, ASHAMED, MOSES, EXHORT, WILL, CLINGING, TREE, DARK, WHITE, PERISH, GATHERED, SORROWFUL, NATIONS.

3

16A - 11:1	20D - 13:10
11D - 11:13	17D - 13:13
1A - 11:25	12A - 13:14
5D - 11:27	13A - 13:9
19D - 11:28	4A - 13:23
7A - 11:29	14D - 13:26
23D - 11:31	29A - 13:34
6D - 11:36	26D - 13:35
15A - 12:2	27D - 13:37
28A - 12:7	21D - 13:37
1D - 12:16	30A - 13:39
8A - 12:17	22A - 13:40
24A - 12:19	9D - 13:42
18A - 12:23	2D - 14:7
10A - 13:6	25D - 14:22
3D - 13:8	

Crossword solution 3 contains: WORD, GRAPES, DESCRIPTION, RECORD, WATER, TWELVE, DEVIL, ABOMINABLE, EAST, SCATTERED, PRAISE, PRECIOUS, WARS, MOUNTAIN, PEOPLE, TRUTH, TEMPTATIONS, JOURNEY, FORTH, ORDAINED, BOOKS.

193

4

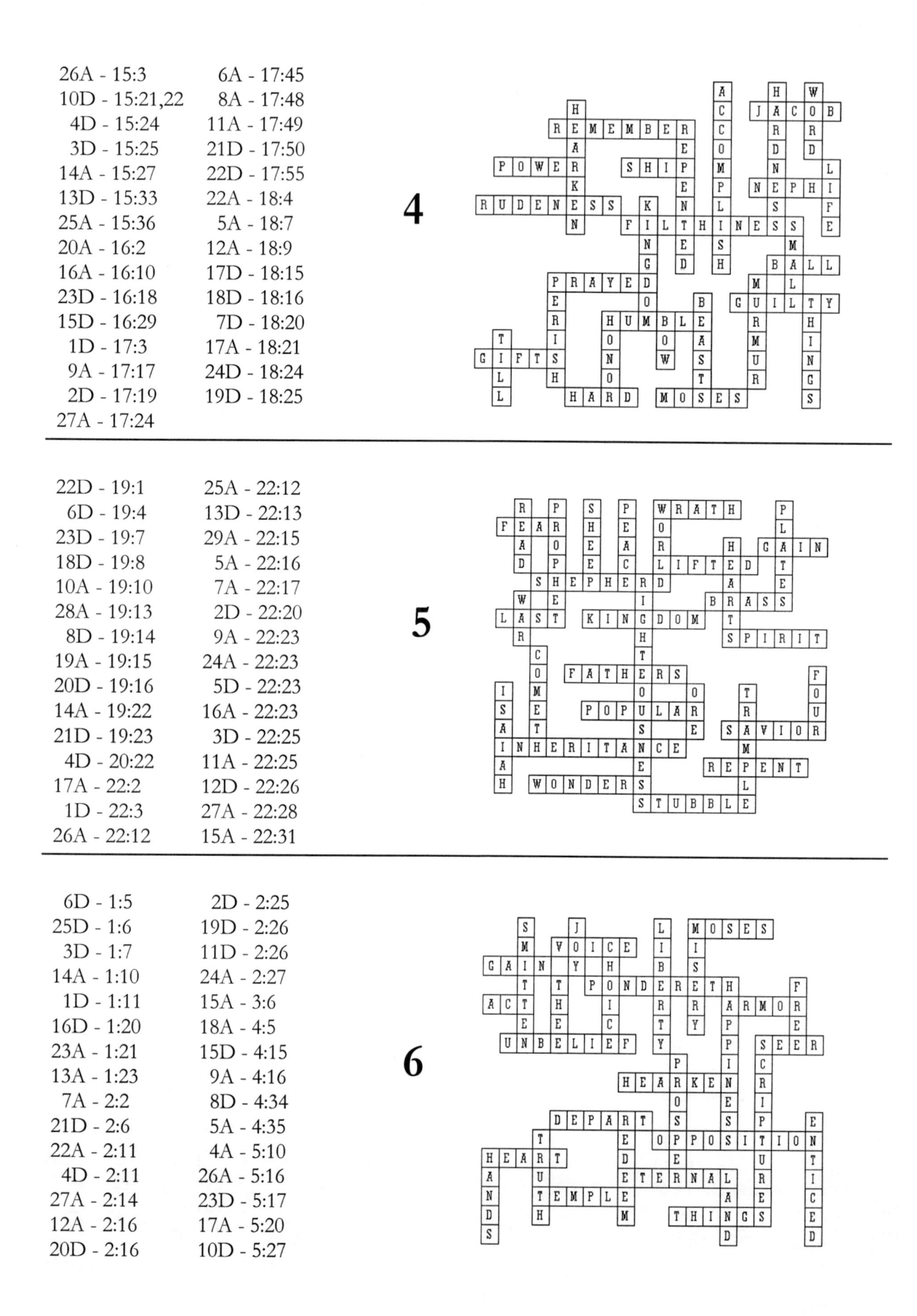

26A - 15:3	6A - 17:45
10D - 15:21,22	8A - 17:48
4D - 15:24	11A - 17:49
3D - 15:25	21D - 17:50
14A - 15:27	22D - 17:55
13D - 15:33	22A - 18:4
25A - 15:36	5A - 18:7
20A - 16:2	12A - 18:9
16A - 16:10	17D - 18:15
23D - 16:18	18D - 18:16
15D - 16:29	7D - 18:20
1D - 17:3	17A - 18:21
9A - 17:17	24D - 18:24
2D - 17:19	19D - 18:25
27A - 17:24	

5

22D - 19:1	25A - 22:12
6D - 19:4	13D - 22:13
23D - 19:7	29A - 22:15
18D - 19:8	5A - 22:16
10A - 19:10	7A - 22:17
28A - 19:13	2D - 22:20
8D - 19:14	9A - 22:23
19A - 19:15	24A - 22:23
20D - 19:16	5D - 22:23
14A - 19:22	16A - 22:23
21D - 19:23	3D - 22:25
4D - 20:22	11A - 22:25
17A - 22:2	12D - 22:26
1D - 22:3	27A - 22:28
26A - 22:12	15A - 22:31

6

6D - 1:5	2D - 2:25
25D - 1:6	19D - 2:26
3D - 1:7	11D - 2:26
14A - 1:10	24A - 2:27
1D - 1:11	15A - 3:6
16D - 1:20	18A - 4:5
23A - 1:21	15D - 4:15
13A - 1:23	9A - 4:16
7A - 2:2	8D - 4:34
21D - 2:6	5A - 4:35
22A - 2:11	4A - 5:10
4D - 2:11	26A - 5:16
27A - 2:14	23D - 5:17
12A - 2:16	17A - 5:20
20D - 2:16	10D - 5:27

7

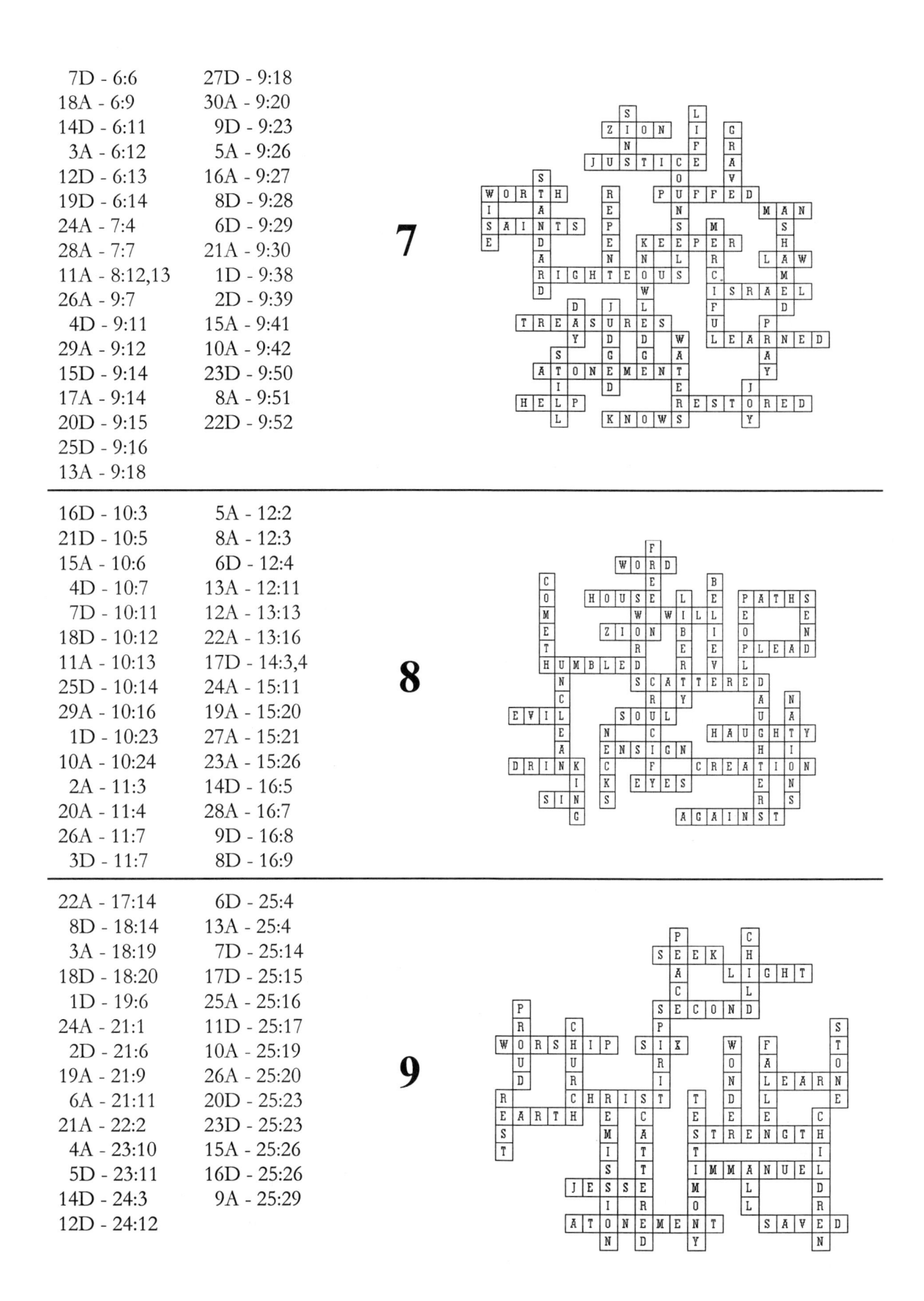

7D - 6:6	27D - 9:18
18A - 6:9	30A - 9:20
14D - 6:11	9D - 9:23
3A - 6:12	5A - 9:26
12D - 6:13	16A - 9:27
19D - 6:14	8D - 9:28
24A - 7:4	6D - 9:29
28A - 7:7	21A - 9:30
11A - 8:12,13	1D - 9:38
26A - 9:7	2D - 9:39
4D - 9:11	15A - 9:41
29A - 9:12	10A - 9:42
15D - 9:14	23D - 9:50
17A - 9:14	8A - 9:51
20D - 9:15	22D - 9:52
25D - 9:16	
13A - 9:18	

8

16D - 10:3	5A - 12:2
21D - 10:5	8A - 12:3
15A - 10:6	6D - 12:4
4D - 10:7	13A - 12:11
7D - 10:11	12A - 13:13
18D - 10:12	22A - 13:16
11A - 10:13	17D - 14:3,4
25D - 10:14	24A - 15:11
29A - 10:16	19A - 15:20
1D - 10:23	27A - 15:21
10A - 10:24	23A - 15:26
2A - 11:3	14D - 16:5
20A - 11:4	28A - 16:7
26A - 11:7	9D - 16:8
3D - 11:7	8D - 16:9

9

22A - 17:14	6D - 25:4
8D - 18:14	13A - 25:4
3A - 18:19	7D - 25:14
18D - 18:20	17D - 25:15
1D - 19:6	25A - 25:16
24A - 21:1	11D - 25:17
2D - 21:6	10A - 25:19
19A - 21:9	26A - 25:20
6A - 21:11	20D - 25:23
21A - 22:2	23D - 25:23
4A - 23:10	15A - 25:26
5D - 23:11	16D - 25:26
14D - 24:3	9A - 25:29
12D - 24:12	

10

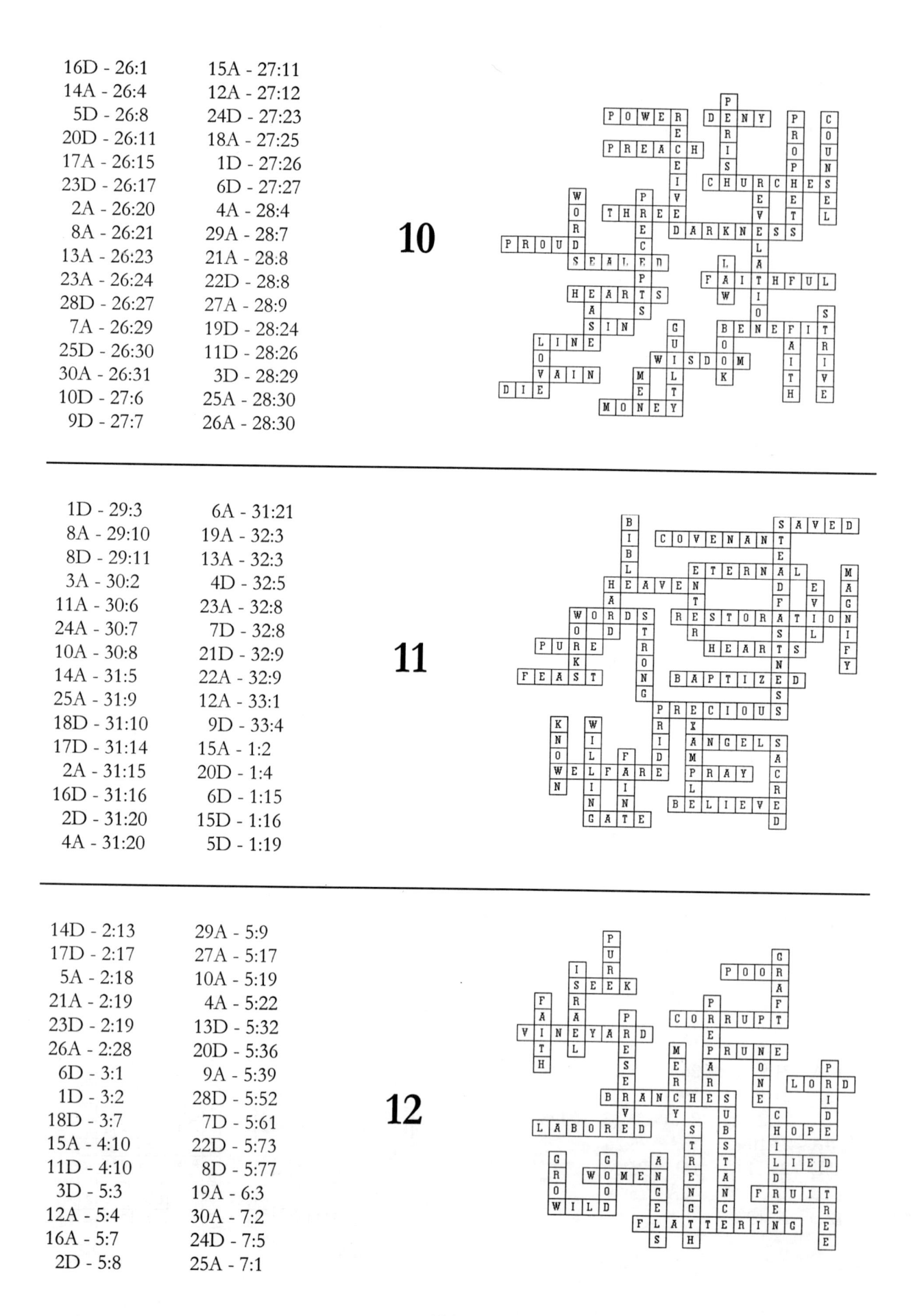

16D - 26:1	15A - 27:11
14A - 26:4	12A - 27:12
5D - 26:8	24D - 27:23
20D - 26:11	18A - 27:25
17A - 26:15	1D - 27:26
23D - 26:17	6D - 27:27
2A - 26:20	4A - 28:4
8A - 26:21	29A - 28:7
13A - 26:23	21A - 28:8
23A - 26:24	22D - 28:8
28D - 26:27	27A - 28:9
7A - 26:29	19D - 28:24
25D - 26:30	11D - 28:26
30A - 26:31	3D - 28:29
10D - 27:6	25A - 28:30
9D - 27:7	26A - 28:30

11

1D - 29:3	6A - 31:21
8A - 29:10	19A - 32:3
8D - 29:11	13A - 32:3
3A - 30:2	4D - 32:5
11A - 30:6	23A - 32:8
24A - 30:7	7D - 32:8
10A - 30:8	21D - 32:9
14A - 31:5	22A - 32:9
25A - 31:9	12A - 33:1
18D - 31:10	9D - 33:4
17D - 31:14	15A - 1:2
2A - 31:15	20D - 1:4
16D - 31:16	6D - 1:15
2D - 31:20	15D - 1:16
4A - 31:20	5D - 1:19

12

14D - 2:13	29A - 5:9
17D - 2:17	27A - 5:17
5A - 2:18	10A - 5:19
21A - 2:19	4A - 5:22
23D - 2:19	13D - 5:32
26A - 2:28	20D - 5:36
6D - 3:1	9A - 5:39
1D - 3:2	28D - 5:52
18D - 3:7	7D - 5:61
15A - 4:10	22D - 5:73
11D - 4:10	8D - 5:77
3D - 5:3	19A - 6:3
12A - 5:4	30A - 7:2
16A - 5:7	24D - 7:5
2D - 5:8	25A - 7:1

13

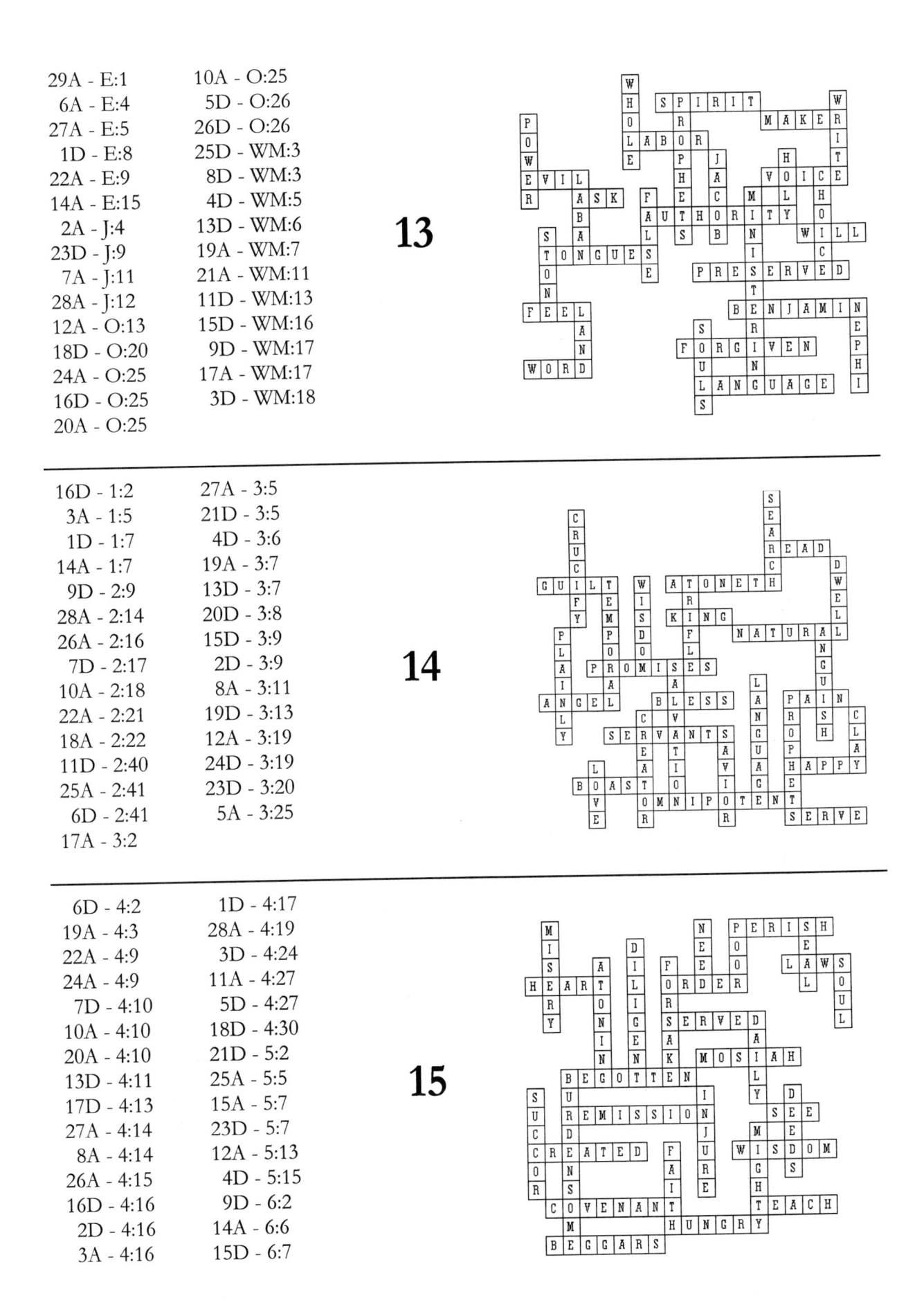

29A - E:1	10A - O:25
6A - E:4	5D - O:26
27A - E:5	26D - O:26
1D - E:8	25D - WM:3
22A - E:9	8D - WM:3
14A - E:15	4D - WM:5
2A - J:4	13D - WM:6
23D - J:9	19A - WM:7
7A - J:11	21A - WM:11
28A - J:12	11D - WM:13
12A - O:13	15D - WM:16
18D - O:20	9D - WM:17
24A - O:25	17A - WM:17
16D - O:25	3D - WM:18
20A - O:25	

14

16D - 1:2	27A - 3:5
3A - 1:5	21D - 3:5
1D - 1:7	4D - 3:6
14A - 1:7	19A - 3:7
9D - 2:9	13D - 3:7
28A - 2:14	20D - 3:8
26A - 2:16	15D - 3:9
7D - 2:17	2D - 3:9
10A - 2:18	8A - 3:11
22A - 2:21	19D - 3:13
18A - 2:22	12A - 3:19
11D - 2:40	24D - 3:19
25A - 2:41	23D - 3:20
6D - 2:41	5A - 3:25
17A - 3:2	

15

6D - 4:2	1D - 4:17
19A - 4:3	28A - 4:19
22A - 4:9	3D - 4:24
24A - 4:9	11A - 4:27
7D - 4:10	5D - 4:27
10A - 4:10	18D - 4:30
20A - 4:10	21D - 5:2
13D - 4:11	25A - 5:5
17D - 4:13	15A - 5:7
27A - 4:14	23D - 5:7
8A - 4:14	12A - 5:13
26A - 4:15	4D - 5:15
16D - 4:16	9D - 6:2
2D - 4:16	14A - 6:6
3A - 4:16	15D - 6:7

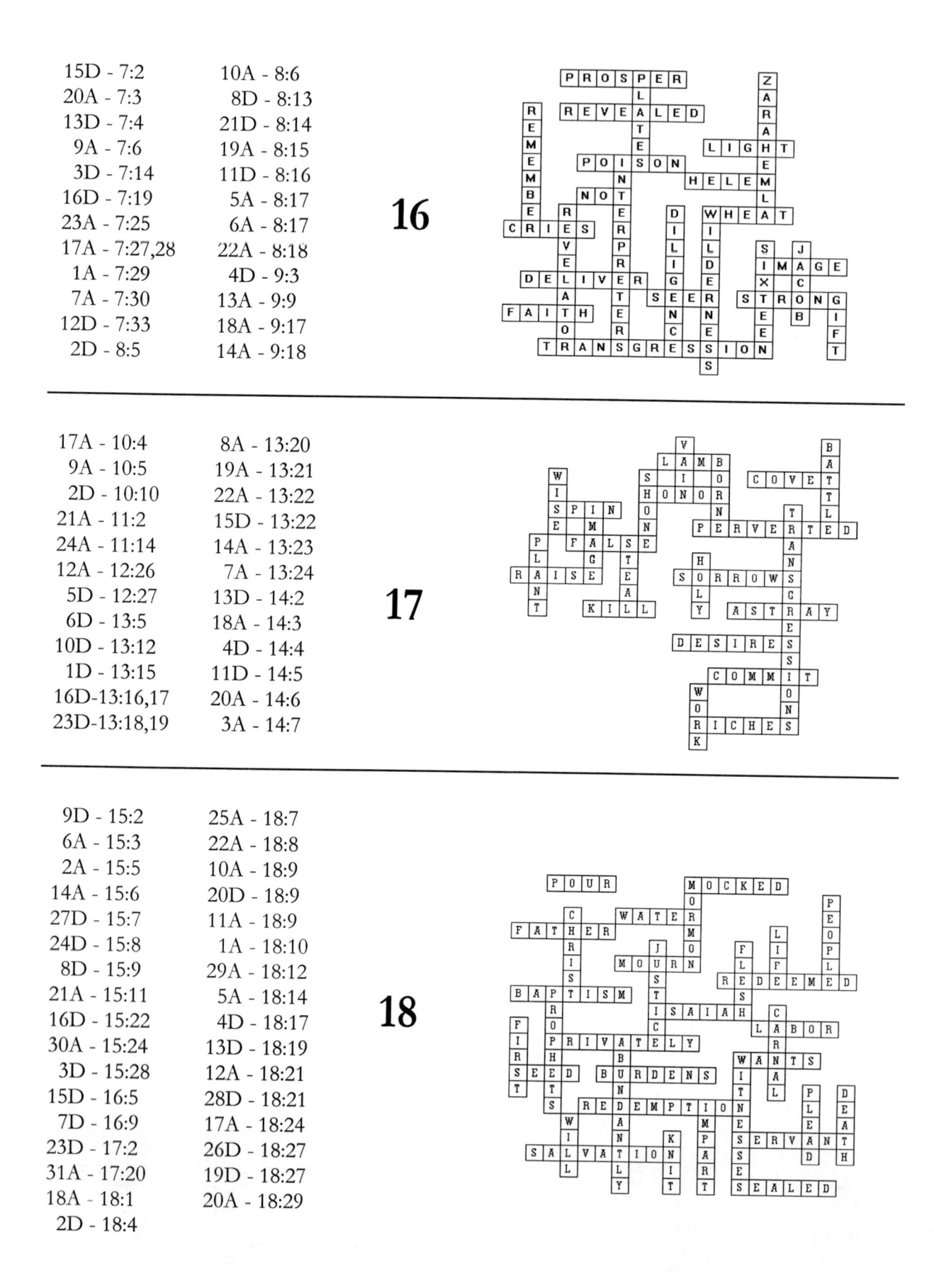

15D - 7:2	10A - 8:6		
20A - 7:3	8D - 8:13		
13D - 7:4	21D - 8:14		
9A - 7:6	19A - 8:15		
3D - 7:14	11D - 8:16	**16**	
16D - 7:19	5A - 8:17		
23A - 7:25	6A - 8:17		
17A - 7:27,28	22A - 8:18		
1A - 7:29	4D - 9:3		
7A - 7:30	13A - 9:9		
12D - 7:33	18A - 9:17		
2D - 8:5	14A - 9:18		

17A - 10:4	8A - 13:20		
9A - 10:5	19A - 13:21		
2D - 10:10	22A - 13:22		
21A - 11:2	15D - 13:22		
24A - 11:14	14A - 13:23		
12A - 12:26	7A - 13:24	**17**	
5D - 12:27	13D - 14:2		
6D - 13:5	18A - 14:3		
10D - 13:12	4D - 14:4		
1D - 13:15	11D - 14:5		
16D - 13:16,17	20A - 14:6		
23D - 13:18,19	3A - 14:7		

9D - 15:2	25A - 18:7		
6A - 15:3	22A - 18:8		
2A - 15:5	10A - 18:9		
14A - 15:6	20D - 18:9		
27D - 15:7	11A - 18:9		
24D - 15:8	1A - 18:10		
8D - 15:9	29A - 18:12		
21A - 15:11	5A - 18:14	**18**	
16D - 15:22	4D - 18:17		
30A - 15:24	13D - 18:19		
3D - 15:28	12A - 18:21		
15D - 16:5	28D - 18:21		
7D - 16:9	17A - 18:24		
23D - 17:2	26D - 18:27		
31A - 17:20	19D - 18:27		
18A - 18:1	20A - 18:29		
2D - 18:4			

19

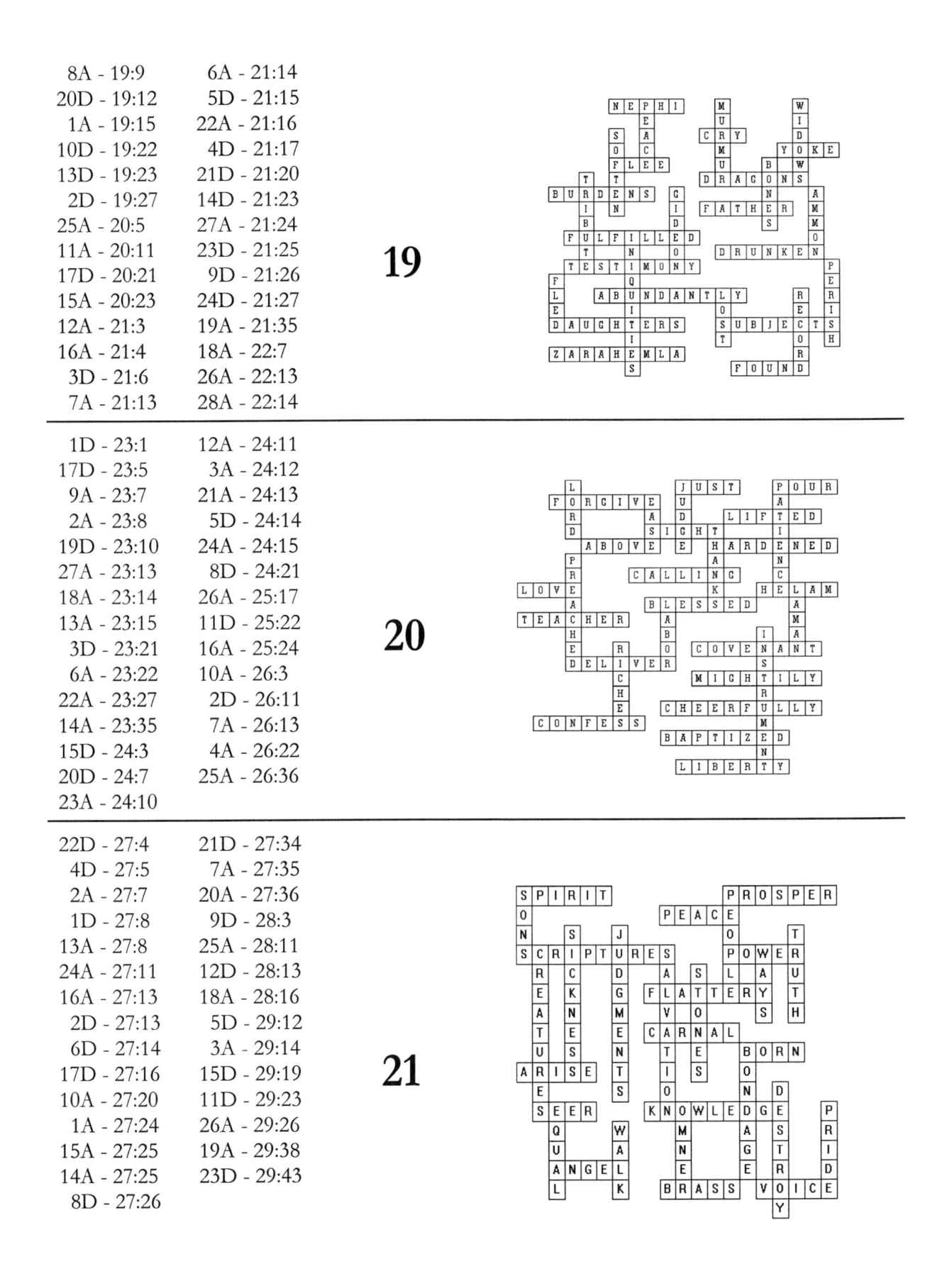

8A - 19:9	6A - 21:14
20D - 19:12	5D - 21:15
1A - 19:15	22A - 21:16
10D - 19:22	4D - 21:17
13D - 19:23	21D - 21:20
2D - 19:27	14D - 21:23
25A - 20:5	27A - 21:24
11A - 20:11	23D - 21:25
17D - 20:21	9D - 21:26
15A - 20:23	24D - 21:27
12A - 21:3	19A - 21:35
16A - 21:4	18A - 22:7
3D - 21:6	26A - 22:13
7A - 21:13	28A - 22:14

20

1D - 23:1	12A - 24:11
17D - 23:5	3A - 24:12
9A - 23:7	21A - 24:13
2A - 23:8	5D - 24:14
19D - 23:10	24A - 24:15
27A - 23:13	8D - 24:21
18A - 23:14	26A - 25:17
13A - 23:15	11D - 25:22
3D - 23:21	16A - 25:24
6A - 23:22	10A - 26:3
22A - 23:27	2D - 26:11
14A - 23:35	7A - 26:13
15D - 24:3	4A - 26:22
20D - 24:7	25A - 26:36
23A - 24:10	

21

22D - 27:4	21D - 27:34
4D - 27:5	7A - 27:35
2A - 27:7	20A - 27:36
1D - 27:8	9D - 28:3
13A - 27:8	25A - 28:11
24A - 27:11	12D - 28:13
16A - 27:13	18A - 28:16
2D - 27:13	5D - 29:12
6D - 27:14	3A - 29:14
17D - 27:16	15D - 29:19
10A - 27:20	11D - 29:23
1A - 27:24	26A - 29:26
15A - 27:25	19A - 29:38
14A - 27:25	23D - 29:43
8D - 27:26	

22

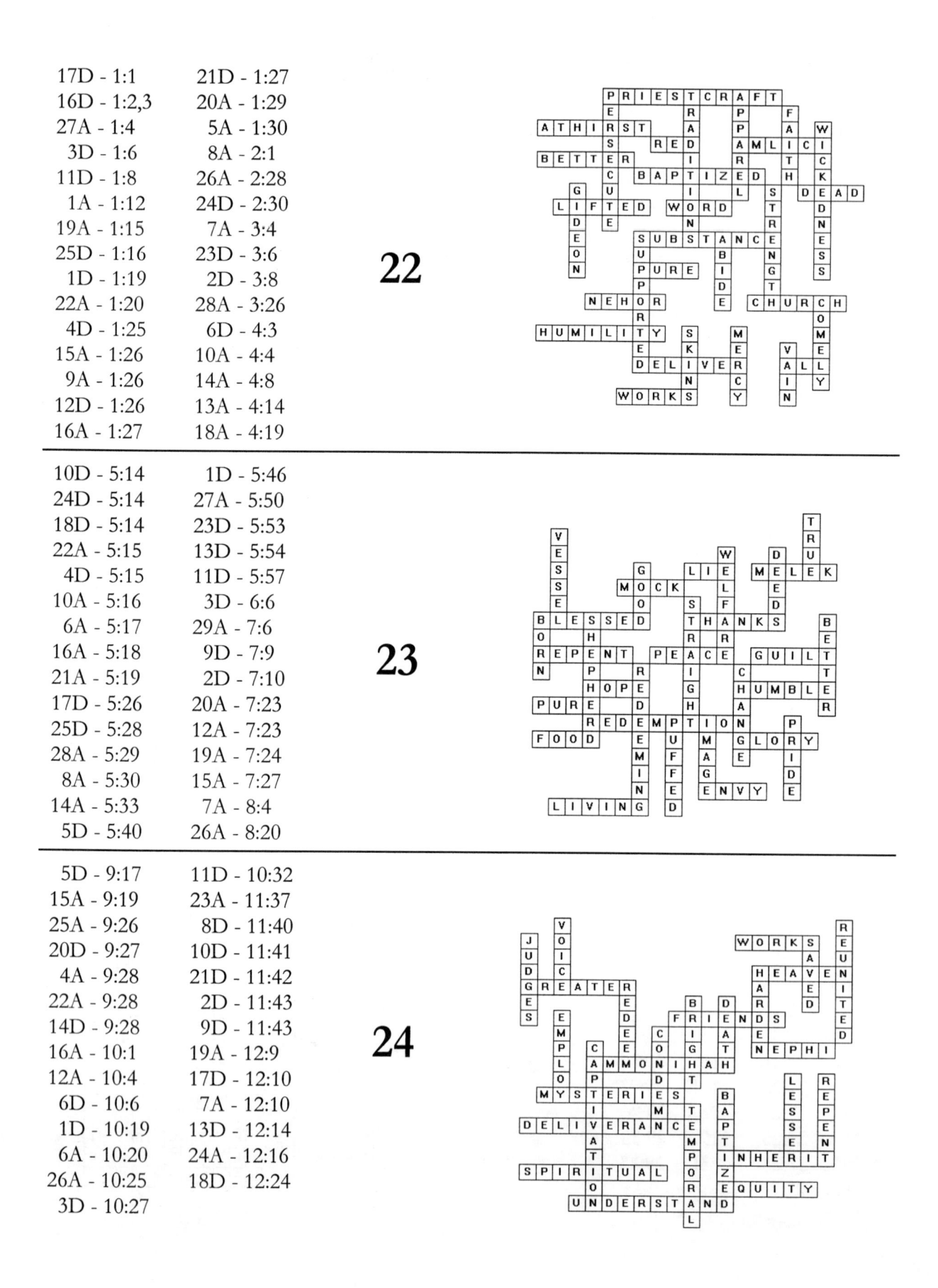

17D - 1:1	21D - 1:27
16D - 1:2,3	20A - 1:29
27A - 1:4	5A - 1:30
3D - 1:6	8A - 2:1
11D - 1:8	26A - 2:28
1A - 1:12	24D - 2:30
19A - 1:15	7A - 3:4
25D - 1:16	23D - 3:6
1D - 1:19	2D - 3:8
22A - 1:20	28A - 3:26
4D - 1:25	6D - 4:3
15A - 1:26	10A - 4:4
9A - 1:26	14A - 4:8
12D - 1:26	13A - 4:14
16A - 1:27	18A - 4:19

Crossword 22 solution includes: PRIESTCRAFT, ATHIRST, RED, BETTER, BAPTIZED, DEAD, LIFTED, WORD, SUBSTANCE, PURE, NEHOR, CHURCH, HUMILITY, DELIVER, VALLY, WORKS.

23

10D - 5:14	1D - 5:46
24D - 5:14	27A - 5:50
18D - 5:14	23D - 5:53
22A - 5:15	13D - 5:54
4D - 5:15	11D - 5:57
10A - 5:16	3D - 6:6
6A - 5:17	29A - 7:6
16A - 5:18	9D - 7:9
21A - 5:19	2D - 7:10
17D - 5:26	20A - 7:23
25D - 5:28	12A - 7:23
28A - 5:29	19A - 7:24
8A - 5:30	15A - 7:27
14A - 5:33	7A - 8:4
5D - 5:40	26A - 8:20

Crossword 23 solution includes: VESSEL, TRUE, MOCK, LIE, MELEK, BLESSED, THANKS, REPENT, PEACE, GUILT, HOPE, HUMBLE, PURE, REDEMPTION, FOOD, GLORY, ENVY, LIVING.

24

5D - 9:17	11D - 10:32
15A - 9:19	23A - 11:37
25A - 9:26	8D - 11:40
20D - 9:27	10D - 11:41
4A - 9:28	21D - 11:42
22A - 9:28	2D - 11:43
14D - 9:28	9D - 11:43
16A - 10:1	19A - 12:9
12A - 10:4	17D - 12:10
6D - 10:6	7A - 12:10
1D - 10:19	13D - 12:14
6A - 10:20	24A - 12:16
26A - 10:25	18D - 12:24
3D - 10:27	

Crossword 24 solution includes: JUDGES, VOICE, WORKS, REUNITED, GREATER, HEAVEN, FRIENDS, NEPHI, AMMONIHAH, MYSTERIES, DELIVERANCE, SPIRITUAL, INHERIT, EQUITY, UNDERSTAND, REPENT.

25

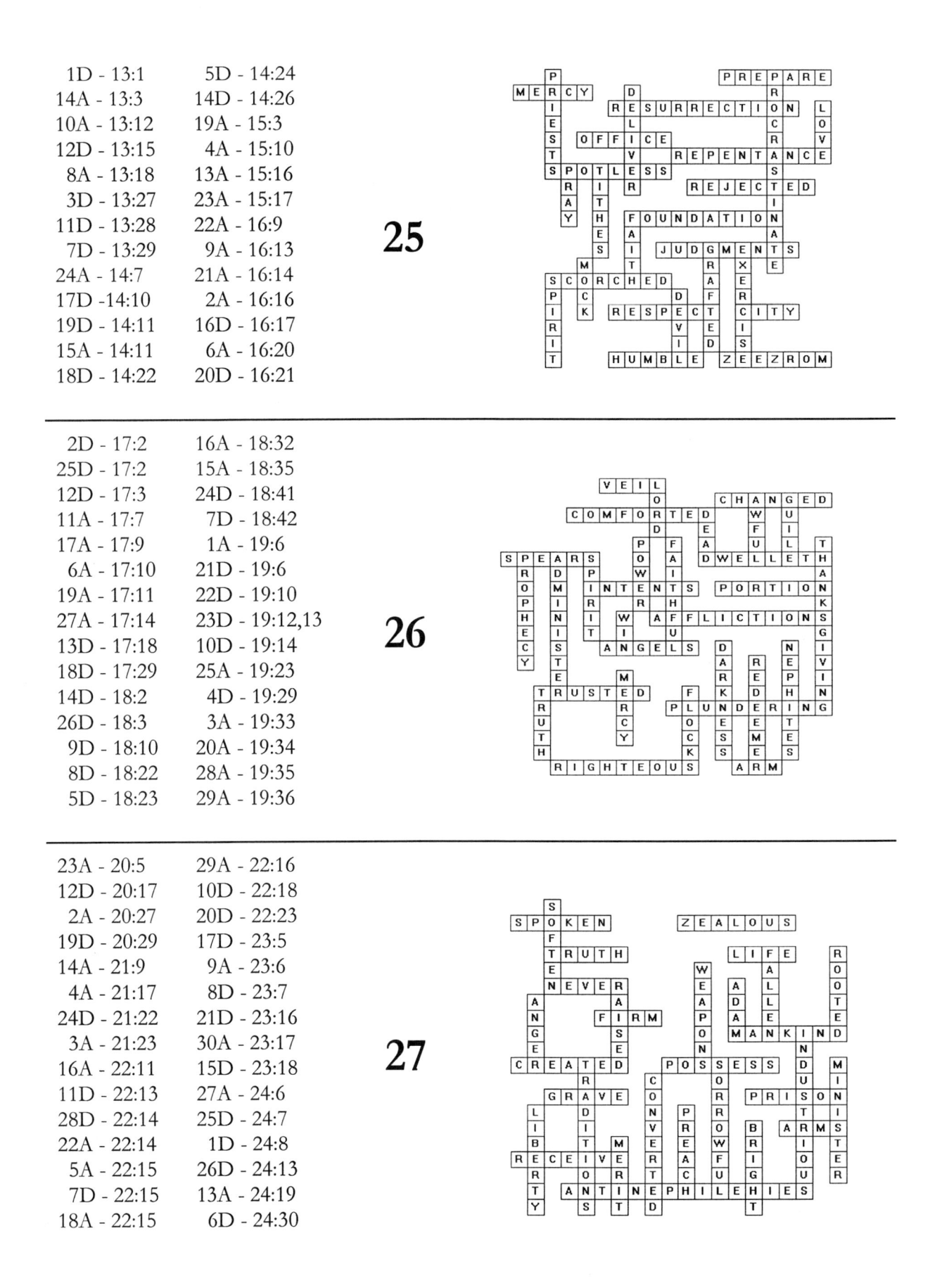

1D - 13:1	5D - 14:24
14A - 13:3	14D - 14:26
10A - 13:12	19A - 15:3
12D - 13:15	4A - 15:10
8A - 13:18	13A - 15:16
3D - 13:27	23A - 15:17
11D - 13:28	22A - 16:9
7D - 13:29	9A - 16:13
24A - 14:7	21A - 16:14
17D - 14:10	2A - 16:16
19D - 14:11	16D - 16:17
15A - 14:11	6A - 16:20
18D - 14:22	20D - 16:21

Grid answers: MERCY, PREPARE, PRIEST, RESURRECTION, LOVE, OFFICE, REPENTANCE, SPOTLESS, PRAY, REJECTED, FOUNDATION, JUDGMENTS, SCORCHED, RESPECT, CITY, SPIRIT, HUMBLE, ZEEZROM

26

2D - 17:2	16A - 18:32
25D - 17:2	15A - 18:35
12D - 17:3	24D - 18:41
11A - 17:7	7D - 18:42
17A - 17:9	1A - 19:6
6A - 17:10	21D - 19:6
19A - 17:11	22D - 19:10
27A - 17:14	23D - 19:12,13
13D - 17:18	10D - 19:14
18D - 17:29	25A - 19:23
14D - 18:2	4D - 19:29
26D - 18:3	3A - 19:33
9D - 18:10	20A - 19:34
8D - 18:22	28A - 19:35
5D - 18:23	29A - 19:36

Grid answers: VEIL, CHANGED, COMFORTED, SPEARS, DWELLETH, INTENTS, PORTION, AFFLICTIONS, ANGELS, TRUSTED, PLUNDERING, RIGHTEOUS, ARM

27

23A - 20:5	29A - 22:16
12D - 20:17	10D - 22:18
2A - 20:27	20D - 22:23
19D - 20:29	17D - 23:5
14A - 21:9	9A - 23:6
4A - 21:17	8D - 23:7
24D - 21:22	21D - 23:16
3A - 21:23	30A - 23:17
16A - 22:11	15D - 23:18
11D - 22:13	27A - 24:6
28D - 22:14	25D - 24:7
22A - 22:14	1D - 24:8
5A - 22:15	26D - 24:13
7D - 22:15	13A - 24:19
18A - 22:15	6D - 24:30

Grid answers: SPOKEN, ZEALOUS, TRUTH, LIFE, NEVER, FIRM, MANKIND, CREATED, POSSESS, GRAVE, PRISON, ARMS, RECEIVE, ANTINEPHILEHIES

28

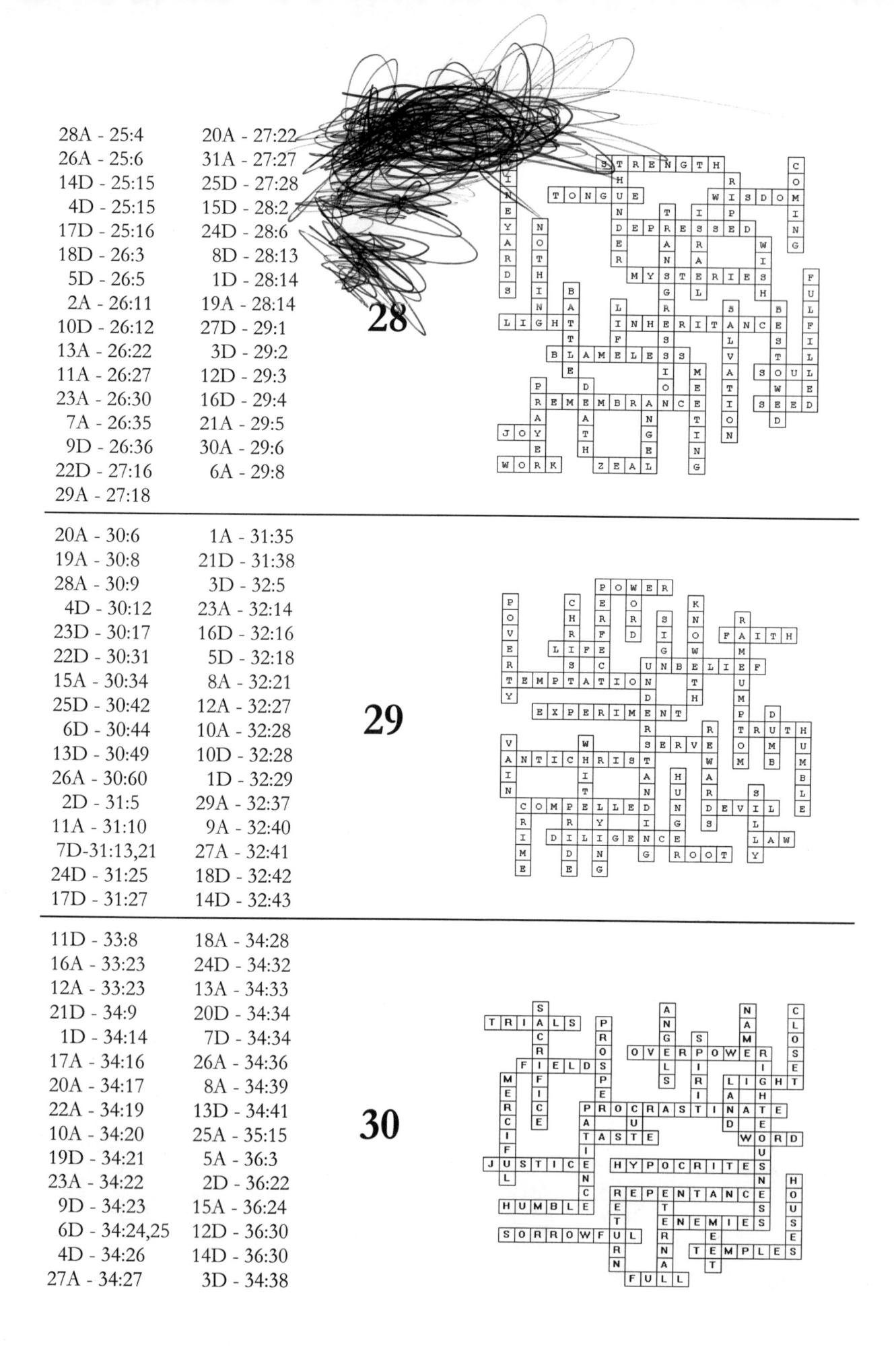

28A - 25:4	20A - 27:22
26A - 25:6	31A - 27:27
14D - 25:15	25D - 27:28
4D - 25:15	15D - 28:2
17D - 25:16	24D - 28:6
18D - 26:3	8D - 28:13
5D - 26:5	1D - 28:14
2A - 26:11	19A - 28:14
10D - 26:12	27D - 29:1
13A - 26:22	3D - 29:2
11A - 26:27	12D - 29:3
23A - 26:30	16D - 29:4
7A - 26:35	21A - 29:5
9D - 26:36	30A - 29:6
22D - 27:16	6A - 29:8
29A - 27:18	

29

20A - 30:6	1A - 31:35
19A - 30:8	21D - 31:38
28A - 30:9	3D - 32:5
4D - 30:12	23A - 32:14
23D - 30:17	16D - 32:16
22D - 30:31	5D - 32:18
15A - 30:34	8A - 32:21
25D - 30:42	12A - 32:27
6D - 30:44	10A - 32:28
13D - 30:49	10D - 32:28
26A - 30:60	1D - 32:29
2D - 31:5	29A - 32:37
11A - 31:10	9A - 32:40
7D - 31:13,21	27A - 32:41
24D - 31:25	18D - 32:42
17D - 31:27	14D - 32:43

30

11D - 33:8	18A - 34:28
16A - 33:23	24D - 34:32
12A - 33:23	13A - 34:33
21D - 34:9	20D - 34:34
1D - 34:14	7D - 34:34
17A - 34:16	26A - 34:36
20A - 34:17	8A - 34:39
22A - 34:19	13D - 34:41
10A - 34:20	25A - 35:15
19D - 34:21	5A - 36:3
23A - 34:22	2D - 36:22
9D - 34:23	15A - 36:24
6D - 34:24,25	12D - 36:30
4D - 34:26	14D - 36:30
27A - 34:27	3D - 34:38

31

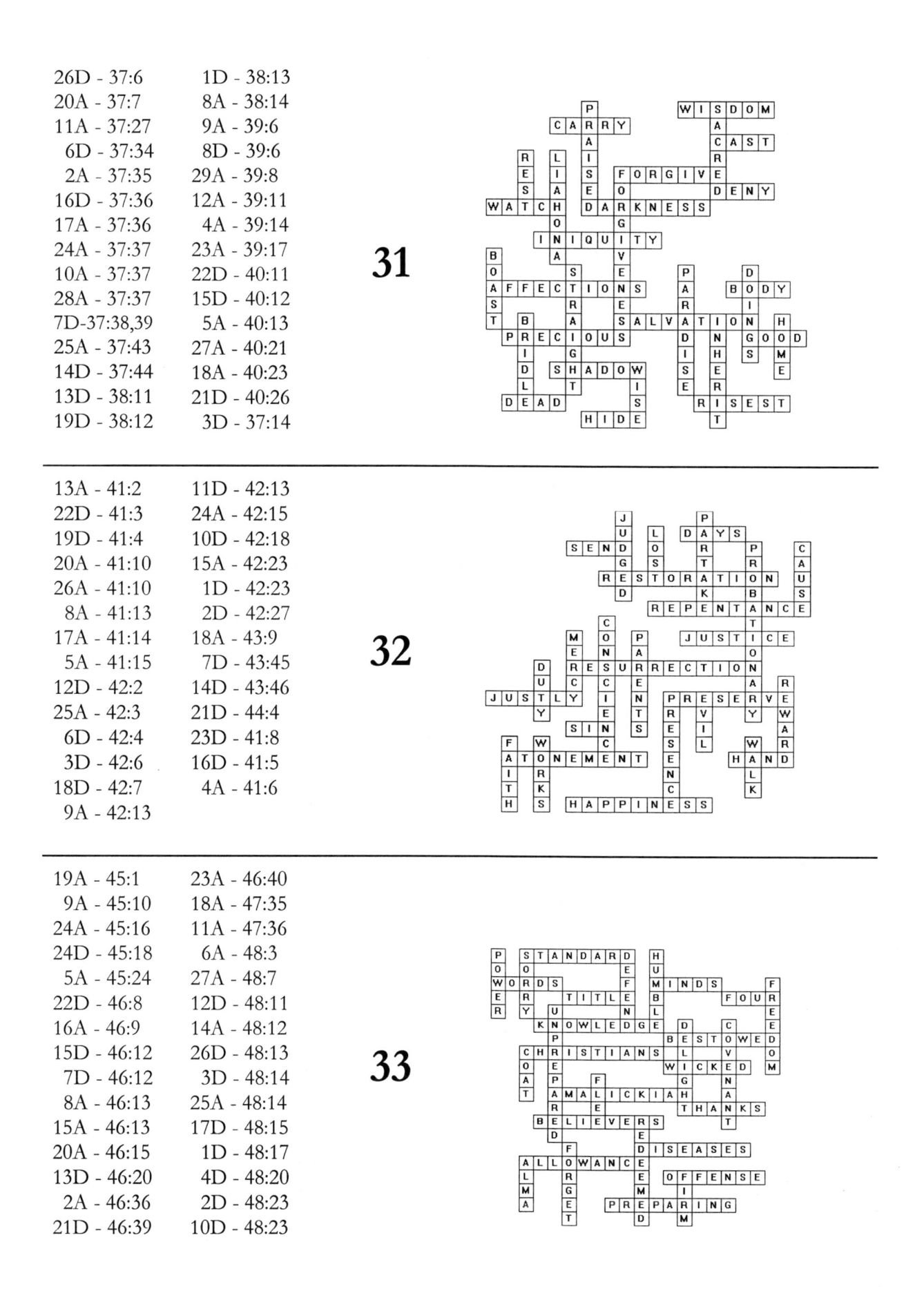

26D - 37:6	1D - 38:13
20A - 37:7	8A - 38:14
11A - 37:27	9A - 39:6
6D - 37:34	8D - 39:6
2A - 37:35	29A - 39:8
16D - 37:36	12A - 39:11
17A - 37:36	4A - 39:14
24A - 37:37	23A - 39:17
10A - 37:37	22D - 40:11
28A - 37:37	15D - 40:12
7D - 37:38,39	5A - 40:13
25A - 37:43	27A - 40:21
14D - 37:44	18A - 40:23
13D - 38:11	21D - 40:26
19D - 38:12	3D - 37:14

32

13A - 41:2	11D - 42:13
22D - 41:3	24A - 42:15
19D - 41:4	10D - 42:18
20A - 41:10	15A - 42:23
26A - 41:10	1D - 42:23
8A - 41:13	2D - 42:27
17A - 41:14	18A - 43:9
5A - 41:15	7D - 43:45
12D - 42:2	14D - 43:46
25A - 42:3	21D - 44:4
6D - 42:4	23D - 41:8
3D - 42:6	16D - 41:5
18D - 42:7	4A - 41:6
9A - 42:13	

33

19A - 45:1	23A - 46:40
9A - 45:10	18A - 47:35
24A - 45:16	11A - 47:36
24D - 45:18	6A - 48:3
5A - 45:24	27A - 48:7
22D - 46:8	12D - 48:11
16A - 46:9	14A - 48:12
15D - 46:12	26D - 48:13
7D - 46:12	3D - 48:14
8A - 46:13	25A - 48:14
15A - 46:13	17D - 48:15
20A - 46:15	1D - 48:17
13D - 46:20	4D - 48:20
2A - 46:36	2D - 48:23
21D - 46:39	10D - 48:23

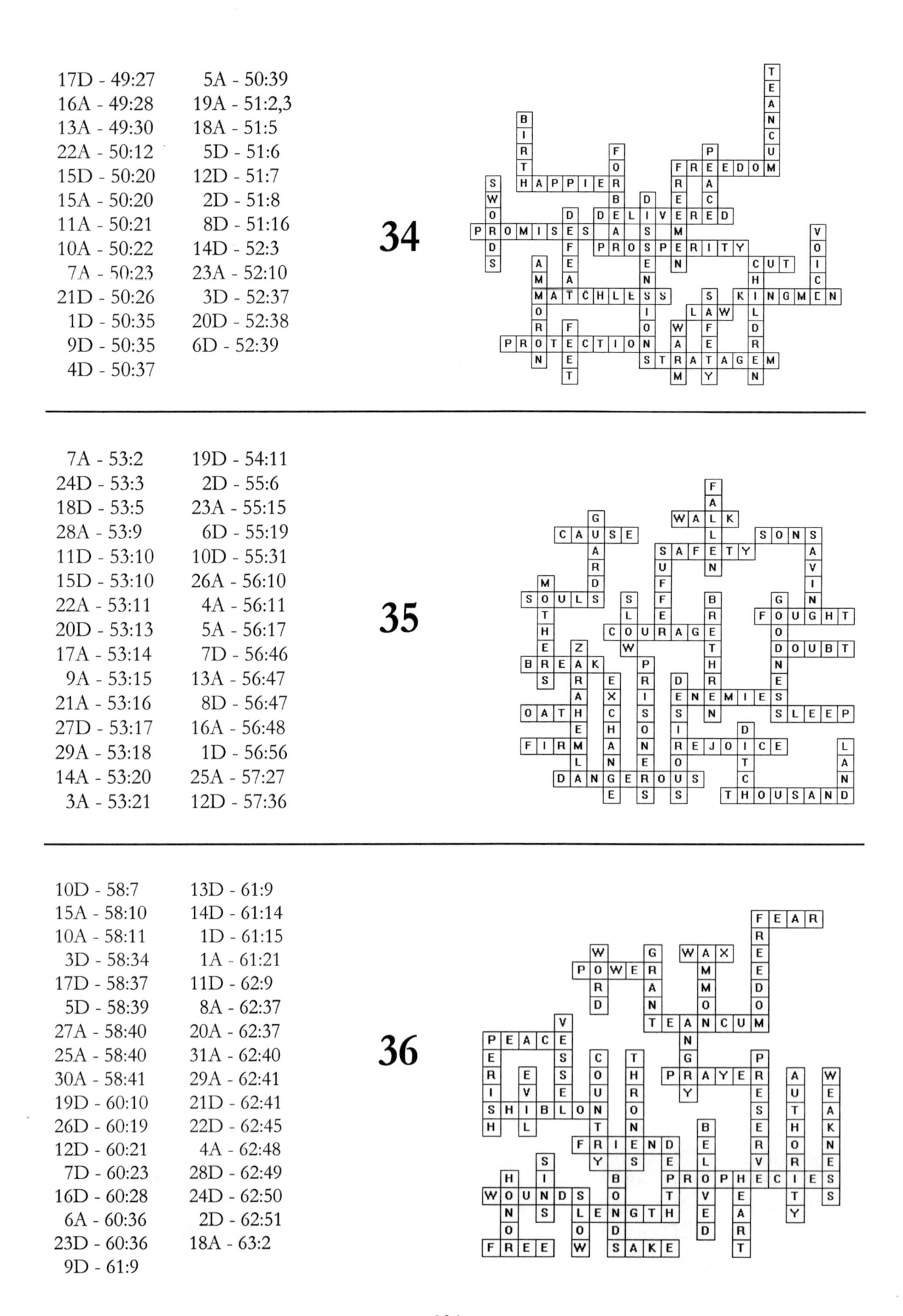

17D - 49:27	5A - 50:39	
16A - 49:28	19A - 51:2,3	
13A - 49:30	18A - 51:5	
22A - 50:12	5D - 51:6	
15D - 50:20	12D - 51:7	**34**
15A - 50:20	2D - 51:8	
11A - 50:21	8D - 51:16	
10A - 50:22	14D - 52:3	
7A - 50:23	23A - 52:10	
21D - 50:26	3D - 52:37	
1D - 50:35	20D - 52:38	
9D - 50:35	6D - 52:39	
4D - 50:37		

7A - 53:2	19D - 54:11	
24D - 53:3	2D - 55:6	
18D - 53:5	23A - 55:15	
28A - 53:9	6D - 55:19	
11D - 53:10	10D - 55:31	
15D - 53:10	26A - 56:10	
22A - 53:11	4A - 56:11	**35**
20D - 53:13	5A - 56:17	
17A - 53:14	7D - 56:46	
9A - 53:15	13A - 56:47	
21A - 53:16	8D - 56:47	
27D - 53:17	16A - 56:48	
29A - 53:18	1D - 56:56	
14A - 53:20	25A - 57:27	
3A - 53:21	12D - 57:36	

10D - 58:7	13D - 61:9	
15A - 58:10	14D - 61:14	
10A - 58:11	1D - 61:15	
3D - 58:34	1A - 61:21	
17D - 58:37	11D - 62:9	
5D - 58:39	8A - 62:37	
27A - 58:40	20A - 62:37	**36**
25A - 58:40	31A - 62:40	
30A - 58:41	29A - 62:41	
19D - 60:10	21D - 62:41	
26D - 60:19	22D - 62:45	
12D - 60:21	4A - 62:48	
7D - 60:23	28D - 62:49	
16D - 60:28	24D - 62:50	
6A - 60:36	2D - 62:51	
23D - 60:36	18A - 63:2	
9D - 61:9		

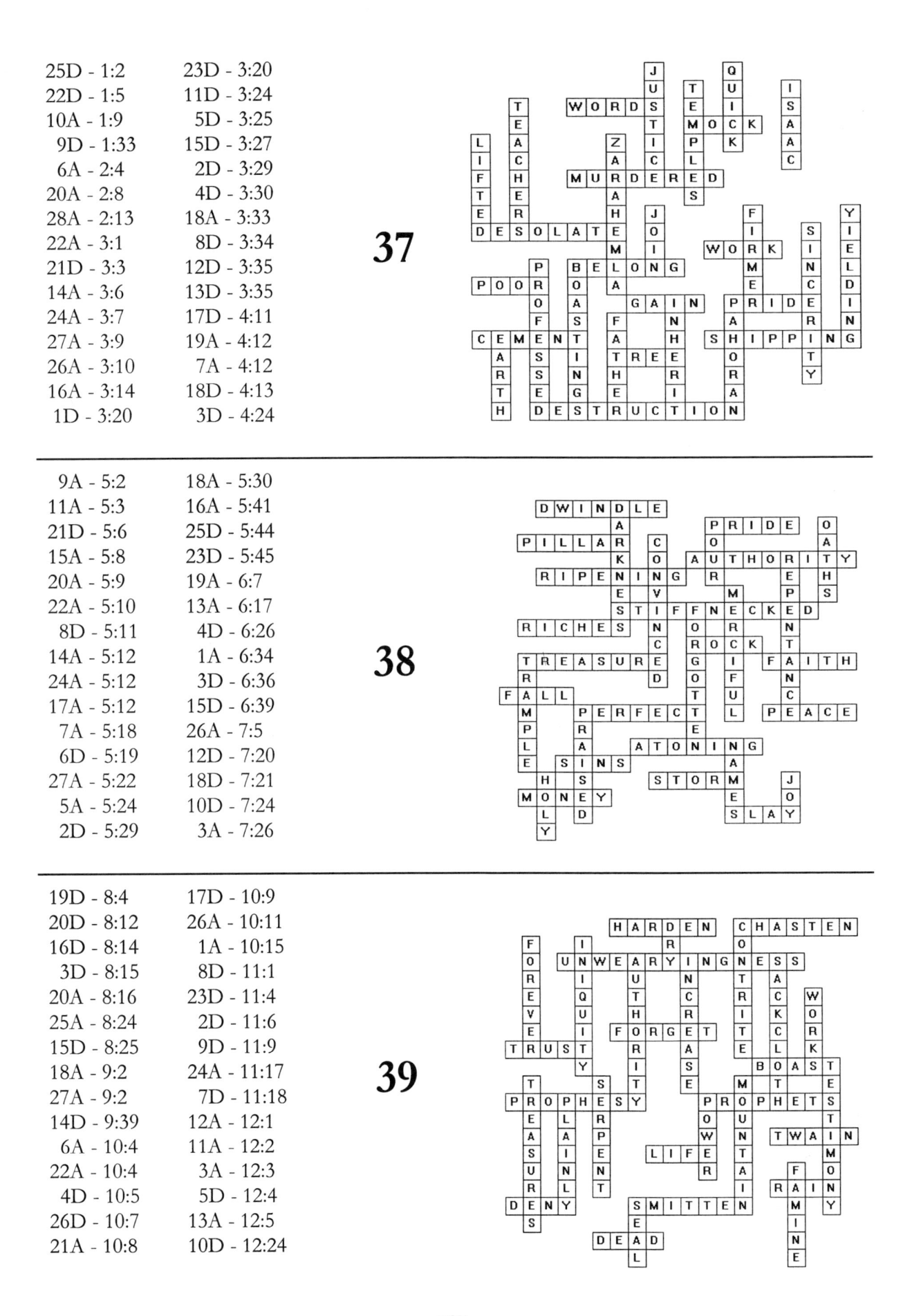

25D - 1:2	23D - 3:20	
22D - 1:5	11D - 3:24	
10A - 1:9	5D - 3:25	
9D - 1:33	15D - 3:27	
6A - 2:4	2D - 3:29	
20A - 2:8	4D - 3:30	
28A - 2:13	18A - 3:33	**37**
22A - 3:1	8D - 3:34	
21D - 3:3	12D - 3:35	
14A - 3:6	13D - 3:35	
24A - 3:7	17D - 4:11	
27A - 3:9	19A - 4:12	
26A - 3:10	7A - 4:12	
16A - 3:14	18D - 4:13	
1D - 3:20	3D - 4:24	

9A - 5:2	18A - 5:30	
11A - 5:3	16A - 5:41	
21D - 5:6	25D - 5:44	
15A - 5:8	23D - 5:45	
20A - 5:9	19A - 6:7	
22A - 5:10	13A - 6:17	
8D - 5:11	4D - 6:26	
14A - 5:12	1A - 6:34	**38**
24A - 5:12	3D - 6:36	
17A - 5:12	15D - 6:39	
7A - 5:18	26A - 7:5	
6D - 5:19	12D - 7:20	
27A - 5:22	18D - 7:21	
5A - 5:24	10D - 7:24	
2D - 5:29	3A - 7:26	

19D - 8:4	17D - 10:9	
20D - 8:12	26A - 10:11	
16D - 8:14	1A - 10:15	
3D - 8:15	8D - 11:1	
20A - 8:16	23D - 11:4	
25A - 8:24	2D - 11:6	
15D - 8:25	9D - 11:9	
18A - 9:2	24A - 11:17	**39**
27A - 9:2	7D - 11:18	
14D - 9:39	12A - 12:1	
6A - 10:4	11A - 12:2	
22A - 10:4	3A - 12:3	
4D - 10:5	5D - 12:4	
26D - 10:7	13A - 12:5	
21A - 10:8	10D - 12:24	

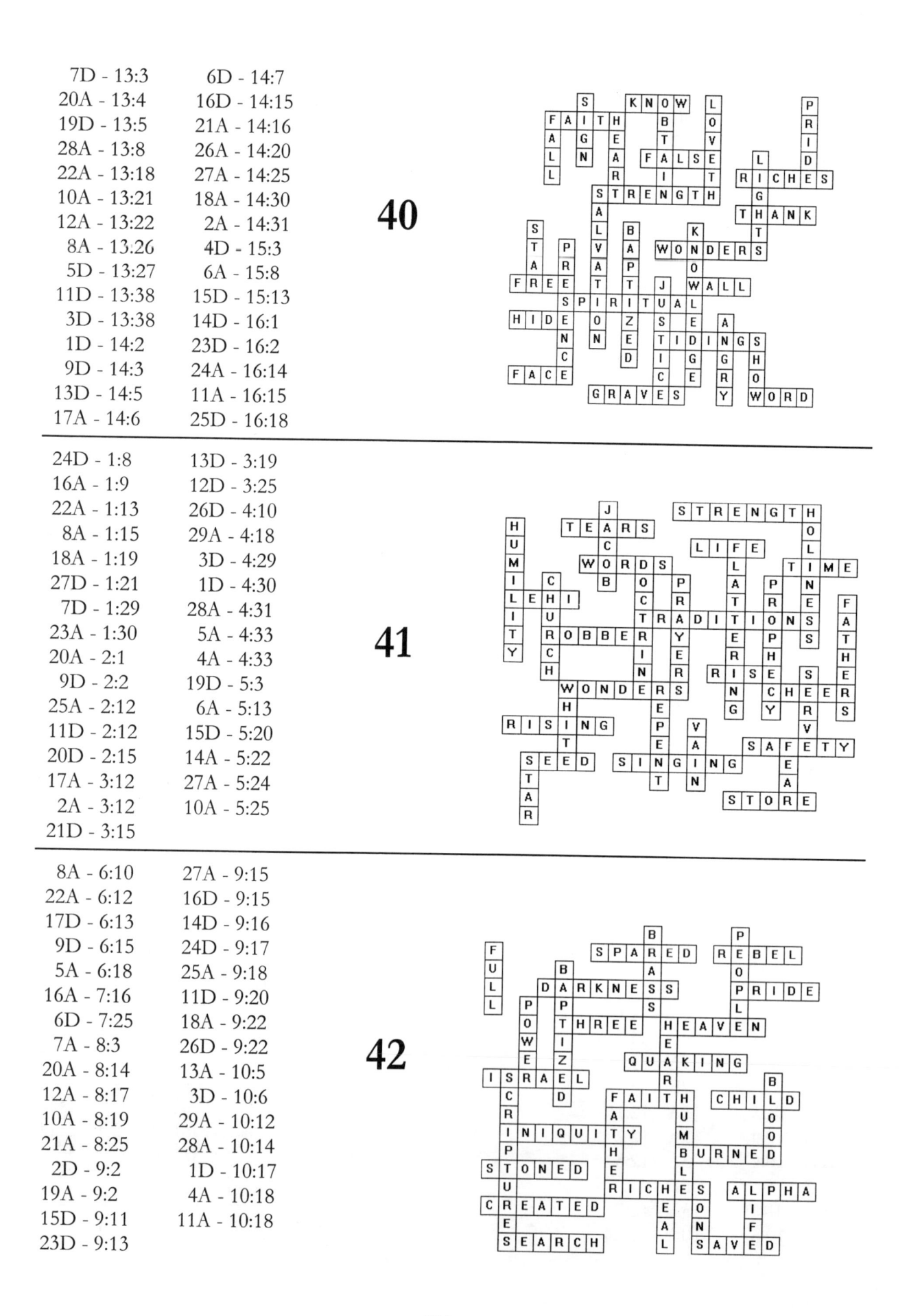

7D - 13:3	6D - 14:7		
20A - 13:4	16D - 14:15		
19D - 13:5	21A - 14:16		
28A - 13:8	26A - 14:20		
22A - 13:18	27A - 14:25		
10A - 13:21	18A - 14:30	**40**	
12A - 13:22	2A - 14:31		
8A - 13:26	4D - 15:3		
5D - 13:27	6A - 15:8		
11D - 13:38	15D - 15:13		
3D - 13:38	14D - 16:1		
1D - 14:2	23D - 16:2		
9D - 14:3	24A - 16:14		
13D - 14:5	11A - 16:15		
17A - 14:6	25D - 16:18		

Puzzle 40 grid contains words: KNOW, LOVE, FAITH, PRIDE, HEART, FALSE, RICHES, STRENGTH, THANK, SALVATION, BAPTIZED, WONDERS, START, FREE, WALL, SPIRITUAL, HIDE, SEE, CONSCIENCE, NEEDED, TIDINGS, GLORY, HO, FACE, GRAVES, WORD

24D - 1:8	13D - 3:19		
16A - 1:9	12D - 3:25		
22A - 1:13	26D - 4:10		
8A - 1:15	29A - 4:18		
18A - 1:19	3D - 4:29		
27D - 1:21	1D - 4:30		
7D - 1:29	28A - 4:31		
23A - 1:30	5A - 4:33	**41**	
20A - 2:1	4A - 4:33		
9D - 2:2	19D - 5:3		
25A - 2:12	6A - 5:13		
11D - 2:12	15D - 5:20		
20D - 2:15	14A - 5:22		
17A - 3:12	27A - 5:24		
2A - 3:12	10A - 5:25		
21D - 3:15			

Puzzle 41 grid contains words: HUMILITY, TEARS, STRENGTH, HOLY, JOCB, LIFE, TIME, WORDS, LEHI, CHURCH, ROBBER, TRADITIONS, PRAYER, FATHERS, RISE, CHEER, WONDERS, RISING, SAFETY, SEED, SINGING, STORE, STAR

8A - 6:10	27A - 9:15		
22A - 6:12	16D - 9:15		
17D - 6:13	14D - 9:16		
9D - 6:15	24D - 9:17		
5A - 6:18	25A - 9:18		
16A - 7:16	11D - 9:20		
6D - 7:25	18A - 9:22		
7A - 8:3	26D - 9:22	**42**	
20A - 8:14	13A - 10:5		
12A - 8:17	3D - 10:6		
10A - 8:19	29A - 10:12		
21A - 8:25	28A - 10:14		
2D - 9:2	1D - 10:17		
19A - 9:2	4A - 10:18		
15D - 9:11	11A - 10:18		
23D - 9:13			

Puzzle 42 grid contains words: FULL, SPARED, REBEL, POWER, BAPTIZED, DARKNESS, PRIDE, THREE, HEAVEN, ISRAEL, QUAKING, SCRIPTURE, FAITH, CHILD, HUMBLE, INIQUITY, BLOOD, STONED, BURNED, CREATED, RICHES, ALPHA, SEARCH, SAVED

43

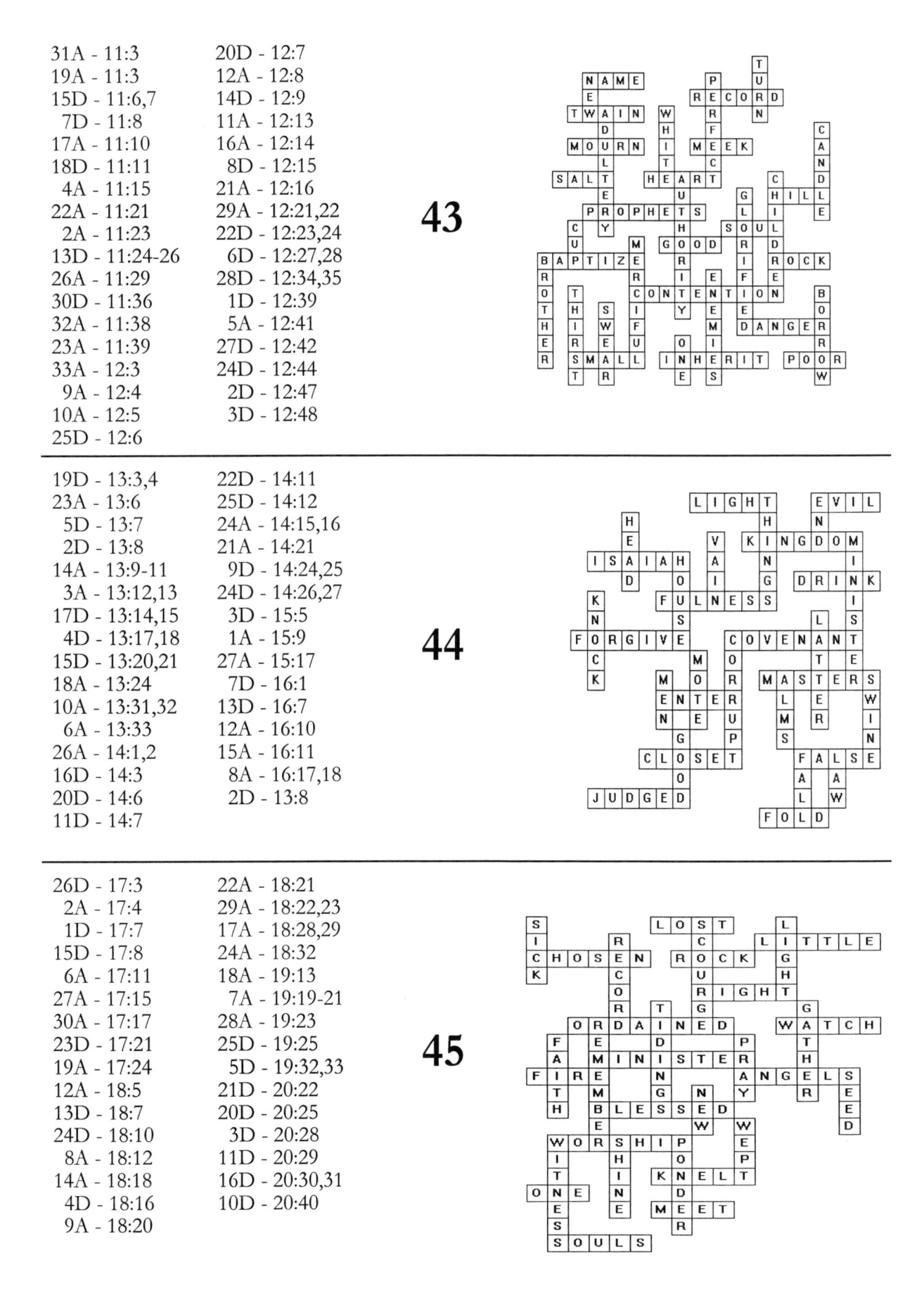

Clue	Ref
31A	11:3
19A	11:3
15D	11:6,7
7D	11:8
17A	11:10
18D	11:11
4A	11:15
22A	11:21
2A	11:23
13D	11:24-26
26A	11:29
30D	11:36
32A	11:38
23A	11:39
33A	12:3
9A	12:4
10A	12:5
25D	12:6
20D	12:7
12A	12:8
14D	12:9
11A	12:13
16A	12:14
8D	12:15
21A	12:16
29A	12:21,22
22D	12:23,24
6D	12:27,28
28D	12:34,35
1D	12:39
5A	12:41
27D	12:42
24D	12:44
2D	12:47
3D	12:48

44

Clue	Ref
19D	13:3,4
23A	13:6
5D	13:7
2D	13:8
14A	13:9-11
3A	13:12,13
17D	13:14,15
4D	13:17,18
15D	13:20,21
18A	13:24
10A	13:31,32
6A	13:33
26A	14:1,2
16D	14:3
20D	14:6
11D	14:7
22D	14:11
25D	14:12
24A	14:15,16
21A	14:21
9D	14:24,25
24D	14:26,27
3D	15:5
1A	15:9
27A	15:17
7D	16:1
13D	16:7
12A	16:10
15A	16:11
8A	16:17,18
2D	13:8

45

Clue	Ref
26D	17:3
2A	17:4
1D	17:7
15D	17:8
6A	17:11
27A	17:15
30A	17:17
23D	17:21
19A	17:24
12A	18:5
13D	18:7
24D	18:10
8A	18:12
14A	18:18
4D	18:16
9A	18:20
22A	18:21
29A	18:22,23
17A	18:28,29
24A	18:32
18A	19:13
7A	19:19-21
28A	19:23
25D	19:25
5D	19:32,33
21D	20:22
20D	20:25
3D	20:28
11D	20:29
16D	20:30,31
10D	20:40

46

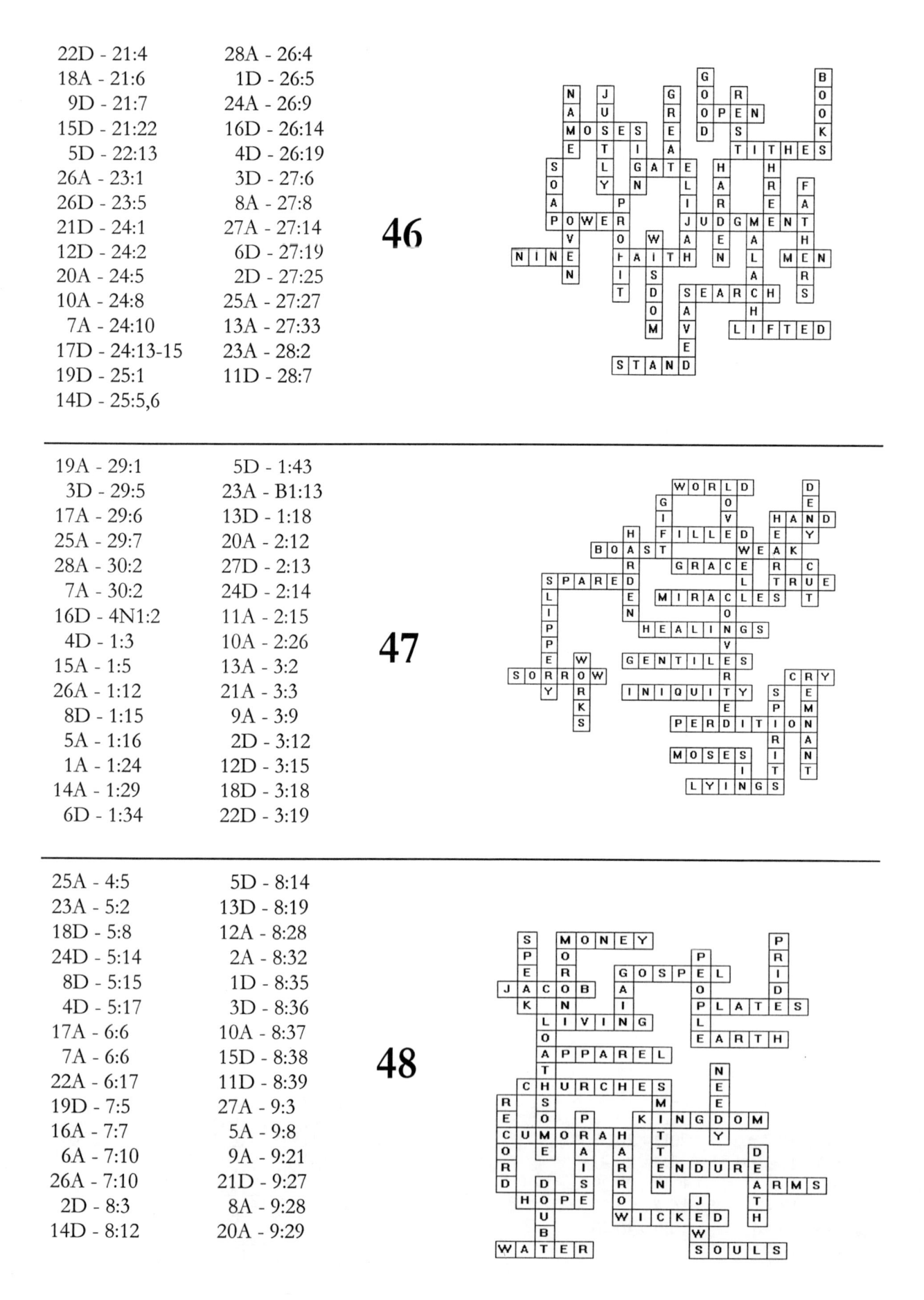

22D - 21:4	28A - 26:4
18A - 21:6	1D - 26:5
9D - 21:7	24A - 26:9
15D - 21:22	16D - 26:14
5D - 22:13	4D - 26:19
26A - 23:1	3D - 27:6
26D - 23:5	8A - 27:8
21D - 24:1	27A - 27:14
12D - 24:2	6D - 27:19
20A - 24:5	2D - 27:25
10A - 24:8	25A - 27:27
7A - 24:10	13A - 27:33
17D - 24:13-15	23A - 28:2
19D - 25:1	11D - 28:7
14D - 25:5,6	

47

19A - 29:1	5D - 1:43
3D - 29:5	23A - B1:13
17A - 29:6	13D - 1:18
25A - 29:7	20A - 2:12
28A - 30:2	27D - 2:13
7A - 30:2	24D - 2:14
16D - 4N1:2	11A - 2:15
4D - 1:3	10A - 2:26
15A - 1:5	13A - 3:2
26A - 1:12	21A - 3:3
8D - 1:15	9A - 3:9
5A - 1:16	2D - 3:12
1A - 1:24	12D - 3:15
14A - 1:29	18D - 3:18
6D - 1:34	22D - 3:19

48

25A - 4:5	5D - 8:14
23A - 5:2	13D - 8:19
18D - 5:8	12A - 8:28
24D - 5:14	2A - 8:32
8D - 5:15	1D - 8:35
4D - 5:17	3D - 8:36
17A - 6:6	10A - 8:37
7A - 6:6	15D - 8:38
22A - 6:17	11D - 8:39
19D - 7:5	27A - 9:3
16A - 7:7	5A - 9:8
6A - 7:10	9A - 9:21
26A - 7:10	21D - 9:27
2D - 8:3	8A - 9:28
14D - 8:12	20A - 9:29

208

49

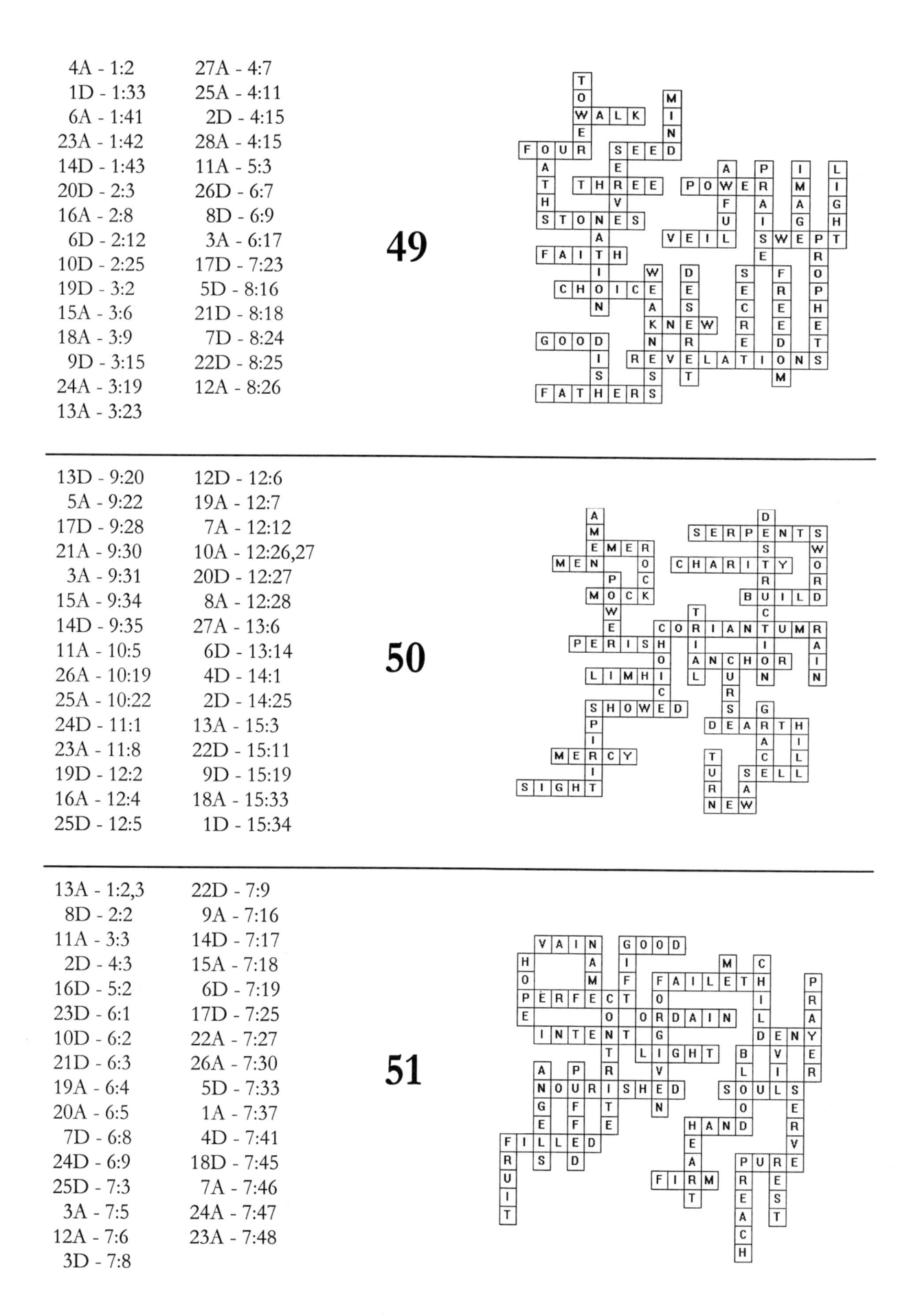

4A - 1:2	27A - 4:7
1D - 1:33	25A - 4:11
6A - 1:41	2D - 4:15
23A - 1:42	28A - 4:15
14D - 1:43	11A - 5:3
20D - 2:3	26D - 6:7
16A - 2:8	8D - 6:9
6D - 2:12	3A - 6:17
10D - 2:25	17D - 7:23
19D - 3:2	5D - 8:16
15A - 3:6	21D - 8:18
18A - 3:9	7D - 8:24
9D - 3:15	22D - 8:25
24A - 3:19	12A - 8:26
13A - 3:23	

50

13D - 9:20	12D - 12:6
5A - 9:22	19A - 12:7
17D - 9:28	7A - 12:12
21A - 9:30	10A - 12:26,27
3A - 9:31	20D - 12:27
15A - 9:34	8A - 12:28
14D - 9:35	27A - 13:6
11A - 10:5	6D - 13:14
26A - 10:19	4D - 14:1
25A - 10:22	2D - 14:25
24D - 11:1	13A - 15:3
23A - 11:8	22D - 15:11
19D - 12:2	9D - 15:19
16A - 12:4	18A - 15:33
25D - 12:5	1D - 15:34

51

13A - 1:2,3	22D - 7:9
8D - 2:2	9A - 7:16
11A - 3:3	14D - 7:17
2D - 4:3	15A - 7:18
16D - 5:2	6D - 7:19
23D - 6:1	17D - 7:25
10D - 6:2	22A - 7:27
21D - 6:3	26A - 7:30
19A - 6:4	5D - 7:33
20A - 6:5	1A - 7:37
7D - 6:8	4D - 7:41
24D - 6:9	18D - 7:45
25D - 7:3	7A - 7:46
3A - 7:5	24A - 7:47
12A - 7:6	23A - 7:48
3D - 7:8	

209

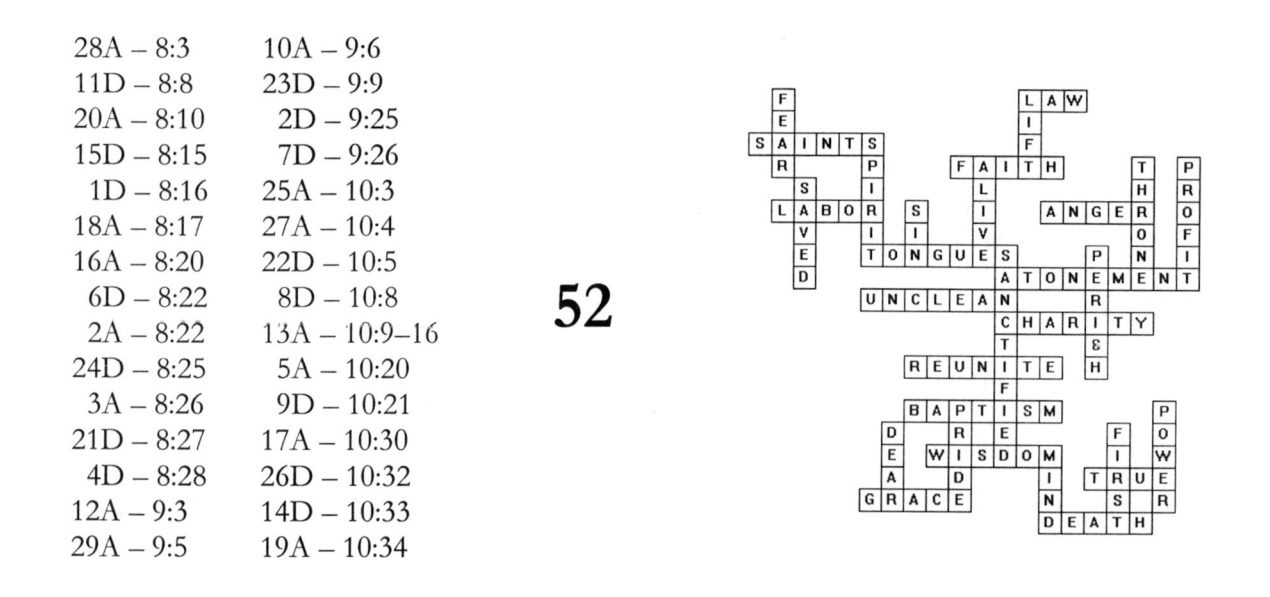

28A – 8:3
11D – 8:8
20A – 8:10
15D – 8:15
1D – 8:16
18A – 8:17
16A – 8:20
6D – 8:22
2A – 8:22
24D – 8:25
3A – 8:26
21D – 8:27
4D – 8:28
12A – 9:3
29A – 9:5

10A – 9:6
23D – 9:9
2D – 9:25
7D – 9:26
25A – 10:3
27A – 10:4
22D – 10:5
8D – 10:8
13A – 10:9–16
5A – 10:20
9D – 10:21
17A – 10:30
26D – 10:32
14D – 10:33
19A – 10:34

52

SCRIPTURE FALLS SOLUTIONS

Scripture Fall:	Answer:	Found in the reading for:
# 1	1 Nephi 3:7	Puzzle ONE
# 2	1 Nephi 19:23	Puzzle FIVE
# 3	2 Nephi 2:25	Puzzle SIX
# 4	2 Nephi 2:27	Puzzle SIX
# 5	2 Nephi 9:28–29	Puzzle SEVEN
# 6	2 Nephi 28:7–9	Puzzle TEN
# 7	2 Nephi 32:3	Puzzle ELEVEN
# 8	2 Nephi 32:8–9	Puzzle ELEVEN
# 9	Jacob 2:18–19	Puzzle TWELVE
#10	Mosiah 2:17	Puzzle FOURTEEN
#11	Mosiah 3:19	Puzzle FOURTEEN
#12	Mosiah 4:30	Puzzle FIFTEEN
#13	Alma 32:21	Puzzle TWENTY–NINE
#14	Alma 34:32–34	Puzzle THIRTY
#15	Alma 37:6–7	Puzzle THIRTY–ONE
#16	Alma 37:35	Puzzle THIRTY–ONE
#17	Alma 41:10	Puzzle THIRTY–TWO
#18	Helaman 5:12	Puzzle THIRTY–EIGHT
#19	3 Nephi 11:29	Puzzle FORTY–THREE
#20	3 Nephi 27:27	Puzzle FORTY–SIX
#21	Ether 12:6	Puzzle FIFTY
#22	Ether 12:27	Puzzle FIFTY
#23	Moroni 7:16–17	Puzzle FIFTY–ONE
#24	Moroni 7:45	Puzzle FIFTY–ONE
#25	Moroni 10:4–5	Puzzle FIFTY–TWO

ONE

TWO

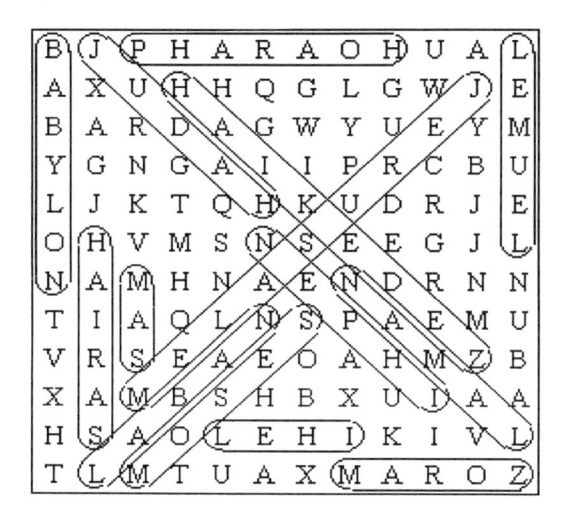

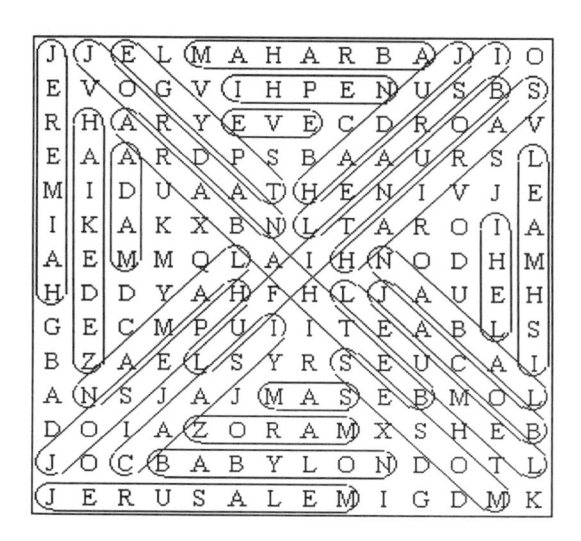

THREE

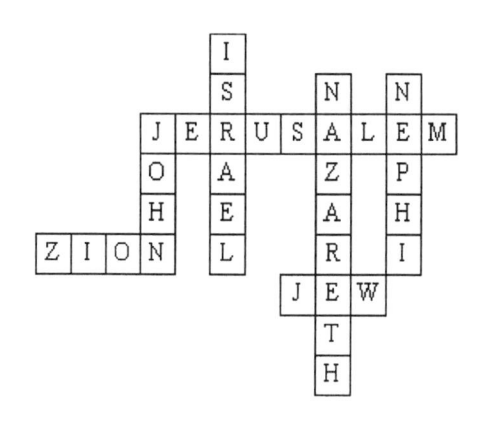

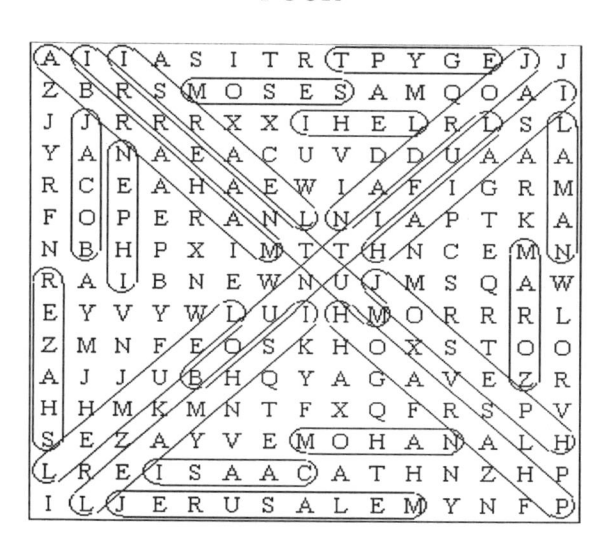

(Crypto:1 Nephi 11:22)

FOUR

FIVE

SIX

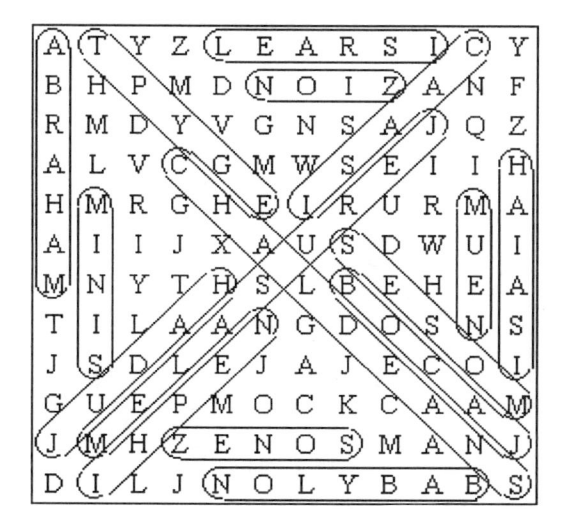

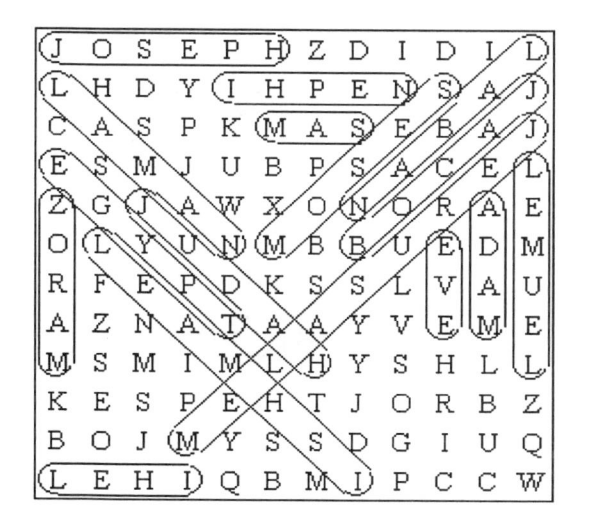

SEVEN

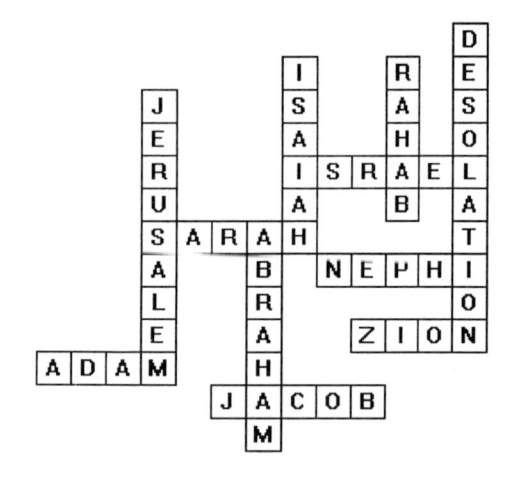

EIGHT

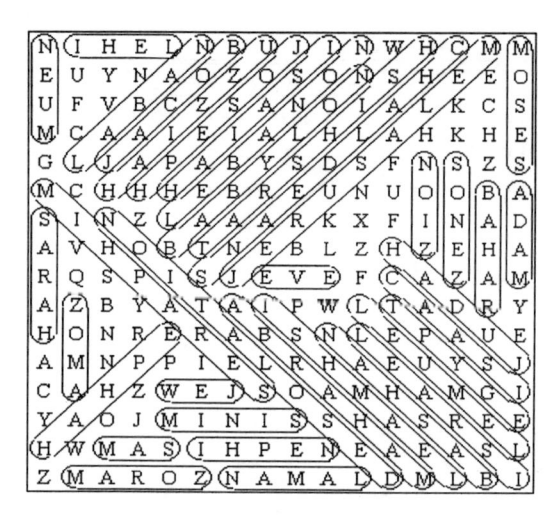

NINE

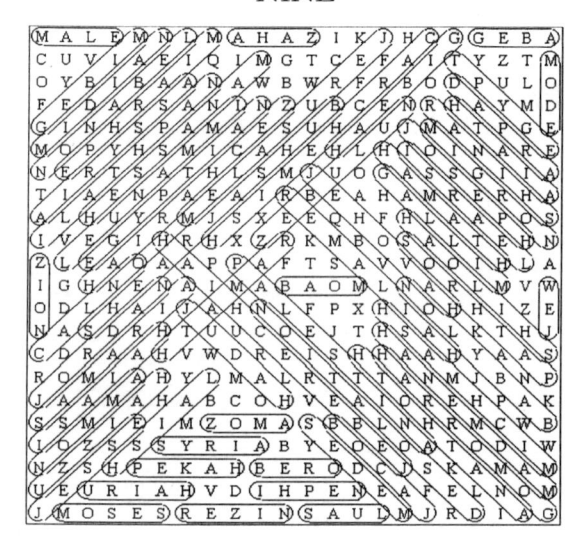

TEN

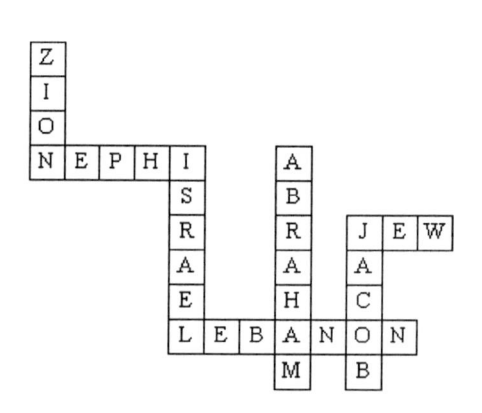

(Crypto: 2 Nephi 27:25)

ELEVEN

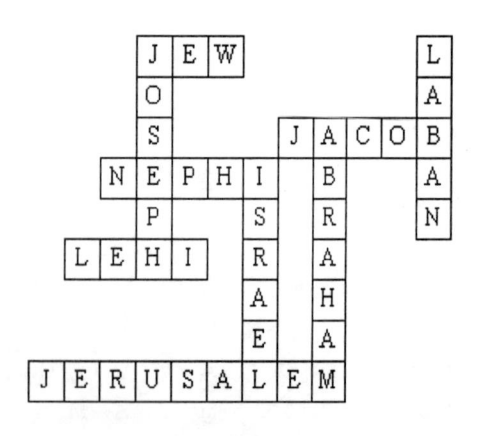

(Crypto: 2 Nephi 31:20)

TWELVE

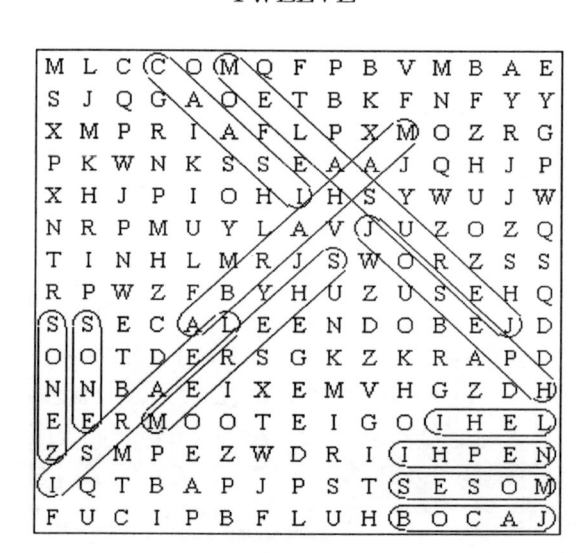

THIRTEEN

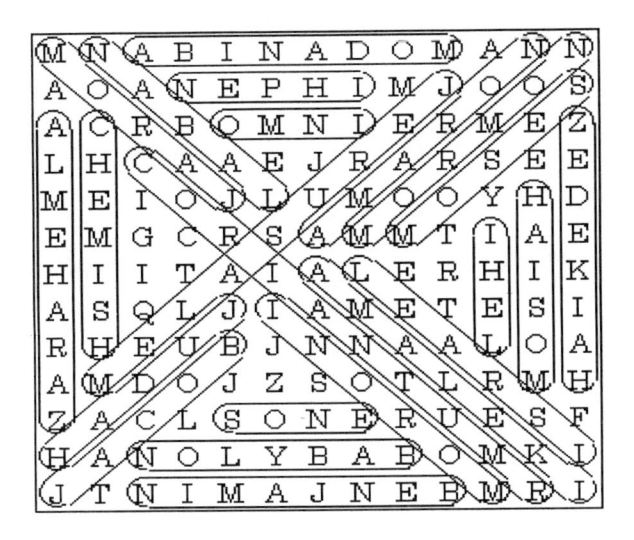

FOURTEEN

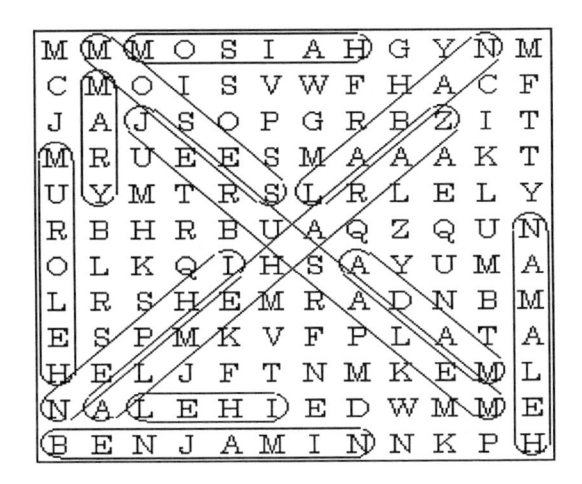

FIFTEEN

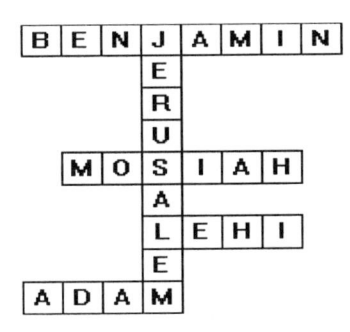

(Crypto: Mosiah 4:15)

SIXTEEN

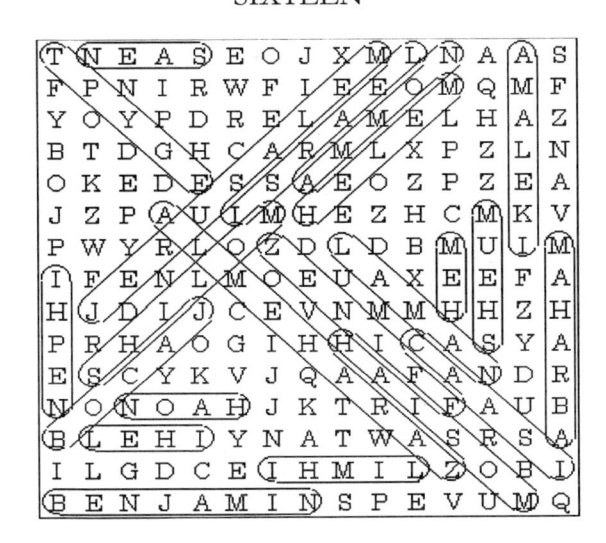

SEVENTEEN

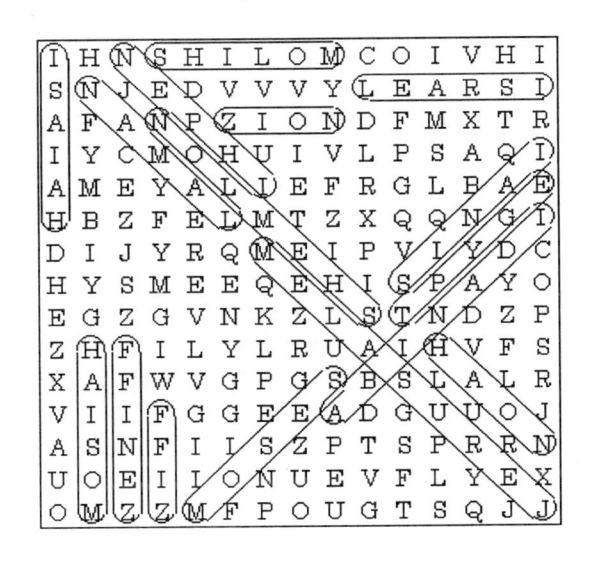

EIGHTEEN

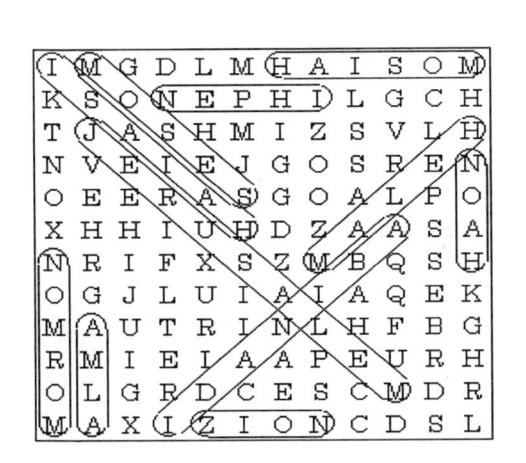

NINETEEN

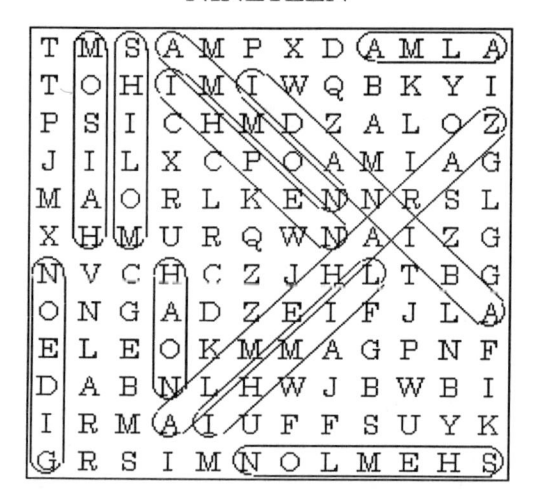

TWENTY

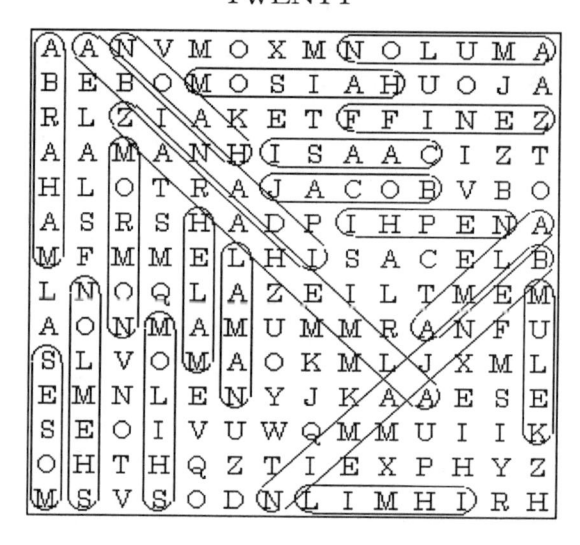

TWENTY-ONE

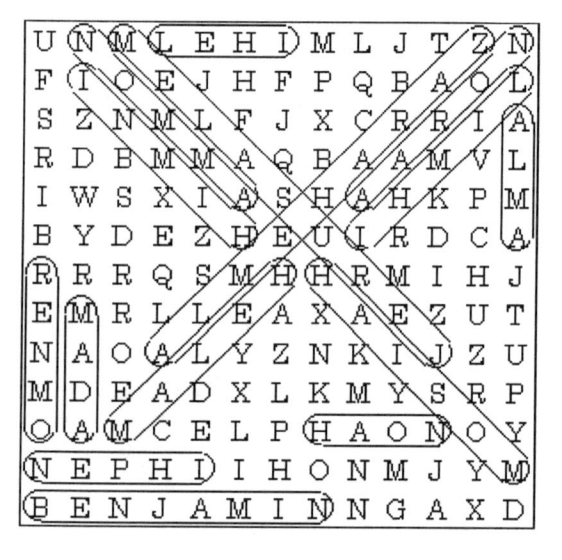

TWENTY-TWO

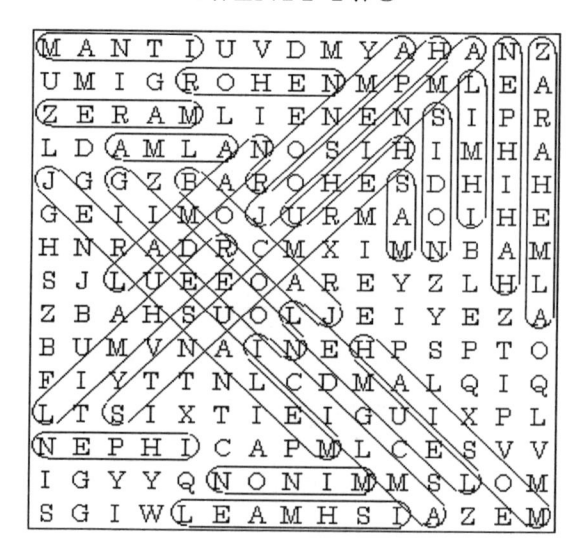

TWENTY-THREE

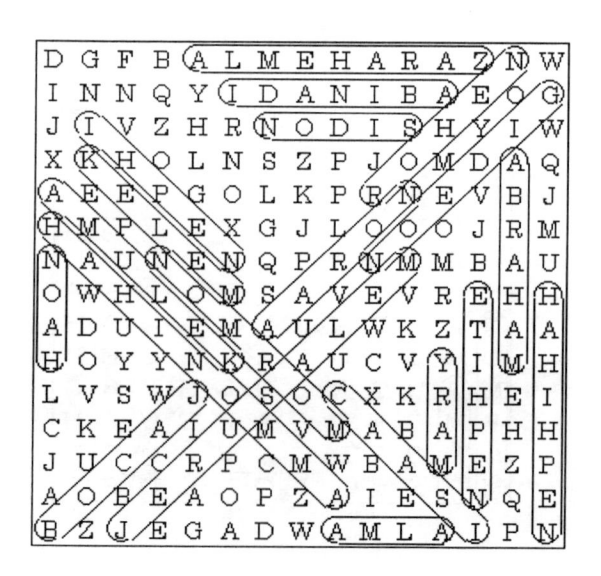

TWENTY-FOUR

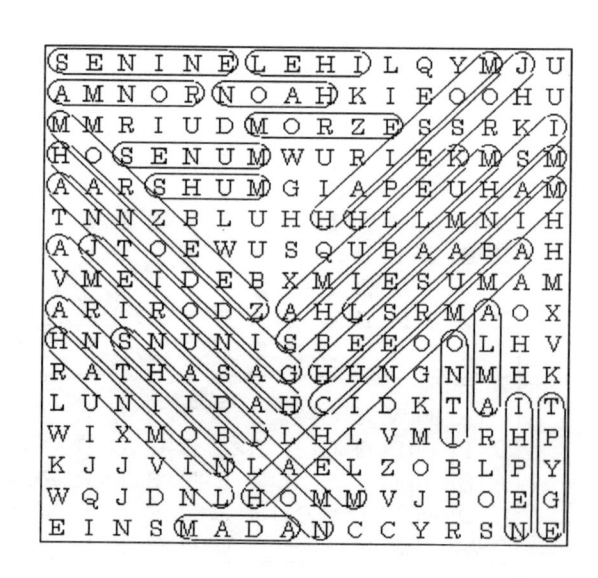

214

TWENTY-FIVE

TWENTY-SIX

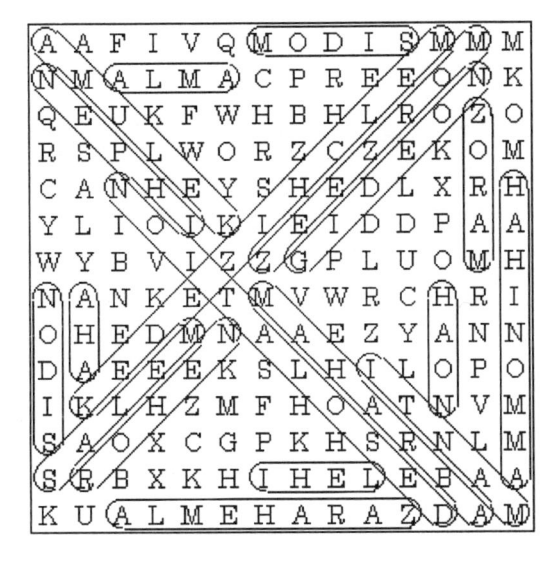

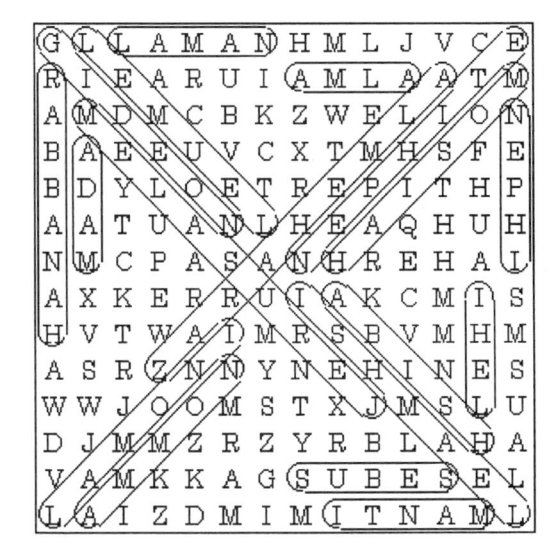

TWENTY-SEVEN

TWENTY-EIGHT

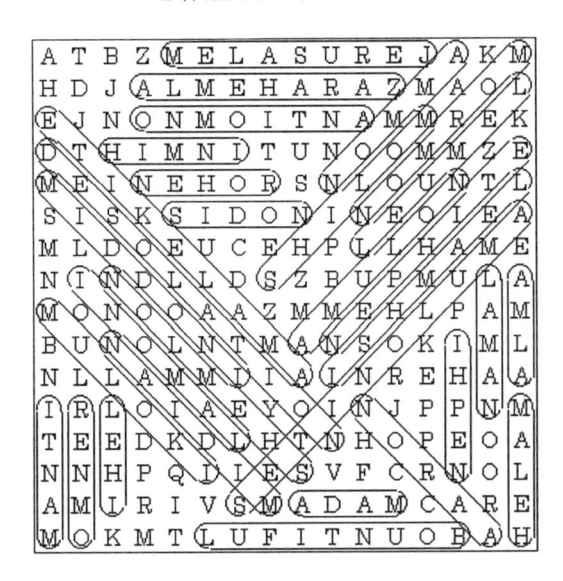

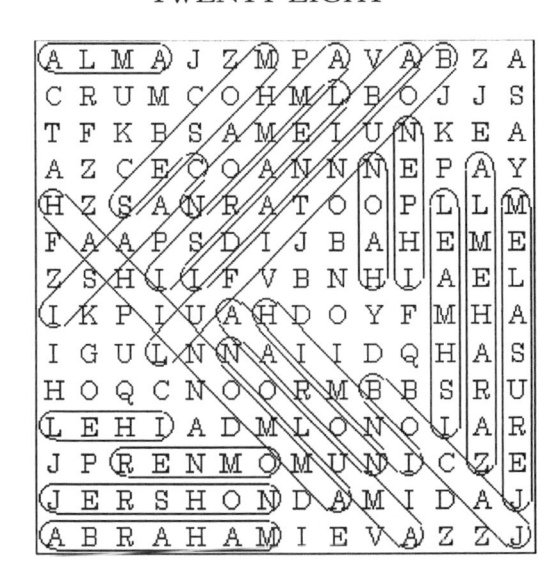

TWENTY-NINE

THIRTY

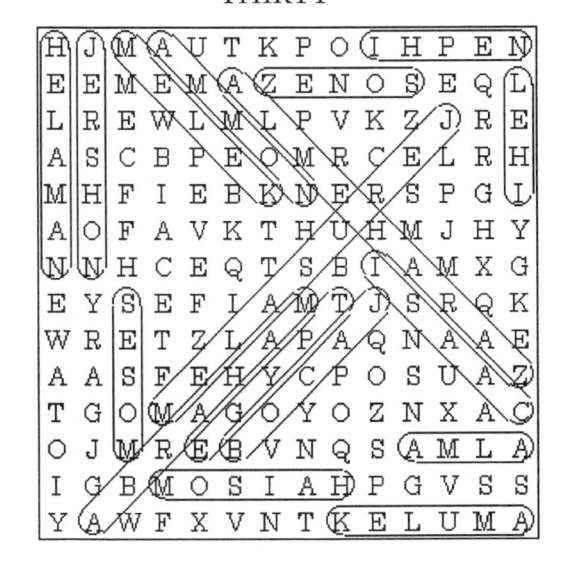

THIRTY-ONE

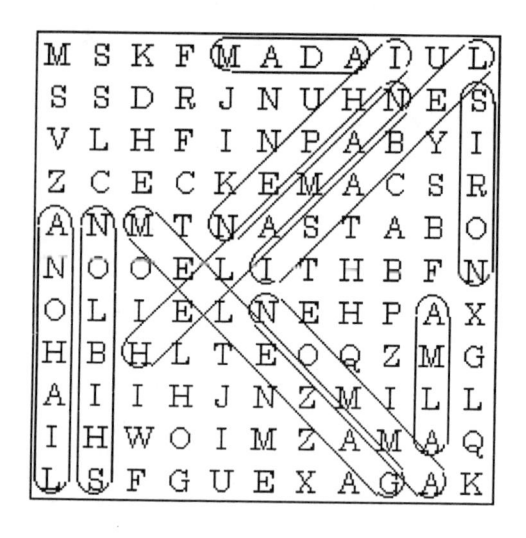

THIRTY-TWO

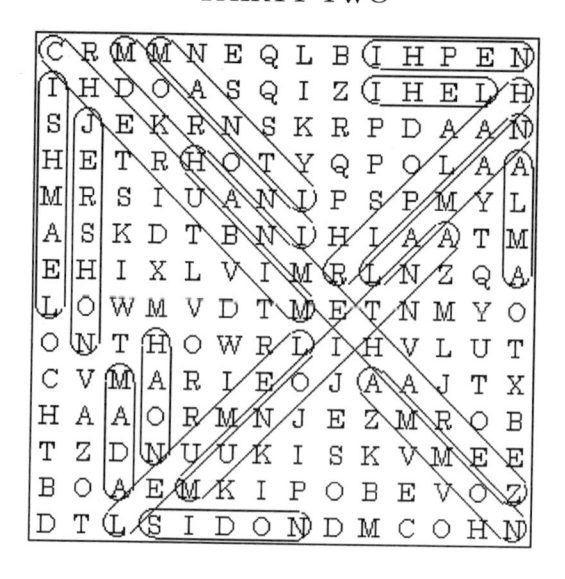

THIRTY-THREE

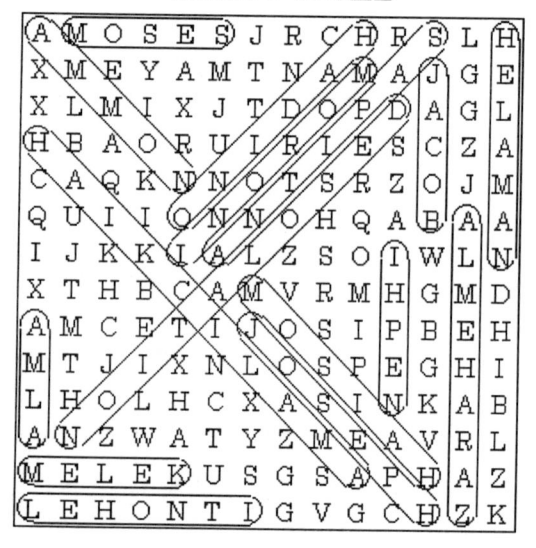

THIRTY-FOUR

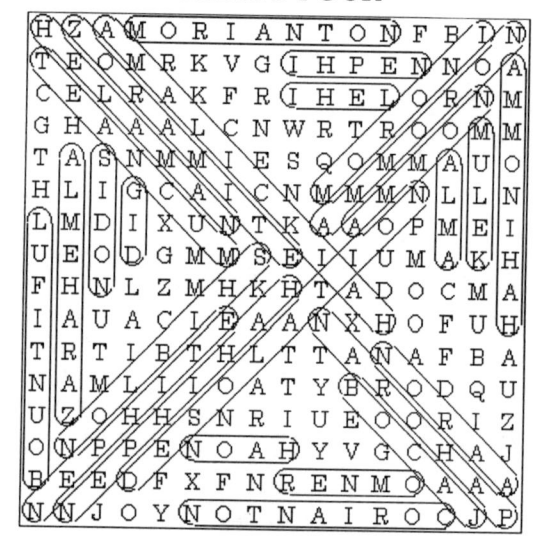

THIRTY-FIVE

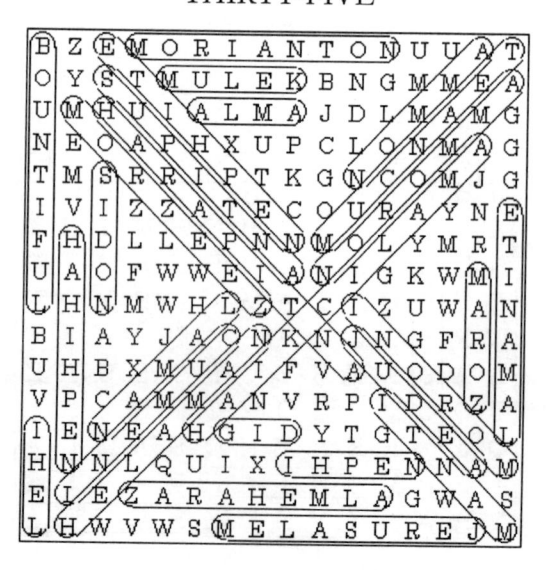

THIRTY-SIX

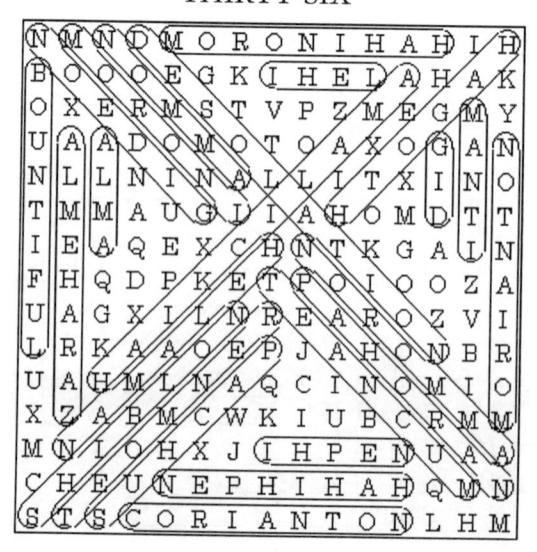

THIRTY-SEVEN

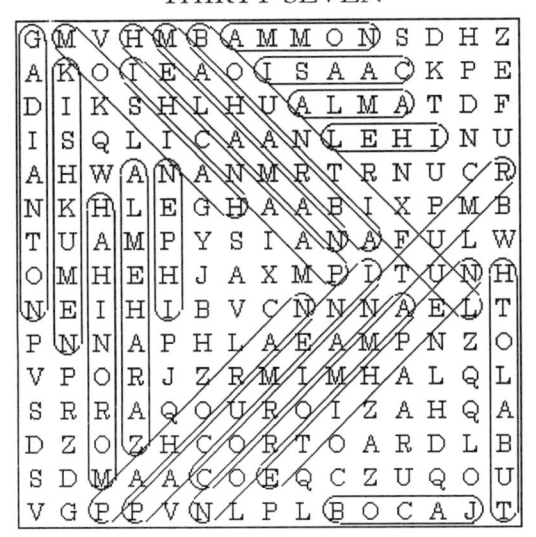

THIRTY-EIGHT

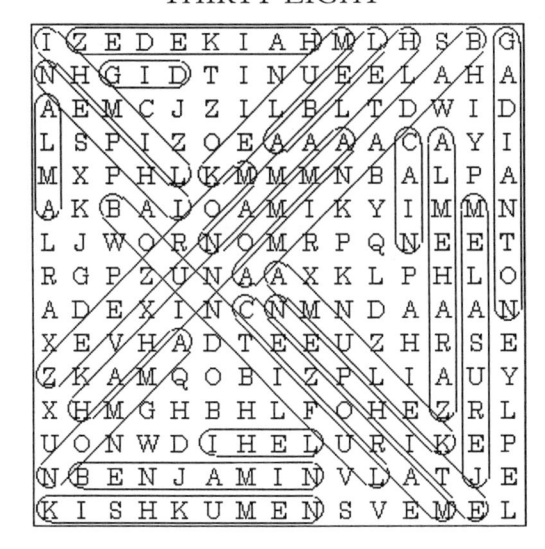

THIRTY-NINE

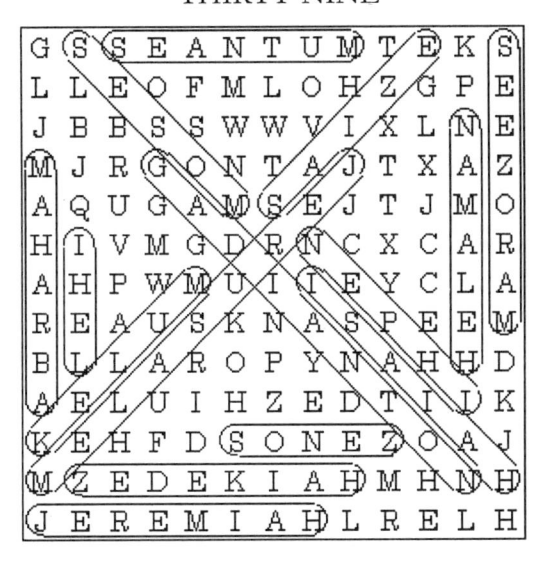

FORTY

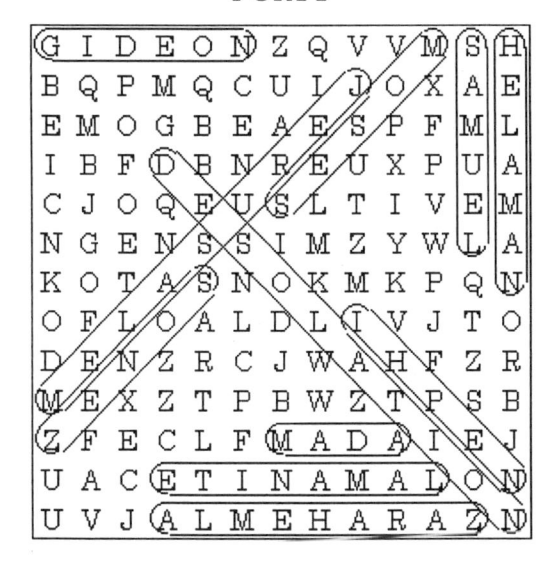

FORTY-ONE

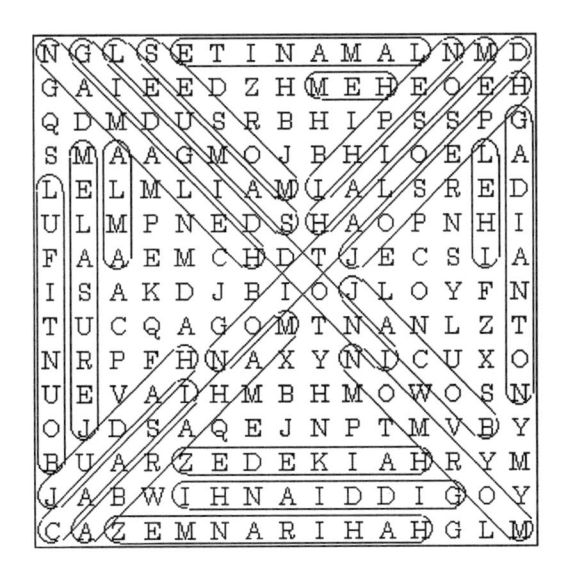

FORTY-TWO

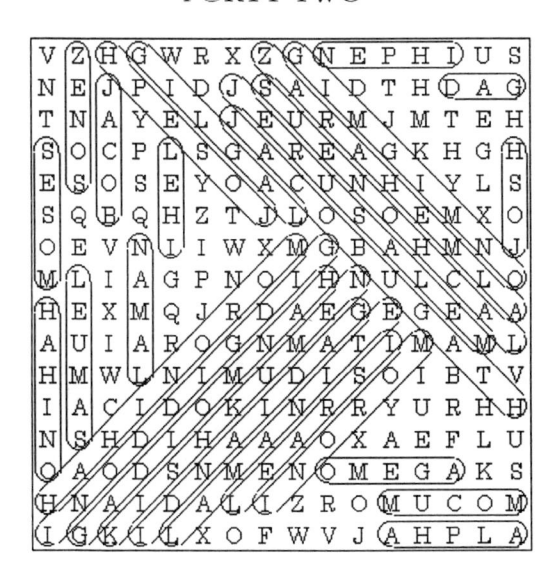

FORTY-THREE

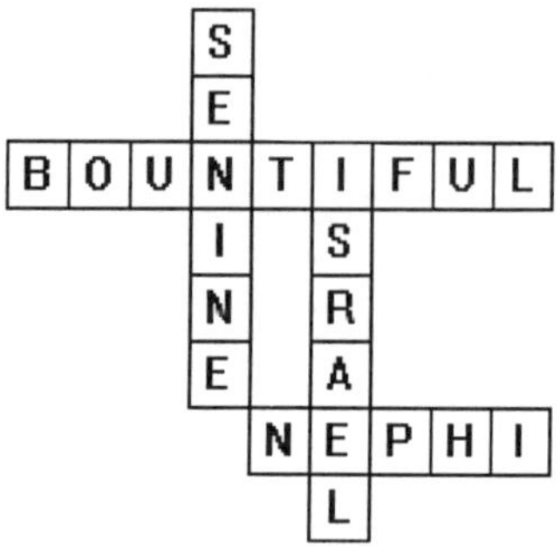

(Crypto: 3 Nephi 11:7)

FORTY-FOUR

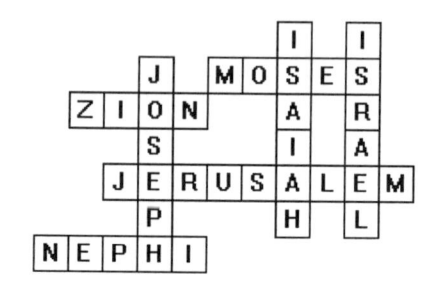

(Crypto: 3 Nephi 13:33)

FORTY-FIVE

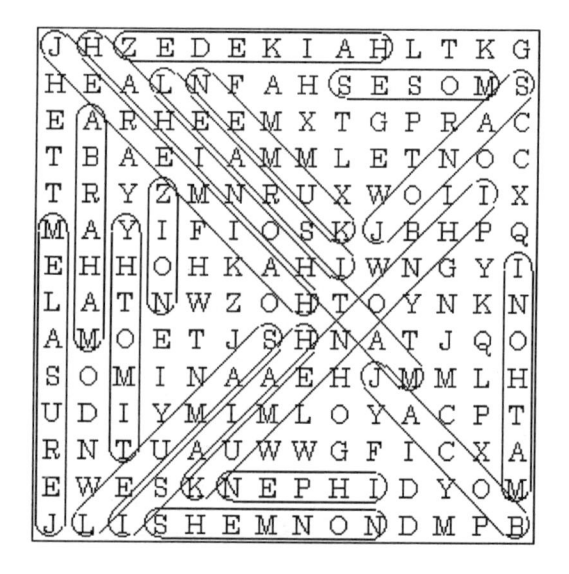

FORTY-SIX

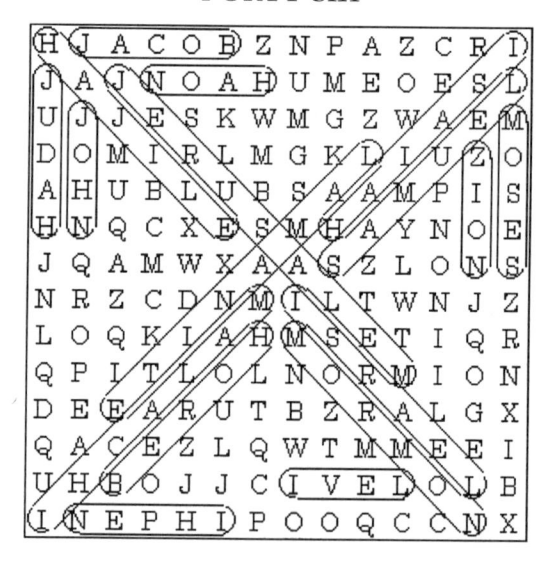

FORTY-SEVEN

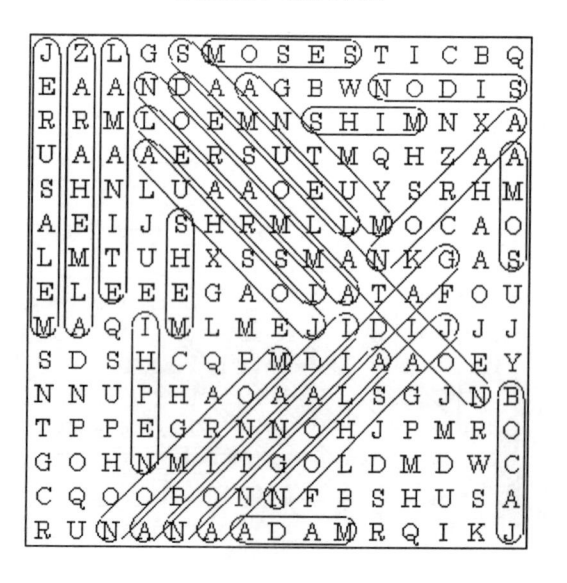

FORTY-EIGHT

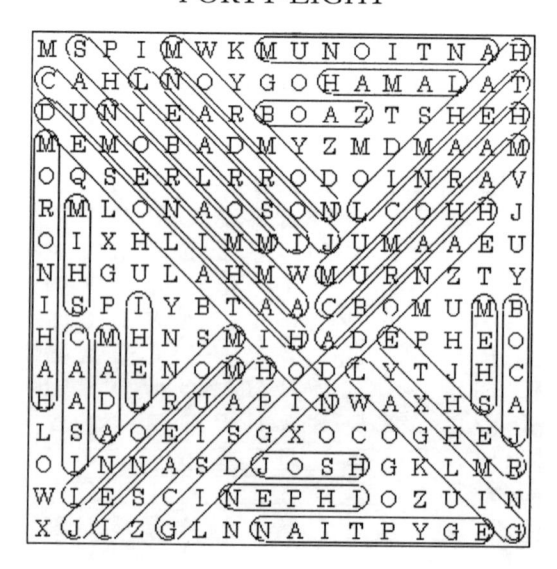

FORTY-NINE

FIFTY

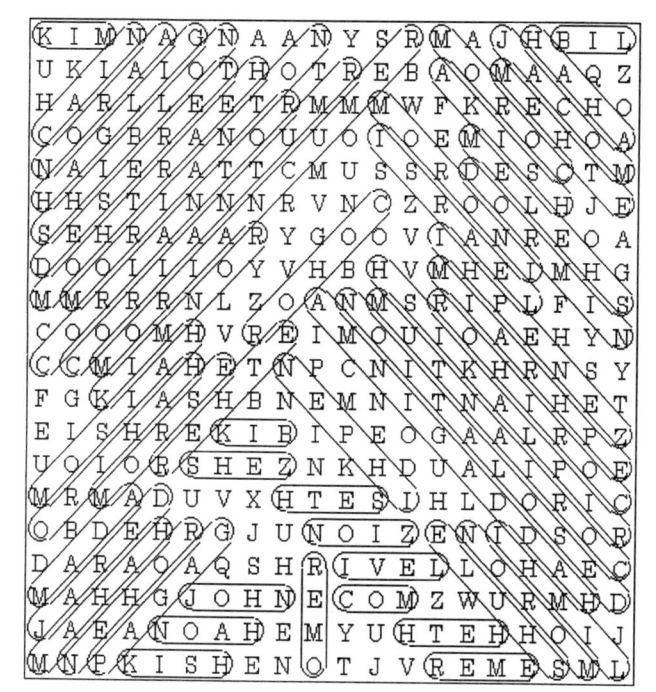

FIFTY-ONE

(Crypto: Moroni 7:47)

FIFTY-TWO

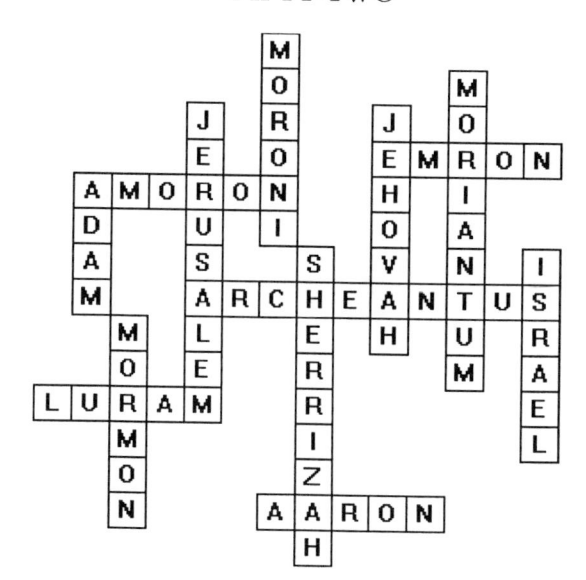

ABOUT THE AUTHOR

The mother of five children, Susan B. Nielsen originally developed the puzzles in this book for her family to help them study The Book of Mormon. She began with a pencil and some graph paper. The puzzles were then further developed and refined over a period of ten years.

Susan enjoys family history, sewing, gardening, camping, and backpacking with her family. She and her husband, Brett, live with their four daughters in Caldwell, Idaho, and have a son on a mission in Chile.

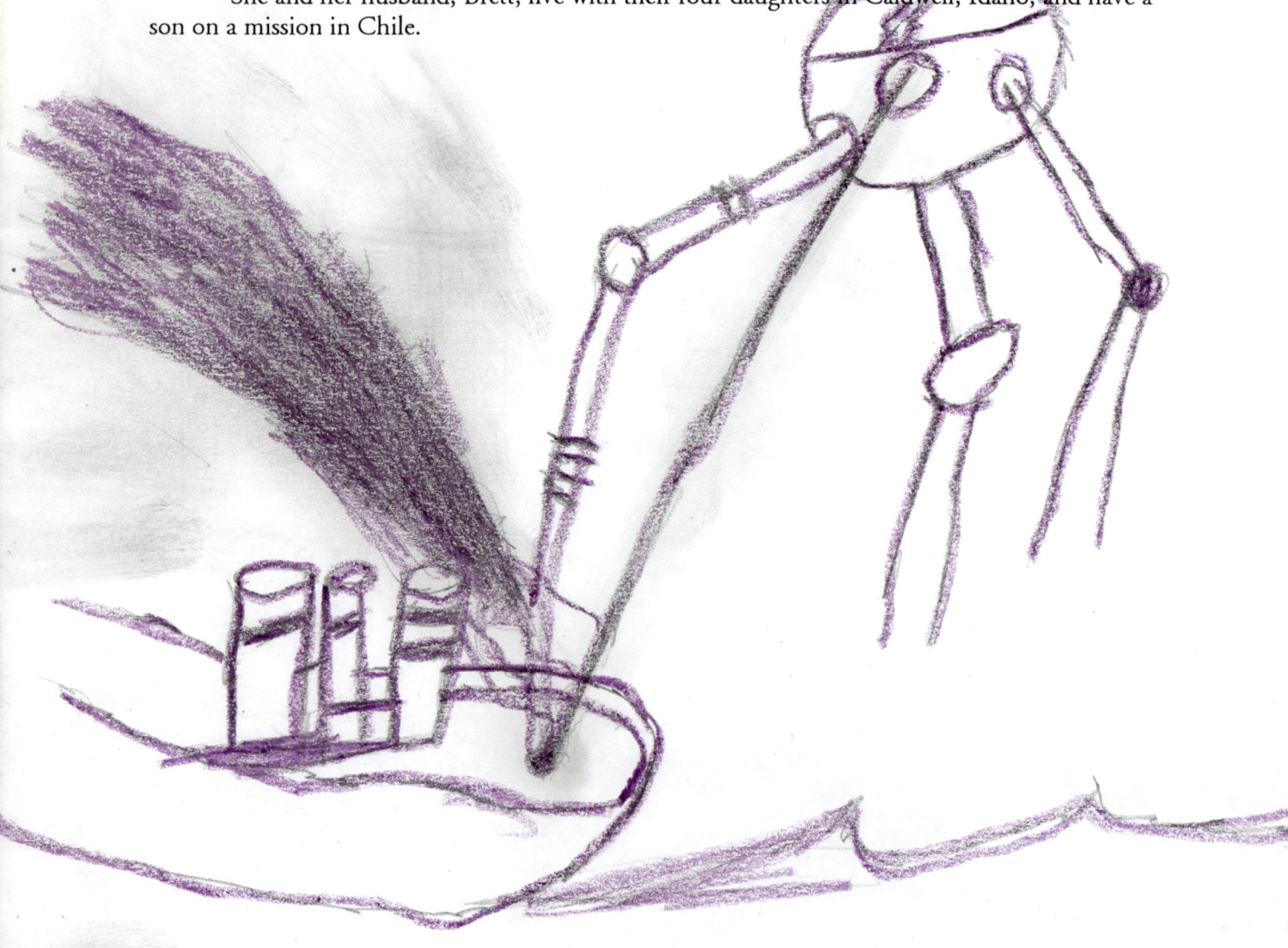